North Of the Line

A Clyde and Neville Adventure

K. Ray Katz

The author will respond to email's sent to:
KRKSoundChoice@AOL.com

NORTH OF THE LINE

Published in the United States of America
Sound Choice Publishers

ISBN:13: 978-1978101746
ISBN:10: 1978101740

Other novels by the author:

World War II
Clyde and Neville Series

Down Under
The Coast Watchers
New Guinea Rescue

Russia / East Asia Series

And Then They Were Kings
My Enemy's Enemy

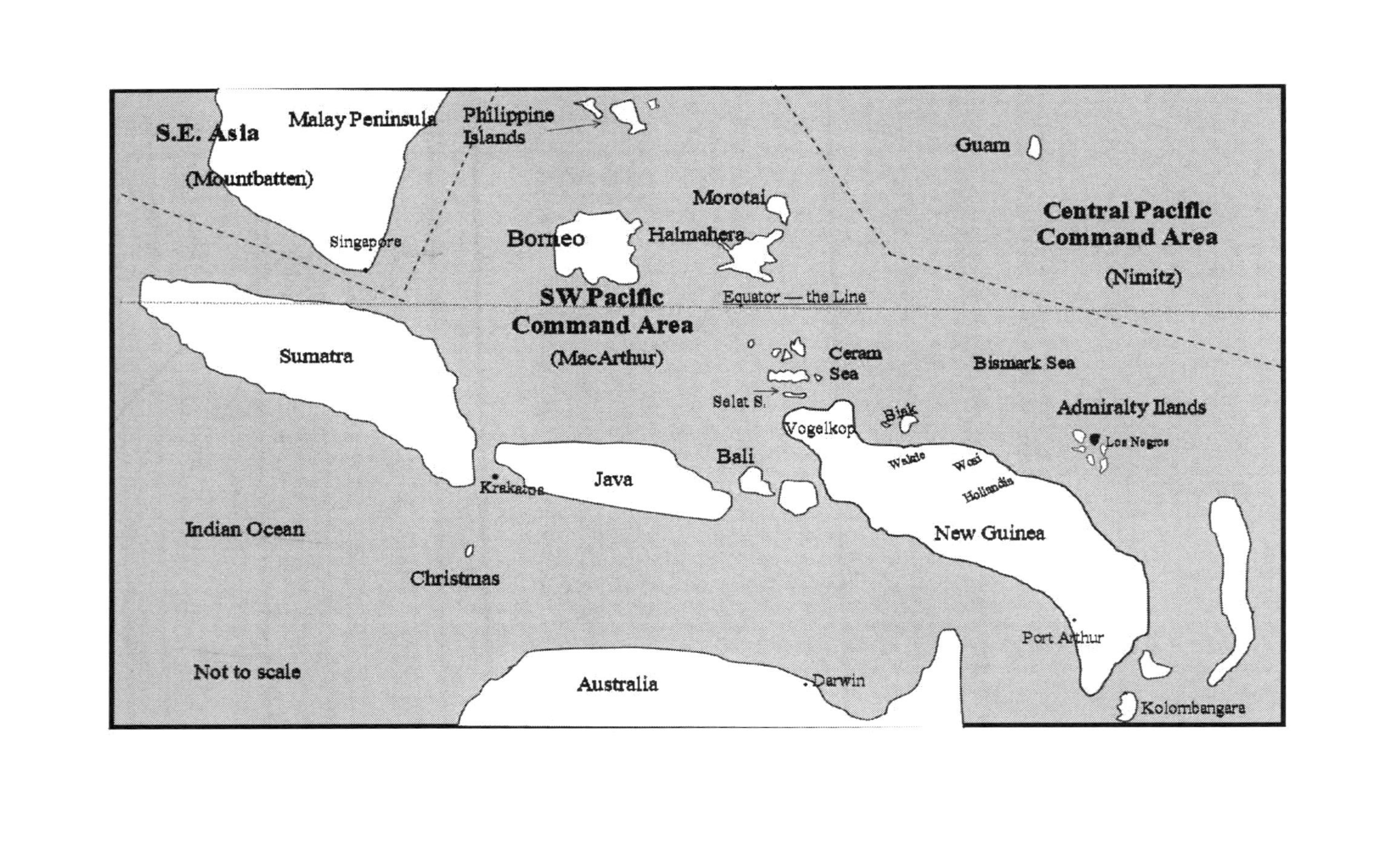
S.E. Asia
(Mountbatten)
Malay Peninsula
Singapore
Philippine Islands
Guam
Morotai
Borneo
Halmahera
Central Pacific Command Area
(Nimitz)
SW Pacific Command Area
(MacArthur)
Equator — the Line
Sumatra
Ceram Sea
Bismark Sea
Selat S.
Admiralty Ilands
Biak
Vogelkop
Los Negros
Bali
Wakde
Wosi
Hollandia
Java
Krakatoa
Indian Ocean
New Guinea
Christmas
Port Arthur
Not to scale
Australia
Darwin
Kolombangara

Chapter 1

Halmahera Sea

September 1, 1944

Neville Saunders screamed in dismay, "Halmaherra? Why in the bloody hell are we going to that miserable island?" His harsh Cockney accent grated on the ears of those closest to him. It was made even more irritating by having to compete with the roar of the B-24 bomber's engines. "I'm not going there, I'm going to Brisbane and then home. Bloody hell, they promised me!"

The short middle-aged Englishman with the beginning of a beer belly was the proud owner of a tropical fruit plantation on Pyramid Island at the southern end of the Solomon Islands. Just having returned from what he hoped was his final mission working behind enemy lines, he slapped his hip. Surprised at not finding his .45 caliber semi- automatic pistol, he looked down. It took him a moment to remember that he had packed it in his carry bag before getting on the plane. He always wore it, when awake or asleep in enemy held territory.

Looking at one of the waist gunners in the plane's belly, he said, "Who changed the flight plan? Why didn't someone wake me?"

"Hey pal, nobody changed nothin. This here plane's a bomber. We drop bombs on Japs and when dead-eye-Dick, up in the nose, ain't three sheets to the wind, we actually hit something. But last I heard, there ain't no Japs in Brisbane."

Neville shook his head trying to understand how he had gotten on the wrong plane. He looked around the cramped interior of the plane for an answer, until his gaze settled on Clyde, his life-long friend lying on a pile of parachutes and life vests.

Knowing when to keep his mouth shut, Clyde Arnold feigned sleep. On a whim, he had guided his friend onto the bomber, instead of a shuttle flight from General MacArthur's forward operating base in the Admiralty Islands, to Brisbane. The two men, newly released from coast watcher duties, had decided to restart the plantations they owned on Pyramid Island now that their island paradise was clear of enemy troops.

Neville thought about kicking his partner awake. However, since receiving a straight answer seemed so unlikely, he turned and worked his way forward to the cockpit, passing the engineer who was also the radioman.

"Who told us to get on this plane?" Neville asked once he reached the cockpit. When no one answered, he continued in a louder voice. "Right then - how long until you drop your bombs and land in Brisbane?"

Suddenly, a deaf and dumb crew was flying the plane. No one said a word. He needed someone to blame for having boarded the wrong flight. Turning, he saw the copilot and then the navigator avert their eyes and look toward the rear of the compartment. Following their lead, he looked back. His eyes blazed when they settled on Clyde standing behind him in the cramped space. Although they were business partners, many people who knew them, gave the two unpredictable Englishmen a different title. In mixed company, accomplice was the nicest word people used to describe either of them.

Saunders stared at his best friend since childhood, his anger growing. "You knew, didn't you?" he shouted, holding a fist up in front of Arnold.

Before his partner could respond, Neville continued, "What is wrong with you? We just barely survived a thousand Japs trying to kill us on New Guinea, not to mention a volcano erupting, and cannibals with poison darts. We're supposed to be going home to our quiet island in the sun, now that the Japs have been run off. But no-o, you still want to play games with these chaps." He pointing at Swede, the pilot, before waving a finger in Clyde's face, "And don't you try to deny it."

No one said a word making Neville sputter, emitting meaningless sounds of rage. Seldom caught without something to say, now, he was so mad he couldn't find words strong enough to express his utter frustration. For the last three months, MacArthur's headquarters had been promising to allow the two men to go home, 'Just as soon as the civil affairs people declare Pyramid enemy free.' In the mean time, when asked, or tricked, as in their last mission, they went behind enemy lines to do things few others could. They survived, so they boasted, by their skill, which must be true, since they were still breathing. They always seemed to draw the right cards, in poker or a jungle firefight. Even when they were pushed out of a plane to parachute into enemy territory with blood-alcohol levels seldom seen in a conscious person, they came away unscathed.

"Why are you flying to Halmahera?" Neville asked the pilot. "The Japs are still there."

Swede nodded. "Yup, that's why this plane is loaded with bombs."

Hearing that, Clyde looked out the window. Not seeing any other planes, he became worried. "You aren't really going to bomb them without any other planes around for support, are you?"

"Sure thing. The squadron's been doin' it every day for the last two weeks. Planes are droppin' bombs on them at all hours. The big brass thinks it makes the little guys nervous. Personally, I think it plain makes 'em mad."

"I hope you're wrong."

"I do, too. So far, they haven't been very good at shooting at us. I guess firing at a single plane is too hard, or maybe it just ain't worth the effort. Anyway, we'll be there in another hour. Make sure you have your parachutes on and stay out of the way, we're within range of their fighters."

Clyde turned and went back to a spot near the waist gunners who were scanning the sky for enemy planes through their wide-open gun windows. Neville, still mad, took a moment to look around the cockpit. After not finding anything, he could hit to help him release his anger without jeopardizing their safety, his eyes settled on the altimeter. It said they were flying at eight-thousand feet above sea level. He waited a minute expecting to see it register their climb to a proper bombing altitude. When it didn't change, his concern came through in voice. "Aren't you flying too low? When are you going up?"

The pilot looked back, surprised to see Neville still in the cockpit. "Everyone goes in at different altitudes. We drew the short straw today."

"Damn right you…we did." Neville muttered as he joined his mate near the waist gunners. "Seems there ain't any long straws left in this world."

When they walked onto the tarmac on Los Negros in the Admiralty Islands, Clyde, the more mischievous of the two, had seen Swede, a pilot he knew, waving at them. Without thinking about the consequences, he guided his partner away from their well-earned flight home and onto Swede's plane for a flight to…he didn't know where. All he knew was, he was enjoying the war and with both of his native wives having deserted him, he needed something more exciting to do than watch mangoes ripen.

The two plantation owners the war had turned into adventurers and unsung heroes, made the best of the situation. Clyde settled into the nest he created with his parachute and travel bag while Neville, grumbling, did the same. The gunners, now all business watching for Japanese fighters paid little attention to the two bad tempered Englishmen. The talking was over. It was time for the war to try and take its pound of flesh.

Halmahera, a misshapen jungle island not far from the equator, equidistant from New Guinea, Borneo, and the Philippines seemed to be a natural next step for General MacArthur. His army had pushed the Japanese out of New Guinea, and now, he had his eyes on the Philippines. The enemy was digging in and the Fifth Air Force had the job of softening him up. Everyday planes took off from the Admiralty Islands and new bases on the Vogelkop peninsula of New Guinea to hit targets over a thousand miles away. The long flights over the island dotted waters of the South Pacific were boring, except for the hour they were within range of enemy fighters and flak guns.

Black puffs of smoke appeared like magic on either side of the plane as it started its bomb run. "Damn," exclaimed the copilot, "it's the middle of the day. What are they doing shooting at us? They should be trying to stay cool in their caves."

Occasionally, they heard the loud boom of a shell exploding close enough for shrapnel to rattle off the plane's skin. Enemy gunners were getting better, but the plane was committed. The bombardier needed the pilot to maintain a straight course to their target, an airbase on the island's northeast coast. The waist gunners relaxed. As long as flak guns were firing at them, they were safe from enemy fighters. Flak didn't discriminate between friend and foe.

Over the din of the roaring engines and flak explosions, they heard the whine of electric motors sliding the bomb bay doors up to expose the reason for their trip. Sixteen five-hundred pound bombs filled with high explosives, some with personal chalk messages written on them, were ready to go. A moment later, its deadly cargo released, the empty bomber rose five-hundred feet as if pulled up by an unseen hand.

Immediately, Swede turned the plane north to evade the flak that was coming ever closer. A shell exploded with a ragged black cloud suddenly blossoming in front of the plane. The copilot's windshield splintered at the same moment several small holes appeared over his head. The pilot looked over expecting to see blood pouring from his friend's mutilated body. To his surprise, he saw a wide grin as his copilot held up his hands to show that he still had everything attached. Swede smiled and relaxed. Lady Luck was on board.

The young second Lieutenant said, "Got to give them credit. They keep trying, but my momma's son ain't that easy to kill!"

The plane continued its turn as it climbed. Without warning, another shell exploded near the right wing. Shrapnel tore through both engines while another piece came through the side window and ripped through the surprised copilot's throat. His head flopped forward. Blood sprayed across the instrument panel as the young man died, a smile still on his face. The plane had sustained a crippling blow. The navigator, who doubled as the bombardier was gone, disappearing through the now non-existent nose of the plane. The rush of air through the gaping hole replaced the roar of the destroyed engines.

Swede struggled to regain control of his plane as the pull of the two good engines made the bomber slip onto its left side. They were seconds away from going into a deadly out-of-control spiral. The engineer cut the fuel flow to the two useless engines trying, without success, to transfer gas out of the tanks in the right wing. Fuel, sucked out of small holes along the underside of the wing, sprayed a visible trail behind them. To regain control, the pilot increased power to the two good engines. Over the intercom, he told the crew, "Jettison everything that isn't bolted down."

Tossed around like a pair of beanbags, Clyde and Neville tumbled over to the left side of the plane. Clyde's head ended up in Neville's crotch. Sitting up, Clyde said, "Don't you ever take a bath?"

"More than you, old chum. Now get off your bum. We need to take a look-see at the people up front."

Clyde scrambled to get a hold of something solid as the plane's tilt to the right became more pronounced. "Hope we don't need to use these bags strapped to our backs." His concern for their situation showed in his voice. "I haven't recovered yet from our last jump."

The two adventurers, old enough to know better than play soldiers in a real war, crawled forward to the cockpit where they found the pilot screaming instructions to the engineer. Neville took a quick look at the copilot, before turning to the pilot. "Anything we can do, Mate?"

Swede yelled to make his words heard over the sound of air rushing in through the missing nose cone. With both hands gripping the wheel, trying to get the big plane to fly level, he said, "Look outside and see if you can spot a place for us to land. I'd prefer that to bailing out over the ocean or back there." He motioned with his head to the island they had just bombed. "They may not be in the mood for company."

Neville stole a quick glance at the altimeter. The plane had dropped four-thousand feet in less than a minute. They desperately needed somewhere for the plane to land in the next few minutes, or…

He squeezed around the pilot and looked out his side window. Clyde did the same to the right, trying not to get blood all over his new clothes. After returning from their last mission to rescue some Allied prisoners from being murdered in a Japanese POW camp, they had taken a detour to liberate several sets of shirts and pants from the Military Civil Affairs office.

"I see an island off to our right. It has a nice long beach."

"That must be Morotai. Can you tell," asked Swede, "is the tide in or out?"

Clyde craned his neck to see the beach as the plane continued to turn away. "I can't see it anymore. You need to bring the plane back the other way."

The big pilot, his shirt soaked through with sweat shook his head. "No can do! I'll let her keep swinging around till we see it again and hope I can keep us in the air for a little while."

The bomber continued its descent spiraling down to two-thousand feet before Clyde's island came into view. It looked promising, but too far away.

"How long till you get us there?"

"How well do you swim?"

"Swim? Him?" Neville pointed at his partner and laughed. "He doesn't even take a bath in water above his knees."

Before Clyde could respond, the plane lurched and fell off to the right. He had to grab onto the blood-drenched rear of the copilot's seat to keep from falling. The bomber dropped a thousand feet before Swede, straining for all he was worth managed to get the plane stabilized and back to almost level flight.

Seeing how hard Swede was working, Clyde asked, "What can I do?"

Through clenched teeth, the pilot said, "Pray."

"Sorry! I haven't been on a first name basis with the guy upstairs since before the first war." Clyde looked at the altimeter and then took a peek out the window. "We ain't going to make it to that island, are we?"

Swede, too involved with his dying plane to talk, shrugged his shoulders, before shaking his head. The laws of physics were not going to be denied.

The plane approached minimum bailout altitude too quickly for all of the crew to get out. "The Flying Coffin," as B-24 Liberator bombers were known, only had one exit, and that near the rear of the plane.

Over the intercom, Swede tried to keep from sounding as scared as he felt. "Assume crash landing positions. Be ready to throw out the life rafts as soon as we stop."

Clyde and Neville didn't need anyone to tell them to get out of the cockpit. One last peek out the pilot's window showed nothing but water. The ocean seemed to be reaching up to swallow the crippled bomber, even as the pilot continued his struggle to keep the wings level and bring the nose up. With the vulnerable nose cone gone, not hitting at a tail down angle would result in the large hole acting as a giant scoop. In that case, the plane flipping over on its back would be the best that could happen. Imitating a submarine–the worst.

The two civilians barely made it back to their belongings when the plane slammed into the water. Swede tried to ease his crippled command down, but at more than a hundred miles an hour, it felt like the fragile metal tube hit a rock wall. The plane disappeared, hidden behind a curtain of spray as it hit, bounced and hit again, this time minus its right wing. With the nose wide open and without the additional buoyancy provided by the missing wing, the plane became another casualty of the war. It started to settle at an alarming rate.

Prior to hitting the water, the pilot braced himself as well as he could, but his head still catapulted into the instrument panel. The impact knocked him unconscious, and resulted in a deep gash in his forehead and a large dent in the metal panel, along with several broken gauges. Swede's inert body hung over the steering column. In the next compartment back, the engineer/radio operator sustained a broken arm and several broken ribs. He could barely breathe, unable to move, he was trapped against the forward bulkhead of his tiny compartment, with the weight of his mangled instrument panel on his chest. The second time the bomber hit the water, the plane's tail dug in. Sheared off, it went its own way, the tail gunner still inside. The other four gunners survived with nothing more than a few bruises.

Nestled as they were in their nest of parachutes, and bags, the two hitchhikers survived without a scratch. With the exception of when they were privates in the First World War, neither Clyde nor Neville ever bothered waiting for someone in authority to tell them what had to be done. As far as they were concerned, they always knew best. They jumped into action, their self-preservation genes telling them everything they needed to know.

"Get those life rafts out and throw our kit in them," Neville yelled to Clyde over the groans of the dying plane as it started to take a nose down angle. "I'm going up front to see about Swede."

"Roger," replied Clyde, as he thrust a life raft out a waist gunner's open window, pulled its inflation handle and stuffed the end of the raft's mooring rope into the waist of his pants. It had barely begun to take a recognizable shape when he started throwing in their personal gear and anything else the crew had that might be useful. One of the gunners threw two more rafts out and began shoving his buddies out the window.

Neville grabbed hold of the plane's airframe ribs and pulled himself forward through the rising water, each step becoming more difficult. After seeing the engineer's predicament and instantly knowing the impossibility of saving him, he closed his eyes and turned away, moving toward the cockpit. He squirmed his way forward, pulled Swede upright and checked for a pulse. Satisfied the man was alive, he released his harness and pulled him out of his seat as the plane tilted forward, the rear rising out of the water, the nose pointing at the ocean floor.

Clyde kept throwing things into the rafts. First aid supplies, personal items, side arms and ammunition, along with a few cans of food, K-rations, and anything else he could lay his hands on, all of which caused him to be the last person to jump out through a waist window. He made a desperate leap for the side of a raft, and missed. He went under, seawater filling his mouth. His splashing drenched a gunner who reached down to grab him. On his second effort, the man caught hold of Clyde's collar and pulled him into the raft like a prize tuna.

Spitting and sputtering, Clyde spun around desperately looking for his partner as the plane disappeared in a swirl of bubbles. He raised his hands to his mouth, and shouted, "Neville, Neville, come on Mate, this ain't no time to be playin' games."

Several more times, he called out. Scared of what might have happened, he pushed his fear of drowning aside, leaned over the right side of the raft, and stuck his face in the water. At the same moment, Neville surfaced on the other side with a now semi-conscious pilot in tow.

Clyde helped pull them into the raft. "It's a good thing you got out of that plane instead of drowning. You know bloody well that I wouldn't have enough time to manage both our properties."

Out of the eleven men who had taken off in the ill-fated plane, seven remained. They thanked their lucky stars as they bobbed up and down in their yellow rafts surrounded by an empty horizon. The dark green island they could see from the air had disappeared below the rim of the sea. To the crewmembers, the island represented salvation. To Neville and Clyde, it had a different meaning. They were going to have to take the crew under their wing and protect them from a group of Japanese soldiers that probably, were just as fanatical as all the others they had fought over the past three years. The crew was going to need to be shown how to live off the land and avoid capture. In the air, the crew, nearly God-like in their ability to keep them safe was in charge. However, on land, Clyde and Neville were the experts at avoiding all kinds of natural and man-made death traps.

With every expectation of going home to their quiet island having become nothing more than a soggy dream, they took inventory of their possessions, and turned the rafts in the general direction of dry land, hoping they would find some deep dark jungle to hide in. Their plane had gone down during the day and probably been visible to an untold number of unfriendly eyes on Morotai.

Chapter 2

Los Negros

September 1, 1944
Evening

In the Admiralty Islands, Los Negros had served as Command headquarters and the hub of Allied activity for the South West Pacific over the previous year. With the final battles to wrest control from the Japanese on the Vogelkop Peninsula, a chicken head shaped area at the end of New Guinea concluded, MacArthur's headquarters was on the move. Its next stop, a temporary location at Hollandia Bay on the northeast coast of New Guinea.

As commander of all operations against the Japanese in the South West Pacific, MacArthur was in a hurry to make good on his promise to the residents of the Philippines, "I shall return." The planning staff, following MacArthur's instructions, looked at Halmaherra and knew it to be the obvious next step. However, being obvious made its capture more difficult. The Japanese could also read a map, and intelligence reported more than twenty-thousand enemy troops were continuing to dig in, increasing their already formidable defenses. MacArthur's plan to divert the enemy's attention away from his next objective seemed to be working. At least, the build-up of troops on Halmaherra pointed in that direction.

Sitting in the mess tent after dinner on Los Negros, the two men, as usual, found themselves talking about their wives, and their plans for after the war. An unlikely pair, U.S. Navy Commander William "Bill" Cullison, and Australian Geology Professor Harry Hopkins, became good friends during the two years they had worked together.

Cullison, previously a submarine commander now worked in the South West Pacific Operations (SWAPO) strategic planning office. However, his work was less about planning, and more about coordinating operations between the submarine command and various groups working behind enemy lines.

At the start of the war, before his current assignment, Cullison commanded several successful combat patrols until he was wounded during an attack on a Japanese naval force believed to be preparing for the invasion of the isolated city of Darwin. His promotion to Commander and transfer to the planning office, allowed him to marry Dusty, a beautiful Australian red head, who ran a cattle station in the *Outback*. After twenty years in the navy and married, he now worked behind a desk rather than a periscope. His desk was his ship and he measured his ammunition in reams rather than by caliber.

Working as a civilian advisor to SWAPO, Harry, the quiet geologist, found himself drawn ever more deeply into dangerous situations. From volunteering to be a Coast Watcher, to parachuting behind enemy lines and rescuing Allied POW's, the middle-aged professor, only a few years older than Cullison, seemed to thrive on danger. Of course, having had the unique and often unenviable experience of being associated with Clyde and Neville guaranteed that whatever he did would be unconventional.

"The first thing I want to do is get to London," said Harry with enthusiasm, "and follow up on the Royal Society's invitation to give a lecture on volcanic activity. Along with being able to survive working with our two walking disasters, my volcanic research on Krakatoa is sure to get me tenure at the university in Melbourne."

Cullison nodded his understanding as he picked up his coffee cup, only to hesitate when he heard his name mentioned by an army corporal holding a message sheet. Cullison waved the cup at the man and took the flimsy message paper. Quickly reading the two lines of information, he looked at the corporal, and said, "Thank you. No reply."

"Another problem, Bill?"

"I hope not, but if there is, with those two, there are no small problems."

Harry's face showed his concern, his eyebrows changing his face into a visual question mark and then to a knowing smile. "You must mean Clyde and Neville. What have they gone and done now?"

"This is a message from McCulloch in Brisbane. He's getting ready to transfer to Mountbatten's command in India, but he went to meet them at the airport, only they weren't on the plane. He put a call in to base operations here, and, as far as they're concerned, both of our boys got on, which, obviously, they didn't. He was hoping we might know something."

"Well…if they didn't get on the flight to Brisbane, I'll bet they found someone flying to Henderson Field on Guadalcanal. That would put them almost within sight of their Pyramid Island."

"Hmm. That makes sense. And, with them, I'm sure the idea of telling someone what they are going to do…"

"Those two?" Harry tried not to laugh too hard. "You know better than that. Letting anyone know what they're doing never occurs to them. They don't even know what they're going to do, until it happens. Sometimes, I wonder how they've managed to live so long."

Cullison thought about it for a moment. The question had come up any number of times. Divine intervention seemed the most logical explanation, even if a little improbable. Then the answer came to him. He slapped his hand on the table to announce his solution to the problem. "I've got it. For all of their simple-minded antics, those two have a survivor's mentality. They rarely consider the fact that they might not be able to do whatever it is they want to do."

"Ergo," continued Harry holding up a finger, "if a person cannot conceive of not being able to do something, they always find a way to succeed."

"As we say back home, 'By hook or by crook.'"

"Having said that, where do you think they are, and shouldn't you have your famously efficient intelligence service start asking around?"

"Now Harry, it isn't like you to be sarcastic. Let's wait a day or so before we make this an official inquiry. But, in the mean time, I will send a back-channel message to both the Canal and Pyramid."

They walked out of the mess tent and stopped. In front of them, the sky slid from blue and gray to pink and orange as the sun dropped into the sea. Off to their right, near the airfield was the twisted and blackened remains of a bomber on the white sand beach, the latest of many that hadn't made it home. To come so close–less than a mile–and not make it back. The bomber's carcass seemed to sum up the frustration of having to fight an enemy you rarely saw. The Japanese were an enemy who gloried in stories of the Samurai and considered compassion an inexcusable weakness.

Cullison couldn't get the sight of the crumpled plane out of his mind as he walked back to his office. Preparing for another meeting, he wondered what the last thoughts of the men inside the doomed aircraft had been. Were they praying to a God of infinite mercy, or cursing those who had ordered them to their deaths?

"It's as dark out here as the bottom of a well. You're sure you have us pointed in the right direction, Mate?" Clyde asked the still woozy pilot. Subtlety had never been one of his strong suits.

"Leave the poor blighter alone, Clyde. He's doing the best he can with his brains scrambled like they are. But, it would be nice to know if we're going to see this Morotai place before my bleeding arm falls off from all this paddling."

"Exactly my feelings, ol' boy."

"Watch who you call old. Our birthdays are only weeks apart."

"But you are older!"

Vermont, one of the waist gunners in the other raft complained while he leaned over the side of the small craft and dug his paddle into the water. "Don't you two ever shut up? With the noise you make, we could run into a coral reef and never hear the surf until it's too late. The more you paddle and the less you talk, the sooner we'll be on dry land. I always thought old people didn't talk a lot, until I met you two."

The second waist gunner grabbed his counterpart. In his unmistakable Alabama accent, he said, "Quick, tell him you didn't mean it."

The first gunner looked at his crewmate, "Didn't mean, what?"

"Tell them they're not old, or they'll never shut up," Alabama said at the same time Neville turned toward them.

"Will you blokes shut your traps? You're making so much noise Clyde can't tell where that sound is coming from."

Marionettes having their strings pulled tight could not sit up more quickly. "What? Where?"

"I said shut your traps," repeated Neville. This time they heard the threat implied by his tone of voice and sat still, listening for something. Their untrained ears, partially deafened by hundreds of hours in the bomber, could not hear anything other than the sound of ocean waves slapping against the side of their rubber raft.

Neville joined his partner hanging over the front of the raft, trying to separate the new, faint sounds Clyde thought he heard, from those of the normal ocean. He put his hands behind his ears and rotated his head. He'd used the same method to locate game when hunting, and sometimes, when was the one being hunted, in the dense jungles of the South Pacific. After what seemed an hour, but might have been less than a minute, he pointed thirty degrees to his left. The dark night prevented anyone from being able to see where his extended arm was pointing.

"Come on now," the irritation Clyde felt at no one doing anything came out in his voice. "Turn these things to the left and start paddling. I need dry land under my feet before my pretty new clothes are ruined."

Neville leaned toward the waist gunners in the second raft attached to theirs by a short rope. Between strokes, in a stage whisper he said, "When Clyde starts to think about how he looks, you can bet he's worried. He's scared a fish will poke a hole in this large airbag. Drowning is his least preferred method of reaching the pearly gates."

Chapter 3

Morotai

September 2, 1944
Early Morning

Drowning had been high on Clyde's list of concerns, closely followed by being tortured or shot. When he and Neville helped rescue a group of Allied POW's scheduled to be eliminated by the Japanese on New Guinea, he saw graphic evidence of the damage that was inflicted on the human body by the twisted minds of people taught they were a superior race. Prisoners told how their buddies were tied to stakes and used for bayonet practice, clubbed to death, or beheaded in training exercises. As he helped paddle, always listening for telltale sounds of ocean waves crashing onto an island or coral reef, Clyde repeated to himself his vow of never being taken alive.

The group, guided by a break in the sound of waves expending their energy against sharp coral heads, squeezed through a gap in the reef to a pristine, hard packed sand beach. Their rafts slid to a stop on the sand as quietly as a turtle making landfall after months at sea. Neville jumped from his and ran up a gentle incline. He assigned himself the job of finding a place for the group to hide until they could assess their situation. They only had a few minutes since the first hint of a rising sun was coloring the horizon behind them. The speed at which an equatorial sunrise occurred, gave them little time to waste.

At times, Swede seemed to be lucid and at others, a breathing corpse. The four gunners each took hold of the first raft with the pilot in it, and ran up the gently sloping beach and into a line of low bushes. They pushed their way through only to stumble into a two-foot deep salt marsh filled with thick, head-high reeds. The marsh turned out to be a narrow area, no more than fifty-feet wide running just behind the beach. As soon as they reached the far side, they put the raft down on the sandy soil and ran back for the third one, as Clyde and Neville followed with the second. After all three rafts were off the beach and all of their tracks were removed, Neville dropped down onto the sandy soil.

"You did real good, Mate," Neville said to Clyde as sarcastically as possible.

"What's wrong, I found the bloody island, didn't I?"

"Right-o, that you did, only there ain't nothing higher than some tall grass and these thorn bushes for us to hide behind for at least three miles, maybe more."

Clyde rose up to a stooping position, his head even with the top of the bushes. In only a few minutes, the night's dark sky had changed with the ever-present clouds turning a brilliant pink. The sun had not yet risen over the horizon, but visibility was already too good to try to get to the distant mountains, or even back out to sea.

Clyde pointed to their left. "I can see a tree over there."

"Wonderful. We'll all hide under the only tree on this half of the island."

Neville knew he had won the latest round in their ongoing battle of words when Clyde slumped back onto the sand and nodded at the rafts. "We need to bury these yellow, 'Here I am, come get me' signs, and then pray no Nip patrols come this way." His voice trailed off, as he said, "If they do…"

"If they do - what?" asked the lanky turret gunner from Alabama.

"What do you mean, what?"

"What happens if a patrol comes this way," he drawled.

Clyde reached into the small of his back, pulled out a flat piece of dark brown wood and held it up. With a flick of his wrist, it became a nine-inch long dagger, both razor sharp edges tapering down to a wicked looking point.

Clyde made sure to retain his smile, which seemed anything but friendly, when he said, "I use this or my pistol. I've seen what those little fellows do to prisoners."

The mild mannered southerner's eyes opened wide for a moment, before he swallowed hard and said, "Right away, Mr. Arnold. How deep you want them buried?"

Chapter 4

The Beach

September 2, 1944

Everyone except the pilot dropped to their knees and rapidly scooped sand with their hands like a pack of dogs in a bone-burying contest. By the time the sun cleared the horizon, the rafts were buried and everyone was settling into the individual burrows they were creating in the moist sand, surrounded by low thorny bushes. "Anyone hears or sees anything, you don't do anything except tell Clyde or me–quietly," said Neville in a loud whisper.

He pointed at one of the gunners. "What's your name?"

"Nevada."

"I'll take the first watch with you. Clyde and one of you others will relieve us in two hours. When it's dark, we'll dig up the rafts and paddle north. We should be able to move up the coast until we get parallel to the mountains. Once there, we'll keep you safe in the jungle from the Japs."

One man asked, "How long are you planning for us to live like mountain men?"

"Until I see one of your lovely gray battleships anchored out there." Clyde nodded at Swede laying under a bush, apparently unconscious, "From what your pilot said, it looks to me like MacArthur is going to attack Halmahera in a week or two, and we're less than twenty miles from there. Soon as he takes care of the Nips over there, he'll have to send a force to take this island, or at the least, dispatch an exploratory force to take a look. That means, we sit tight, do some reconnaissance, and listen for his big guns."

"What about food? We only got enough for a day or two."

"You must be one of those city fellas." Clyde chuckled. "These islands have food growing on almost every tree. All you have to do is reach up and grab it."

Trying not to laugh, Neville added, "And hope you have a good supply of toilet tissue..."

"Or nappies," said Clyde.

Neville continued, If you ain't accustomed to eating mango, coconut and papaya, morning, noon and night, with an occasional bread fruit thrown in for variety."

Hearing someone move, Neville swiveled to his left. Swede tried to sit up. Making sure not to show themselves above the level of the surrounding bushes, the group gathered around him. Vermont, the turret gunner, the only sergeant in the group, helped the pilot sit up and gave him a drink of water.

"Thanks," Swede mumbled. After a second drink, slurring his words, he said, "Did we get off a Mayday?"

"Yes sir–but no one responded. Our only hope was for another plane to hear our Morse code call. We were too far from any of our bases for a voice message to get through."

The pilot nodded his agreement, and then looked at Clyde and Neville. "I guess there's a reason you two came along, after all." He took a moment to look at each of his crew, before saying, "From here on out, these two old…" He stopped when he saw the scowl on Clyde's face. "I mean these two coast watchers are in charge. You do whatever they say and we'll be okay."

"Right you are, Mate. Now you lie back and get some rest. We'll keep you just as safe as if you were in your own bed back in the states." Neville smiled at the pilot who looked young enough to be his son. "The way you look, your head must have done some real damage to the plane."

He looked at the crewmen spread out around them. "The rest of you, do what you can to protect yourselves from the sun. We have a long day and we need to conserve our water. We won't be able to get any more until we're in them mountains."

Clyde moved over and whispered to Neville, "You want to tell them or me?"

Neville's face said, "What are you talking about?"

"You know." He pointed back to the marsh.

"Oh! I forgot. I didn't want to scare them. Hoped they'd relax a little."

"I think we should. You know the old saying, 'Better safe than sorry.'"

Neville grudgingly nodded his agreement. He looked at the plane's crew. All of them had been watching the two civilians. He took the time to make eye contact with each of them. "One more little thing…if you see anything looks like a floating log, or hear something moving through the reeds, best you tell Clyde or me. There's a good chance it could be a croc. They can be quite tasty if you cook them right."

"That they can," agreed Clyde. "Make mighty fine eating, although, with the old ones you need to boil the meat, they're too tough to cook on the Barbie. But, don't you worry. Anybody sees one, we'll catch it. Wouldn't want it to get away when we're short of food."

"Wouldn't want it to get away?" the sergeant blurted out. "What about us not wanting to get eaten. I heard those things can get real big."

"Naw-only in Australia or India. On the islands, they don't grow to more than fifteen feet. Now get yourselves some rest. The less you move around, the less water you'll need."

Clyde nodded his agreement, and then added. “Neville’s right. I haven’t seen one bigger than that in three of four years.” Clyde turned to his partner. “You remember that big one Neville. He was the one killed that water buffalo when we were on Kolambangara. Came up out of the river, grabbed that buffalo in a blink of an eye and pulled him under. It were a nice size buffalo–eight-hundred pounds if an ounce.”

Not willing to believe the loudmouth Englishman, the Sergeant said, “Come on, now. How could one of those attack an animal that big?”

“Have you ever seen a Saltie? I mean a mature male. They weigh over two-thousand pounds. He can get his head ten feet out of the water faster than you can clap your hands. Anything they grab onto is gone, and that’s a fact.”

Neville shook his head, seemingly resigned to keep quiet and let Clyde have some fun, although, everything he said, so far, was true.

Clyde had one more choice fact to impart to his stunned audience, but then decided he’d said enough. Instead, he finished with, “But don’t you boys worry your young heads. We know a few tricks if a Saltie shows up, so just lay yourselves down and get a good rest. Tonight we’ll find us a nice place to hide out until your General MacArthur gets here.”

In the middle of the afternoon, it was time for Neville to relieve Clyde again. They used the single stunted nut tree twenty-yards farther inland as their guard tower. When he saw Neville crawling towards the tree, Clyde climbed down and on his knees, started doing some stretches to loosen up while his bomber crew companion was already crawling back to their encampment.

Neville said, “Anything interesting happen?”

“Not much, except for a large group of them buggers carrying a lot of equipment and dragging a weapons cart moving along the beach toward the mountains about a half hour ago.

Could be the same ones you saw earlier. They looked pretty sharp, clean uniforms and all."

"No, I saw a small group, about a dozen. How many of the little blighters were in your group?"

Clyde, started to answer, stopped and with a question mark on his face raised his hand and started stabbing at the empty sky trying to visualize and count the number of enemy soldiers he had seen. When he reached seventy, Neville broke into his running commentary, saying, "Are you sure? That's more than a beach patrol."

"That it is. In fact, as much as I want to get to someplace safe, I think we should stay out of them mountains till we get a better idea of what's going on."

"Do I hear you acting cautious? I don't know how big this island is, but those mountains go for at least twenty miles, and seventy isn't that many soldiers."

Finished with his stretches, Clyde sat cross-legged and gingerly moved a branch covered with curved stickers away from his leg. "Who said there weren't more than that? I stopped counting when you interrupted my train of thought. You can call me cautious if you want, but every time I get scratched by these bushes it reminds me that I'm not bullet proof."

"I still think we should get into those mountains tonight, otherwise, we're going to run out of water tomorrow morning."

"Forgot about that, now didn't I?" Clyde mumbled.

"Right! Now you get back to our Yanks and I'll go imitate a monkey climbing that tree."

Time in the tree passed slowly for Neville. It wasn't big enough to have large comfortable branches. No matter how he tried to sit, he always felt like he was going to fall. He finally gave up and was moving to another branch when Kansas, the young man with him located ten feet higher, called down. "Mr. Saunders, I can see another group coming up the beach."

Neville quickly settled himself into his new position wedged in a crotch of the tree, and looked up. "How many?"

"Hard to say," replied Kansas while watching their enemy through Neville's binoculars. "They're spread out across the beach from high water up to the bushes."

Neville's mood changed from curious, to concerned. "Are any of them coming off the beach?"

"Don't look like it. But there sure are a lot of them."

"Start counting them as soon as you can, but don't use the binoculars. Don't want sunlight to reflect off the lens. Can't be too careful, can we?"

When Clyde returned for his next shift in their watchtower, Neville was sitting with his back against the tree. He looked up, surprised to see his friend pushing his way through the final few stalks of tall grass in front of him.

Seeing Neville with a scrap of paper and pencil in his hands, Clyde said, "What're you doing, making your Christmas wish list?"

Neville held up a hand asking Clyde to keep quiet for an instant, before returning his concentration to the paper. He scribbled something in the only clear space remaining, and looked up. "I think you're right. We should stay out of the mountains for awhile."

Clyde's eyebrows went up. "What made you get smart and see things my way?" When he didn't receive an immediate answer, he pointed at the slip of paper. "What have you been doing?"

Neville waved the paper at his partner. "I've been tallying up all the unfriendly people that have been trooping up the beach since you left."

With perfect timing, Kansas still up in the tree, called out in a loud whisper, "Sir, another fifty-plus are going to be here in less than a minute."

Neville looked up and acknowledged the call with a hand wave. He turned to Clyde as he wrote a new number over what was already on his paper. "That makes over five-hundred and fifty of them heading toward the mountains since you went for a nap. Too many for a quick patrol and too many for us to take a chance on heading in the same direction."

"Glad to hear that I'm not too cautious. But we still have a problem. If we can't go north, where do we go? We've got a bloody great deal of water behind us, and the same thing in front of us if we cross to the other side of this little peninsula."

"No choice old boy. We go south."

"You do remember, I hope, that that's where all of these little fellows are coming from."

"Exactly right. They can't be in two places at the same time."

"What makes you think they didn't leave a bunch behind, or that they aren't all coming back?"

Neville stuffed the paper and pencil in his pocket and called for Kansas to climb down. "I imagine they did leave some people behind, but my money is on the rest of these fellows staying up in the mountains. They're probably thinking the same as me. The Yanks are coming and they don't have near enough men to defend this open end of the island.

"If this had happened two years ago, your neighborhood bookmaker would lose money if you bet on them defending their base to the last man. But now, I don't think they're so anxious to meet their maker. That's why, when the time comes, I'll bet they're going to try and mount a guerrilla type of defense from the mountains like the people are doing in the Philippines."

"Damn! That makes sense, but even if you're right, it won't take a large guard force to make Swiss cheese out of our little group."

"Come now, where's your sense of adventure? There has to be food, and water, and who knows what else, just waiting for us to come get it."

Clyde shook his head. "I don't know if it's worth taking the chance."

"Not even for some sake?"

"Don't like the stuff."

"Well the Nips drink beer too. Maybe they left some for us. At least we know they're base is somewhere on this sand spit, not in the mountains. I know I was looking forward to getting out of this war and enjoying a well-deserved rest, but we'll need to do things a bit different with these Yanks along. No starting our own little war like we've done before. This time, once we find a hidee-hole, dull and boring is the name of the game."

Clyde scuffed some dirt with a boot. "Think I'm an idiot or something? You ain't telling me anything I don't know. But, we'll still need to lead some patrols to get a lay of the land and find food for this bunch."

Before Neville could break in, Clyde held up a hand. "I know, I know, don't take any chances."

"Look, you got us into this situation because you didn't want to go home to our quiet island. We do this right, show the Yanks they need us and you'll be able to get back in the action. That's what you want, right?"

"Only if you come, too. If you say no, we'll both go back to Pyramid. With the Japs gone and you planning to rebuild your place, maybe your wife will decide to come back."

Neville didn't immediately answer as he tried to bring his desire to return home into balance with Clyde's need for…he wasn't sure what. Trying to walk a fine line between the needs of his life-long friend and the question, that after three years apart, did he really want his wife to return? "I'll think about it. First, let's make sure these Yanks are ready to move south when it gets dark. Once we get a look at what we'll have to do, we can decide what comes next."

"Fair enough, but remember, we need food, and more to the point, we're going to need water. They put their base where it is for a reason, and I'll bet water is part of it. That means we either take their base or turn around and head for the mountains."

The group followed Neville's instructions and stuffed everything they had into their pockets. When they were ready to head out, Neville called over to Vermont, a squat man with broad shoulders, seemingly, born without a neck. "How is your pilot? Can he walk or will we have to carry him?"

The sergeant looked back at Swede, eyes closed, laying in his sandy depression. "It all depends on how far we have to go. He'll try to stay on his feet, but someone will always have to be next to him…just in case he blacks out."

They moved back to the salt-water marsh and kept the water between them and the beach as they began to walk south, Neville in the lead with Clyde bringing up the rear. Without any moonlight, pushing their way through the tall reeds and occasionally stumbling into depressions with water ankle deep was disorienting–the darkness–suffocating. They started out with each man twenty or so feet behind the man in front. Within ten minutes, they were bunched together close enough to touch. Neville looked back a few times without seeing anything. Some things were black, while others were a dark gray. Unhappy with the way the group was acting, he held back from saying anything. While he had been working behind enemy lines since the beginning of the war, he could only imagine what might be going through the minds of the crew. Working in enemy-controlled territory was never routine, but experience had given him the confidence he needed to control his fear.

Everyone knew how important it was to keep quiet, but little sounds kept escaping when someone stumbled, or the fear of the unknown could no longer be contained. For all they knew, more Japs were walking in the opposite direction on the beach to their left not a hundred yards away. Vermont walked beside

Swede, frequently lending a helping hand and at other times, convincing him to stay down when he moaned or talked to himself about girls he met in college.

It didn't take long for the crew to become tired. Neville called a halt to their travels every half hour, hoping to keep them from getting too worn out. They were all young men who, for the last several months, did little but sit around in their hot tents and cold plane. Acknowledging how stressful and dangerous their jobs were, the squadron's commanding officer never put a priority on physical conditioning, and it showed.

The salt marsh curved to the left where the almost flat terrain changed to a steep sandy hill. Neville whispered for everyone to sit down and wait for him to return, before he started climbing. Keeping just below the top of the thirty-foot high hill, with Clyde by his side, he had a good view of the white surf marking where land and sea melded together on their left. Other than the surf below and a few stars peaking through a thin cloud cover above, they could not see anything in front of them. The uniformity of the void in front seemed unnatural. Their entire world appeared to have a soft black curtain draped over it.

Clyde's head jerked around. "What was that?" he blurted out, pointing to their right.

"What? Did you see something?"

Remembering to whisper, he said, "I don't know. I thought I saw a light. Just for a moment. I think it was moving."

"How far away?"

"What say you make the next question an intelligent one? How could I tell? I only saw it for a second. It could have been just the other side of a cricket pitch or a mile away. Without some frame of reference…"

"No need to be sarcastic! The moon should be coming up in a little bit. I suggest we don't go any farther until we know more. I'll go back to the men and get them to settle in."

Clyde wiggled until he created a comfortable spot next to a bush on the hilltop, never looking away from the direction where the brief light had appeared. Too dim for an electric light, he felt sure it was either an oil lamp or possibly, someone lighting a cigarette. In either case, someone was out there, and where there was one…

Following the dictum, a "watched pot never boils," Clyde almost had himself convinced the moon had gone on a walkabout. Finally, with excruciating slowness the clouds to the east started reflecting the silvery white light. The moon seemed almost as brilliant as the sun when it shouldered aside the darkness and the few remaining clouds to make the ocean become a parade of sparkles moving toward the island. By the time the moon was high enough to give the land some definition, Neville was settled in beside him.

Clyde answered Neville's one word question, "Well?" with a shake of his head.

"Maybe they're all asleep."

Neville poked Clyde in the ribs. "We can't be that lucky! You know bloody well that if some of the Emperor's finest are out there-they are not all asleep! We used up this month's luck ration escaping the crash."

"Fine then, but what if the boss man took his best men into the mountains and left his bottom of the barrel troops back here?"

"Why would he do that?"

"His sense of honor-duty. Someone has to defend the place. He can't let the Yanks take over his base without a fight."

Neville couldn't believe his ears. "In other words, you're saying the men still at the base are simply cannon fodder. No officer would do that, not even a Jap."

"No officer? What about the times we saw whole battalions chewed up by machine gun fire when we were in the Great War. How much do you think those officers cared about ordering their men into no man's land?"

Neville pursed his lips and slipped his set of binoculars out of its pouch. Slowly he scanned the darkness. "You may be right, but it don't matter. Good soldiers or not, we need to find out as much as we can." He concentrated his scan on one spot. "I can see the tops of some buildings sticking up over the next hill."

"In that case, I must have seen a careless lookout lighting up on top the hill."

"Some men never learn. People keep telling me that cigarettes will be the death of me, only tonight it' going to be his. What time is it getting to be, Mate?"

Clyde looked at his watch. The faint glow of its hands said twelve-thirty. "If there is still a large bunch at the base, they'll change lookouts every two hours, probably at two o'clock. Otherwise, it'll be at four. We need to be ready to take the man out around four-thirty, get our boys up there and figure out what to do before they sound reveille."

"Slow down a minute. We can't go charging in there as if it's an aboriginal village in the back of beyond. We need to do some reconnaissance. Remember, all we have are a few men who have no ground combat experience armed with a handful of pistols. We run into one machine gun or a dozen half-decent soldiers and that's the end of it."

Miffed at Neville for not seeing the elegant simplicity of his plan, Clyde rolled onto his right side and looked out over the landscape as the rising moon revealed its contours. He could see several small hills, and then a silvery thread coming from farther inland toward the enemy camp.

"Well I'll be…now I know…of course!"

"Still learning the English language, are you?"

"What are you going on about?"

"Clyde, I know you can't be as dumb as you make out, Mate, but then, you always manage to prove me wrong. Come on now, give me a clue as to what's in your, so-called, mind."

"Water, that's what. We need it and that's why the Japs put their camp right in front of us." Clyde pointed off to the west, careful not to expose himself above the ridgeline. "There's a stream out there and it runs toward those buildings. All we have to do is circle around and fill our canteens. Then we can take our time figuring out what we want to do."

Chapter 5

Dark of the Night

September 3, 1944

Stripped of everything but their canteens and pistols three of the crew followed Clyde and Neville toward the enemy camp. Vermont stayed behind, keeping watch over Swede. He kept a piece of cloth handy since the pilot's delirium fits were becoming more frequent. As a last resort, he might have to stuff it in his mouth.

As lost as the group had been stumbling around in the dark, they now wished God had never invented the moon. They each felt as nervous in its ghostly light as strippers hiding behind large soap bubbles with a stagehand about to turn on a fan. Clyde led the way with Neville bringing up the rear. With hand gestures and an occasional friendly tap on the shoulder, he tried to keep them calm, while all the time working to convince himself that they were still too far from the Japanese camp to be discovered.

Clyde chose a zigzag route, as they crawled through enemy territory. He made use of every bit of vegetation and irregular land contour he could find to keep them invisible. An hour of crawling toward the stream had everyone ready to jam a fistful of sand down Clyde's throat. Nevertheless, while their thirst continued to build, looking at the good side...they were still breathing.

Clyde squirmed around to face the man behind him. "Stay here and relax, I'm going to the top of this hill for a gander. That stream ought to be around here...somewhere."

Kansas, scratching at sand flea bites on both thighs, mumbled, "After you find the water, how about some bug repellant?"

Clyde shook his head in disgust. "Babies...you're all babies. I told you to cover yourself with mud."

"Maybe you did, but I ain't got that much spit."

Fully aware that any response would cause the airman to continue talking, Clyde suppressed a retort that easily came to mind, and crawled up the hill. From his new vantage point, he could see the parade ground in the middle of the enemy base, as well as the stream off to the right. After looking around to see if there were any lookouts on his hill, Clyde took the time to commit the camp layout to memory.

Lacking any distinctive features, the place could have been built by half the armies in the world–twelve buildings arranged like spokes of a wheel radiating out from the center hub, the parade ground. Through the non-existent windows in one building, he could see shadows that resembled rows of tables and benches, most likely the mess hall. Another, with real windows had the appearance of officer's quarters. The remaining structures were open-air barracks constructed with local materials. They had supports fashioned from tree limbs, palm fronds for walls, and miles of tough vines holding everything together. The place wasn't elegant, but with all the slit trenches running around the perimeter and between the buildings, the place could be defended by a force of a hundred or so.

Clyde slid down the hill and gathered the group together. He quickly told them what he had seen, before leading them on to the stream. The water was brackish, but drinkable, if you didn't have an educated palate. With their canteens full, Neville led the way back to Vermont and Swede while Clyde went back up the hill and dug a trench under a bush creating a well-concealed spy-hole from which he could watch the quiet enemy camp without fear of discovery.

His eyes growing heavy after watching nothing happen for several hours, a sudden sound jerked Clyde awake. A novice musician, missing half his notes was trying to sound reveille with his bugle. The camp came alive. Two squads of men and one officer, a total of twenty-one soldiers took their places, equipment and ammunition belts strapped on, rifles at their sides. Too few to be able to put up a meaningful defense, still, they were too large a group for Clyde and Neville to take on, head to head. The officer in charge yelled at his men, displeased with something, he hit one in the face with a swagger stick, before having them run around the camp perimeter for fifteen minutes, rifles held high over their heads. When the group finally filed into the mess hall, Clyde slid out of his burrow and returned to his own men.

They found a raised mound deep in the reeds of the salt-water marsh behind the beach as an out of the way place to wait out the daylight hours. Before letting everyone settle down for the day the two amateur soldiers gathered everyone together.

Kansas blurted out the one thing they all wanted to know. "What did you find out?"

"It's like we thought. About twenty men are there to die for the Emperor whenever MacArthur gets around to it."

"What kind of defenses? Machine guns, mortars, booby traps?"

"None that I could see. They do have slit trenches all over the place. Might be more for protection against being bombed, although I didn't see any evidence of the Yanks having tried to ruin their beauty sleep. I think we could sneak in there tonight and hit them tomorrow morning when they're all lined up for reveille. All we need do is take care of that one lookout."

Clyde's plan made sense, and even if it could be improved, questioning it in front of the others was a bad idea. Neville nodded his agreement. "We'll stay here today and move back to thc base of the hill at sundown."

Vermont straightened up from taking another look at Swede. "What about the Skipper? I think he's getting better, but we can't leave him here."

"Right you are. He'll have to come with us, at least to the hill. Then we'll see."

Clyde, unable to stifle a yawn, said, "Make yourselves some shade. It's going to be a hot one. I'll go back up the hill before sundown to make sure nothing has changed."

With the sun about to settle below the western horizon, Clyde crawled under his favorite bush, parted the grass in front and began examining the camp below. The cook was stirring a pot of something over a fire next to the mess hall with two men nearby breaking up and feeding the remains of wood packing cases into the fire. An officer walked to the center of the parade ground with his bugler. The rest of his command suddenly appeared. They drew up to attention with the first off-key note, and one man lowered their flag. Under his breath, Clyde once again counted his targets. As far as he was concerned, they weren't men. They were simply targets needing to be neutralized. To assuage any guilt he might feel later on, he reworded a well-known scripture. "Do unto others, before they can do unto you."

The first soldier in line to get his food ate quickly, went to the latrine and climbed the hill to take his post. A darkness as dense as a velvet curtain and a second brief shower descended over the island as Neville joined Clyde near the top of the hill. They took turns napping with only the sound of a few lonely crickets breaking the silence. The guards changed at midnight. After the new man had time to relax, and before the moon came up, Clyde and Neville moved into position. They waited, twenty feet apart and a little below the hillcrest with the guard post between them. For silent work, Clyde preferred his lethal looking dagger, while Neville, more of a traditionalist, preferred a heavy Marine K-Bar knife.

Another replacement guard arrived a few minutes after four, and received some sharp words from the man ready to be relieved. Several times the new man paced back and forth along the crest. It only took the man a few repetitions for Neville to gauge when to make his move. As soon as the sentry turned to walk away, Neville moved to a kneeling position, only to have a foot slip. The sound was softer than that of the nearby crickets, but it was enough.

The man stopped, turned and started to un-sling his rifle. With no time to get to his feet, Neville lunged at the guard's knees, wrapped his arms around the man's legs and pushed him over. His knife in his right hand was pinned against the ground. Neville couldn't get it free as the guard tried to swing the butt of his rifle at Neville's head.

Neither man could land a telling blow against the other as they rolled off the crest of the hill facing away from the camp and came to a stop against a thick thorn bush a few feet below. Getting his hand free, Neville brought his knife down in a savage thrust, only to have it knocked out of his hand when it hit the stock of the rifle. The soldier worked himself free and now on his knees started to swing the rifle around in a brain-crushing blow that never made contact. Grabbing a handful of the man's hair from behind, Clyde yanked the guard's head back and with one stroke cut his windpipe and jugular. A fountain of blood erupted from the guard's throat, his head almost severed from his body.

The man fell forward, his lifeless body rolling down the hill. Neville sat down and took a few deep breaths. Clyde chuckled as he wiped his knife clean on a tuft of grass. "Who taught you how to ambush a man?"

Concerned for his reputation, Neville reached out and pulled his partner close. “Not a word. Not a bloody word or I’ll stake you to an ant hill and smear your face with honey.”

“Right, you are, but you really should be more careful. I was worried I was going to have to lead these Yanks to safety all by myself.”

“Hmmph. Just you wait. Next time…” Neville’s voice trailed off as they started down the front of the hill toward the enemy base following a narrow path that avoided the heaviest undergrowth. They hunched over when the ground flattened out and moved quickly seeking the security of the mess building. Once screened by the building, they took a moment, to scan the area for danger. “This is too easy!” Clyde whispered into Neville’s ear.

Neville inched to the corner of the building. He poked his head out and quickly pulled back. He waited a moment, then did it again, taking more time to verify that no one was awake. He motioned for Clyde to take a look. Satisfied that the camp did not hold any unseen obstacles, they made their way back toward the hillside path. Passing by the dead coals of the cooking fire, Neville stumbled on a piece of wood and fell to his knees. Clyde dropped down beside him. “You Okay?”

“I’m fine–just stupid,” Neville whispered, as he reached out and picked up the piece of wood. Part of a packing case with a symbol and Japanese characters printed on it.

Clyde got up and took a few steps before looking back at Neville still on the ground. He hurried back, “Let’s go, we have to get the others down here.”

Neville nodded, but did not move, his eyes still on the wood. The thin light cast by the quarter moon made it difficult to see the markings clearly. Knowing the danger they were in, Neville grabbed Clyde and pulled him close. Pointing at one symbol on the wood, he said, “I’ve seen this before, but…what do you make of it?”

Irritated at Neville for wasting valuable time, Clyde's head swiveled around like an owl scanning the area for danger, before grabbing the wood out of Neville's hand. He turned, placing the moon behind him and held the piece of wood up to the light. He squinted hard and shook his head, trying to understand what he was looking at. Part of the symbol in question had been rubbed off, but with imagination, he understood what it meant. Clyde put the wood down and whispered, "You got it right, Mate. This was part of a crate of land mines. Saw them burning a stack of wood like this earlier."

"How many do you think they planted?"

"A hundred, two-hundred? Who knows?"

"Good thing we had that path, otherwise…"

"I know, I know. It all comes from living right, only we ain't going to be able to get our fellas' around to the other side of the camp. Too likely someone will step in the wrong spot."

"You stay up on the hill and make sure things don't change," said Clyde. "I'll go back and get the others. We'll have to hide them under the mess hall and that other building. It'll mean being farther away from the parade ground than we want, but that's the way it has to be. Sure hope they can shoot straight!"

Six men with five pistols and fifty-six bullets planned to assault twenty trained soldiers equipped with rifles. In a camp that was probably surrounded by a minefield. There was only one sure way to escape–the path they had come in on. The odds of something going wrong were high. Too high. A bookmaker would lick his chops at someone placing money on their survival.

The group nervously crawled under the closest two buildings with people starting to move around above them. Some shouting and the entire camp quickly came awake. Feet ran down the three steps to ground level and everyone headed out onto the parade ground. The scene was a duplicate of every other army in the world. One man stood at the flagpole, next to him, the wanna-be bugler moistened his lips with the officer in charge standing in front. The remaining enlisted men lined up at attention in two rows facing forward.

Sweating hands pulled pistols from holsters and flipped off the safeties. A bullet already chambered in each weapon with the hammer drawn back, the five shooters tried to brace themselves for the heavy recoil of the .45 caliber pistols. The jarring off-key first note of the bugle came, releasing the pressure, the nervous tension of men facing the unknown. Only Clyde and Neville had ever had the opportunity of looking into the eyes of a man they were going to kill. For the others, shooting at a fighter plane had been scary, but impersonal. This was war on a personal level.

Three bullets found their targets followed by one more spinning a man around. Caught off guard, the remaining Japanese dropped to the ground fumbling to bring their weapons up and chambering rounds in their bolt-action rifles. Hidden in the shadows under the two buildings, the only targets the Japanese could see were flashes as each pistol fired. Clyde and Neville, aware of their advantage, moved around after almost every shot. The airmen, concentrating on trying to hit their targets remained rooted to their positions.

Clyde ejected his first magazine, slapped another into his pistol, pulled back the slide chambering a round. Two more Japanese soldiers slumped over, as had one of the flyers. Kansas, the lowest ranking crewman, the only one without a pistol, reached over and picked up the weapon Texas dropped. Taking a lesson from his teachers, he rolled over twice, held the gun with both hands, took aim and dropped two men with two quick shots. Rabbit hunting on the Great Plains had its benefits.

The Japanese officer, by some miracle untouched, stood, drew his sword and shouted at his men to charge the intruders. Neville tried to control the adrenalin surging through him. He took his time, aimed and shot the young man in the chest. The lieutenant's face registered surprise and then shock as the powerful slug plowed through him and lodged in the brain of the man behind. The other soldiers, caught in positions halfway between prone and standing made easy targets for the assault by the unusual attack group, the crew of a Yankee bomber led by English coast watchers. When the shooting ended, their thumping hearts sounded as loud as a base drum. It was over. Smoke and the smell of burnt powder drifted across the parade ground and the Japanese flag lay crumpled in the hands of a dead soldier at the base of the flagpole.

"Well I'll be a…" cackled Vermont, surprised he was still alive. "We did it. We really did it."

Kansas crawled back to Texas and hesitated before feeling for a pulse. He'd never touched a dead body. His heart was pounding. Expecting the worst, his face lit up when his hand felt a strong beat. Laying in the deep shade under the building made it hard to see where his friend had been shot. He bent down close to Texas and saw a pool of blood under his head. Getting closer, he saw a deep gash running from the top of his forehead to the crown of his head. A steady flow of blood dripped into a dark red puddle beneath, before being sucked down into the sandy soil. For Texas, the only difference between life and death…a half-inch, a new way to part his hair and the world's worst headache.

Picking his way through the pile of mangled bodies, Neville kept alert for any signs of life. His dread of finding one of the Japanese injured, but not dead, began to disappear until his foot nudged an inert body. A soft moan escaped the man's lips. Neville spun around, aimed his weapon at the man wearing a blood-red shirt and then lowered it. With each weak breath bubbles formed on the soldier's chest. Shooting a man who could shoot back was part of war, but shooting an injured man, who could not defend himself, even if he was a Japanese soldier, seemed wrong.

While Neville hesitated to administer a coup-de-gras, Vermont walked over, looked at the mortally wounded soldier and shook his head. When he again raised his pistol, the gunner, said, “What are you going to do?”

“We can’t take care of him, we can’t take him with us and leaving him here like this…well that doesn’t seem right either.”

Vermont took a deep breath and turned away. Over his shoulder, he said, “Better you than me.”

The soldier seemed to know what they were saying. His eyes widened as his face showed the pain he was in along with contempt for his enemy, when he saw Neville raise the pistol. He pulled the trigger and was rewarded with a loud click. The battle, or was it a slaughter, had used every last bullet. He holstered his weapon and picked up the man’s rifle. The weapon discharged, seemingly of its own volition. A jolt shook the body and a rush of air escaped the suddenly flaccid lips. Another soul was on its journey to the shrine at Yakusuni.

Looking around the parade ground and feeling proud of himself, Kansas said to no one in particular, “That sure was easy.”

“We were lucky!” stated Clyde. “Dumb luck, but I’ll take it.” He turned to Neville, “Good show, Mate. Now, answer this question. Do we keep the place, or…?”

“Or, sounds like the smart thing. Let’s grab what we need and get our bloody arses out of here before any of their friends stop by for a cup-a.”

Vermont quickly scavenged among the bodies for medical supplies, knelt on the ground and got busy bandaging Texas’ head. “Why not stay right here and wait for MacArthur? There isn’t anyone left to bother us.”

Kansas chimed in. “We might even get a medal.”

“There’s a couple of hundred ‘why nots’ up in them mountains and we killed their buddies. How would you feel if you were in their shoes? Eventually, they’re going to send out a patrol. When that happens I intend to be someplace else.”

Clyde settled his pistol back in its holster and took a moment to look around the camp. "We need to make it look like a raiding party came ashore and then left. We don't want the Nips in the mountains to think we're still on the island."

"That sounds like a plan I can live with," said Neville. "I'll take these boys back, pick up Swede and get our rafts. We'll paddle down the coast and then up the stream. You start putting together a pile of material that we can use. All the food, water, medicine and weapons you can find, along with whatever else makes sense. When we're done, it will look like a raiding party came ashore and left the same way."

Vermont used the crumpled flag to wipe the blood off his hands. "What do you mean, left? The mountains are full of Nips? If we ain't staying here, where we going?"

"Back where we started, next to the salt marsh. Two, maybe three trips and we'll have enough to keep us going until the Army shows up."

"If MacArthur follows your game plan. What if he doesn't? How long can we last?"

"At least two weeks, maybe more. All we have to do is keep quiet, drink a lot of water and not get sunburned. As you Yanks say, 'It's a piece of cake.'"

"Uh, huh…sure." Vermont's response validated why he was the crew's resident skeptic title. "You guys are in charge, so I hope you know what your doing. But until our guys show up, I'm going to keep worrying about Emperor Douglas getting distracted and sending his ships somewhere else!"

"I like the way you think. Hope for the best, plan for the worst."

Chapter 6

Sound and Fury

September 15, 1944

Island time does not have hour or minute hands. It isn't concerned with the little things that make one day different from the next. Island time is divided into sunrise–time to scratch the night's fresh accumulation of bug bites. Daytime–digging deeper dugouts to hide from the sun. And finally, sunset–cooking some of their meager selection of food on an alcohol burner, along with some tough meat from the tail of an old Saltie that wandered by one morning.

Day followed day with little change, except for the day the first patrol came down from the mountains. About to take his turn in the lookout tree, Vermont glanced up to see Clyde motioning toward the beach, and then, with a hand signal for him to stay on the ground. He watched a Japanese patrol walking on the hard packed sand at the water's edge, heading for the camp by the stream. Thirty minutes later, they saw two men running back up the beach. It took almost three hours for a full company of men to come jogging by, rifles at port arms.

Over the next day and a half, small and large patrols fanned out over the peninsula searching for any sign of the invaders who had killed their comrades.

Some patrols came close to the hideout near the salt marsh, but the group's luck held, in more ways than one. Swede, recovered and refreshed, came back from his mind travels, while Texas started moving around wearing a turban of woven grass to disguise his white head bandage.

Patrols continued to come down from the mountains three times a week walking along the same paths and looking in the same areas every time. The Japanese were going through the motions, but seemed resigned to the fact that the invaders had escaped. Everyone on Morotai was waiting for the big invasion of Halmahera a few miles away and wondered how it would affect them. With the bombing of that large island becoming more intense, the invasion had to happen soon. The results were likely to be rescue for one group, while the other died fighting for the Emperor.

A soft swishing sound woke Clyde out of an uneasy sleep. Neville's hand touched his friend and pulled back, followed by Neville fitting his body into a slight depression in the sand.

"You hear that," whispered Neville.

"What?"

"Don't move, don't talk, just listen. I can hear engines."

"Don't be daft. We know the Nips don't have any motor vehicles on this island."

"Maybe so," acknowledged Neville cocking his head, "but, I hear something."

Clyde looked at his watch. "It will be sunrise in another hour. After that you can take a look around, as long as you promise not to get shot."

"Glad to hear you're so concerned."

"Of course I'm concerned. What am I going to do on Pyramid with twice as much land and half as much help? Plus, I already have two wives, somewhere. Don't need yours."

About to slip a verbal knife into his mate, Neville twisted around to look at the dark early morning sky as a flash lit up the clouds. Blossoms of orange and white light glowed briefly before they heard and felt it. "What kind of storm is that?"

Clyde, elated at what he heard and saw said, "That's a Yankee storm! It looks like MacArthur finally made up his mind to take Halmahera." The two men stood up only to hear a dangerous mind-piercing whistle and a geyser of sand explode into the air two-hundred yards away. They dove for the protection of mother earth, with the explosion rattling their teeth. Before they could say anything, several more explosions occurred.

"I know those fellas don't always hit what they're aiming at, but I thought they were getting better, until now." Neville got to his knees to see what was happening and heard another shell whistling down toward them. He quickly imitated a groundhog.

Cautiously coming up for air after the blast stopped bouncing him around, he said, "Bloody hell, don't they know they're shelling the wrong island? I think you should go over and tell them they're ruining my beauty sleep. The island they want is a little farther south."

Kansas crawled into his hole. "I thought we sank all the Jap ships."

"Nice thought there, only these are your countrymen."

"Those are our guns? How do we tell them to stop?"

"Very carefully!"

"And from somewhere else," added Neville.

Having exhausted their repertoire of smart-aleck remarks, each of them grabbed a shovel and tried to find China. The naval shelling continued for another hour with most of the shells landing near the opposite shore of the peninsula. When the bombardment ended, the silence was broken by the sound of landing craft plowing through the surf and depositing a full brigade of soldiers on the beach. Larger landing craft followed disgorging tanks and trucks into the shallow water where they promptly bogged down. Aiming for a total surprise, that's exactly what MacArthur's headquarters got.

A pre-invasion reconnaissance team had not been allowed to evaluate the landing area. Bulldozers and other construction equipment arrived before the beach master could call them off. Every vehicle heavier than an unloaded Jeep bogged down to its axles in the soft ooze hidden under the calm water. In the case of the heavy vehicles, they continued sinking until the crews abandoned them, watching as their mechanized marvels disappeared under the two-foot deep clear blue water.

Noon came and went before Neville felt it safe to take a look. The group assembled, tied several white rags to some long branches and started walking across the peninsula. As soon as they saw movement in the bushes ahead, they stopped, held their hands up and vigorously waved their flags. Swede, whose clothing looked as much like a uniform as anyone's, stood in front to greet the group's rescuers.

"Yes sir, that's right. We've been on the island for two weeks," answered Swede, between mouthfuls of bacon, eggs and hot coffee. Still dressed in their island clothes, the group sat at a table in the officer's mess of the heavy cruiser Nashville answering questions from a Naval Captain and two Colonels. The officers, part of MacArthur's planning and intelligence staff, wanted the island's resident spies to tell them everything they knew about the place.

Still upset at how close the naval gunfire had come to eliminating them, Clyde broke in. "Who taught you Yanks how to invade a place?" He said angrily, to the small group of officers, who were taken aback by the Englishman's lack of gratitude for being rescued. "First you're supposed to send in some Rangers or somebody, to find out where to come ashore and what to bomb. If you had, you wouldn't have wasted all those lovely artillery shells, plus you landed on the wrong beach."

"What do you mean, the wrong beach?"

Neville continued as he held up his empty coffee cup for a steward to refill. "You landed on the wrong side of the island. If you're smart, you'll tell your people to move around to the other side. Good firm sand there. You won't have to go digging to find those lovely tanks, not that you're going to need them."

The older of the Colonels, pointed a finger at them, his well-tanned and deeply lined face showing his anger. "Look you two. We've been doing this a lot longer than you, so why don't you show a little gratitude. You're damn lucky we found you before the Japs."

"Lucky? Maybe. But we found them first. Didn't you wonder why none of your men got shot at when they landed? We…"

Clyde put his hand up to calm his partner. "You want to know where the Japs are right now?" The officers nodded. "Up in those mountains. They've been up there for two weeks waiting for you to show up. We cleared the rest of them off the island."

"You what?" None of the officers could hide their disbelief.

Clyde decided the time had come to put these Yanks in their place as he and Neville had done on several other occasions. "It was either them or us and we didn't feature living in them mountains, what with having to take care of your injured pilot and all. If a Jap is alive over there, he's in the mountains."

Seeing how the situation was going downhill in a hurry, Swede said, "That's exactly right, sir. Mr. Arnold and Mr. Saunders took care of us and the Japs, just like they said."

The Colonel gave Swede a hard stare before softening his expression. "Well…that, that's great. We don't need the mountains. We don't even want the mountains. All we want is the open area on the southern end of the island for an airbase to support upcoming operations in the Philippines. We'll cordon off the area we don't want and let the Japs eat all the coconuts they can find."

"What about them fellas over on Halmahera. You been bombing them pretty regular."

"Oh, that was a diversion to keep them from sending reinforcements over here. We don't need that island. When they run out of food, they'll give up or commit hari-kari. No point in losing men for nothing."

With MacArthur and his staff on board, the Nashville had barely arrived in time for the invasion. The big ship stayed two days, long enough for the Supreme Commander to be sure the invasion was a success before turning around and taking him back to Hollandia.

The staff learned to treat Clyde and Neville like rich, annoying relatives, showing gratitude and respect while looking forward to shifting their care to some other branch of the family…and the sooner, the better. The Philippines were the next target and things were going to happen even faster than originally planned.

Admiral Halsey commanded task Force 77 and generally worked in the Central Pacific under Nimitz. However, his massive fleet of carriers and support elements sometimes crossed into MacArthur's theatre of operation to support his activities. In early September, Halsey attacked various targets in the southern Philippines as preparations for the Philippine campaign moved forward. The Japanese response from the areas targeted was so anemic that Halsey, in his brash manner, fired off urgent messages to his superiors and MacArthur.

Skip Morotai and Mindanao, along with a number of other targets and attack Leyte.

Several all-night sessions occurred in Washington when Halsey's recommendations and supporting information arrived. His advice would advance the war schedule by several months.

Could they do it? Was there time to reorganize air, land, and sea personnel numbering in the hundreds of thousands? Could the supply chain meet the demands? Nerves were on edge and even the President voiced some doubts, but in the end, though the Morotai operation had already begun, word came down through channels...Invade Leyte in thirty days. It might be a life or death decision for thousands of men, with the decision makers flying by the seat of their pants.

Hearing that his two wayward friends were safe, Cullison knew they should be sent home, but…maybe not. The entire character of the Pacific war was about to change and Cullison might find it handy to have a pair of wild cards in his hand.

Chapter 7

Hollandia

September 19, 1944

By definition, fighting can result in injuries, or death, and the closer to the front lines, the more dangerous the situation. Hollandia, originally a small Dutch settlement located in a narrow valley hemmed in by steep hills, sitting on New Guinea's north coast, was no longer a battle zone. A thousand miles from Morotai or any other active fighting, the place was an active outpost of the war. For the time being, it was MacArthur's new headquarters complex. Following their boss, senior officers and their paper pushing staffs began arriving by the boatload. The support troops were pushed to the limit to create the physical facilities to make the place operational. The number of people quickly outstripped the facilities. Land that could be built on was at a premium requiring the Engineers to build new accommodations farther up the narrow valley, many miles from the water.

Neither Cullison nor Harry could get to the harbor when the Nashville dropped anchor. The only thing Cullison could do was send a corporal to meet the first invaders of Morotai when they stepped onto the beach from a landing craft. Wearing their mix and match semi-civilian clothes with side arms and carrying what remained of their personal items in two small duffle bags, the corporal immediately recognized his passengers.

The unusual attire, civilian shorts and naval officer shirts made the corporal wonder if he should salute. He decided not to, and stuck out his hand instead. "Mr. Arnold, Mr. Saunders, the Jeep is over here. Can I help you with those bags?"

Always looking for an advantage, Clyde dropped his bag where it settled into a shallow depression in the wet sand. He acted as if it weighed a hundred pounds. Assume control, keep the other fellow off balance, was how he lived. It also helped explain his lack of friends. "Right you are, sonny. You can carry my bag to the car." Without waiting for their escort, the two men walked to the Jeep and got in.

The Corporal, who looked too young to have a driver's license, started the engine, jerked the gearshift lever down and the vehicle lurched forward. After he found second gear, he said, "Commander Cullison said I'm to take you to the BOQ, Bachelor Officers Quarters. He said he'll be by later today. By then he hopes to have arranged your transportation home."

Buildings in the original Dutch settlement were built with wood planking and as few nails as possible. Glass windows were non-existent, but the openings did have screens. The settlement covered ten blocks, give or take. With the massive influx of personnel and material, the base now extended almost twenty miles up the narrowing valley that ended at thousand-foot high cliffs protecting the island's unexplored interior. The farther from the harbor they drove, the more temporary looking the buildings. Many of them appeared to have been built by the Japanese during their three-year occupation of the area.

Signs attached to wood poles along the road pointed to the many different offices and commands needed to support a large army. Mess halls, supply depots, enlisted quarters, officer's quarters, jail, repair shops and several BOQ's. After they drove past BOQ #3, Neville said, "You missed the turn."

"What?" the driver said trying to avoid a pothole with a supply truck heading right for them. The Corporal swerved to miss the truck and pothole. Instead, he found an even larger hole. The jarring impact had Neville wondering if all his teeth were still in place.

"I said, thc BOQ is back there on your left."

"Oh, no Sir. My orders were to take you to number five. All the others are full. I think they've already started putting up number six. This place sure has grown since I got here."

"When did you arrive?"

"Almost two weeks ago. Have you been here before?"

"Here and other less memorable places on this damn island." Clyde's voice left little doubt as to how he felt about New Guinea. The driver was young, but the meaning of Clyde's words and the tone of his voice, along with the look on his face made the young soldier stop talking and concentrate on his driving. Clyde's face looked as if he had been forced to eat a rotten breadfruit, a bland tasting diet staple of some of the island's natives–the headhunters probably ate it during lent.

The Jeep came to a stop in front of a palm-thatched building where a soldier was nailing up a sign. "BOQ #5" They were at least ten miles from the harbor and fifteen-hundred feet above sea level. The valley had narrowed to nothing more than a two-hundred foot wide cleft in the mountains that seemed to go straight up into the clouds. The driver grabbed their luggage, dropped it on the porch and hurriedly started back down the valley. Clyde took a moment to look around, shrugged his shoulders at Neville and walked into the all-purpose office-lounge-dining room.

"You've been assigned hut number six," said the clerk pointing out the side of the open-air building. The construction crew promised they would add walls to it in the near future. "Your hut is the last one up that path to the right. We serve three meals a day right in here, if the supply truck doesn't run out before it gets this far up the valley." Holding out a pencil, the clerk said, "Please sign here."

Clyde signed the book. While waiting for Neville to finish signing in, he said, "Where's the bar?"

The orderly looked up from his desk. "This is a temporary BOQ, sir. The only place that serves beer is down near BOQ number one."

"Beer?" Clyde's eyes opened wide. He hadn't had any of his favorite beverage in several weeks. "You have beer?"

"Stick your tongue back in your face. This ain't Sydney!"

"One can always hope." Clyde looked at the orderly. "Ain't that right son? Now, where is the beer?"

"It's near number one sir. The building behind the trees at the left end of the beach. A new supply arrived by ship the first of the week, direct from Houston."

A balloon stuck with a pin could not deflate as quickly as did Clyde's anticipation of getting drunk. "In cans?" he asked, already knowing the answer. "That's unsanitary."

"Sir?"

"Just because they boiled the stuff doesn't mean its okay for a fellow to drink canned piss." Clyde and Neville had very particular tastes in beer. They had been known to get quite vocal and physical when it did not come up to their standards of taste and alcohol content. American Army beer most definitely did not meet those standards. "What about liquor? Surely…"

The clerk shook his head. "None, that I know of. I hear the base commander don't drink."

Neville raised his hand in a calming gesture to keep Clyde from blowing up. "Let's find our hut, unload our kit and take a walk around. Remember, this place is run by the Army. They aren't as smart as the Navy or Marines when it comes to liquid refreshment, but I'll bet you if we look, we'll find us some."

Clyde's face instantly changed with a big smile appearing. "My, my, how your brain has grown. Soon as Cullison shows up we'll get him to pay us for saving his flyboys and then start sniffing around."

"What do you mean, pay us?" Neville asked as they walked up to their hut.

Clyde looking as innocent as a choirboy. "Someone put us on the wrong plane, now didn't they? Without us, those young boys would have been captured or dead. The least the poor chap can do is get McCulloch to reinstate us as Coast Watchers. That means we'll be able to draw at least a month's salary plus a hazardous duty bonus, preferably in Yank dollars."

Warming to the idea, Neville added, "Now hold on a minute before you start giving our services away on the cheap. How much do you think those flyers are worth? What with all of their special training, each one of them could be worth a grand or more."

They found their hut, a raised floor and a roof protecting some cots covered with mosquito netting. Clyde walked around testing the mattress on each of its six cots. "You do have a point. Let's think about it and see how grateful the Yanks are once Cullison gets here. In the mean time, I'm going to claim the cot in the corner for a well-deserved nap."

Clyde and Neville had done a little exploring after waking up, but stayed near the BOQ waiting for Cullison to show up. When he did get there, he didn't waste any time on pleasantries. "We have a rule in the Navy, when asked a question, you give a clear and honest answer." Cullison pointed his finger at Neville, and then at Clyde. "Do you understand?" They both still had smiles on their faces as they nodded.

"Now…how did you come to get on the wrong plane?" Before either of the self-proclaimed saviors could answer, he continued, looking directly at Clyde. "I've already talked with the man who dropped you at the airfield on Los Negros, but I want to hear your side of it."

"There goes our hazardous duty pay," Clyde said under his breath.

Cullison leaned forward. "What was that? Did you say something about pay?"

It was time for either a stout defense or a strong offense. Clyde chose a route somewhere in the middle. "I know that in the past, we've volunteered for difficult assignments, but we were always paid for our efforts. Commander McCulloch took care of us. Now, as I see things, we saved most of a bomber crew, eliminated a Jap base, protected your troops from being killed during the landing and advised General MacArthur on where to bring his equipment ashore. Surely you can see that we are due some compensation for taking such risks."

"That is not what I asked. The subject is, how did you get on the wrong plane?"

Clyde took a deep breath. He wasn't in the habit of sticking to the truth when what he had to say might be considered, by some, as a character flaw. He took another moment before saying, "I saw the pilot waving at us from his cockpit and thought we should take advantage of the nice weather. I thought, why not take a look at what's going on? It might be our last chance."

"Ahh." Cullison smiled knowing that finally, he was hearing the truth. "So, getting on the wrong plane wasn't the fault of your driver, or anyone else on base, was it?"

"No it wasn't. I thought we needed one more…I don't know…something, before going back to civilian life."

"Okay. And now that you've had some excitement, do you want to go home, or do you want to do some good?"

Neville's eyes opened wide. "Where, when and how much will you pay us?" he said, cutting Clyde off.

Their expectations rose as Cullison told them the situation. Clyde had visions of a wad of money large enough to pay for whatever liquor they could find, even if it happened to be a General's private stock. Then Cullison said, "McCullough can't put you back on the payroll. He's been assigned to Mountbatten in India, which unfortunately means…"

Their spirits hit bottom before hearing, "I'll get you your back pay, but I expect you to follow orders. Is that understood?"

All smiles, Clyde pumped Cullison's hand while Neville slapped him on the shoulder. "We won't let you down. We'll be ready for an assignment in two or three days, Bill. Just need a little time to recover from being chased around by the Nips."

Neville shot a questioning look at Clyde. He wanted to say, "What in the world?"

Cullison turned to leave. Before he could take two steps, Clyde reached out and gently touched his arm, making his new employer turn around. Holding Cullison's attention, he put a hand in his pocket and drew it back out holding the pocket's lining. "About our pay? We lost what we had in the plane crash. Don't even have enough money to buy a toothbrush."

"Toothbrush?" Cullison asked sarcastically as he dug into his pocket and drew out his billfold. He took one look inside, pulled out all of his folding money, fifteen dollars, and handed it to Neville. Pointing a finger at his newest employees, he finished with, "You have three days…and you better be sober!"

"But…"

Using his best commanding officer voice, Cullison repeated, "No buts. Three days, my office, zero-eight-hundred, both of you…sober!"

Chapter 8

Decisions

September 20, 1944

The high-level conference started right after breakfast. Mess attendants came into the large tent once an hour with urns of fresh coffee, while the men, many with a galaxy of stars on their shoulders, tried to adjust to a new reality.

"Gentlemen," said General MacArthur in a relaxed tone as he tapped a pencil on the table for emphasis. "We've come a long way in the past several years. We all wish things had progressed more quickly, but we now have all of New Guinea, the Admiralties and Morotai. You are to be congratulated." The ten generals at the table smiled at the compliment.

Behind the generals sat two rows of officers, none with a rank lower than Major. At the beginning of the war, they served as Army, Air Corps and Naval officers of the United States, Australia, New Zealand and the Netherlands. The Japanese onslaught brought them together as nothing else could. They represented the upper echelon of the Southwest Pacific Command with five star General MacArthur as their leader.

MacArthur knew how to extract the most out of a few words. He took a moment and dramatically looked at the men who translated his orders into military victories. "We have recently learned that our enemy is worse off than we thought. Admiral Halsey has provided information that makes us believe that we no longer need to invade Mindanao."

The allied plan scheduled the large Philippine island at the southern end of the country for invasion in November. It was to have been MacArthur's long awaited, 'I Shall Return' moment. The large group stayed silent, although many of them turned to look at other staff members with a question on their faces. The Joint Chiefs and the President had approved the schedule for the invasion over a year ago. Jokingly, it had been said, that only God carried a rank high enough to change the plan. It seemed someone had been wrong.

"Admiral Halsey's information has convinced Washington and me that we can bypass Yap, Ulithi and Mindanao. The men that will not be used in those landings, along with our reserve forces will allow us to strike for the heart of the Philippines, with a landing on Leyte.

"Besides our own seventh fleet, we will also have support from the Third Fleet's fast attack carrier units. Therefore, I am ordering an invasion of Leyte for October twentieth. That means thirty days from today we will be storming a Philippine beach. I want to see a plan of action for the major commands on my desk tomorrow morning, and a final operations order for all units down to company level in four days." MacArthur smiled as he picked up his battered hat, its brim covered with gold braid tinged green. "You're all good men or else you wouldn't be here, so get to work."

He looked at his Chief of Staff, General Sutherland. "Dick, they're all yours."

Everyone stood as MacArthur made his way out of the tent erected the previous week to accommodate staff meetings. MacArthur's headquarters had only arrived at Hollandia that week. In fact, some personnel were still in transit from Brisbane.

Sutherland made a motion for everyone to take his seat. "All right. We have an assignment. Let's get to it!"

Time available to make good decisions was at a premium. The conference participants ate spam on white bread for a hurried lunch washing it down with more coffee. The intermittent rain showers outside went unnoticed with the meeting finally ending as dinnertime stared them in the face. The decision to change the Philippines invasion schedule had been made in haste with messages flying back and forth between MacArthur, Nimitz and Washington.

MacArthur could hardly contain himself as he paced around his office. His plan for the conquest of Japan had been ignored in favor of the plan put forward by the navy, but now he had a chance to show what he could do. He was finally getting the opportunity and the resources to become the center of the war in the Pacific…where he belonged!

War, the most uncivilized activity of civilized man, required meticulous planning and a good deal of luck. If everything went as planned, the end of the war with the invasion of Japan might happen as much as six months ahead of schedule. However, that was the future. Right now, each of the affected units stretching from Australia to Seattle needed to adjust thousands of details, reassign hundreds of ships and tens of thousands of troops to attack a new target, and make it all happen within thirty days.

Problems with transportation, naval and air support, supply and thousands of other questions, large and small, needed to be solved. Cullison continued as the coordinator for submarine and small surface-craft support, along with the establishment of land-based observation posts.

If Japan decided to use this invasion as a do-or-die effort to stop the Allies, the navy needed to be ready. An early warning net of planes and submarines needed to be put in place to provide advance notice if Japan decided to challenge the operation. The enemy still had a substantial fleet dispersed in the home islands, Viet Nam, Borneo and other locations in the South Pacific. Cullison faced a challenging month trying to get assets such as the fast attack PT Boats as well as destroyers, assigned to locations where they could intercept inter-island reinforcements while still being available for other missions. Fixed-position observers might also be needed for reliable observation of activity in the region's restricted waterways meaning, he needed to talk with Harry.

A fleeting question of, how his two problem children were fairing all the way up near the top of the valley ran through Cullison's mind as he and Harry walked into his office tent. It was something he knew he should check on. With so many other problems needing his attention, he decided to trust them not to get into trouble, this time. When it came to Clyde and Neville, he was the eternal optimist, even though the pair always managed to disappoint him.

Trying to put his two middle-aged disasters out of his mind, Cullison and Harry sat for a few minutes in the entrance of the squad tent located under some coconut trees at the fringe of the jungle with a view of the water. They watched lights on the various ships in the harbor coming on, one at a time. It was a calming sight that almost made them forget why they were there.

"Damn this is pretty. Too bad it won't last."

Without looking at Cullison, Harry nodded in agreement. A big sigh escaped the professor's lips when he turned his attention to the desk and picked up a small-scale map of the Philippines. "If I understand what you've been saying, your brass expects the Jap navy to oppose the landings."

"They have to. The Philippines are part of the inner defense ring protecting the Japanese home islands. They must know that loss of the Islands will be the beginning of the end. Their fleet, in fact the whole country, is short of fuel. Losing the islands will make it almost impossible for them to ship raw materials home from southeast Asia."

"But you don't know from which direction they'll attack, which strait they'll try to transit or in what strength?"

"That's our problem. What I need you to do is pinpoint the best locations to use as observation posts. We need locations where a minimum number of men can monitor all of the choke points the Jap fleet might use."

Still looking at the map, Harry shook his head. "I don't know Bill, there are a number of routes they can take. How about a little guidance?"

"Sorry, Harry. It's better if you work on this without my prejudicing your results."

"Not asking for much, are you? Especially, since I've never set foot in the Philippines."

"Don't worry about that, Harry. Geology doesn't change. You did this once before and set yourself up very nicely. Who other than a nut in love with volcanoes, would have thought to establish a lookout post on Krakatoa, not to mention saving some Dutch planters and finding himself a wife. I simply want you to look at your maps and pick out the locations where we can make the best use of a few observers. I'll do the rest, which reminds me, I need to get the latest information on sub deployments from Captain Richards."

"If that's the way you want it…okay. Only, one thing before you go, can you tell me about the area's vegetation?"

Cullison thought about Harry's question, trying to remember what he had seen on the islands before the war, when he was a bachelor and his interest in women ran a close second to the navy.

"You remember what you had to deal with on Sumatra?"

Harry groaned in response, remembering all too well the dark, almost impenetrable jungle he bumbled his way through to find Marieke."

Cullison smiled. "I'll take that as a yes. Leyte is about the same, with a little less rain."

He knew that many of their decisions would be by-guess-and-by-God. With the operation, only thirty days away Cullison was going to do a lot of praying. Considering the time crunch and the challenges posed by the island nation's restricted waterways, the decision to not send in reconnaissance units had been easy–they might be captured and made to talk. It was something the Japanese did exceedingly well. Relying on the use of a map-reader to select the vantage points, versus having someone on the ground, meant the map-reader had to be good. Harry was good. However, the question remained…was he good enough?

Chapter 9

J. J.

September 21, 1944

The day started in much the same way the previous one had ended–raining. New Guinea was famous for its humidity, heat, bugs and headhunters. Everyone had an equal opportunity to experience the first three. The last one, headhunters, were more than a rumor, but thought to be limited to the unexplored jungles in the center of the island, although no one knew for sure–only ten percent of the huge island had ever been seen by a white man. Maps of New Guinea carried the notation, "Unexplored" for the thousand-mile long central mountain range.

In an effort to keep the thousands of troops pouring into Hollandia under control and safe, officers promoted the idea that headhunters controlled the area the other side of the mountain at the head of the valley. It served to keep most of the men who were bored living under an almost permanent rain cloud from wandering off into the jungle. Most new arrivals had never seen a jungle, and some, like little boys, could not resist the temptation to go exploring.

Exploring was fun and getting lost was the last thing on a man's mind until he turned around and realized he could not tell where he had come from. Panic quickly took over followed by yelling for help. Thrashing around looking for a path or heading off in the wrong direction soon followed. If he was lucky, he found the coast or a friendly native, although the natives all looked the same and most carried a short spear, ideal for use in the thick jungle. The men who did get back to camp never strayed off again.

Neville and Clyde rarely acted as if getting older meant acting like grown ups. As they returned to their BOQ quarters from a forgettable lunch, Clyde summed up a unique opportunity. "We have three days, Right?"

Without waiting for Neville to finish nodding in agreement, he continued. "We learned on our last visit to this lovely island, that almost every tropical plant known to man grows here."

Neville interrupted, with, "What's this about plants ol' boy? You planning on becoming a botanist? If so, you've been in the sun too long. We have enough plant work waiting for us if we ever get back to Pyramid."

"Will you shut your trap and listen to me? You remember when we spent a quiet few weeks up the coast at Wakde last year?"

"Of course I do, and it wasn't quiet. What with us training those soldiers and leading an ambush against that Jap unit that showed up in the middle of the night. Of course I remember the place."

"I thought you would, but do you remember the most important thing that happened?"

"I have no idea what you're talking about, but I'm waiting with baited breath to be told."

"We met J.J. You remember him, don't you? The native that came walking out of the jungle."

Neville shook his head. "Not really. I was too drunk, although I remember the liquor he showed up with."

"Right you are. That scrawny fellow sold us his Jungle Juice and the way he bargained, we weren't his first sale."

"Yes, I do remember that. Wouldn't it be nice if we could find him now?"

"Not very likely, Wakde must be over five-hundred miles from here, but he told me his recipe and I always remember things that are important."

Neville's face lit up in a broad smile as he grasped what Clyde was driving at. "You remember what he said? That's unusual, however, we do have three days free of interference and if we can find all of the ingredients…"

"That's what I've been trying to tell you, and with enough sugar and yeast we can hurry things up. J.J. said he took a week to make a batch, but I bet you I can make something by tomorrow night that'll be stronger than that piss they call beer that came all the way from Houston."

"Well, you took your bloody time telling me. How much money are we going to need? All we have is what Commander Cullison gave us."

"We won't need much. We go shares with a couple of sergeant majors. We should be able to make a gallon a day. One quart per day for us…" Neville's smile disappeared. Seeing the change in his partner's attitude, Clyde changed his next words to keep his partner happy. "Oh, all right…two quarts for us. The rest we can divide between our suppliers."

Neville looked at his watch. "It's close on to three o'clock. What say you make a list of what we need, and then we go scrounging. Meet back here at six? I'll find a cook, you locate some of those construction fellows. If we get started manufacturing tonight, we can get drunk tomorrow night."

"Jolly good. We get what we need to start things off and then talk to a couple of the sergeants, quiet like. If anyone knows how to keep things quiet, it's those fellows. They can take charge of the scrounging and our security. Don't need any do-gooder officer sticking his nose into our business."

Before turning in for their first night alone in the BOQ, on real beds equipped with mosquito netting, they were able to accumulate some specialized building materials from the construction battalion that were easily converted to a better use. They found all the cooking equipment they needed in a truck fresh off a ship and hoped no one would miss any of it for at least three days. With modification, it promised to put them in the spirits business. New Guinea had little to recommend for itself other than, all the right ingredients for grade-A Jungle Juice. It was all available to anyone willing to thrash around in the thick undergrowth. They easily found coconuts, needed as a taste enhancer and then act as portable containers of the finished product. A visit to the one bakery on the growing base and a promise of some of their product yielded several pounds of yeast. Limes, the final ingredient in Clyde's recipe were promised for the following morning.

"I wasn't looking forward to staying up all night tending the fire," said Neville, lying on his cot, protected from a swarm of mosquitoes by a double layer of screening. "It certainly was nice of that Sergeant Loring to lend us two privates to work the night shift."

"Can't agree more, ol' fellow, but it does mean we're going to have to increase production again."

"True, but one of the sergeants brought us several boxes of sugar cane and wheat grass. Along with papaya, aloe vera and some petimezi that came in rather late this evening, I think we have things well in hand, don't you?"

"Maybe, but you never can tell about these things till the end, and then it's too late." Clyde stopped talking, a question on his face.

Neville looked up and recognized his friend's confusion. "You forgot what petizemi is, didn't you?" Without waiting for an answer, he continued, "It's that stuff that looks like a carrot." He shook his head. "Can't remember what it tastes like."

Neville yawned and turned over in his cot trying not to touch the mosquito netting that kept the noisy insects at bay. "We should have some idea in the morning of what the final product will taste like," was his final comment of the night.

Clyde woke up with his nose twitching. The jungle had a new smell. It was more rotten than the usual smell of decay that permeated the area. He shook the dead bugs off his netting and then his boots before walking to the edge of the hut's floor. Without exterior walls, the floor simply ended at a two-foot drop down to the dirt. He stuck his nose up to get a good whiff of the smell, then shook Neville awake.

"I think we have a problem."

Neville rubbed at his eyes removing the crust that formed while he slept. Not understanding what Clyde could be talking about, he started to roll over when his nose came awake. The rest of his body quickly followed. "The juice!" he exclaimed as he tried to get up, forgetting to remove his netting. He thrashed around for a minute, finally succeeding in extricating himself from the material's embrace as Clyde leaned against a post, watching and laughing.

"What are you laughing at? The juice is burning!"

"Burning? That should be interesting. I've never seen a liquid burn, except that is, for petrol."

"All right, so it isn't burning, but it smells like it's too hot. We better get over to the clearing before someone gets curious."

The two conspirators hurried into the jungle. Several hundred yards away, on the other side of a small ridge was a clearing where Clyde and Neville put their mad chemist shop together. Their two pot-watching privates were sitting against a tree talking, while flames from the fire under three large kettles were dancing as high as the lips of the pots.

"You two," Neville yelled at the young men while making a sweeping gesture with his arm, "get over here. The fire is too high. Everything is going to boil off before it's ready."

The four of them used long sticks to wriggle some of the burning logs away from the pots. Neville looking in one pot could see the liquid at a rolling boil. He shook his head in disgust and walked over to take a seat on a downed tree. "This is the last time I choose cheap labor for something this important," he mumbled to himself.

"When you want something done right, you have to do it yourself," preached Clyde.

Neville looked at his partner. "If that's the case, mister smart pants, why weren't you here to make sure we got a good batch, first thing? But no-o, you needed your beauty sleep, didn't you?"

Trying not to laugh, Clyde said, "Talk about calling the kettle black."

Neville looked at the three large pots and smiled. "They are black, aren't they? Think we should throw this batch out and start over?"

Shaking his head, Clyde walked over and looked inside the pots. The liquid in all three was back to gently bubbling, and the smell, similar to a week old dead skunk had softened as well.

Some might compare the smell with that of a long deceased animal, while others would say the aroma had qualities similar to the breath of a water buffalo. Whichever description seemed the most accurate, the smell filled the air and later in the morning the first drop of their moonshine sizzled its way out of a long copper tube. They continued the process through the day and into the evening filling a number of glass jars. They had discussed using canteens, but judging from the liquid's smell, they did not know if the metal would be thick enough to withstand the corrosive quality of the potent liquid. Their refreshment was not for the faint of heart.

Time was of the essence in getting finished with the first batch, since everyone knew that it was more enjoyable to get drunk at night than in the morning. Only when they ran out of glass containers did they compromise and start using brand-new canteens donated by a supply sergeant, praying the metal would be thick enough.

Neville carefully poured several ounces of the liquid into a coconut shell.

"How does it taste?" asked an excited Clyde.

Neville screwed up his face as he gagged on the almost clear liquid. "Not as good as the stuff we had in Wakde. It needs more lime juice." A shiver ran down Neville's spine as he talked himself into a second taste. With the nerve endings in his throat having gone on strike, the second swallow went down more easily, although he could have used a nose pin to combat the smell. Before Clyde had a chance to grab the coconut shell, Neville drank the remainder of the fluid.

"Now, you're not being very friendly," complained Clyde.

"Oh no, I really am. I'm protecting you. You have no idea how strong this is."

"That is something I would like to find out for myself."

Neville's body shook as another chill traveled from his throat down to his feet, and up again. He poured a generous amount of the liquid into a coconut shell, handed it to his partner and quickly stepped back.

Clyde took a deep breath preparing to take his first sip when a sergeant walked out of the jungle smoking a cigarette. He started talking, only to be cut off by Neville yelling at him. "Get away. You want to kill him?"

"I just..."

"Put out that cigarette before you cause an explosion."

The chastised sergeant took a step back, dropped his butt on the ground and stamped it out. "Hey Neville…sorry, okay? I couldn't find any more papaya, but I did pick two boxes of almost ripe pomegranates. I mean, one fruit's as good as another, right?"

Neville nodded, "They should work. Might even improve the taste."

Clyde's faith in their ability to find something stronger than three-point-two beer was rewarded when he took his first swallow and immediately wished he was closer to a large water supply. Glad that the sergeant had extinguished his cigarette, like Neville, he needed to take a moment to catch his breath. Innovation and determination, often called stubbornness, was part of their makeup.

The potent formula they created guaranteed to provide many hours of unconscious bliss. The two men preferred good English beer to all other types of refreshment, nevertheless, the quality of their product and its unusual taste was going to give them many enjoyable hours arguing over which attribute was more important, taste or alcohol content?

They put a second batch of ingredients on the fire with the same two sentries there to watch it through the night. Before they returned to the BOQ and climbed into bed for a night of liquid induced bliss, Neville looked around the clearing to make sure that all of the jungle juice had been removed, otherwise they would have two unconscious fire watchers.

He slapped at his left arm. "Damn these insects are getting bad. The smell must have upset them."

"How would you feel if someone made your house smell like this stuff. I wonder…"

"What?"

"I was wondering if we could reduce the smell by running this gift from the Gods back through the distiller again."

"That might be worth a try with the new batch. It can't make it any worse and maybe ageing it a bit would help. We could slow things down and let it sit for a half-hour. You know, like wine…let it breathe a little."

Carefully holding their coconuts so none of the precious liquid could spill out and damage the floor or their hands, the owners of the island's newest distillery settled down, looking forward to not being in any condition to remember the coming night.

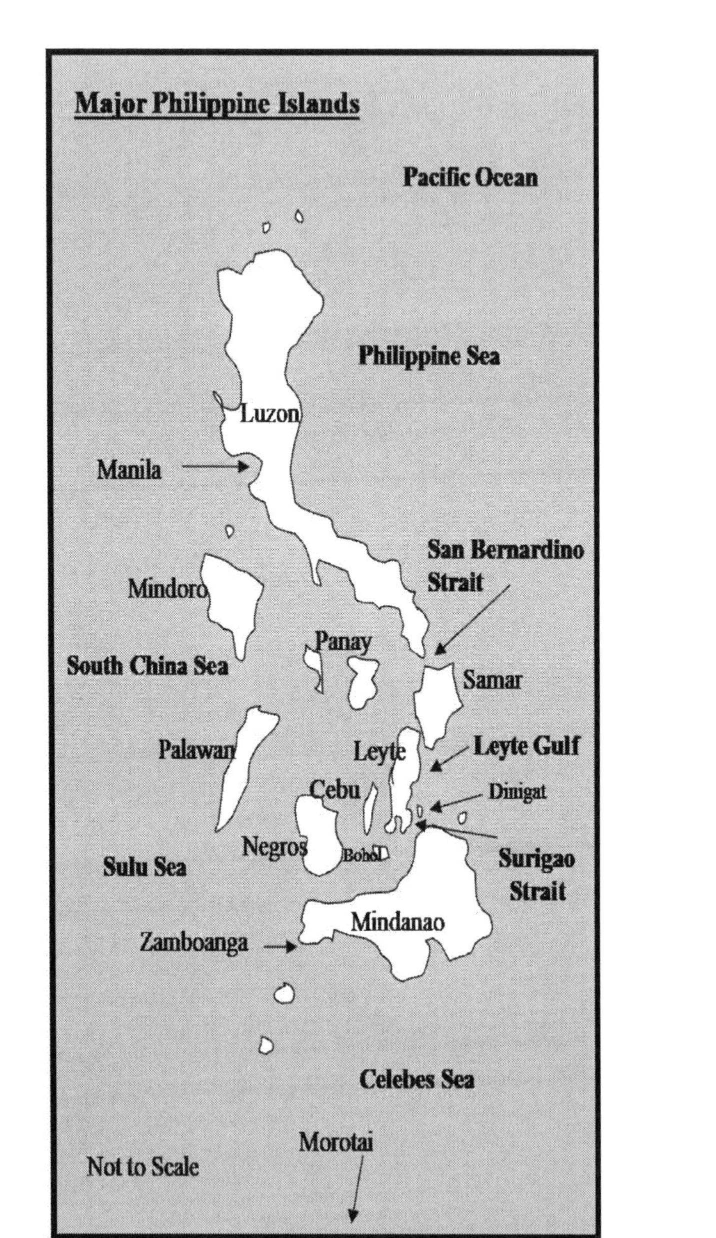
Major Philippine Islands
Pacific Ocean
Philippine Sea
Luzon
Manila
San Bernardino Strait
Mindoro
Panay
South China Sea
Samar
Palawan
Leyte
Leyte Gulf
Cebu
Dinigat
Negros
Bohol
Surigao Strait
Sulu Sea
Mindanao
Zamboanga
Celebes Sea
Morotai
Not to Scale

Chapter 10

Count on Them

September 23, 1944

The largest operation of the war in the Pacific was going to happen in less than four weeks. The planning had everyone working all day and most of each night. Cullison needed to be everywhere attending one meeting after another. The briefing Cullison was attending this morning discussed the expected response from the Japanese Navy. Colonel Willoughby, MacArthur's G-2 Intelligence Chief, summed up what was known, what was suspected and what was pure guesswork. There wasn't much difference between the three.

The Colonel concluded, "I'll finish by saying we know the Japs have about ten battleships, six aircraft carriers, two-dozen light and heavy cruisers and at least fifty destroyers they can throw at us." He hesitated and removed his glasses to wipe the sweat from his forehead. The day's heat and humidity were building as a light rain continued outside. With his glasses back in place, he continued, "They could send everything they have at us. However, coordination will be a problem since these ships are located in a half-dozen different locations separated by thousands of miles."

"Sir, what is your best guess as to what they will do?" asked a naval Captain.

"We think any response will involve about half the ships I've mentioned. It seems likely they will try to hit you from both the north and the south."

An army Major with a pair of wings pinned to his chest signifying that he was in aviation asked, "Do we have any idea what we can expect regarding their air units?"

Willoughby again removed his glasses and rubbed his eyes to relieve the burning he felt while successfully stifling a yawn. "I'm sorry gentlemen. I haven't gotten much sleep this past week and I suspect neither have you. We believe their naval air units are almost non-existent. Our boys have done a tremendous job and the Jap flyers they have left are so new they can barely recognize the ships they're assigned to. The land-based units are a different story. Although we will be targeting their airstrips from now until we land on Leyte, their shore-based planes could pose a problem, especially for the transport ships that have to anchor off the invasion beaches. This means we'll be using all three divisions of our small Jeep, convoy escort carriers, Taffy one, two and three to maintain a strong air-cap over the invasion beach. Admiral Halsey will hold the fast attack carriers in reserve to go after the Nip fleet's capital units when they appear."

Cullison listened carefully to what the Colonel said. When the Intelligence Chief finished, he raised a hand. Willoughby nodded at him, "Commander?"

"Sir, do I understand you correctly? You do not expect them to attack our forces through the Surigao or San Bernardino Straits?"

"All I can say Commander, is that the Japs are unpredictable. What they will do will greatly depend on the situation at that moment. When it comes to military action, we know they are gamblers. That means you better be ready for anything, no matter how crazy it may seem to us. They have a different mindset and a different set of values.

Smiling at those closest to him, Willoughby continued with his obligatory cover-your-ass – CYA - statement. "The Navy expects the primary resistance to come at us through a simultaneous attack from the north and south. Trying to approach us from the West by transiting either strait would likely end up a disaster for them."

Willoughby, a man whose advice MacArthur put great stock in, looked at Cullison. "Does that answer your question?"

Cullison nodded to him while thinking, *That certainly was a CYA briefing. It isn't worth spit, but whatever happens, he can claim that we were warned.*

*   *   *

Cullison often felt like a man without a country. He rarely had his own staff. Each new problem or mission made him seek a solution using a new group of people. Harry couldn't refuse when Cullison asked him to follow up on a possible problem that occurred from time to time and of which, he had intimate knowledge–it was called Clyde and Neville. Although employed by the army for his expertise, Geology, Harry often found himself working as Cullison's go-for, chasing down information or solving problems his friend did not have time to pursue.

The two Englishmen were told to report to Cullison at eight in the morning. Their three-day recuperation time was over. Harry sat in Cullison's tent, waiting. Irritated, he looked at his watch for the third time in the last ten minutes. They were over an hour late. He wondered what unbelievable excuse they would use to justify being tardy whenever they did decide to show up, or if they showed up at all.

Rarely was Harry without a book close at hand, no matter the situation. Having run through all of his professional books for the second time, he settled into Cullison's chair with a dog-eared spy novel. Time stood still as he followed the hero through a maze of streets along the Shanghai waterfront until he heard a truck horn and looked at his watch. It was almost eleven and no English planters were visible in the muddy street. Should he sit around and wait some more, or report to Cullison? Rejecting both options, he decided to go in search of the two misfits. It would be better if he found them rather than Cullison sending out MP's as he had done last year when he found out they were playing poker on an LST in the Admiralty Islands.

With all the trouble they caused, he still cared about Clyde and Neville. If asked why, he would only shrug his shoulders. It was hard to put into words. As capable as they were of amazing acts of bravery and self-preservation when fighting the enemy, they seemed incapable of self-control when an opportunity to get into trouble appeared. Why he and Bill kept expecting the two to change was beyond him, although everyone was irrational about something.

With his decision made, Harry stuck the dime novel in his pocket and walked out to the road, where he thumbed a ride up the valley to BOQ #5.

* * *

When talking about things that could be relied on, a person often said, "Like mom and apple pie." They were two things that were constants in a rapidly changing world. Two other things also went together, drinking and gambling. Clyde and Neville worked hard producing a liquor that brought gasps from all those privileged to get some. Whether the gasps were in astonishment or appreciation was an open question. When sober, the two men kept trying to improve their product and fulfill the needs of the people who provided its ingredients. To pronounce their product as "Grade-A J.J." was to pay them a high complement. Still in its early stages, Neville always made notes on each batch in an attempt to come up with a consistently superior product.

* * *

Slogging through the mud, Harry reached their BOQ hut expecting to find the two plantation owners still asleep, only their beds were empty. At first, the orderly professed ignorance. "I'm sorry, Sir, they go out a lot without telling me anything." Hoping to get rid of Harry, and the annoying civilian dressed like an officer, he said, "Why not leave a message, Sir? I'll give it to them as soon as they show up."

The orderly continued trying to get him to leave a message as Harry's attention was drawn to a couple of Sergeant Majors carrying several boxes toward the jungle. Sergeant Majors were as rare as Generals. It was highly unusual when they did something physical. Harry walked to the far side of the BOQ office and watched the two men confidently trudge down a narrow trail and disappear–swallowed by the thick jungle.

The two men appeared to be sure of where they were going, which seemed curious to Harry. As far as he knew, there wasn't anything in that direction except more jungle and possibly, some headhunters. Concerned for their safety as well as curious, Harry stepped out into a light rain and started down the path. The nervous attendant called after him, trying to get him to turn around. The attendant knew, without a doubt, that even though Harry was a civilian he was bad news for the local distillery.

Soon after the BOQ huts disappeared behind a wall of dripping greenery, Harry picked up an unusual aroma, but ignored it. His thoughts were occupied with the question, *where could those men be going and what are they up to?*

Thick green walls of trees and bushes encased in vines sprouting leaves as large as dinner plates bordered the path reducing visibility to a few feet muted any sounds coming from the road. The isolation he felt at being visually cut off from anything man-made was enhanced by the eerie quiet. The sound of Clyde's harsh voice yelling at someone around the next bend in the trail brought Harry to a stop. He listened for a minute and then slowly moved to a position where he could see down the trail to a jungle clearing.

The two sergeants were sitting on the ground talking to Neville and several other soldiers. He could see Clyde trying to get up from a stooping position in front of something cooking on a fire. He was not quite erect when he took two halting steps to his right, then two more backwards and plopped down on his ass, all the while laughing. He held a glass jar in his right hand maintaining it in an upright position even as he fell and braced himself, left hand on the ground.

Suddenly Harry's internal light went on. The smell, the way all of the people were acting and Clyde carefully sipping liquid out of the jar, told him why his two friends had not reported for duty and were not likely to for some time to come. He watched them for another minute before backing up, turning around and heading back to the road.

After getting a ride down the valley, Harry went to Cullison's office, but he was not there. He left a note and walked over to the mess tent for a late lunch. His conscience was clear. He knew, full well, what would happen once Cullison read the note. Clyde and Neville had no one to blame but themselves. Harry knew that anyone who got into as many tight spots as they did, must have a special guardian watching over them, and yet…

Harry took his time eating, appreciating how much better the food had gotten in only a few days. The Yanks certainly knew how to follow through on the old belief that an Army traveled on its stomach. In a perverse way, he was glad the two planters had gone AWOL. Cullison would be fuming. Instead of sending them to the Philippines as seemed likely given the shortage of good coast watchers, his outrage at being played for a fool was likely to result in their being quickly shipped home. For their sake at least, that's what Harry hoped would happen.

Dumb luck was just that–dumb! It could only carry them, so far and Harry was sure they had used the last of it on Morotai.

He hoped Cullison would do the right thing, since he wanted to see the two retire to their small island with all limbs and questionable mental faculties still intact.

Chapter 11

Dry Times

September 24, 1944

A rare thing happened early in the morning–early at least by Neville's standards. Of all days, the sun picked this one to shine directly into their hut through a small gap in the trees near the road. The normal morning cloud cover had come and gone. It was going to be a glorious, hot, steamy day with the clock about to strike noon. Without being held in check by clouds, the heat and humidity was climbing quickly providing everyone with their own personal New Guinea bath.

Sweat trickled down his forehead, dripped onto his eyelids and slid down his nose. The annoying sensation made Neville wipe his eye and increase the burning sensation he was trying to stop. He grabbed a corner of the bed sheet and wiped his face. Slowly sitting up, he stretched and then groaned. It took considerable effort for him to keep his enlarged head from falling off.

After feeling good, drinking in moderation for several days while perfecting their liquid refreshment, he decided it was time to get falling-down drunk. He loved getting drunk but hated the morning after, which was a good reason never to get completely sober and to simply skip the first part of the day–it always led to pain and disappointment. Neville again rubbed his eyes and after blinking several times, noticed Harry sitting on the edge of the next bed.

On cue, Clyde, still asleep started to snore–loudly. Both men looked at him, before Neville, slurring his words, said, "Whatcha doin' here, Harry?" Without waiting for an answer, he looked at the floor around the bed while saying, "I put a canteen around here, now didn't I?"

"You mean this one?" Harry picked it up from beside him on the bed, held it out and turned it upside down.

Neville tried to stop him from emptying the container, but grabbed his head and moaned instead.

A few drops of liquid splashed on the floor. "I already poured out the rest of this stuff and I emptied those pots in the clearing out back. Like it or not, Neville, you and Clyde are on the wagon–at least until you leave New Guinea."

"Aw, come on Harry. You can't do that to us. We just got the formula right. You don't want us to waste all that time and knowledge, now do you?" Neville grinned, sure that his argument would convince Harry to see the error of his ways.

"That is exactly what I want and you're lucky I got here before the MP's. You should have heard Bill yesterday when I told him exactly how you've been spending your time off. You really got him mad. Both of you should be ashamed after all he's done for you. Why'd you do it?"

Not ready to grasp how he and Clyde had screwed up, Neville said, with as much feeling as he could muster, "There ain't any good beer here. All they have is that stuff from the States and you know how bad that is. Now I ask you, how's a man supposed to feel good about himself drinking that piss? Why a bloke would drown before he was able to drink enough to do any good."

Harry started to respond, but Neville waved a hand to cut him off. Unsteadily, he stood up and stumbled to the edge of the hut's floor where he leaned over and noisily threw up on the ground. The sounds he made were loud enough to pull Clyde back into the land of the living.

"Oh, hello Harry. Come to join us?" said Clyde, as he squirmed around on his cot and pulled a canteen out from under him. "Come by for a drink?" Clyde held the canteen out and Harry reached for it.

"No-o." Groaned Neville, but before he could say anything else, Harry took the metal container and walked over beside Neville and poured the potent drink on the ground.

"Harry, that wasn't nice. Now I'm going to have go to the factory and get some more."

"I've already been there Clyde. How could you two stand being around that smell all day?"

"It ain't hard–not when we can make stuff this strong." Clyde's head jerked up and he looked at Harry, his mouth opened and closed without a sound coming out, before angrily saying, "Don't tell me you emptied everything in the clearing. Do you know how hard we worked?"

Harry didn't try to answer the question. He looked at his watch and said, "You better get dressed. Bill will be here in ten minutes with your escort." The word "escort" really made the two amateur distillers pay attention. When they served in the Great War, that word was frequently linked with "firing squad."

"It ain't like you, Harry, to joke about something like that. All the Commander needs to do is tell us which ship is going south. We won't even hold a grudge for what you just did."

"That's right," added Neville. "Let bygones be bygones." He looked at his partner. "Come on now, get your clothes on. We don't want to keep some lovely ship waiting, now do we?"

Two Jeeps pulled in off the dirt road as Clyde finished lacing his boots. Cullison, trailed by three MP's, stepped up into the hut and watched as the sources of his irritation reached for their travel bags.

"I hear you two have been making liquor. That's against regulations." Cullison looked around the hut. When he didn't see any liquor bottles he picked up a canteen, shook it and turned the container upside down. He put it under his nose only and quickly jerked his head away as the foul aroma assaulted his nasal passages. "What did you do wrong to make it smell so bad?"

"We didn't give it time to properly age. That's what I forgot to do, but we didn't have time anyway, what with you only giving us three days."

Cullison was only half listening as he tossed the canteen onto Clyde's cot in disgust. "Okay, where is it? I can smell it so it has to be around here."

Innocently Neville said, "What might that be?"

Cullison shook his finger at Neville, his face turning red at being played for a fool. "Oh no you don't, not this time. I'm going…"

Harry interrupted, "I'm afraid you have to blame me, Bill. I destroyed all the evidence."

Deftly changing the subject, Neville asked, "When does the first ship leave for Brisbane, Commander, or even better, Guadalcanal?"

Cullison looked at Neville, unable to disguise his amazement at being asked for transportation out of the war zone after blatantly ignoring his instructions. He looked fit to be tied, and then suddenly, his mood changed. Turning to Harry, he said, "Remember what I said about how well some things work out?"

Not knowing what his friend was talking about, Harry shook his head.

"Oh come on, Harry, you remember…the transport ship schedule."

Clyde and Neville brightened up, forgetting for the moment about all of their hard work now irrigating some weeds or more likely, sterilizing the dirt.

Cullison continued, "Two days ago I told you about revisions to the shipping schedule because of the upcoming operation. Now that the entire Brisbane headquarters is here, all of our supplies will be coming either from the States or Gava Vutu. Whatever we left in Australia was turned over to Mountbatten and is being shipped to Burma. A hospital ship in the harbor weighed anchor last night. It was the last ship bound for Brisbane." He turned to Neville. "That is why you were supposed to show up yesterday morning and you blew it! So the question is, what do we do with you now that no one is going in your direction for at least the next couple of weeks?"

Neville jumped to his feet, for the moment forgetting about his swollen head. "That ain't fair. You could have sent someone to get us." Pointing at the ground and stamping his foot, he said, "We were right here."

"All day," Clyde added for emphasis.

"No, you weren't," said Harry in a quiet voice. "When you didn't show up, I came looking for you. You were out back brewing or distilling or cooking or whatever and having a grand old time. You made a choice and it was the wrong one, just like the last time and the time before that. Each time, you make a mess of things. Bill and I think, oh well, next time will be different, but it never is, is it?"

"I think Harry's summed things up nicely, don't you?" said Cullison. "So now, what do we do? We can't have you hanging around the base trying to make a buck off of innocent soldiers a long way from home, but…I do have an idea."

Clyde started shaking his head. "Not again. Oh no. The last time you had an idea you took advantage of us, dropped us out of an airplane, you did."

Without knowing what Cullison had planned for the pair, Harry cut in. "Clyde, you enjoyed every moment of that operation on the Vogelkop. Being in charge of everyone, saving those men from certain death. Come on, admit it."

"Well…"

Cullison kept at it, not wanting to leave them an opening where they might make their own arrangements. "That's the spirit, and when you get back, your island will still be there. By then we may even be able to find you a flight all the way to the Canal."

"Where, what and when?" said Clyde who could not help expressing some interest in a new assignment, although he was getting homesick for their little island.

"Harry's picked out a few places where we'll need some coast watchers for our Leyte Gulf operation."

"I ain't going in by parachute, and that's my last word on the subject."

"Agreed," said Cullison. "We…I mean you, are in luck. This time I found you a sub. It should be coming into the harbor in a couple of hours."

"That okay with you, Neville? I like submarines." Clyde looked at Cullison. "Is it the Nautilus?"

"No. She wasn't available. This one is the Dace. She's a regular attack sub, but just as fast. Tell these men," Cullison indicated the MP's standing behind him, "where your gear is and they'll help you pack up. Then we'll go to my office. I'll give you all the details of your assignment and you can check the equipment I pulled together for you."

Skeptical of how fast everything had changed and yet, seemed to work out to Cullison's satisfaction, Neville said, "Don't let any grass grow under your feet, do you Commander?"

"Or for that matter," added Clyde, "under ours."

* * *

Walking down the pier with Harry, Clyde said, "I ain't never been to the Philippines before. You sure the place you picked out is going to work?"

Trying to sound as positive as he could about the primary location he chose for them, Harry said, "I think it will work out just fine. That little island should give you a good view of both ends of the Strait. The only thing I'm not sure of is whether any Japs are there. That's why I gave you two alternate locations–just in case. Make sure you do a good reconnaissance of the area before you release the sub. You'll be lucky if the captain will give you more than two hours at each location, so use the time wisely."

"You know, Harry, when I looked at the map, I thought I was looking at that little place where you did your coast watching two years ago."

Harry didn't say anything for a moment, thinking back to when he'd worked as a coast watcher. "You mean Krakatoa?"

Clyde nodded.

"That worked out nicely, using an unstable volcano as an observation post. The Japs didn't want any part of that place. But don't worry. No volcanoes for you this time, at least no active ones, not for at least fifty miles."

Neville stood at the end of the pier near the brow leading to the Dace's deck. Cullison shook his hand and watched the first half of his English headache go aboard. After Clyde went aboard, Cullison climbed the side of the sub's conning tower and had a few quiet words with the Captain. Forewarned might not equal forearmed, but his conscience was clear, no matter what the two planters might try to do on their weeklong trip back to the war.

Chapter 12

Secret Mission

October 1, 1944

Sitting at a table in the crew's mess compartment of the submarine, Clyde held a coffee mug in both hands waiting for the temperature of the dark liquid to drop low enough not to remove the inside of his mouth. The mess area was one of the largest compartments on the Dace. It felt nice to be in a place where he could spread his arms and not touch both walls at the same time.

Clyde stared at the cup for a while losing himself in the steam shrouded mug. Someone walked by breaking his trance-like state. He looked up at his partner sitting on the other side of the narrow table. "It took us two weeks to get to Hollandia after leaving Morotai and here we are right back again at this miserable island." He nodded to the world outside. "Blimey, for all the good it did us, we should have stayed right here."

"Why is it, every time you open that big mouth of yours, you're wrong?" replied Neville, taking pleasure in plunging his verbal knife into his best friend while finishing another of the cook's excellent cookies.

"Wrong? What are you talking about? That's Morotai out there, ain't it?"

"That it is, and that's a fact."

"Well then?"

"Just take a moment and think before you get on your high horse. If we had stayed here, we never would have enjoyed the results of working out the finer points of making jungle juice. And that information," he pointed a finger at Clyde for emphasis, "is going to make living on Pyramid–if we survive this next assignment–a lot more profitable. Think of all the beer we won't have to buy."

"I don't know if I agree with that. I'm not ready to give up having a half dozen bottles after working all day. I'm not saying our jungle juice sometimes ain't good for what ails a bloke, but I need the feeling of having my hands wrapped around a large mug. A small canteen that smells like last years underwear don't seem as friendly."

Clyde brought the mug to his lips and blew on his coffee before gingerly taking a sip. About to take a second drink, he looked up as five US Army Rangers filed in. They took their carbines and Thompson sub-machine guns off their shoulders and carefully laid them on a table while several sailors placed backpacks in a pile against a bulkhead.

Not bothering to hide his feelings, Clyde said, "It's about time you blokes showed up. It's boring enough traveling inside a tin can without having to just sit here. We've been waiting for half the day. What took you so long? Get lost? The island ain't *that* big."

All five Rangers wearing clean, sweat-soaked combat gear and almost new boots, were big men, muscles bulging in all the right places. The biggest one, a sergeant name Forester, stepped over to the two Englishmen. He stared down at them, his face showing his displeasure at their being aboard. "Until you know what you're talking about, Pops, zip it. That place is bigger than it looks and we was on a transport ship on the other side."

Knowing that to stand up might lead to something physical, Clyde kept his seat and laid a hand on Neville's arm to make sure he didn't do anything rash. Two weeks earlier, they had gotten on the wrong side of Commander Cullison. Getting into a fight now, before even starting their mission, might not sit well. Keeping his voice calm, he simply said, "We liberated the place long before you boys showed up, so we know that sand trap of an island better than we'd care to. But since the place ain't important, we'll put that behind us."

Clyde stuck his hand out. "I'm Clyde Arnold. What are your names?"

The Rangers grudgingly introduced themselves and grabbed mugs off a tray next to the coffee pot. Two of them yelped when they tried to drink the scalding hot liquid.

Introductions done and everyone's hand filled with a heavy white mug, Neville innocently asked, "Where you boys going?"

The sergeant looked a couple of his men in the eye, making sure none of them said anything before looking at Neville and shrugging his shoulders. "Damned if we know. We're supposed to report to some lieutenant."

"He's around here, somewhere?" offered Clyde. "He's the quiet type. Says so few words you can be in the same room with him, and not know it."

"Either in his quarters or outside," said Neville, trying to be helpful. "Although that don't make any sense to me. Nice and comfortable in here, no bugs."

Turning to the other Rangers, the sergeant said, "You men stay here. I'll find Lieutenant Spann and see if anything has changed. Don't any of you wander off and make sure you watch what you say."

Ten minutes of awkward silence passed slowly, the Rangers wondering what two strangely dressed Englishmen were doing on the sub. Several noises coming from the deck above made everyone look up. A moment later, a Second Lieutenant trying to grow enough hair to start shaving, walked into the compartment followed by the sergeant. He ignored Clyde and Neville, and spoke to the Rangers. "Get your gear, follow the sergeant, and keep your traps shut."

The Lieutenant stood out of the way, as his men filed by on their way to bunks in the forward torpedo room. Once they were gone, the young man walked over to Clyde and Neville. Without bothering to say hello to the two men he had been traveling with for the past week, he said, "My men and I have been assigned a mission behind enemy lines. Where we are going and what we'll do when we get there is none of your business."

Clyde's head swiveled and he looked at the Lieutenant with disgust, showing his disdain for the man he considered a rank amateur.

Unfazed by Clyde's look, he continued, "I'd appreciate it if you don't talk to my men about our mission." Without waiting for a reply, he turned and followed after his men.

"If that young man gets through the war he should do well as a foreign service officer. For the past week, he's acted as if the weight of the world is on his shoulders. I'll bet this is his first time fighting anything other than a straw dummy. He should be a real asset to some ambassador."

Neville smiled his agreement. "He does have the perfect personality for a horse's-ass diplomat. If he survives he might be able to start a new war all by himself."

Clyde almost choked as he finished his coffee, laughing at one of his partner's better comments. Standing to place the mug on the drain board, he added, "There you have it, ol' boy–if someone doesn't shoot him. Hope he ain't going the same place as us. I don't want him drawing Japs to us and have to make a choice between saving his arse and getting our job done."

"You shouldn't be too hard on the young man," admonished Neville. "After all, he might be just what we need to win the war. He is a Ranger."

"He ain't no real Ranger. He's a wanna be. We knew that the minute he came aboard. His boots still have a shine on them.

Officers like him think they know everything. They didn't do well in the last war, except to get promoted for issuing stupid orders and getting men killed. I'll bet he don't do any better in this one."

"Never can tell with those glory boy types."

Neville looked up, his eyes seeming to penetrate through the submarine's hull to the activity on the bridge as he felt the engines change pitch and the Dace start to move away from the temporary dock. "Next stop, the Philippines," he announced as his nose led him to the galley where the cook was pulling several pies out of the oven.

Never one to let a financial opportunity get away, Clyde said, "Those blokes don't like to talk, but since there ain't any beaches on this ship..."

"Boat," said Neville. "Don't want to get the Captain upset again. This is a boat."

"Right you are...boat. However, as I was saying, without a beach to run around on, they are going to need something to keep them busy. Think we could convince them to play a few friendly hands of poker? The Captain said we won't get to the Strait for another week."

Already behind schedule, the Dace headed north at flank speed, on the surface. In war, there were no sure things. However, SubPac had determined that the threat of Japanese air attacks more than two-hundred miles from enemy held territory was low enough to allow surface travel during daylight hours. When near the Philippines, the sub would travel submerged, out of harm's way during the day, at a much slower speed. Clyde and Neville resigned themselves to the monotony of the trip. Even with the reduced threat from the air they knew the only time the Captain would allow them on the bridge, one at a time, was at night.

Lieutenant Spann, almost six feet tall, blond hair, blue eyes and peach fuzz on his chin watched his men get settled in the large, but still cramped, forward torpedo room. When they had their gear out from underfoot, he called them to form a circle in the access well near the starboard torpedo tubes.

"Our mission is straight forward. Land on the coast of Leyte, find a guerilla leader named Kangleon and pass on sabotage instructions. We tell them what to hit and when. In case I get hit," he pulled a small notebook out of his shirt pocket, "it's all in here, but I won't tell you any of the specifics until I'm sure the Japs can't capture us."

One of the Rangers hesitantly raised his hand. "Sir, don't these guerrillas have a radio? I mean, can't headquarters send them the info instead of us risking our necks. The Japs don't take prisoners."

"I don't know if they have a radio or not, but these are our orders. Each of you men has made an impression on your officers. I presume that's why you were chosen for this mission. But, no one is to talk about the mission if those Englishmen can hear what you're saying. I don't know why those two old men are going ashore, but whatever the reason, the Japs will probably catch them. I don't want the enemy to learn anything about us from a pair of old rejects who are too slow to get out of their own way.

"And one more thing–if you have any money with you, be careful. One of those guys is a card shark."

"Which one, sir?"

Still dead serious, the lieutenant, without cracking a smile, said, "The one that has your money in his pocket."

Chapter 13

Solid Ground

October 13, 1944

The Rangers had not been prepared for the confinement of living in a submarine, and it showed. After months of training, on the go from dawn to well past dusk every day and sometimes all night, the five Rangers were raring to go. In fact, they were past that point as they sat at a mess table on the Dace hoping to feel the submarine start moving.

How to keep their minds occupied during the slow voyage had been difficult. When they left Morotai, their goal was to reach the Surigao Strait by the eleventh. It was a narrow waterway between the Philippine Islands with Leyte on the north, and Mindanao on the south. They were to go ashore near the southern tip of Leyte and pass on final sabotage instructions to the local guerillas. Once contact had been made, they were to coordinate local resistance activities with the upcoming invasion scheduled to occur in a few days.

Unfortunately, the two noisy, abrasive, rude and argumentative Englishmen, had to be dropped off before the group or they would already be walking on dry land. Although each of the Rangers had experienced variations of the same dream–throwing the two men off the rear of the sub–the opportunity never presented itself since most of the time the Dace traveled submerged.

Private First Class Bjork, half to himself, said, "How long have they been gone?"

One Private, Stenseth, a nineteen-year old from the Kentucky hill country, his mouth full of pie, looked at his watch, "An hour and a half. That's got to be long enough, don't ya think?"

Sergeant Forester sat at the end of the table idly spinning a quarter. He slapped it down on the table, drawing everyone's attention. "I want to get going as much as you guys, but it ain't goin' to do any good bellyaching about those two. The Captain has his orders and we'll get goin' when he's satisfied. We waited three hours the first time, before finding out that the place where they wanted to set up camp was in the middle of a Jap outpost. All we can hope for is that it doesn't happen again."

In a strong Brooklyn accent, Corporal Weber said, "I'm hoping they don't find a good spot for their lookout post and come back to the sub. I'd like one more chance at getting my hands on some of my money."

"Fat chance," said Bjork. "The way those guys play, they gotta be cheatin', but nobody can figure out how. I'm hopin' we seen the last of them. Both my ears and my wallet need a rest."

"You think we got it bad? Lt. Spann has to eat with them in the Officers Mess," replied the sergeant. "This is the Lieutenant's first time leading a mission in combat. He's got to be as nervous as Stenseth when he came face to face with that croc on Morotai. Listening to those two old men spout all that nonsense about outracing a volcano and ambushing a whole company of Japs probably has him wanting to strangle them. So just be thankful for small favors and if they come back, hold on to your wallets."

"Hey Sarge, you think any of that stuff is true? I mean–either they think we're really stupid or they really did those things."

"Bjork, don't worry about those two loud mouths and what they did or didn't do," Forester said as he nervously flipped his quarter again. "This won't be my first time in combat. You only need to know one thing–do what I say when I say it. Don't try to analyze anything, just do it!"

"You mean the way Stenseth started shooting at that croc?" Bjork looked over at Stenseth who kept his head down, trying not to start shaking as he relived the moment.

"Well, that wasn't the smartest move I've ever seen. You shoot one of those things, it just makes it mad. Next time, climb a tree and then shoot it between the eyes." The sergeant looked at Stenseth and smiled. "I don't think a single bullet hit that baby."

Stenseth had been taking a ribbing about his reaction for a week. Trying to put the best face he could on his actions, he said, "Maybe I didn't hit him, but he sure did turn around quick and head back to that creek."

Lt. Spann entered the compartment and said, "Sergeant, it seems our companions have decided to leave us. Have the men carry that pile of gear those Englishmen need up to the forward deck. Load it in the rafts and be careful. It's dark as the inside of a cow up there and just as slippery."

Using a small flashlight with a red lens, Neville inspected each of the bundles brought on deck before indicating where they should be put in the two rafts, one tied behind the other. Making things easier, the rafts were sitting on the forward deck instead of in the water. All the captain had to do was submerge the Dace and the rafts would float free. When all was ready, the Captain came down from the bridge and shook their hands. Quietly, he asked Clyde, "All of that stuff about running around behind enemy lines, stealing boats and leading a Jap destroyer in the wrong direction–was it all true?"

"Scouts honor." Clyde held his hand up similar to the way he'd seen boy scouts do in a movie.

"Are you sure you can do it again? How old are you? You must be over fifty. If you want to rethink this thing before I submerge, this is the time."

"Thank you for your concern, Captain, but I ain't that old, yet. Me and Neville, we can take care of ourselves–and if we run into trouble, you'd be surprised how fast we can disappear. Why once I outran a Roo."

The Captain laughed. "Now, that I'd like to see." He shook their hands and climbed up to the bridge.

"All personnel are off the deck and hatches are sealed," the bridge talker repeated for the captain, as information reached him from inside the sub.

"Control room, flood down five feet," ordered the Captain.

Large bubbles appeared along both sides of the Dace as it settled in the water. The entire submarine sank lower in the water until only the conning tower remained visible. The men on the bridge listened as Clyde and Neville struggled to get the two rafts moving using a pair of paddles. Not yet concerned about their noise, the sound of their splashes slowly moved toward shore.

"Surface the boat," said the captain. "Ahead one-third, come left to two-nine-five."

* * *

"How many times have we done this, Clyde?"

"I think this makes five. That's four more times than we've had the good sense to say no."

"Where's your spirit of adventure?" Neville whispered as he scanned the darkness in front of them, broken only by a white line where the almost non-existent waves slid up on the beach.

"My spirit of adventure is back at Hollandia, which is where we should be right now."

"In that nice new jail they just finished building? You know, as much as we like the Commander, he would have put us in there for thirty days if we hadn't taken this assignment. When it comes to business, that's all he knows!"

With deep water close to shore, it only took them fifteen minutes to get from the sub to the island. Neville dug his paddle in for one more stroke, hit the sandy bottom and fell over as the raft lurched to a stop in less than a foot of water. They hopped out. With Neville pulling the raft, it slid up on the beach followed by its twin. Cullison had stocked them with enough equipment and supplies to survive for up to two months, instead of the two weeks, after which, they were going to be relieved…if possible. Harry's sight-unseen, second choice was a location on top of a ridge near the coast of Limasawa.

"Right, now that we're here, let's do this the same as when we landed on Selat Sagawin. You go right, I'll go left. Look for a good place to hide all of this material and both rafts before sunrise. Meet you back here in fifteen minutes."

"I just hope this place isn't like Sagawin. We barely made it out of there…" Clyde's words became garbled as he held his hand over his mouth to try and control a fit of spontaneous giggling. Doing the wrong thing at the wrong time was another quirk of his, and this was definitely the wrong time.

"What are you doing? This is no time for you to go bonkers on me."

Clyde finally answered. "Oh nothing, I was simply remembering how you got stuck under a tree on that island. Your bottom-half was hanging out over a cliff and the Japs were looking up to see why rocks were falling."

Fortunately, for Neville, it was too dark for Clyde to see his red face.

"Come on, get to it," Neville growled to cover his embarrassment as he started down the beach. He knew Clyde was never going to let him forget the incident. He had slipped on the side of a hill and except for getting wedged under a fallen tree, he would have slid off a cliff and landed in a creek at the foot of a Japanese camp. It was his second most embarrassing incident, on that not-very-peaceful island.

Chapter 14

The Cleft

October 14, 1944

The distance from Limasawa where Clyde and Neville were exploring their new home, to a point near the middle of Leyte's large peninsula pointing south into the Strait, was less than one hundred miles. The Dace could easily make it from one to the other on the surface in the hours remaining before dawn, except for the moon, an almost cloudless sky and a number of faint sonar contacts. In the Strait, the sounds of an enemy ship might be masked by the noise from the foaming surf hitting rocks, coral reefs and cliffs. Choosing to be cautious, the Captain kept the boat submerged and found an out of the way piece of deep water where they spent the day. The Lieutenant and his Rangers would be another day late, and the Captain might live to see his two-year old daughter.

Lt. Spann stuck his head through the hatch into the forward torpedo room. His voice raised, he called out, "Sergeant Forester."

The sergeant looked up from where he was watching his men strip and clean their weapons. It was the third time each man had gone through the procedure in the last hour. Being nervous because of their impending mission didn't help their confidence, but the Sergeant had to agree that they knew what they were doing. Forester made a motion for the men to continue as he stood up, walked to the rear of the compartment and stepped through the hatch. "Yes, Sir?"

"Are the men ready?"

Forester briefly looked back at the men before answering. "Yes, Sir. They're getting jumpy, but that's to be expected. None of us likes being cooped up in a traveling sewer pipe. At least those Englishmen are gone. Now they can concentrate on the mission. Once we're out of here and on dry land...well, they'll be okay."

The sergeant's answer didn't fill Spann with confidence. How could he be confident? He was still looking for the answer to the question, 'Why he was taking untried men on a mission behind enemy lines?' Although any operation behind enemy lines was dangerous, their plan was straightforward. When he received the assignment, he expected to be leading men with at least as much combat experience as himself, which wasn't a lot. In truth, the only person on the mission with any significant combat time was Forester, and he seemed to be trying hard to look relaxed–maybe too hard.

"The Captain says we're here and it looks quiet. Get everyone up on deck."

"Glad to hear that, sir. Can't say I'll be sorry to see the sky again, no matter what happens."

"All right then, get them moving."

The six men stepped into the rubber boat. They expected to travel fast and light. Two days' rations and a radio were the only items they carried other than their weapons, ammunition and backpacks. The guerillas could be relied on to supply anything else the group might need once they made contact. The air corps had been dropping supplies to them once a week for the past two months, although the last plane to drop supplies had not been able to make radio contact. The problem could be as simple as a bad radio tube. That was one of the reasons for bringing a replacement radio with them. Get ashore unobserved, make contact and pass final instructions to the local guerilla leader. After that, the plan was to help the locals draw the Japs away from the invasion area before hooking up with friendly forces. No one wanted to sound like he was scared, but each of them was thinking and praying for the same thing–meeting people who did not have slanted eyes.

*　　*　　*

Ten miles long, thin and relatively flat, except for a central ridge, the island of Limasawa, at first glance, appeared to be a green wall rising out of the water. The crest of the thickly overgrown jungle ridge looked out over the multi-hued waters of the Strait from a height of almost four-hundred feet. Deep foliage-choked ravines gouged out by frequent heavy rainfall scarred its sides. The uninhabited island lacked easy to negotiate trails up to the crest. They had to cut and hack their way up a ravine still dripping from the last storm.

"Where the bloody hell are the engineers when you need them? I'm an ol' man," mumbled Clyde while trying to wipe his face and swat bugs at the same time.

"Who says? We're the same age and I ain't old," countered Neville.

"I must be old. That's what all those young men kept saying."

"When it's time for you to be old, I'll tell you. Until then, stop complaining and get back to work."

Clyde grunted and took a swing at a thick bush with his machete. He jumped back, startled by a blood-curdling scream. Neville reached for his carbine as the two men stepped back a few feet. They waited a moment for it to repeat. The only thing they heard was a half-dozen colorful birds chattering away. Cautiously, Clyde reached out with his machete and poked at the bush. The entire thing seemed to come alive, branches moved in every direction as the screeching sound startled them anew. This time, Clyde did not pull back. He held his ground and poked deeper into the thick foliage determined to find out who, or what he had disturbed.

A monkey weighing at least thirty pounds jumped from the bush to an overhanging tree. He climbed high enough to feel safe before hanging by an arm and his tail and spitting at the two men while continuing to voice his displeasure at being disturbed.

Neville laughed so hard at the startled look on Clyde's face he almost fell over. The monkey seemed to expect the intruders to go away. When they didn't, several others poked their heads out of coconut trees farther up the hill. They chattered back and forth until Clyde and Neville resumed their climb. No sooner did they reach the trees than several of the monkeys turned around and aimed their bowel movements at the intruders. A smelly, semi-liquid brown rain hit two wide-brimmed hats.

Slow, deliberate steps climbing the ravine were replaced by the two men yelling and cursing as they scrambled to escape. Two monkeys jumped from tree to tree keeping pace with the men until they were well past the monkey habitat. At last, they let out a screaming howl meaning, "don't come back" and returned to their group.

"If I had a shotgun, we'd be having fresh meat for supper," Clyde mumbled as he removed his hat and wiped it clean on some grass.

Three hours of work finally paid off. They stood on the ridge top and peered through dense foliage at the surrounding waters. At the best of times, visibility in the area could be a problem due to the heavy humidity. Late in the day, the haze had thickened and hung over the water like a gauze curtain over a window.

In between deep breaths, with his hands on his hips, Clyde looked west into the setting sun. "What do ya think, six miles?"

Neville took his time trying figure out how far they could see. He pulled out his chart of the region to match the marks on the paper with what was visible. "Six?" He shook his head. "Maybe only five, but no more than six."

"That ain't very far, is it?"

"Don't know. It may be far enough. We should know better in the morning. Anybody uses this side of the Strait, we'll see 'em daytime or night, if the moon is up. One of the reasons Harry picked this place is because the Strait is deeper on this side."

"Let's hope the Nips don't come through tonight. It's going to take us a full-day to haul all of our stuff up this hill and make radio contact."

Neville looked around and then pulled up a few small bushes creating a clearing at the edge of the slope where they could relax. "Right you are! Tomorrow we haul everything up here and set up our communications, but tonight I'm going to sit back and enjoy the view."

Clyde slowly turned around studying the area. He shook his head as he rotated around a second time. "Sorry ol' boy, you've got the wrong end of the stick. This is a grand location to watch the water, but we need to put our radio and such farther back." He pointed along the top of the ridge behind them, "We should establish our base near the top of a ravine, where we'll be protected. You do remember, the old saying, 'Better safe than…'"

"I know, I know, only it seems more work than necessary. We should be on our way back home in one or two weeks and there really ain't any Japs on this island."

"That's what you said about Selat Sagawin, and look what happened to us there."

Neville took a moment to consider what his partner said. They had barely escaped from that quiet little island with their heads and other associated parts still attached. No one had ever accused Neville of being smart, except when being compared with Clyde. However, in war, expecting the unexpected amounted to the same thing. He nodded, "I'm going to enjoy the view for a few minutes while this old body recovers. Why don't you find us a good spot to set up in? I'll be along as soon as the sun is down."

Clyde shouldered his travel pack and carbine. Carrying his machete, he wended his way through the thick brush along the top off the ridge moving north, directly away from the Strait. He passed three small ravines before seeing one that looked right. Lowering himself from one rock to another, holding onto various bushes and tree limbs, he dropped down the almost vertical slope to where he found a cleft in the rocks less than fifty feet below the ridge line. It wasn't large enough to be called a cave. However, it did offer some protection from the elements, and with one large rock hanging over the top to act as a diversion for the rainwater that would pour down from above, it promised to keep them dry. Lastly, by hanging a net across its open face, they would have protection against observation from the air. With a little work, the place had the potential of becoming a cozy hideaway/ headquarters.

Satisfied with his discovery, he started back up to the top. Halfway up, he placed his hands on two rocks to climb to the next level. He heaved himself up, placing one foot between the rocks. He released his grip with his right hand and reached for the base of a bush growing out of the hillside. Pulling on the plant, he heaved himself up. As he reached out his left hand to grab another rock, the bush's shallow roots tore out of the hillside.

Clyde quickly transitioned from an experienced rock climber to a neophyte as he fell backwards, his foot still wedged between the rocks. Time slowed as each piece of his mistake registered on his wandering mind. Hands slipping - bush pulling loose - left foot finding nothing but air – falling backwards – trying to pull his foot free - muscles in his leg screaming at being forced into an unnatural position – the back of his head bouncing off a large rock, three times, although he only felt the first two. Instantly, the lovely evening turned black, a second before his foot slipped out of his personalized, cut down boot. His inert body landed with a thud on a pile of loose stones washed down from above.

Some time later, a harsh voice, not unlike a braying mule, cut through Clyde's foggier than usual mind. "Here," he called back, although it amounted to little more than a whisper. He called out a second and then a third time, his voice growing stronger with each repetition. He stopped when he heard his partner cursing as stones he kicked loose tumbled down from above. Neville stumbled over Clyde's prostrate body before dropping to his knees beside him.

Clyde tried to wiggle around without using his throbbing leg. Neville grabbed him under the arms helping him into a sitting position against a large boulder. Opening his mouth to speak, Neville stopped when Clyde said, "Don't ask."

"Right–then. Moving on, anything broken?"

Clyde shook his head. "Don't think so, but my leg hurts like bloody hell."

Neville looked at the rocks above them, then scrambled up and pulled Clyde's boot loose. "Here you go, Peg leg." He held the boot out to Clyde. "Now let me take a look at your leg. We need to get you walking again. Don't like the idea of having to carry everything up this hill by myself."

Every word dripping with sarcasm, Clyde said, "Now that's exactly the kind of bloke everyone says you are. For better or worse, it's share and share alike." He waived his boot at Neville. "I can't wait till this shoe is on the other foot."

Chapter 15

Incompetence

October 16, 1944

His mind frequently filled the space between sleep and being conscious with dreams. Today's episode began well with Clyde sitting in his favorite tavern in Manchester where he could not believe his eyes. The bartender pouring a beer could not turn off the tap. He saw the man rush to fill mugs as fast as his hands could move. Overflowing with good dark beer, a line of mugs ran the length of the bar. Patrons fell over each other to grab the full containers, one in each hand. Clyde found himself swept into the middle of the crowd fighting to get to the bar. Every time he came near his goal, someone snatched it from him. With his mouth so wet he felt in danger of drowning in his own saliva, his dream quickly morphed into a horror story where the crowd continued to grow pushing him out into the street.

Hearing a splash of liquid nearby, he opened his eyes expecting to see beer running across the floor. Instead of the low ceiling of the public house in Manchester, he saw Neville watering a nearby rock. The urge to cry at such an injustice almost overwhelmed him.

"Damn, what did you do, sleep all night with a cork in it? You sound like the ocean flooding that sea cave we almost drowned in on Kolombangara."

Neville looked over his shoulder, grunted an acknowledgement and turned back to finish his business at hand. After squeezing his cloud dry, he turned toward Clyde. "How's the leg feeling? Do you need a hand to get up?"

"Don't know. Guess I better find out." Clyde turned around and got to his knees. He took Neville's hand and pulled himself up to a standing position, all of his weight on his left leg. Gingerly, he applied weight and stood like that shifting around a little at a time until his right leg bore its full load. He flexed his knee a few times, then carefully took a step, wincing when he came down on the ball of his foot. Taking another quick, small step, he returned to a position where three-quarters of his weight was on his good leg. The foot hurt more than expected and his calf somewhat less.

"It's sore as hell, but it works!"

"Always knew you were incompetent. Can't even break your leg right."

"Now that's the Neville I know and…"

"Love?" Neville added with a smile.

"Not quite the word I was looking for, but give me a moment, it will come to me."

"While you're trying to get that brain working, why don't you limp over here and water a rock. Now that you're awake, I can make a trip down below and start bringing up the supplies."

"Capital idea and don't forget that tin of biscuits Harry gave us. That, along with some hot tea and bacon, sounds like just the thing to start our day."

"What about I bring along some fresh eggs and buttered toast?"

Clyde smacked his lips.

"That would be grand."

"That it would–if we had any." Neville picked up his carbine and climbed up the ravine. Over his shoulder he said,

"Don't get in any trouble. I'll be back soon as I can."

While keeping an eye out for the island's long-tailed diarrhea-prone residents, Neville brought food and cooking utensils up the hill, along the ridge top, and down to their new nest. After breakfast he carried up their radio, followed by two more trips, the last with their bedding. At the top of their ravine, he put their sleeping bags on the ground for a moment to adjust his grip. In the blink of an eye, one of the bags flew up into a tree, a monkey chattering away at its success. Neville jumped to grab it back, and lost track of the other bag. In a flash, it also became a monkey's flying carpet. It didn't take long for Neville to admit defeat, the bags disappearing into the thick green canopy above accompanied by the chattering of a dozen monkeys.

"They did what?" Clyde asked, incredulous at what he believed was his partner's lax behavior.

Neville simply shrugged his shoulders and walked away muttering about looking forward to some monkey stew. At mid-afternoon, he decided the time for a break from helping Clyde had arrived. He took a short nap on some fresh palm fronds while Clyde busied himself putting their remaining possessions away, all the while staying off his bad leg.

Their routine radio contact times were six in the morning and five in the evening, with sighting reports called in whenever needed. Clyde looked at his watch, settled the earphones on his head and flipped the power switch. Greeted by silence, he sat and waited. Thirty seconds later, the radio tubes glowed warmly, meaning the radio passed its first test. Smiling to himself, he adjusted the volume to bring the static down to a comfortable level and sent out their coded call sign. He flipped the main switch to receive, waited thirty seconds, then repeated the process.

After seeing him try one more time without success, Neville leaned down next to Clyde and pulled off his earphones. "Nothing?"

Clyde shook his head and pointed to the antenna wire strung from several coconut palms on the hillside. He didn't need to say anything for his partner to start sliding his hand along the wire checking for breaks. In a half-crawl half-stooping walk on the steep hillside he followed the wire to the first tree and then to the second, tugging on it every few feet. When he tugged on the wire between the second and third trees, it came apart. Only the exterior insulation remained intact. He pulled out his knife, peeled back the covering, and started to reconnect the delicate copper wire when he dropped the knife. His foot slipped while bending down to get it. Still holding onto wire, he fell on his ass and slid down the hillside until he met a tree, trunk to crotch.

He yelled a string of profanities so loud it scared the monkeys into silence. When the pain subsided to a dull roar, he carefully picked his way back up the hill while trying to massage the pain out of his buttocks. The thin wire did not appear to be any the worse for his experience. Still cussing a blue streak, he finished his splicing and crawled back to Clyde.

His partner didn't waste any time and was copying down an incoming message by the time Neville sat down next to him. Neville took the paper as soon as Clyde signed off. They followed their normal routine–Clyde handled the radio and Neville took care of the coding/decoding.

The short message said:

ACTIVITY YOUR AREA STARTS IN 24. KEEP ALERT.

Bill hasn't changed," quipped Clyde, "still uses one word when three would actually say something. Wonder what's going to happen?"

"If we'd had some time before boarding the submarine I could have found out more about the overall plan. As it is, someone else is going to score the winning goal while we twiddle our thumbs outside the stadium waiting for a passerby to tell us who won."

"Couldn't have said it better myself," Clyde mumbled as he finished stowing the radio. Old habits died hard. He always made sure the equipment, except for the antenna, was ready to travel. The island was still an unknown. They had to be prepared for unwelcome guests to pop in at any time. He fell silent while discussing the situation with himself. *Should he milk his sore leg for a few days of rest, or should he get on with it? It was a satisfying feeling to watch Neville do all the hard work, but his leg felt better when he stayed active. Moving about seemed the thing to do.* "Help me up," he said as he reached for Neville's arm.

Clyde flexed his leg before taking a few hesitant steps. The ball of his foot seemed better and now his calf felt worse. He looked down at his leg and then at Neville. "I think I need to keep using it or it's going to get really tight. Let's take a look around the island, make sure no one is taking a walk-about and going to drop in while I'm enjoying a sun bath."

A sour look covered Neville's face at the visual image of Clyde laying out nude. "Good idea. Don't want to shock the natives, now do we?"

Clyde broke a dead branch off a bush and pantomimed throwing it at Neville.

Not able to pass up an opportunity to rib his partner, Clyde said, "That is, if you can keep your footing?"

"That'll be enough about my balance, Mr. Clumsy. Come on now, as long as your leg is up to it, we need to find us a stream."

"You're right. It's best to keep our drinking water supply topped off, just in case."

"Who's talking about drinking? A good soaking might help you smell better."

"No reason for that," Clyde retorted. "My nose is working just fine."

"Unfortunately, mine is, too."

With Neville's help, Clyde managed to climb to the top of the ridge. They slowly walked to where it ended and looked out over the Strait. Even through binoculars, visibility seemed to be no better than the day before, or even a little worse. A small single-mast sailboat struggling to sail north against a fitful headwind along the island's west coast was the only visible movement. It could be a local fisherman heading for his village on Leyte's southern coast or a family returning from a trip to the local grocery store.

Although unable to see anything moving, they could hear the far-off rumble of a number of large diesel engines somewhere out on the water. One possibility, a sub traveling on the surface–Japanese subs were notorious for their loud diesel engines–or it could be American PT Boats or even a few of the enemy's patrol barges. Lacking competition, sound could be heard several miles away over open water.

Neither of them said anything as they considered the situation. The Strait wasn't all that wide and yet they could only see part way across. A variation of Murphy's Law ordained that whatever they needed to see was likely to happen on the other side of the Strait. Knowing there wasn't an easy fix for their problem, they turned around to head back along the ridge.

After a few steps, Neville stopped. "Will you look at that?" He pointed at a cloudbank to the east.

"Looks like some nasty weather out there. We best get back in our hidey-hole unless you fancy taking a bath standing up."

Approaching the ravine where their camp was located, Neville again looked at the storm front. "I think we're about to find out how dry the spot you picked for us is."

Knowing how Neville could complain when uncomfortable, and sure of being the butt of his unkind words, Clyde tried to head him off. "Well, it looked good when I first saw it."

"We'll see, we'll see." Neville's voice said it all. He expected to get soaked and be miserable. A few more steps and they reached the ravine, where Neville moved in front of Clyde and allowed his partner to lean forward on his shoulders as they headed down to their camp.

First the wind came, not gentle like a lover's whisper, but strong, brutish, even scary, like a bookmaker's collection agent. It hit with an unnatural suddenness in advance of the heavy clouds in the east. Their camouflage privacy curtain became the wind's first casualty, and then it rained as if God had kicked over a bucket of tears. The raindrops were so large, they looked like they could do a man permanent damage when they bounced off the rocks, some rebounding a foot in the air. Clyde and Neville pulled ponchos over their heads and pressed themselves against the rear wall of their shallow cleft. Within minutes, they found themselves staring at the inside of a waterfall as a torrent roared down from above, cascading from the overhanging rock. Anything not firmly anchored in the ground became a casualty of the storm.

Surprised at the storm's intensity the two men stared at the flowing water rather than at their camp supplies. Movement at their feet drew attention and before either of them could grab at their personal items and some kitchen utensils, it was sliding down the hillside.

No deluge of such intensity could last very long and in a short time, it changed into a gentle rain more common for this time of year. The wind, however, was another story. It continued to howl, swirling around their little nest and reducing their dinner to a couple of food packets along with a canteen of plain, metallic tasting water. They were going to have to learn to enjoy uncooked food or find the items strewn around on the ground below.

Watching the waterfall change from a roaring cascade to a thin stream, Clyde, now able to hear his own voice, said, "I wonder who was in that sailboat we saw. Hope they made it to land before the storm hit."

"If they weren't good sailors they're probably fish food. I know that's exactly how we would have ended up if we'd been out there."

"Maybe we should check the shoreline in the morning. What do you think? Even natives can make a mistake."

Never letting an opportunity to see the darker side of things get away, Neville said, "Who says they were natives? This is Jap territory, at least for a couple more days."

"Japs in a boat like that? Not their cup a tea, Mate. We were going to take a look around in the morning anyway, after we check in with Bill. We can still do that and check out places where they might have taken refuge."

"Fine," said Neville, disgusted with their situation and Clyde's infatuation with the boat. You look for your sailboat, I'm going to try and find some of our newly departed possessions."

Thunder accompanied the approaching daylight. Clyde looked out to see flashes of light on the underside of the clouds over the east end of the Strait. Complaining to himself, he said, "What good does that do? Thunder is supposed to happen before it rains, to let everyone know a storm is coming, not after."

Neville walked up beside him. "Once again you're showing your lack of basic education. What did you do in school besides sleep?"

"What in the hell are you talking about?"

"That my good friend ain't thunder. It's some great bloody armada creating a number of holes in the ground on one of these lovely islands."

"Battleships?"

"Nothing else sounds like that…and that's a fact!"

"Who do you suppose it is?"

"My money's on the Yanks, although, the Nips still have some ships just as big. The Yanks raised those ships out of the mud at Pearl Harbor for a reason. Now they're using 'em."

"Glad I'm here and not over there, even with being wet most of the night and feeling like a newly caught tuna."

Clyde looked at his watch. "Almost time to check in. Maybe they'll tell us what's happening."

"I guess one of us has to be a dreamer. But, what I'm hoping for is a nice clear sky and good visibility."

"Look who's dreaming now."

"I ain't dreaming, I'm being practical. We can't report what we can't see."

"Now that is something I can agree with." Clyde hesitated a moment as a new idea came together before saying, "Next time we send a message, why don't we ask for a better island? Something with a useful view."

Chapter 16

New Mission

October 18, 1944

The day started in a routine fashion with Neville getting a small fire going. Clyde set up the radio for their morning contact. Neville looked up when Clyde, surprised, softly said, "Hello there," while continuing to copy an incoming message. Neville leaned over his shoulder, curious to see what had sparked his partner's interest.

Clyde glanced up from his copy pad. "It's in code and too damn long a message to be anything good."

Neville shrugged his shoulders and returned to the fire. When he was finished copying the message, Clyde sent an acknowledgement, and switched off. He began closing up the equipment after removing his headphones and handing the coded message to Neville.

When Neville finished his decoding, he shook his head in disbelief, and handed off the slip of paper. Clyde read their instructions and quickly became equally unhappy.

"I knew it. Didn't I tell you, didn't I?" Clyde's voice rose as he spit out each word. "Those damn idiots! Getting those boys into a situation like that. Someone ought to make those so-called brains go in there themselves. But no-o, who do they call when they hang men out on the end of a line like that? You and me, that's who!"

Knowing his mate was right, nevertheless, Neville tried to calm him down. "Who would you send? We're the best, ain't we?"

"Well of course we are," Clyde quickly agreed. "That ain't the bloody point."

"Then what is? The way you're talking, you sound like you're afraid you might get your boots dirty."

"To hell with my boots, it's my skin I'm worried about and the older it gets, the more I like wearing it smooth like–no extra holes. Remember those Yank Marines we met? They were fond of saying that when things get tough, it's time to send in the Marines. I can't agree more," he said, while reaching down to unfasten his radio's cover. He pulled his hand back and stuck a finger in his mouth. "Damn, I just pinched my finger on that silly buckle."

"Why? What are you doing?"

"What's it look like I'm doing? I'm opening the radio case. How do you expect Bill to know when to send us those boats unless we tell him?"

"But, I thought you said…"

Clyde stopped fiddling with the radio and looked at his partner. "I know what I said, and I meant every word of it, but if we're the only ones close enough to get the job done then we bloody well better go do the job. It's not the fault of those young lads if someone dropped them into the deep end of the pond."

"Good on you, Mate. I'll write up the message. What time do you think we should tell our personal fleet to arrive?"

Clyde stopped setting up the transmitter, looked up at the sky, and thought about their situation and that of the Rangers who were in need of their help. When on the submarine, the six men had treated the two Englishmen with disdain, but that was then and now was now. "Normally I'd say after dark. However, it sounds like those boys need us as soon as possible, or sooner. Tell Bill to have his PT Boats collect us at noon."

"If any Japs are around and see us leave, they may come over for a walk-about afterwards. We better make sure we do a good job of hiding our stash. That means we won't have any time to look for your sailboat."

"Right you are. Who knows, it might have sunk, but if it didn't, we can look for it when we get back."

Clyde stopped for a moment and thought about the current situation, and specifically, where the Rangers were reportedly trapped. He nodded his head, agreeing with his own estimate of the situation. "Yes, that will work," he said under his breath, and then more loudly, "Go on, write up your reply to Bill. Noon will work just fine."

With engines roaring, PT Boats 245, 255 and 272, in a V formation, moved through the deep blue water on a northeast heading at better than twenty knots. They planned to make landfall at a point on Leyte's southern shore only a few miles from where Lieutenant Spann and his men had run into a strong enemy patrol and become trapped. Clyde and Neville, with the wind tearing through their hair held on to grab bars standing behind number 255's small windscreen. PT Boats were beautiful to watch, but passengers rarely had time to enjoy the scenery as they worked to maintain their balance and not get thrown overboard. The three boats plowed through, or bounced over the rough water. Each increase in speed made the water react like freshly forged steel, rather than a flowing liquid.

"We need to get one of these when we get back to Pyramid," yelled Clyde trying to make himself heard over the engine and wind noise.

Less than thrilled at the idea, Neville replied, "I'll ask the Admiral for one, next time we see him."

Responding to his partner's lack of enthusiasm, Clyde continued, "If we take the guns and torpedoes off, and add a roof and benches, this could be a grand little ferry. Think how much wc could make running it up and down the islands."

Knowing another pie-in-the-sky idea when he heard one, Neville stopped paying attention as he concentrated on their new mission.

After negotiating the loan of one crewmember from each of the three boats, the leaders of the ad-hoc rescue unit agreed to the mission. The job was similar to the operation they conducted on New Guinea. All they had to do was lead a small group, in the dark of night through several miles of jungle filled with hostiles. It made them feel needed, despite what Clyde said. The call made it apparent that the army knew how good they were, or how they lacked good judgment, depending on a person's point of view. Even so, they were realists, meaning they were nervous. After accomplishing the simple assignment, they needed to help the Rangers locate the local guerilla leader. Once that was done, Clyde and Neville could return to their small island and resume their normal duties.

Not until the sun touched the horizon behind them did the small flotilla come in sight of their landing area. The Lieutenant, j.g. commanding the boat, a twenty-two year old who had grown up along the Oregon coast, signaled the other two boats. Each boat had three diesel engines. With his signal, each one turned off two engines and routed the exhaust of the third through a muffler. Within seconds, they were assaulted by the silence they had been wishing for. Their engines burbling at little more than an idle, the boats cautiously approached the apparently deserted beach.

Turning to the Lieutenant, Neville asked, "Where will you be if we need you in a hurry?"

Pointing back over his shoulder, the Lieutenant said, "We passed a group of rocks about five miles back. We'll tie up out there. When we get your pickup message, we'll be less than thirty minutes from the beach. And by the way," he looked directly at Neville, "when we do pick you up, I'd really appreciate you bringing back all three of our men, undamaged."

Before Neville could think of a smart response, Clyde stood up as tall as his slightly-rounded body allowed and pointed over the bow. "I can see a beach." He turned toward the Lieutenant. Dropping his voice, he said, "I hope it's the right one."

"Don't worry about that, Mr. Arnold. You just get everyone back here in one piece."

On a hair-trigger, the gunners continued traversing their 30-caliber machine guns right and left as the three boats approached their destination. Their bows touched the sand, and the engines held the boats in place while the three gunners dropped over the bow into two feet of water. Other crewmembers handed down guns, equipment and the all-important radio transmitter. Clyde and Neville, as befitted their age, slowly lowered themselves over the side, each hanging from the lip of the bow. They watched a wave recede and dropped the last few feet. They were in and out of the water so fast, there wasn't time to get their feet wet.

No sooner did the men reach dry land, than all three boats backed away. The sun, already below the horizon, disappeared with its normal equatorial speed, leaving only enough light for the men to scramble up to the tree line and identify a small opening in the thick canopy. Headquarters said they thought the wide slow-moving stream threading its way through the jungle would get them near their target, but right or wrong, it appeared to be as good a place to start as any.

Neville took the lead. Clyde automatically took the tail-end-Charlie position, leaving one of the sailors in the middle of the line to carry the transmitter. They followed the stream, sometimes walking in the water, at other times in the bordering jungle. Following its meandering route back into the hills, they didn't walk in any one direction for more than a minute. The moon had not yet shown itself, and even if it had, they would still have been walking in almost total darkness. Neville's ability to find his way was nothing short of magical, or so it seemed to the sailors who kept stumbling along. The man with the radio remained in the middle of the group, maintaining his footing with constant help from the other two. Trying to keep alert for the enemy soon became an afterthought.

A strong shower drenched the tree canopy and moved on, hardly reaching the soft jungle floor. The stream narrowed and the jungle closed in, the farther they traveled away from the sea. The width of the stream, initially clear of interfering foliage, soon narrowed. They constantly brushed branches out of the way. The increasing steepness of the terrain caused the gently flowing water to move more quickly, pulling at their feet and adding to their difficulties.

Neville started using his machete. Simultaneously, he worried about the noise, while taking pleasure at being able to slice through plants whose tough sharp leaves and thorns scraped his arms and plucked at his clothes, eyes and other tender places. When he banged his knee into the large trunk of a tree that had fallen across the stream before he saw it, he knew they had gone as far as they could without some light. Common sense said the odds of any Japanese being nearby were miniscule. On the other hand, his desire not to be staked out over an anthill, or skewered by bayonet-wielding sadistic little men made him call a halt until first light.

The never-silent jungle grew more raucous to announce the start of a new day. First light revealed that one end of the tree trunk blocking their way had come to rest in the notch of another tree. Neville pointed to the youngest and smallest of the sailors. "Young man, climb up this tree and the one it's laying against. Take a good look around and then come back down. Do not," he waged a finger in the man's face, "try to tell me what you can see until you're back down here. Understand?"

The sailor looked up. The top of the second tree hidden from view, disappeared into a mass of branches a hundred or so feet above their heads. Seeing a worried look on the young man's face, Clyde said, "Where are you from, lad?"

"Kansas."

"How big are the trees in Kansas?"

Not sure how to answer, the sailor finally said, "Um…we don't have any, Sir."

It wasn't the answer Clyde expected. "You mean in your yard? What about your neighbors? You must have enjoyed climbing their trees when you were young?"

"Kansas is different, but I read Huckleberry Finn when I was in school." He could see that Clyde didn't understand that trees in Kansas, tall enough to climb, were unknown to the sailor. To cover the awkward silence, the young man quickly added, "It don't look as hard as climbing that damn greased pole in boot camp."

He shrugged out of his backpack, hung Neville's binoculars around his neck and climbed onto the fallen tree. He tested his footing and quickly walked along the inclined trunk. Twenty feet off the ground, he reached the upright tree. Taking a moment to see what his next move would be, he grabbed a limb and started up. In no time at all he disappeared from view. Invisible to the group on the ground, they followed his progress by watching the leaves of various branches shake.

"SHIT!" The word rang out from up in the tree, followed by, "Oww, damn, get off, damn, okay, okay," and then the chatter of monkeys celebrating their victory. His clothes torn, deep scratches on his facc and arms, he hurriedly dropped down several branches and moved around to the other side of the tree. He carefully inched up past the family whose bedroom he had invaded, grateful to have avoided their sharp teeth.

"What the hell is happening up there?" asked Clyde, looking at Neville for an answer.

Neville knew and smiled to himself, happy to have someone else become acquainted with some of the less than mild-mannered residents of the lush island.

By the time his legs came back into view, most of the group had finished eating their cold breakfast. Sweating profusely, the young sailor sat down on the fallen tree and rested before working his way to the ground.

Clyde held out a canteen that the sailor drained without stopping for a breath. "I never knew a tree could grow so high. I could see all the way back to the ocean."

"Never mind the ocean, we already know where that is," growled Clyde. "What you went up there for is to tell us what we don't know, what's in front of us?"

"Such as Jap soldiers," added Neville.

The sailor shook his head. "Hard to say–everything is so green. Never seen so much green, but I did see some smoke in front of us, over to the left."

"What about a cliff?"

"Nope." He shook his head again. "No cliff. Although, I saw a steep hill about a mile or so in front of us. And it's hard to have a cliff if you don't have a hill."

"The young man has a point, now don't he?" Neville observed, while adjusting his binoculars.

"Maybe." Clyde grudgingly admitted before adding, "Our boys should be keeping a low profile if they have any brains. That means the smoke is coming from the Japs. Let's stay with the stream for awhile, then we can bear off to the right."

The three sailors simply listened. They were in an alien environment. They didn't know much, but they did know when not to offer an opinion. All they wanted was to get back to their boats.

"All right lads. Saddle up and put those machetes away. Instead of cutting things down, we slip between them. No one says anything. Mum is the word, and be ready to get lower than the bloody dirt if you hear anything. Clyde and me will lead the way, you three stay back a wee bit in case we start shooting."

With the ability to see where they were going, the group made good time, even with the added precaution of trying not to make any noise. Neville continued to lead the way with Clyde, carbine at the ready, close behind.

They began hearing gunfire after they angled away from the quickly disappearing stream. The crack of Japanese Nambu rifles came from their left and the flatter sound of carbines from directly ahead. Neville changed direction, angling more to the right, hoping to come up on the Ranger's left flank.

Clyde touched his mate's shoulder. "You go ahead and meet up with these blokes. I'll take these men around behind the Japs." He looked at his watch. "I'll give you one hour and then we'll bang away as fast as we can for two minutes. They'll turn to meet the new threat. You and the Rangers can charge at them from behind. It don't sound to me like there's more than a dozen of them." Confidently, he continued, "It'll be a bloody shooting gallery with them playing the ducks."

Clyde didn't wait for his partner to agree. He simply waived his arm at the three sailors to follow him and pushed through the branches of a short palm tree to move toward an ambush position behind the enemy. Silence was their friend and protector.

Neville moved off on his own, confidant yet cautious, carbine at the ready, safety off. It never seemed to matter that he wasn't actually in the army. Whatever the two of them did, they always ended up in combat situations without being paid extra for putting their lives at risk. The score after three years of war, including the bomber fiasco totaled, Clyde and Neville five, Japan still at zero.

* * *

The information Neville had on the Ranger's situation was close to nil and sadly, even that was likely to be out of date. Still, he couldn't help wonder if this time, things might end differently than expected.

The Rangers were backed up against a cliff. Instead of dropping away, it rose up behind them almost a hundred feet high. The less-than-ideal location was where they decided to make a stand after being pursued by the enemy almost since they first came ashore. Several Japanese sharpshooters shooting down from above were slowly making headway at finishing them off. A clearing in front of the cliff, strewn with boulders dislodged from above looked to be about a hundred feet wide. Taking some time to get a complete picture of the battlefield, Neville saw several crumpled Japanese bodies sticking out from behind the boulders. He could also see at least one Ranger sitting with his back against the cliff, head down on his chest and missing his helmet.

The only good thing about the situation appeared to be the location of the Rangers, close up against the base of the cliff. It made the job of the sharpshooters quite difficult. They had to expose themselves, leaning out over the cliff face to get a shot. Several Japanese bodies spread-eagled on the rocks below gave evidence of their vulnerability. Neville, however, could see that he would be equally vulnerable if he tried to reach the Rangers across the cleared space.

While he watched, two men above quickly leaned out, took shots and ducked back. Out of sight of the Rangers, they were still clearly visible to Neville. He squirmed around making himself comfortable behind a tree and took aim. His shot was on the mark and a sharpshooter slumped over. Having heard carbines firing for the last twenty-four hours, the sound did not attract any attention from the Japanese. However, it did not go unnoticed by the Rangers, one of whom stuck his head up to see who was out there.

Neville waved his carbine in the air, then pointed at his watch and twice flashed five fingers. The head nodded, and dropped down behind its protection an instant before a bullet ricocheted off the rock beside him. Then, another shot rang out. Its sound died away, replaced by a high-pitched scream. The sharp crack from another Nambu rifle followed and the scream changing to a short gurgle and then, silence.

With less than five minutes to go before Clyde's noisy entry, Neville took aim and wounded an enemy soldier creeping toward the Ranger's left flank. Admiring his shot, Neville was slow to get behind his tree. A shot from above found the top of his right shoulder. Grabbing at his wound, Neville dropped down and skittered laterally to another protected location. He surmised from his shoulder only burning, rather than a lightning-bolt intense pain, that he had been lucky, although he dreaded what Clyde would say. Up until now, neither one of them had been wounded by the enemy, not even during the Great War in France. He pulled a field dressing from its pouch and grimaced when he pushed it down on the wound, all the time keeping his ears peeled for Clyde's noisy entry.

Distracted as he was by being shot, Neville still didn't lose interest in the battle going on at the cliff. He laid the barrel of his carbine in the notch of a thick bush hoping for one more shot. The sharpshooter on top of the cliff obliged him by moving just enough to disturb the limb he was hiding behind. Neville didn't hesitate. He pulled the stock of his weapon into his good shoulder, set his front sight on the limb and fired. The bush erupted as his adversary fell forward through the bush and dropped over the cliff screaming all the way down. The last man known to be on top of the cliff had been eliminated.

The man's body hit the jungle floor next to the only Ranger still fighting. Startled, the Ranger jumped to the side exposing his body. One shot rang out. The lone remaining Ranger died, sprawled out in the low ground cover. The information the group had been sent to pass on to the guerillas dying with him, unless they could find the Lieutenant's small notebook.

Stunned at how the situation had changed, Neville sat there for a moment. When he saw the Japanese start to advance across the clearing he aimed his carbine at them, but something told him not to fire. In all likelihood, neither he nor Clyde had been discovered. The realization of how futile it would be to continue the battle squeezed its way into his consciousness. He reluctantly took his carbine out of the bush and grimaced at the pain in his shoulder. It was hard for Neville to accept defeat as he crawled away to find Clyde. He needed to keep his mate from shooting.

Neville had not moved more than fifty-feet toward Clyde, when to his dismay he heard the on-time ripping sound of three Tommy guns, one after the other firing a full magazine in the general direction of the enemy. When the third one finished, they repeated their routine a second time, this time giving the top of the cliff some attention. Caught at close range out in the relatively open area below the cliff face, the Japanese hesitantly returned fire. The cracking sound of their single fire bolt-action rifles said the diversion, now the main attack was working. Too late to stop his mate, Neville found a good position to hit the Japanese from their flank. He was close enough to throw a hand grenade, but didn't have any. Instead, he settled in the notch between two boulders identified the officer in charge and sent him to meet his ancestors.

The Japanese realized the difficulty of their situation when a second man's head snapped back surrounded by a large pink cloud. They broke ranks to charge their new enemy, fully exposing themselves. The withering fire was merciless. The sailors were in their element. Tommy guns did not require a person to be an accurate shot. When on the PT Boats, their primary duties were to operate the rotating thirty caliber machine guns against enemy air attack. The attrition the Japanese army and naval air units experienced throughout the war zone meant the gunners were out of practice shooting at the enemy. But, at such close range, Clyde's prediction of a shooting gallery proved true. Within seconds that seemed like hours, the only people he knew to be alive were the sailors, Clyde and Neville.

After checking each of the bodies on the ground, the group reassembled near the cliff. To everyone's surprise, Sergeant Forester, his head wrapped in a dirty bandage, groggily greeted the two plantation owners. "Why does seeing you two not surprise me, although I'd like to know where you picked up your three keepers?"

Ignoring the Sergeant, Neville looking around. "Lieutenant Spann?"

"That's him by the cliff." Forester pointed at the body that looked like it had fallen asleep sitting up. "He took the first bullet. Never knew what hit him."

"Didn't care much for the blighter, but still…sorry for the young man." Neville shook himself back to the matter at hand. "It seems you're the only one left, Sergeant. Afraid all we can do is cover your men, we don't have time to bury them."

Forester nodded. This wasn't his first time in combat and he accepted the reality of it.

"I guess I'm in charge of this operation now. Did you bring me any information on the guerillas?"

"Sorry to disappoint you, old chap. Your headquarters put us in charge, not that either of us asked for the job, but…well, there you are."

While Neville talked to the sergeant, Clyde stood behind him working to pull the bloody dressing off his friend's shoulder. Already in a foul mood, Neville started to pull away, only to be forcefully grabbed and held against a boulder.

"What damn fool thing did you do to yourself? Can't leave you alone for any time at all, can I? Now stop your squirming while I do you up proper like."

Neville tried to stay still as Clyde sprinkled sulfur powder on the wound and applied a large bandage. While being bandaged, he looked up to see one of the sailors hand a small bundle of dog tags to Forester and a small notebook to Clyde.

Clyde took a moment to leaf through the information in the notebook before looking at each of the dog tags. They were all that was left of five young men who had been looking forward to the rest of their lives.

Chapter 17

Encounter

October 20, 1944

Lieutenant Spann's tactical awareness and knowledge of the enemy never impressed any of his men, possibly he tried too hard to do things perfectly. Unfortunately, he seldom ended up getting things right. Keeping his head down when under attack was the smart thing to do, and basic to staying alive. Unfortunately, he thought being a leader meant taking risks instead of always following the combat manual. Sticking his head up for too long when under attack turned out to be the last wrong thing he did. His reward–not living long enough to see the result of his poor decisions.

Gleaning what they could from Forester, along with the information provided by Cullison, gave the co-commanders a reasonable idea of where they needed to go. The last reported position of the guerilla's traveling camp was to the southeast, near the east coast of the large peninsula they were on. If the mapmaker was accurate, they only needed to go ten miles. On the map, the location of the cliff meant they needed to move south a little to get over the central ridge. From there it would all be downhill.

By mid-morning the group was ready to go. Clyde took the lead followed by Forester, the sailors and Neville bringing up the rear. Walking away from the cliff, a few of the men paused to pay their respects to the men laid in a row, each covered with a poncho. Forester turned and yelled as a single shot rang out. They all dropped behind rocks or trees as if hit by a giant club. The echoing sound of the shot and ricocheting bullet faded into the distance, swallowed by the dense foliage. One of the sailors gingerly reached his hand out for his helmet that now sported a deep groove down its right side.

Clyde yelled in a hoarse whisper, "Did anybody see where that came from?"

The sailor who had acquired an instant headache pointed at the cliff top with his helmet. "He has to be up top. Must have been waiting for us to move away from the cliff."

Clyde glanced up. He didn't expect to see anything, but it was always possible that the sniper they had missed might make a mistake. Nothing moved. If the man was smart, he was already on his way to a new position, the same thing his targets should be doing. "Keep your noses in the dirt and crawl into the trees. We stay out here, he has the advantage."

Once in the trees, they resumed their positions in line and Clyde led off, jogging as quickly as the undergrowth allowed. He found a small game trail that crossed over the hill and once on the other side they increased speed. Neville drew the unenviable position of tail-end-Charlie. Constantly looking back over his shoulder, his position made him the one most likely to receive a bullet in the back. Twice in the next half-hour, a shot rang out. After the second one, a small limb fluttered down from a branch inches above a sailor's head. The bullet was all the encouragement any of them needed to increase their speed and forego a ten-minute break at the top of the hour. Fortunately, for them, their pursuer was having difficulty tracking them and shooting straight at the same time.

It was embarrassing for a six-man squad to be chased by a single shooter, but they didn't have the time needed to set a trap for their antagonist. Into their third hour of a hurried march across unknown terrain, Clyde happened to look at the ground and did a double take. He stopped so fast the other men imitated a rush-hour chain-reaction collision. He almost missed a thin line of trampled down weeds when he crossed it. Clyde extended his arms pointing at the surrounding area. The men untangled themselves and settled down, nervously eyeing the thick jungle. Neville huddled with Clyde discussing the new situation in whispers. It was a quick discussion. Agreeing with Clyde, he quickly motioned for the men to form a tight group around them.

Clyde pointed at the weeds. "Some people came through here in the last few hours. It looks like they took care to leave as little evidence as possible."

"That means they're guerillas, right?" said a sailor.

"Quiet," growled Forester trying to reassert his authority.

"That's right," agreed Neville. "Or, at least, we can hope so. We're going to follow the trail, but be ready to hit the ground fast. These fellows are more likely to shoot first than invite us over for a Bar-B." He held up a finger to emphasize his words. "Remember this, no one shoots unless we say so. With a little luck..."

Sarcastically, Clyde said, "A little?"

"All right, with a lot of luck, this trail might lead us to their headquarters."

Following behind parties unknown made a sudden meeting with the people ahead of them more likely than for the group to be surprised from behind. Neville changed position putting himself behind Clyde–a better place for when they met whoever they were following. He told Forester to take the tail-end position. The faint trail Clyde first saw stood out like the Sydney to Brisbane highway compared to other sections. The two men with skin the color of burnt parchment used all their tracking abilities to keep from losing the trail. Casting about for visual signs, at times Clyde was down on his knees examining individual blades of grass. More than once he or Neville found what they believed to be the trail, only to lead the group off in the wrong direction. Valuable time had to be used backtracking and eventually, finding where they made the mistake.

"These blokes are good, bloody damn good." Neville's statement was high praise indeed.

"Too good," replied Clyde. "Too good to be Nips, and too good to be natives making a quick trip to the local market."

"Which begs the question, ol' boy. What are they going to do when they find us climbing up their proverbial ass?"

"They'll either kiss us, or…"

"It's the 'or' that can get us killed, Mate. Any ideas?"

"A brass band might be useful." Clyde slapped at his pockets, "but seeing as how I seem to have mislaid mine, a flag would be nice. A big flag."

Neville turned around to the sailors behind him. "Any of you men carrying a flag? American, British, Aussie? I'll even take one of your confederate union flags. Anything that don't say Jap!"

Negative, was their only reply. No one had a flag and their combat uniforms were designed without any easily visible insignia. With that idea dismissed, they continued through their green on green world until suddenly they were into bright sunlight. Clyde dropped to one knee before he poked his head back up and looked over the tall grass in front of him. To walk through the now overgrown field that some one had painstakingly cleared would be impossible without leaving a telltale path. The field screamed ambush, as did trying to bypass the area and picking up the trail on the other side.

Neville squatted next to his old friend. "Want to flip a coin to see who leads."

Clyde shook his head. “They ain’t far ahead of us. See the way the grass is still flat in places.” He pointed at the weeds in front of them. “Probably some of them are on the other side of this field. We need something to tell these blokes we’re on their side.”

“Tell me, oh Great White Hunter, what fantastic idea do you have? I’m all ears.”

Clyde shrugged his shoulders. “Don’t know. I must have skipped that class.”

“Asleep, more likely.”

“How can you say that about a wounded veteran?” Neville pointed at the bandage on his shoulder.

Clyde said, “Give me that.”

“Why? You looking for some sympathy?”

“We need a flag, right? We stick your bloody bandage on a pole. It don’t matter if we’re Japs or whirling dervishes, somebody sees that, they’re at least going to want to know whose fool enough to be carrying it, before they shoot.”

“Maybe…” Neville’s skeptical reply wasn’t exactly a rousing vote of confidence, although, he couldn’t think of anything better.

Clyde knotted one end of the bandage to the pole, made a stay-here gesture, and walked into the field with the pole held high, the red and white flag swinging in the wind. Nervously he looked everywhere when he stopped and waited halfway across the field. All was quiet. He took a deep breath and continued on, wondering when someone would challenge his approach.

Prepared for something bad to happen, he approached the trees on the far side of the field. He stepped from bright sunlight into the jungle and stopped, waiting for his eyes to adjust to the semi-darkness. The pole in one hand, he raised the other and turned in a circle to show himself to the hidden eyes he knew were watching his every move.

When nothing happened, his nervousness changed to irritation. He had been a gentleman, waiting for his would-be captors to show up. "Bloody hell. You can't be that scared of one ol' man," he yelled at the wall of greenery around him as he continued to turn, hoping to see some friendly faces appear. The longer he waited, the more irritated he became. After two more rotations, he said, "That's it. I'm done with this." He dropped the flag, disgusted with himself for acting like a Nervous Nelly. He shouted back across the field for Neville and the group to join him, knowing the type of unkind remarks that were sure to follow.

Clyde faced the field to wait for his motley group to appear. He could easily hear them tramping through the tall grass as they approached. Neville appeared closely followed by one of the sailors with the others a few feet behind, still hidden from view. The initial smile on Neville's face froze in place as he suddenly dropped his carbine and raised his hands. The sailor followed his lead, shocked at being captured so easily.

Standing in a semi-circle behind Clyde were over twenty men, none taller than five foot four dressed in Japanese uniforms. Clyde's smile disappeared when he saw Neville's action. He slowly turned around, "God damn it!" he muttered as he laid his carbine on the ground. *How could he have been so stupid?* Instead of being captured out in the open field, he had been fooled and dropped his guard when nothing happened. Their enemy had turned the tables on them by doing the unexpected.

The other two sailors came to a halt, wondering what had happened up ahead. They broke from their single line formation and poked through the tall grass. Each of them did the same as Neville when they saw so many guns pointed at them. Only Sergeant Forester, the last man in the line remained hidden in the grass.

Seeing the sailors drop their carbines and raise their hands, he ducked down and worked his way twenty feet to the left before he crawled to the edge of the field. One of the Japanese soldiers broke away from his group and approached Clyde. He was less than ten feet away when Clyde started to smile and lower his hands. The uniforms, many of them with blood stains, were Japanese, but the people in them were not.

The man began to speak, only to have his words cut off by a gunshot. Flung back and spun around, he fell to the ground. A barrage of gunfire quickly responded to the single shot. Scything through the tall field grass, several bullets and a lot of buckshot impacted on a point to Neville's left. Grass stems filled the air. Seconds later, the shooting stopped. When all of the grass thrown into the air had fluttered to the ground, everyone saw that Forester had tried to be a hero. Covered with severed stems of field grass, his body laid still, blood oozing from its wounds.

A woman in a Japanese uniform rushed out to the man Forester had shot. She ripped his shirt open, saw a bullet wound high on his right side, rolled him toward her and looked at his back where she saw a matching wound. Two more men rushed out to help her, as Neville ripped open his battle dressing pack and offered it to them. They hesitated until the woman said something unintelligible and went about the business of bandaging the wounds.

Clyde slowly walked over to Forester. The upper half of his body, and especially his head had taken the brunt of the barrage. His face all but gone, blood hid several bullet wounds and nearly a hundred double-ought shotgun pellets. Hands covered in Forester's blood, he pulled off one of the dead sergeant's dog tags.

Neville picked up his makeshift flagpole and rammed it into the ground marking the location of Forester's body. One sailor walked over, pulled a poncho out of Forester's pack and spread it over the body. Forester had not been looking forward to the operation thinking, he had already done his share in the war. The poorly conceived operation validated his worst fears, and now, if he was lucky, someone might bury him before nightfall. As much as Neville wanted to do the right thing, the mission had to come first.

The woman wiped her bloody hands on her pants as she walked over to Neville who thought she was a nurse. She pointed at Forester, "He stupid."

"Yes, he was," agreed Neville sadly, surprised to hear the woman speak English.

She turned away to talk to the men closest to her. Before she became distracted by something else, Neville said, "We are Americans. We're trying to find Ruperto Kangleon. He's the leader of the resistance on Leyte. Do you know him?"

The woman turned to once again face him. Seeing her up close, Neville saw a softness beneath her hard exterior.

"Of course. All people know Ruperto. He not here." Having stated the obvious, she called out to one of the men in a strange language. He ran over and after a minute of conversation that included more hand gestures than vowels, he took another man and the two of them ran back into the jungle in the direction of the field. One minute they were there, the next, a line of barely disturbed palm fronds pointed to where they had disappeared.

Neville, who was far from tall, looked down at the woman. "Did you ask that man to get Ruperto?"

Annoyed at the question, she answered, "He not here. They bury dead men."

"Thank you, but can you take us to him?"

"Why you want see Ruperto? He on other side of island."

Neville didn't think it wise to tell the woman about the upcoming invasion. Instead, he asked, "How long will it take us to get there?"

"Many days. Talk to me. I send words to Ruperto?"

Neville looked at the Filipinos surrounding the area, apparently waiting for the group's leader to make himself known. When no one seemed to want to take charge, he asked, "Is your leader nearby? It's important that I talk with him."

"Talk with me. I leader," said the woman. "I Nieves Fernandez. What you want?"

Neville stood there, his disbelief evident. He knew this little, middle-aged woman who looked like everyone's favorite history teacher had to be joking. She must be trying to protect their leader…just in case.

"Good on you," he said, accompanied by a small, nervous laugh. "Come on now, we don't have time for games. Where is he?"

Nieves rolled her eyes in disgust, her thoughts easy to read, *another one*. "I leader," she repeated, as she turned around and said a few words in her native Tagalong language, waved her arms, and walked away. The rest of the Japanese dressed guerillas followed her.

Seeing the last of the rebel group disappear into the trees, Neville motioned for his group to follow along behind. Obviously, Nieves was going to lead them to her group's leader.

Walking together while keeping the last of the Filipinos in view, Neville said, "They do jump to it when she says move, now don't they? I hope she ain't the boss."

Clyde scoffed at the idea. "Not a chance. She's probably the head man's live in."

"If so, it don't say much for his leadership style. She can't be the prettiest Sheila on the island…not even in this jungle."

"Hold on there, Mate. She has a nice face. Put her in some girl clothes instead of that old Jap uniform and she might look pretty good. Especially after you've been in the jungle awhile."

About to be on the loosing end of the discussion, Neville smoothly changed the subject. "Did you notice the guns a lot of those fellas had? Never seen anything like em. Have you?"

"No factory ever made those things. Looked like pieces of water pipe clamped onto some pieces of wood they whittled down to fit like a rifle stock. But, they make a lot of sense. Shooting buckshot in the jungle where your target isn't too far away, they can tear up a fella real good. You saw what they did to Forester."

"I wouldn't mind..." Clyde stopped what he was about to say when he saw the jungle become brighter. Just as when they had approached the field. The transition from heavy jungle to open space occurred within twenty feet. They walked into a wide-open central courtyard of hard-packed dirt surrounded by more than a dozen thatch huts on stilts. Pens for chickens and goats and one covered with metal mesh to hold monkeys were all located between the huts. Nieves stood on the porch of the largest dwelling waving for them to join her, offering wicker chairs to the two men. The sailors were led to a shaded area nearby where they were given refreshments and some kind of stringy meat on sticks.

Neville and Clyde easily downed mugs of warm fruit juice before accepting small, hand-wrapped cigars. Clyde happily inhaled the rich smoke. By the time half his cigar had turned to ash he started getting fidgety–he needed to be on the move. To his way of thinking, time was being wasted waiting for the guerilla boss to show up. He leaned forward, looked at Nieves and said, "Will your group's leader be here soon? We really need to talk with him."

Nieves shook her head, and said, "I tell you, I leader all guerillas south end of island. You American. You talk, I listen."

Clyde started to make a smart remark that they would be sorry for. Neville knew his mate only too well, and stopped him with a wave of his hand as he had an unsettling revelation.

Maybe, thought Neville, the woman was the 'head man.' After all, everyone seemed to jump when she said to. Neville looked his partner in the eye, shifted his eyes to Nieves and ever so slightly bobbed his head. Clyde understood his mate's almost imperceptible gesture, saying without words, that strange things happened in war. "Miss Fernandez, we are British. The American

Army sent us to tell you what they are planning to do, and ask for your help."

"You want kill Japanese? We help." Her ear-to-ear smile lit up her face with anticipation. She turned in her chair and grabbed one of the water-pipe shotguns leaning against the wall. Despite it having been carried through the jungle for some distance, the crudely built but lethal weapon was clean and well oiled. Brandishing the home-made gun, she said, "We kill many soldiers this year." She extended her arm, pointing at her people. "Have three-hundred men. More tomorrow. We chase Japanese back to Tokyo. What you need?"

The oldest of the sailors, not yet twenty-two, assumed command of his three man unit. He had been trained in Morse Code and became the operator of the transmitter set up in Nieves hut. Neville gave him a short course in coding/decoding before handing over the code book. His final instruction, "Always ad some extraneous words at the beginning and end of each message. In case the enemy finds a way to break the code, the unrelated words might ad some confusion."

* * *

Cullison breathed a sigh of relief when he received a contact message from his traveling maniacs. He agreed to have the PT Boats pick them up before nightfall, right where Nieves suggested.

It was a rare pleasure for them to have the cooperation of the government, through Cullison, and not get yelled at. Operations involving Clyde and Neville had a way of making officials nervous. Always ready to look a gift horse in the mouth, and get bitten in the process, the two men maintained a healthy skepticism for anything arranged by the government. Whenever possible, they told officials as little as possible about their activities until after the fact…well after the fact.

When Clyde signed-off, Neville asked, "You didn't slip in any last minute comments about that little island out in the Strait, did you?"

"Now why would I do that? You know how Bill would react. No point in getting him upset all over again when he's a thousand miles away. If we remember, you can tell him, later."

Nieves and several of her men guided them to a beach only an hour's walk from the camp. The three sailors were so glad to see their floating homes, only the sight of two shark fins slicing through the water restrained them from swimming to them. The Boats waited for them just the other side of a coral reef that prevented vessels from getting to the beach. Clyde and Neville shook Nieves hand. In return, she gave each of them a hug but then gave Clyde a kiss he wouldn't forget for quite a while, before they stepped into a dugout canoe for the trip out past the surf line.

Boat 255 slowly backed away from the reef before turning around and heading out to sea. Standing on deck the two men waved to the people on the beach, most of whom had already melted back into the jungle to continue their battle against a harsh occupier.

"I don't think those people look at all worried about attacking the Nips."

"Nope, not at all," agreed Neville. "If you were them, would you? They've been waiting three years for this. They want their country back."

The two coast watchers took hold of the grab bars as the boat's stern dug into the water with its increased speed. Over the rising level of noise, Clyde said, "Wouldn't mind coming back here after the war. I think Nieves could look real nice with a dress and a little makeup."

"She just might, at that, as long as you treat her gentle."

"What do you mean? I treat all my women right. You know that."

"The reason I said that is simple. She handles that shotgun as easy as most women hold a baby. And, just what would you tell your wives if they decided to take up where they left off playing Mrs. Arnold? If my old brain remembers right, they change their minds more than most women change their shoes."

"Not likely, Mate. They left me for greener pastures. Haven't heard from either one in over a year…maybe two."

"I know they left you, same as my woman did me, and you're better for it. The thing is, I heard that a couple of my wife's Aussie cousins are keeping her informed on what I'm doing. So you remember this old chum, they could be doing the same thing. Until you come up with enough money to bribe a judge, common law says they still have the inside track to your money. And one more thing…they ain't what you would call understanding about other women. In fact, if they weren't first cousins, you might not be alive right now."

"I'm sure you mean well, Neville, but I know a thing or two about women. I can take care of myself."

"Sure you can, but if we ever meet up with Nieves, remember our little conversation. Hate to see my partner torn into pieces by three women after the Japs failed to get you."

Chapter 18

The Idea

October 21, 1944
Early morning

Commander Cullison's pair of recurring headaches relaxed in the 255 boat's small cabin. Unhappy at the thought of not rescuing the Rangers, the two men took comfort in how they were able to make contact with the guerillas. However, when recounting the encounter, they decided one feature might conveniently be forgotten. A woman being the leader of the guerilla group that surrounded them had a decidedly poor sound, and they did have a reputation to uphold.

Although they would never admit it to anyone else, they were bone-weary tired after having gotten less than three-hours sleep during the past two days. It felt good not to be slogging through the jungle, even if riding in the PT Boat did not allow a person's body to relax. That, combined with the adrenalin draining experience of combat, meant they were looking forward to returning to Limasawa and getting some rest.

Neville's mind drifted along with thoughts of a mug of good beer slipping into his consciousness, only to be swept away by reality, and the cup of fresh American coffee in his hand. Clyde, also with a cup of hot dark liquid, leaned over a navigation chart of the area. Idly, he slid his finger along the channel the boat had to negotiate before turning west. His unconscious action changed when he noticed a feature that wasn't on the less detailed map in his backpack. He put down the mug and bent a small goose-necked lamp down closer to the chart. The feature grabbed at him when he saw their intended course. Clyde stayed bent over the chart for so long Neville became concerned, and joined him.

"You alright, Mate? Need to lie down?"

Clyde acknowledged the question with a brightness in his voice that had not been there moments before. "Blimey." Followed by a cheerful, "Never better old sod, never better."

The quick, short answer, his voice full of life after such a grueling mission told Neville something was up. Seldom did Clyde talk in short sentences and his interest in the chart was out of character since young Lieutenant Boyd, steering the boat had already exhibited his ability to not get lost. Clyde kept his voice down, not as soft as a whisper, but definitely too soft for any of the crew to hear him.

"I was thinking…" even with his renewed alertness, he could not stifle a yawn. "In all our assignments since we left Pyramid, I can't remember us ever returning to a post once we left. We didn't go back to any of them, did we?"

"You're right, but what made you think about that?" He looked at Clyde with a combination of concern and curiosity. "What's going on? I can almost hear those gears in your head banging against each other, and it don't sound good."

Clyde tapped a pencil against his front teeth appearing to try and work out a difficult problem. "Like I said, we've never gone back to work at a lookout sight once we pulled out. This will be the first time. I was thinking, it would break our streak."

"What streak? It ain't like we planned most of those departures and since when was there an award for not going back to a lookout post?" Neville waited for his mate to keep talking.

Greeted by silence, he made a, tell-me-more-motion with his hands. "Come on. Out with it. What's going on?"

"Well…as I said, we never go back. This would be the first timc unless we get off this cruise ship a bit early."

"Little man, you've got me curious." Neville pointed at Clyde's head. "What is it you're trying to get me to do? And, how mad will our dear Commander be when he finds out? He's already thrown us in jail for gambling on that ship in Los Negros, and Wakde was supposed to be punishment as well."

"Don't I know. Never did understand what made him do that, sticking us in that forgotten hellhole. Most of the time the Commander is a nice fellow."

"Exactly right. No matter what we do, he can't do us any worse than Wakde."

Clyde started tapping his finger on the chart. Neville turned away to reach for his coffee cup. The longer his mate didn't look at where he was tapping, the harder Clyde poked at a spot on the chart.

How could he get Neville to agree to a change in plans if he refused to look at the chart? Clyde and patience had less than a passing relationship. Frustrated with his partner, he put his hand on Neville's shoulder and turned him back around. With Neville's full attention, he grinned and used his pencil to point at a spot on the chart.

At a loss to understand what his co-conspirator could be so interested in, Neville finally paid attention and looked more closely at the naval map. Suddenly he understood. The grin on his face quickly mirrored Clyde's. "You lovely… When? How?"

Clyde took a pair of dividers from a tray above the navigation table and measured the distance from his pencil point to their current location. "We have less than an hour before the young man up there needs to make a slight course correction for us."

"How are you going to get him to change course. He doesn't strike me as being the adventurous type."

Without an easy solution to the problem, Clyde sat down. "That is a problem," he admitted.

Sure that he was being set up, Neville said, "That means you expect me to solve it and make your idea work. I seem to remember that your ideas always end up with us at the bottom of a well without a ladder. Now, tell me the truth, this one won't be any different, will it?"

"You're my best friend, right?" Clyde hurried to answer his own question. "Of course you are. I certainly hope you don't think I'd share so many good ideas with someone I don't like, and this one," he again pointed at the chart, "is just what we need to get the job done. Limasawa is a nice place for a vacation, if you're a hermit, but we haven't been able to see a bloody thing. It's too far from where we need to be." He took a pencil and drew a circle around his discovery. "This is where we need to be to get the job done."

The hook–a better lookout post–that Clyde dropped into the water did its job. It snagged Neville as easily as if he was a salmon passing by on its way upstream to spawn, and Clyde reeled him in. With the hook set, they only needed to do one more thing. How were they going to make the Lieutenant change course?

While contemplating the problem, he looked over to see Reynolds, the radio operator copy down a message, tear a sheet off his pad and take it up to the Lieutenant. He returned a moment later followed by the young Mr. Boyd, who looked at the chart. "Send an acknowledgement with our ETA, zero-seven-hundred."

Always curious, Clyde and Neville looked up. Almost in unison, they asked, "Change in plans?"

"Yes, and unfortunately it's going to affect you. All four squadrons, thirty-nine boats have been ordered to rendezvous south of Bohol tomorrow morning. Headquarters must think the Japs are going to try and break through the Strait."

"Where is Bohol?"

"It's the first choke point the Jap Navy hits if they try to get at the invasion fleet by forcing their way through the Strait. Bohol on the north and Mindanao on the south are forty-miles apart. They define the point where the Sulu Sea meets the Bohol Sea."

"Forty miles sounds like a lot of ocean. Why don't you bring 'em to this area?" Clyde pointed at the Surigao Strait's narrowest point. It was a hundred-miles east of Bohol, and the location where he thought two brave but impulsive coast watchers ought to be, instead of on Limasawa. "This place is only about four miles wide. The Japs come through here, you can't miss. They'll be sitting ducks, and if they come through too fast they'll go aground when they try to make a sharp turn to port to get past Dinigat and this other small island to get into the Gulf of Leyte."

"Good idea, Mr. Arnold, only the Admiral says we go to Bohol."

"What about our getting back to Limasawa?"

"We aren't going to have time to get you there. That means you'll have to stay on board for awhile, unless we see a destroyer you can transfer to."

Neville tried not to show his thoughts. He acted disappointed. Resigned to the change, he said, "Ah well, can't be helped, Sir."

The two men dropped into their opposing roles as easily as a shark can smell fresh blood. With the easy-to-please roll already taken by Neville, Clyde said, "Can't be helped? My ass it can't be helped." He banged his hand down on the chart table for emphasis, startling Boyd. "We didn't put off going home to our safe little island only to be shunted aside because we're inconvenient."

The Lieutenant said, "What would you have me do Mr. Arnold? My hands are tied."

Derisively, Clyde replied, "Your hands are tied? Not if you don't want them to be tied. You're simply hiding behind your orders. You young people don't care, like us. We been in two wars and know what it takes to win. You fellas' have had it too easy."

Before the startled Boyd could open his mouth to defend himself against Clyde's outburst, Neville stepped between the two. "Come now, Mate, that ain't fair. The poor boy has his orders. It's not like he wouldn't help us if he could, right Lieutenant?"

"Of course I would, if I could."

His arms folded, Clyde stuck out his jaw, "Prove it."

"What do you mean? I just said, I have my orders."

"Right you are, Mr. Boyd, there isn't any way you can get us to Limasawa," agreed Neville. "But, there is a place almost as good that's only a few minutes out of your way. Granted it ain't the best, but I think Clyde and me could do some good if you drop us off," he pointed at the place Clyde had circled, "right here."

The Lieutenant bent over to see what Neville was pointing at. "You want me to drop you there? You're not crazy, you're insane. The Japs would spot you before you had time to unpack your radio. There isn't any way I'm going to get court-martialed because you two have a death wish. Without orders, you'll simply have to take it easy for a day or two until I can get you transferred to a destroyer."

Clyde reacted to his mate's idea as if Boyd had never said anything. "I like your idea, Neville. That looks like just the place for us. Why don't I send a message to the Commander. I'm sure he'll agree."

Clyde's idea, his willingness to send Cullison a message confused Neville. He didn't know what to say, although he felt sure he knew what the Commander would say to the idea. But, Clyde hadn't proposed sending the message, without a plan…he hoped. Still, whatever the outcome, he decided to play along secure in the knowledge that the Americans didn't have a jail close by to throw them in. At least, not yet.

Clyde stepped over to Reynolds, the radio operator, tapped him on the shoulder and motioned for him to get up. He took the man's headphones, sat down and began examining the setup. It was a lot more complicated than the simple unit he was accustomed to using. Boyd motioned for Reynolds to take a break, whereupon the radioman went up the short ladder to get some air.

Neville grabbed a message pad and quickly scribbled out a message asking for a change in assignment location. By the time he finished the task of converting the short message into their abbreviated code Clyde knew what he needed to do.

"I'll let you know the minute we get a reply, Lieutenant." Clyde hoped Boyd would take his subtle hint and go back on deck.

"Thanks, I'll be in the galley. Can I get you anything?" Both men shook their heads. "All right, just lean around the bulkhead and let me know when you hear something."

Clyde fiddled with the radio trying to make it look like he knew what he was doing until Boyd walked into the galley a few feet forward of the main cabin. As soon as the Lieutenant was out of sight, Clyde motioned for Neville to bend down. He whispered a few words in his friend's ear and then started sending out a message. The radio had the capability of being tuned to both short and long-range frequencies. He knew enough to pick a frequency used for short-range transmissions and crossed his fingers that no one would respond. Since Reynolds had not had the receiving unit's speaker turned on, the reply, if any, would only be heard in the radio operator's headphones.

Clyde flipped the master switch from send, to receive and started to write down the reply he wanted–a simple acknowledgement.

Without warning, Boyd stepped back into the main cabin, "Did you get through?"

"Said to expect a reply in ten minutes or so. They knew it was me and answered right away. I'm told I have a distinctive transmission style. It's called a..."

"Fist," responded Boyd, "you have an unusual fist. I was listening from the galley, and they're right. You send code with some unusual breaks. You sound a little like a ham operator I corresponded with when I was in high school. He lived in Cyprus."

Boyd reached around the bulkhead, grabbed his coffee cup, and headed for the ladder. "I'll be on deck. Let me know when Commander Cullison says no."

As soon as the Lieutenant's shoes disappeared from view, Clyde motioned again for Neville to lean down. He handed him two sheets from the message pad. "Write out Cullison's okay along with a caution not to take any chances, and then convert it into code. Boyd's going to want to see it before he'll change course."

Ten-minutes later, Boyd poked his head down from above. "Anything?"

"Not yet. How long do we have before it's too late?"

"Fifteen. After that, this is your home for awhile."

"Wait another five-minutes before you start to receive Cullison's reply," said Neville. "We don't want to give the Lieutenant too much time to mess around with our plan."

"Plan? Let's call a spade, a spade. A plan is something a person takes time to think about. What you're getting us into doesn't even qualify as an idea."

Clyde angrily took his headphones off. In a whisper, he said, "If this ain't a plan, a good one at that, then what are you doing going along with it?"

"Only God knows the answer to that, but you're my mate, and a man don't walk out on his mate."

"Thanks, ol' boy."

A laugh in his voice, Neville said, "In for a penny, in for a pound. Now, you better start receiving our go-ahead."

As soon as Lieutenant Boyd heard about the change in plans, he thought Commander Cullison must be one cold hearted son-of-a-bitch, willing to throw men's lives away for almost nothing. "My God, do you know how exposed you'll be? Let me send a message to the Commander and get him to reconsider."

"Now don't you worry about us," Neville replied. He needed to keep the young man from giving the game away by contacting Cullison. "We've been in and out of worse spots than that little island, now haven't we, Clyde?"

"We're the best coast watchers in the business, lad. Like my shadow here says, this is the kind of assignment we expect to get."

"I think you two are crazy, but if that's what you want to do, we'll have to drop you with an inflatable at the edge of the channel. That's as close as I can get and still make it to my squadron's rendezvous on time. You're going to have to paddle a couple of miles. Are you up to it?"

Clyde had a hard time not groaning. Why was it that islands were always surrounded by water…a lot of water?

The spot on the map didn't qualify as being small. Miniscule seemed a better description. So small, Clyde needed a magnifying glass to read its name, Danawan. The island, not much more than a large pile of rocks and scrub brush, had the great advantage of being located on the south edge of the main channel where ships needed to turn left or go aground on Dinigat. The new coast watcher location looked perfect, although, it did have one defect. The size of the place might require some innovative thinking–it was that small. Even so, they felt confident of being able to create a hideaway since all of the other islands in the area were encased in thick jungle growth.

Boyd turned to Reynolds. "Get the men to break out that rubber boat and make it ready. We're getting close to the drop off point." He turned to Clyde and Neville. "If you need anything on the boat, just grab it and stick it with your gear."

"Awfully good of you, Lieutenant." Clyde put his friendliest face on. "Your men really helped us with those Tommy Guns. We would be in your debt, that is, if you can spare a pair?"

The crew rapidly inflated the rubber raft while Clyde and Neville piled what they wanted on the rear deck. The crew scurried getting things ready until the moment when the Lieutenant dropped the throttles to idle. Number 255 drifted out of the main channel. The darkened boat didn't look much different than the black water that made it rock from side to side. The shallow water and an east wind trying to force all of it out of the Gulf and through the narrow strait caused the boat's erratic motion. The waves weren't steep, just confused and choppy, coming from any and all directions. It wasn't the smooth, glass-like water Clyde prayed for as his second choice…after dry land.

The crew handed down carbines, pistols, a pair of Tommy Guns, and hand grenades wrapped in oilskin tarps. Also in a tarp was the radio followed by several backpacks filled with food, medical supplies, general survival gear, and enough batteries to keep the two delinquents in contact with their commanding officer for several weeks. The bottom of their undersized cruise ship bulged downward, slowly pulling the entire boat lower. Even the smallest of waves slopped over the air filled sides soaking the two men trying to make room for everything. Reynolds threw several fifty-foot lengths of rope into the boat as the Lieutenant waved and yelled, "Good luck." Anything else he might have said disappeared in the roar of the three diesel engines as he pushed the throttles forward.

Clyde and Neville picked up their paddles and dug them into the black water pointing the blunt bow toward the small island. Even without any light to speak of, they could tell the rubber boat was moving and finally decided to go in the correct direction. As tired as they were, it took awhile for them to settle into a routine.

Some time later, a noisy line of white surf appeared. As with so many other locations around the South Pacific on a dark night, the first indication of an island was water churning over a line of coral. The waves grew as they approached the shallows. An unexpected surge pushed them toward the island at an alarming rate. One instant the boat was moving at a reckless speed, and then it felt like someone had dropped its non-existent anchor. The front of their delicate craft snagged on a small outcropping of coral and came to an abrupt stop. Both men tumbled forward banging into equipment. The precious radio fell over. It missed the other equipment and hit the boat's inflated side to remain wedged in place and almost dry. The newly acquired Tommy Guns did not receive the same full-measure of good luck. The weapons placed on top of the radio for easy access… just in case, dropped into the dark waters with a splash and gurgle, unnoticed by either man.

The next wave to hit them spun their boat around and pushed it over the obstruction to rush, rear end first, toward the beach. Neville managed to climb back onto his perch sitting on the rounded side of their inflatable an instant before it came to a stop in shallow water. The flat bottom of the overloaded raft bulging downward acted as another non-existent anchor when it hit the sandy bottom. Everything stopped moving except Neville. No one could be more surprised than he. In the blink of an eye, he found himself floundering around on his back in the shallow water. His open mouth looked as if it was trying to drain the entire Pacific Ocean. The irony of it all hit him as he realized he might drown in less water than he needed for a bath.

He tried to push up from the soft sand bottom only to find his hands sink into the silt-like mud. His head briefly came out of the water before his arms sank deeper into the fine material. He coughed, spewed out a fountain of seawater, gasped some life-saving air, and disappeared from sight. Surrounded by darkness, his thrashing feet turned the shallow water white providing Clyde a target to grab at.

Clyde reached down, found a foot, and pulled. He unwittingly dragged Neville away from the beach and into deeper water. An incoming wave twisted Neville out of his grasp and pushed him partway under the rear of the boat in water deep enough to float.

His arms no longer constrained by the soft sand, Neville flipped over onto his knees and stuck his head up to rejoin the air-breathing world. His wheezing gasps, punctuated by bone rattling coughs, announced his safe return to a friendly environment.

The two men staggered onto dry land, and allowed their clothing to drain while reverting to their well-trained whispers. They conveniently ignored the fact that the sounds Neville emitted while in the water could have given most foghorns significant competition. With no more than a dozen words between them, they pulled the boat and their remaining equipment out of the water and hid everything behind some rocks above the beach. They made the boat quickly disappear under a covering of thorn branches torn from bushes, they unhappily discovered while blundering around in the dark.

Believing they were the only ones on the small island, Neville's whispers disappeared, replaced with his patented brand of unnecessary banter. "Unless I miss my guess, we're on Danawan. Home sweet home, the jewel of the Surigao?"

"Where else would we be?"

Through clenched teeth, Neville asked, "Do you really want me to answer that?"

"What's the matter? You're here, ain't you?"

Neville's voice left little doubt how he felt. His mate had botched an effort to drown him. "You know damn well, what's wrong. Next time, grab me under my arms, not by my feet."

Twisting and turning as Neville continued complaining, Clyde had things on his mind other than answering his mate–primarily, pulling thorns out of his hands, arms, and other tender parts.

"Well…what's your answer?"

Clyde looked at Neville. "Course I will, I'm your mate, ain't I, on one condition, if you get out the thorns that are stuck in the back of my legs."

"How the devil did you do that? All I had were a few in my fingers."

"Simple. A person can back up into all manner of things when he can't see a hand in front of his bloody face."

"Turn around and let me get to work." Neville ran his hands over Clyde's legs, conveniently forgetting any bedside manners he might have learned by mistake. Neville enjoyed every single thorn he removed, losing count when he passed twenty. "Right you are now. Your legs are as smooth as Betty Grable's, but if you have any in your ass, you're on your own."

"Don't think I have any there. At least I hope not, but now that I think of it, how is that shoulder of yours doing after being in salt water?"

"It burns some, that's all."

Clyde shuffled around in a circle making sure he had a clear space to sit. He rubbed his hands over his buttocks one last time before gingerly settling onto the sand. A contented sigh escaped his lips when he didn't feel anything sharp. He asked, "Did you have a chance to see if we lost anything out of the boat?"

Quite matter-of-factly Neville said, "Nothing important that I know of, other than those bloody Tommy Guns." Already lying down, he felt around until he knew where Clyde had stretched out. With an updated picture of his surroundings in his mind, he finished answering Clyde's question. "As long as we don't run into a full-company of Nips it won't matter."

"And if we do?"

"Not a problem We simply run around this scrap of land until they get tired. As dark as it is, they're sure to get lost. Can't say when I've seen a blacker night. Might be a storm coming, can't see any stars. We'll have to take a walkabout at first light."

"If we ain't soaked to our skins or drown when it rains," replied Clyde lying there waiting for one more smart comment. Instead, he heard a snort and then, the soft snoring that he knew so well. As far as his partner was concerned, they were safe, or at least, safe enough, wrapped in the security blanket of a dark night, on an island too small to be of use to anyone. Whatever problem lay ahead, it would be solved, avoided, or talked to death once daylight arrived.

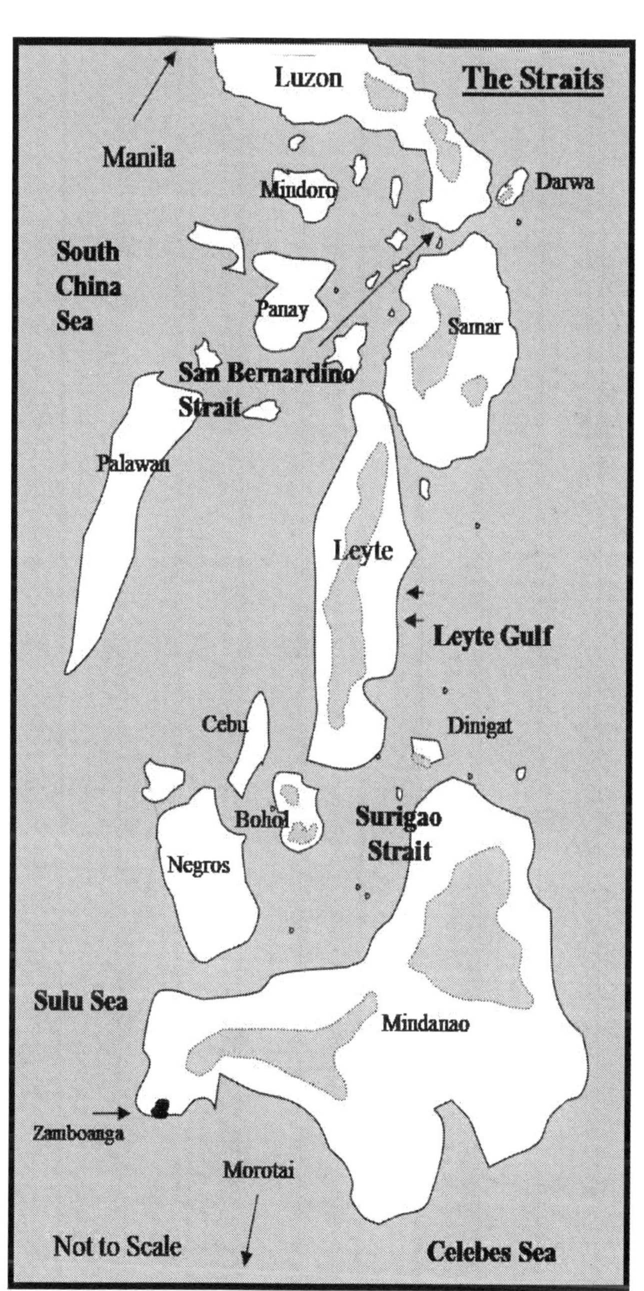

The Straits
Luzon
Manila
Mindoro
Darwa
South
China
Sea
Panay
Samar
San Bernardino
Strait
Palawan
Leyte
Leyte Gulf
Cebu
Dinigat
Bohol
Surigao
Strait
Negros
Sulu Sea
Mindanao
Zamboanga
Morotai
Not to Scale
Celebes Sea

Chapter 19

Danawan

October 21, 1944
Pre-dawn

A stranger stumbling across Clyde and Neville might believe, with good reason, that they were dead. Wrapped in a cocoon of darkness, the two men were sound sleep. Pretending to still be twenty years old could only get a person so far and they were well past that point.

The Seventh Fleet had drawn the honor of being the primary Philippines invasion force. Since being targeted by the Japanese at Pearl Harbor, it had grown to be the largest fleet in the world with over seven-hundred ships. At four in the morning, several resurrected battleships and cruisers began a bombardment of the Japanese troops remaining on Dinigat.

On little Danawan, several miles from where the large shells landed, the explosions were audible, but not disagreeably so. The vibrations coming through the ground were what bothered the two inert bodies. Their beds were being rocked, and not by a kindly nanny.

Neville fought the disturbances as long as possible before sitting up to look around. He felt that half the sand on the beach had worked its way under his eyelids. His muscles also felt overused and under-appreciated. Another set of explosions occurred on Dinigat and several seconds later, he felt and heard them. Kind thoughts regarding the U.S. Navy did not immediately come to mind. He rolled onto his side, reached over and gave Clyde a shove.

An unintelligible sound emanated from the body followed by a hand slapping at whatever was trying to wake him. A second and then a third shove had their desired effect. Clyde opened one eye. The pain of opening his sleep deprived eye along with the pitch-black night made him think he had been wounded in the head and lost his sight. His heart skipped a beat, making him sit up just as another set of shells landed on the island across the water. The flash relieved his anxiety. He could see again. He turned to his partner. "What's going on now?"

The diffused light of an explosion illuminated Neville's shrug. "Don't know, the morning paper ain't been delivered yet."

Both eyes now open, Clyde looked at his watch. "Blimey, we only had two-hours sleep. I know war can be hard on a bloke, but do they have to do it night and day? I need my beauty sleep."

"You certainly do, but not right now." Neville got to his feet and stretched before saying, "Come on." He made a follow me gesture and began picking his way up the Island's one big hill.

Clyde grumbled all the while they maneuvered around and over the boulders, bushes and small trees in their way. Once on top, they had a good view of where the shells were landing on the island two-miles away across the channel.

"Only one thing to be glad for in a war," philosophized Clyde, who flinched when a large barrage impacted on the side of the island facing them. "That you ain't the target. A bloke could almost feel sorry for the Nips over there."

Neville's head snapped around. "What did you say?"

From the tone of Neville's voice, Clyde understood what he was questioning. "I said…*almost* feel sorry."

"You had me scared. For a moment I thought you were going soft."

"After what we've seen? Not hardly."

The very beginning of a new day appeared to be only minutes away. The black night was changing to gray. Aided by the exploding shells, Neville thought he saw something move. He used his field glasses to get a better view, even though the lack of light made it difficult to properly focus them on the area in question. It took him several minutes to be sure of his initial impression. He lowered his binoculars. "I do believe it's time for us to get back to our little boat."

"What's the hurry? It looks like the storm missed us. Why don't we stay up here and watch the war for awhile?"

Neville answered, "Not enough room."

Clyde spread his arms out to indicate the area around them. "Of course there is. There's more than enough room for the two of us."

"Maybe so, but not for both of us…and them." Neville pointed at several Japanese barges pulling away from Dinigat.

"Why?" Clyde yelled at the sky. "Why is it us…always us. Just once I would like to see somebody else dropped in the shit."

"That's what happens to do-gooders. The nicer we are, the bigger the challenge. We need to come up with a solution, fast!"

"Maybe they're going somewhere else."

The tone of Neville's sarcastic response removed any need to guess how he felt. "Sure, and maybe, some rich American wants to buy our land because he found gold while bumming his way around the world. My money's on the Japs coming here."

Clyde finished the argument with, "You ain't got any money…now, get your bum moving."

They scrambled down the hill, aware they could see their way without any difficulty. Moving downhill as fast as possible with an assist from gravity, Neville stumbled, Clyde couldn't slow down and slammed into him making them both fall and roll down the hill. Arms and legs sticking out in all directions, they barely avoided braining themselves on the rocks that whizzed by as they shouted warnings of impending doom while trying to grab at bushes they passed. With all bones still intact, they dropped over the edge of a three-foot high ledge. Neville's shout halted in mid-syllable when he came to an abrupt stop wrapped around a tree trunk. Adding insult to injury, Clyde slammed into his back. Every remaining molecule of air in his lungs whooshed out.

Both men were stunned, unable to move. Neville silently prayed for the ability to breathe again. Clyde couldn't believe his luck–his body felt like everything still worked. Finally able to stand he brushed dirt and weeds off his lightweight shirt and Bermuda shorts, before motioning for Neville to follow suit. "Come along ol' boy–time, tide, and the Nips wait for no man."

Unable to breath properly, Neville could only make a gasping sound. In answer to his mate's desire to get moving, he shook his head while pointing at his chest. Clyde stooped down next to him, and pulled on the waist of Neville's pants, hoping the extra space would help him catch his breath.

Neville's chest expanded and after taking several more breaths, he pointed to the other side of the island. "I need to rest a bit. Go on around and take a gander. See how much time we have before the place gets crowded."

"On my way." Clyde jumped up and moved horizontally around the island until he could see the barges. They appeared to be in the same place as when he first caught sight of them. Five patrol barges grouped together, only a couple of hundred yards from Dinigat. Maybe, thought Clyde, they were going to go somewhere else, or a flight of fighter-bombers might drop by. No pilot could dream of an easier target.

The bombardment of Dinigat continued, with an occasional shell flying off target and creating a beautiful hundred-foot high fountain in the ocean, orange flames lighting it from the interior. Come on, come on Clyde thought to himself, trying to will the battleships to attack the barges. He remained crouched behind a rock, watching until all five boats turned onto the same course heading straight for Danawan. Not good, thought Clyde who had a hard time tearing himself away from the sight of his approaching problem.

He finally managed to look away and turned to get back to Neville. When he heard the ripping-cloth sound of several large shells traveling across the sky he looked up. His eyes refocused on Dinigat in time to catch a bright flash out of the corner of his eye. Three large explosions occurred. Parts of Japanese barges and men were borne skyward on columns of water. Guns and engine parts flew in all directions, mixed equally with arms, legs, and bodies, minus their heads. When the man-made water spouts disappeared, one barge remained afloat, almost swamped by the downpour of seawater. It turned and started to zigzag through the floating carnage, the scent of which drew a number of large sharks eager to gorge themselves on the product of war.

One load of Japanese soldiers was better than five, and on any other island, would have been of little concern. The likelihood of finding a secure place to hide on Danawan seemed as poor as finding a keg of English beer. The first rays of the morning sun hitting his face killed the possibility of being able to paddle away. Do that, and their only achievement would be to provide the sharks with a tough, crunchy dessert. It didn't seem the best way to use what he thought of as his unique talent.

The time Clyde took to see what their new neighbors were doing worked well for Neville. He looked into their various backpacks and rucksacks making a mental list of what they still had. When he heard "Tally Ho," he knew that either Clyde was riding to hounds or the hounds were after him.

"Over here," Neville yelled and waved his arms in the air.

"The Yanks sank four of those barges, but one of 'em is still headed this way."

Neville's one word reply summed up the situation. "Brilliant!"

"Don't get mad at me. I didn't invite them."

Neville looked out at the surrounding water. "We can't get off this island until dark. That means we need to find a place to hide, unless you want to make a fight of it right now."

Clyde shook his head. "Don't know how many are in the damn boat and we lost those Tommy Guns."

"What about using hand grenades? That should reduce the odds."

"Maybe…but first we need to find us an out of the way place."

Clyde looked around, put his hands up and said, "Where? We had to pick the one island in the area that don't have any jungle. All we got are rocks."

"They're big rocks. We can do something with 'em but, first, we've got to do a better job of hiding our ocean liner. Let's get down there, put it in the water and pile some rocks in it. Then carry all our stuff up here. We can fit most everything under the ledge we fell off of. Then we can pile some rocks over what's left." Neville looked at his partner.

Clyde shook his head in disgust. "Right. If that's the best you can do, we might as well do it." He clapped his hands for effect. "Let's get going, only make sure you take your carbine down to the beach. I don't plan on being a prisoner of war."

Once the rubber boat was in the water, Clyde took charge of partially deflating and sinking it, while Neville took care of grooming the beach. For two tired middle-aged men, they moved with surprising speed. Next, they enlarged the rock hollow under the ledge and filled it with all of their worldly possessions. Clyde jumped from rock to rock to prevent leaving any footprints as he searched for a spot where he could watch their enemy. Neville joined him as soon as his housekeeping chores were complete.

Lying side by side, Neville with his binoculars, they watched the barge approach. When it was only few hundred yards away it turned to the right and began circling the island. "that's a good size tin can they have there." Clyde looked at his partner, "Any idea how many are in it?"

"Why? One or a hundred, Japs are all the same. The only way to get rid of them is to shoot 'em"

"Odds, ol' boy. We've learned to play the odds. One or two men in that thing…we win. Fifteen or twenty…we run, agreed?"

"Agreed, but not for more than three-minutes."

Clyde looked at Neville as if his partner thought he was stupid. "I'm not daft, man. I know how big this island is. We go more than three-minutes, we'll be getting closer, not farther away."

Neville put one hand up to quiet his partner while holding his binoculars with the other. "Five–I count five men in that barge. What odds will your bookie give us on five young men against two old ones?"

"We ain't old…just experienced."

Neville motioned over his shoulder to where everything was hidden. "Hide now, attack later. Come on, let's burrow into that patch of thorn bushes we found a couple of hours ago."

"Lead on, but I wish they had waited a few hours. I was hoping for us to send off a message. Commander Cullison must be getting a bit nervous."

"Maybe…but it can't be helped. It's either his ass or ours. Now, let's get moving, and this time, watch the thorns."

Chapter 20

A Little Island

October 21, 1944
Evening

The little island of Danawan did not look like any of the other nearby islands. Similarly, the rain late that morning was unlike the sudden cloudbursts common to the region. It rained softly and steadily for almost an hour. Clyde and Neville reacted to it by pulling their ponchos over their heads. They slept the sleep of the innocent late into the afternoon under a protective roof of thorn bushes, oblivious to the small Japanese detachment that decided to set up camp less than a hundred-yards away. A second rain, the type that can wash a truck off the road brought them back to the land of the living.

A poncho is, by its nature, a compromise. The wearer sacrifices total protection for the freedom of having relatively unrestricted movement–quick access to his weapons and equipment being of prime importance. Each man found himself soaked from his head down to the middle of the chest and up to mid-thigh. Other parts of their bodies remained dry, until the sound of rain triggered Neville's call of nature. He rolled over creating a small wave in the muddy water trapped next to him. The water traveled under his poncho from knees to shoulders. The cool liquid soaking through his clothing brought him awake better than his old alarm clock ever could. When the water slopped back, it gave Clyde a similar sensation.

"Who the bloody…" Clyde said, before Neville could shush him by placing his hand over his mouth.

Neville admonished Clyde with words spoken more softly than a whisper. "You ever hear the expression, 'Loose lips sink ships?' Well Mate, we ain't a ship, but them Japs are here, somewhere. They could sink us right into this mud if you don't put a cork in it."

With his voice thirty decibels softer, Clyde said, "Sorry about that. I started talking before thinking. How close are they?"

Neville shrugged his shoulders, then got onto his haunches and relieved the pressure on his bladder. With one problem solved, he slowly raised up high enough to see through the top of the bushes around them. He made himself ignore the scratches and sharp stings from thorns embedding themselves in his skin when he moved branches out of the way. There were times, few in number, when he could concentrate on one thing and ignore everything else. He let the thorns do their worst as he searched for the Japanese who must have landed on the island. By the time he saw the small group, he was standing erect with only the lower half of his body concealed behind the bushes. "I can just see them around the other side. Don't look like more than five or six of 'em."

"What are they doing?"

"They're cooking dinner."

"What about the rest? Are there five or is it six, or do you need more fingers to count the blighters?" Having to wait for important information made Clyde more impatient than normal.

Neville looked down at Clyde sitting on the ground at his feet. "Take it easy, I'm evaluating."

"How long is this evaluating going to take? We need a plan."

"All right, now," Neville said, and then, half to himself, added, "Ain't that something. They're here for the same reason we chose the place. The last fellow is the lookout. He's watching the Strait with binoculars." Neville took his eyes off the lookout for a moment to see what had grabbed the man's interest. Several indistinct blobs–ships–were barely visible. The big unknown, were they friends–increasing their command of the strategic waterway? Or foe–about to reclaim the area they had conquered?

Remembering what he was supposed to be doing, Neville turned back to check on the lookout. "Uh, oh." He stooped so his head was even with the thorn branches. "One of 'em is walking this way." Neville raised up just enough to be able to see the man uncover his radio, switch it on and start listening for messages. He watched for several minutes until the man finished, switched off the radio and went back to the campfire. One of the other soldiers handed him a tin plate of food. The lookout gave his binoculars to another soldier, and with a nod of his head indicated that the man should take the lookout post.

"I was hoping these fellows would move on, but it looks like they're planning to stay. You know what that means."

Clyde looked at his watch. "Sundown in less than an hour. They'll settle down once it gets dark. I say we hit 'em about eleven tonight. You can attack from this side, I'll go around the island and work from over there. If I take out the guard without a lot of fuss, we'll be sure of getting the rest of them before they can create an organized defense."

Neville shook his head. "Sorry, old sport, the guard is my job." He looked at the sky before continuing. "It don't look like we'll have any clouds tonight. That means the only way for you to attack from that side, even at night is to go out in the water far enough not to be seen and then work around behind them. We both know I'm the one for that, right?"

Upset at not being cast in the role of the dashing commando attacking from out of the water, Clyde grumbled a little before agreeing. His aversion to deep water, anything over his knees, meant his argument was only so many words meant to preserve his ego.

"Look at it this way," said Neville. "You'll get to shoot a lot more of them than will I. If you don't, I'm going to be as dead as a Christmas goose on New Year's. That means you need to make sure that you point the right end of that carbine at 'em."

"What about capturing a few?"

"And have one of them pull a hand grenade out from under his shirt when you ain't looking? That ain't the way I want to remember you. After we finish with 'em, if one ain't completely dead… well then, I'll consider it."

It rarely mattered what the two of them argued about, as long as they enjoyed it. However, Clyde didn't think continuing this argument would be any fun. No matter how many men he saw die, killing was not a subject he took lightly. Instead, he crawled around the base of another bush where the mud wasn't as thick, and slipped his backpack under his head after un-snagging himself from the protective canopy of thorns. Still trying to make up for the sleep lost over the past few days, he prepared for the challenging night ahead the best way he could.

A light breeze blowing in from the East carried the promise of a quiet, dry night. The two Englishmen standing in the middle of their thorn bushes saw an occasional flash in the sky to the north where the main Leyte invasion had occurred. Across the water on Dinigat, everything remained quiet. Thinking they were alone, the Japanese invaders settled in for the night with one man remaining on guard duty walking around between the fire and the shoreline.

"My watch says twenty-two-thirty. I'll wait for you to take out the guard around twenty-three-fifteen. As soon as I see him go down, I'll start to work on the rest of 'em."

Neville nodded, shook his partner's hand and dropped to the ground to crawl out of the thorn bushes. When he reached the water, he held his carbine over his head and walked in until it was chest high, turned to his right, and started circling the island. Clyde went in the opposite direction, uphill, and to his left, aiming for a position overlooking the enemy's small camp.

The campfire continued to consume all of its fuel until its feeble light did little more than mark the center of the Japanese camp. The lookout kept his attention focused on the water. He protected his night vision by never looking back toward the fire. Clyde frequently checked the luminous dial of his watch while waiting for Neville to attack. At twenty minutes past the hour, he was silently urging his partner to get on with it as he simultaneously realized the problem. The lookout wouldn't look away from the water. Neville must be stuck out there, unable to get close.

Neville had been so sure that his plan would work, they didn't come up with a just-in-case backup. The Japanese lookout, like so many other enemy soldiers they had encountered in the past, knew how to follow orders–exactly. Following orders was what they did best. The beatings they received in basic training taught them that above all else.

Neville needed the guard to look away for a minute. He'd even settle for thirty seconds. Understanding Neville's predicament, Clyde felt around and located several large stones, each one the size of a cricket ball. He stood up, took a couple of practice throws to loosen his arm, brought the first stone to his lips, kissed it, offered a prayer, and let it fly.

The stone arced out toward the campfire and dropped three feet away. It rolled to the edge of the dying fire where it clattered against a partially consumed smoking branch. The resulting sound, swallowed up by the bed of ash, did not provide the distraction Clyde had hoped for. The man on guard duty either didn't hear the noise or didn't think it a sufficient reason to turn around.

Clyde took the second rock, bounced it up and down in his hand recalibrating his mind and arm. Instead of a high lofted throw, he hurled the stone like a cricket ball, low and fast. It hit dead center in the fire, skipped up and hit the guard in the middle of the back. The intended distraction had become a threat.

The guard grunted, whirled around, pulled his rifle down from his shoulder to a position of port-arms, and set his feet to meet the unknown.

From the water's edge, Neville saw the rock skip through the fire and hit the guard. He instantly knew what his partner was doing. His muscles coiled, he sprang into action the instant the soldier turned away. Clyde tossed his third missile, letting it roll towards the fire to keep the guard's attention away from Neville.

Hurried footsteps on wet sand are virtually silent. That isn't the case on dry sand. The guard heard Neville coming far enough in advance to be able to turn and attempt to protect himself. Surprised by the suddenness of the attack, the guard concentrating on staying alive forgot to yell out to the rest of his group. The knife thrust intended to enter his back between his third and fourth ribs and then his heart, now pointed at his lower chest. The rifle, held diagonally in front of the man became an obstacle to a successful attack.

The guard swiped at the knife thrust with the barrel of his rifle, reversed its movement, and aimed the butt at Neville's head. Unprepared for the new situation, Neville's instincts took over. The rifle butt missed its target and disturbed his thinning hair as he slid, feet first onto his back. His forward motion took him directly between his enemy's legs. Before the man could react, Neville thrust his long double-edged blade straight up into the exposed groin and belly. The excruciating pain caused the man to drop his rifle. A scream of agony echoed off every rock on the island as the razor-sharp knife sliced into soft flesh, ripping at vital organs. Neville continued his slide to the man's rear, twisting the knife and doing more damage as he pulled it out.

Pandemonium broke out as the rest of the Japanese soldiers were startled awake. Clyde grabbed his carbine the instant he saw the results of his throw. The Japanese however, needed a few seconds to understand the situation. Clyde and Neville were ready and opened up on the Japanese before they could do anything. Semi-automatic carbines were excellent weapons for close-in work. The heavy caliber bullets eliminated three soldiers in less than ten seconds.

Neville crawled up next to the soldier he had stabbed and used his body for cover. The man lying curled up in a fetal position, moaned, but did not move. His body made a good support for Neville's carbine as he tried to hit the remaining soldiers who took cover behind some nearby boulders. They were in a difficult position with one attacker to their left, the other to their right.

The two groups traded shots as the campfire sputtered. Darkness would aid the defenders more than the attackers. Neville raised his head to take another shot, but dropped down when he heard a dull thud a short distance in front of him. He jammed himself tightly against the man he had stabbed. In the little time he had remaining he tried to push the man up and burrow into the sand under him. The grenade exploded a moment later, covering him with rocky debris. His ears rang as loudly as Big Ben. The body he hid behind quivered, gave a death rattle, and went limp.

The soldier who threw the grenade prepared to throw another. He came up on his knees, arm cocked, ready to throw the explosive an additional twenty feet. His head unexpectedly snapped back as both arms flew forward. Clyde's bullet caught him in the back, directly between the shoulder blades. The grenade dropped from his hand as he fell forward to lie next to it.

The other Japanese soldiers, their attention never wavering from where their targets were hidden, had no idea what was about to happen. Three seconds later the grenade exploded between them. Their bodies shredded, both men died not knowing they had been killed by their comrade.

His legs felt like licorice sticks about to snap under his weight as Clyde hurried toward the spot where he last saw his partner. "Neville… Neville old chap. Where are you?" With his night vision destroyed by the explosion, Clyde could not see where he was walking. The few red coals that remained from the campfire were his only guide. He stubbed his foot on the grisly remains of the Japanese lookout and fell forward sprawled across the body. His hand slipped on blood-drenched flesh as he tried to get up. He pulled away in disgust from the warm body that resembled fresh hamburger.

He quickly scoured his hands clean in the sand and again called for Neville. His heart had not yet slowed down from the excitement and fear of battle when a hand touched him on the shoulder. He reacted so violently he fell over backwards as he tried to bring his carbine into position.

"Don't shoot… I give up," Neville yelled with a nervous laugh, "I think we got 'em all."

"I need a cigarette and something to drink. That was close."

Neville leaned over to catch his breath. He felt as if he'd just run a Marathon. "Relax, Mate. It was a near run thing, but we won. Soon as my heart slows down I'll take a look around. One of these fellows might have brought something to drink stronger than tea."

"Good thinking. I do seem to be a wee bit thirsty. While you're doing that, I'll start bringing our gear over so we can send the Commander a message before he tries to send condolence messages to our wives."

As Neville checked to see how much ammunition he still had, he said, "It would be just like those women to spite us and be someplace where he could find them. If they think we're dead, they would sell our property and be gone with the money before you could say Winston Churchill."

Chapter 21

Messages

October 22, 1944
Early

The signals office on Morotai received the message at 0225, a slow time for the radio operators. A crypto specialist decoded it and had a messenger take it to Cullison's office. The thin piece of paper sat there until the first of the morning staff checked in at 0400. No one knew how important the information might be and it didn't matter. The staff followed standing orders. Cullison needed to see anything received from his coast watchers–without delay.

A sergeant walked around a large tent checking each cot. He tried not to shine his flashlight in each man's eyes while he searched for the Commander. As he moved around the tent, several seemingly inert bodies cursed him before he reached down and nudged Cullison's shoulder. When a set of eyeballs replaced tightly shut eyelids, he said, "Commander, you left orders that you wanted to see anything from the Surigao Strait as soon as it arrived . A message came in a few minutes ago."

Cullison feebly waved a hand, and sat up. He grabbed his glasses off a discarded packing crate and looked at his watch before extending his hand for the message. The sergeant kept his flashlight aimed at the paper while Cullison's foggy mind tried to make sense of the information.

He understood the words, but the message didn't make sense. Maybe Harry could figure it out. He thanked the sergeant, walked over to Harry and got him up. The two men quickly dressed and went to the office they shared in a newly built Quonset hut. Each man grabbed a cup of coffee and reread the information.

Stripped of all the army's routing data, it said:

> **Arrived Danawan 0300-211044. Eliminated enemy outpost 2345-211044. No casualties. Surigao coast watcher position established. Will operate all daylight hours. Have supplies for five days. Monitoring radio on regular schedule.**

Harry's face mirrored Cullison's look of confusion. "I don't understand. Weren't they supposed to go back to Limasawa after trying to help those Rangers?"

"That's what I told them to do. I don't know what this is all about." Cullison ran his hands through his uncombed hair. "That PT Boat driver was ordered to take them back there."

Harry pulled out a map of the Strait and ran his finger across it before pointing to Danawan. "It's not far from where the Boat had to go on its route back to Limasawa, and don't forget, we are talking about Clyde and Neville. They frequently regard an order as a mild suggestion open to interpretation."

Cullison shook his head in disbelief. "You mean our two idiots are on Danawan, an island that is scheduled for us to assault in…" he looked at his watch. "In less than an hour."

"Oh shit! Our boys won't know they're there. As far as you Yanks are concerned, the Japs are the only ones on that island."

"If they're still alive. The pre-assault bombardment starts at zero-five-thirty."

Harry walked away from the map wondering if there was a way to save the two brainless wonders. He looked at Cullison. "Why don't I get a warning message to them, while you try to delay whoever is going to invade their island."

Dubious about getting anything done in time, Cullison said, "We can try. They said they'll be on their regular radio monitoring schedule. That means they'll be listening at zero-five-hundred."

Harry turned to leave for the message center but stopped when Cullison said, "Their message said they eliminated an enemy outpost. Ask our witless wonders if there are any more Japs on the island. I know that's the first thing the mission commander is going to want to know before he agrees to call it off."

* * *

Message traffic began to pick up with the approach of another day. The continuation of operations on day three of the Leyte Gulf invasion meant men moving inland were waking up in hastily dug trenches. Most of them would gladly trade their first born not to be there, but orders were orders.

On Morotai, Harry leaned over a table and hastily wrote out his message.

> **Assault force will land Danawan 0600. Bombardment begins 0530. Take cover. Are any enemy troops on island? Trying to get assault cancelled. Advise status.**

He handed the message to the center's outgoing message clerk. "This needs to go out at zero-five-hundred."

The clerk stamped the paper with a time/date stamp. Harry could see the man do his job with all the feeling of a robot. Concerned that the clerk had not heard him, Harry repeated his instructions to which the man said, "Yeah, yeah. I hear you." He held the message up for Harry to see. "Everybody's in a hurry, mister, but you ain't got a priority stamp so it'll go out when we get a chance."

Harry grabbed the sheet of paper out of the man's hand and scribbled in large letters, 'Transmit promptly at zero-five-hundred.'

He placed the paper in the middle of the clerk's small desk. "If this doesn't go out on time those guys will die and you're going to wish you were with them. Understand?"

* * *

Cullison leafed through the massive operations book for the entire Leyte invasion. He found the Danawan operation on page 544. The time and date were spot on, but the book didn't designate which naval units and ground forces had been assigned the chore. The assault was too small. Whoever the big brass found lying around would be tasked with the operation, probably with only a few hours notice. The only way to stop them from trying to kill Clyde and Neville would be to find the gold braid in command.

He placed calls to every operations section on Morotai, over a thousand miles from Danawan. He found that the units detailed for the assault would be selected by some naval officer commanding ships guarding the southern approaches to the invasion beach. Still, a copy of the order would be logged into the master files on Morotai. It took twenty-some minutes to find the appropriate files, after which he still needed to make contact with the Captain named as operations commander. He commanded Destroyer flotilla 3. In the overall scheme of things, its designation was, DesDiv3, of Fleet 7.45.21. Captain Rawlings had responsibility over six destroyers, one (LST) Landing Ship Tank, four tracked assault landing craft, and a hundred and fifty soldiers. The assault plan only envisioned having to root out a small force of enemy soldiers. Most of the enemy were expected to be dead or cowering in their foxholes at the end of the destroyer division's bombardment.

Cullison knew the likelihood of being able to establish reliable voice communications with Captain Rawlings over that distance was somewhere between not-at-all and don't-bother. This time it fell to Cullison to hand the signals clerk a time sensitive message.

> **Some allied forces under command this office already on Danawan. Some-possibly all enemy eliminated. Request postponement of Danawan operation until verified.**

The clerk time stamped the piece of paper, 0507. The ships would start firing in less than thirty minutes. On the good side, a destroyer's five-inch shell didn't grab a person's attention like a battleship's two-thousand pound, sixteen inch shell, unless it landed right on you.

Harry ran into Cullison near the entrance to their tent. "I'm going back to the message center to make sure my message went out. Want to come along?"

"Sure." Cullison made an after-you gesture with his hand.

The lieutenant in charge of the message center looked like a character in a cartoon. A small man in a sweat stained uniform with his sleeves rolled up sat behind what appeared to be a desk. What ever it was, it threatened to disappear under a stack of file trays overflowing with paper and several piles sitting on the floor nearby. Any idiot could recognize a personnel assignment error when he saw one. The officer looked completely lost, hopelessly unsuited for his position.

Lieutenant Gradzinski popped to attention as Cullison approached.

"At ease Lieutenant. We gave your clerk two messages that needed immediate attention. One to Commander, DesDiv 3 and the other to coast watchers in the Surigao Strait." Preparing himself for bad news, he asked, "Did they go out, and have you had any replies?"

Gradzinski leaned over toward one of the piles of paper on the floor, thumbed through the first dozen on top and pulled two pieces out. He looked at one and then the other. "Both messages were received by the addressees, sir," he said with a smile.

A corporal came up behind Harry, "Excuse me, sir," reached around and laid a handful of messages on another pile.

The Lieutenant picked up a full tray from his desk and handed it to the corporal who replied "Yes, Sir," to the non-verbal command to get on with his work.

Initially at a loss for words at the Lieutenant's efficiency, he simply said "Busy morning?"

"Yes, Sir. I think the Japs are getting upset about losing the Philippines."

"We've won already, have we?"

"We will, sir." The Lieutenant hated being distracted. He looked at his desk the way a marooned sailor looks at a woman when he first reaches land.

"Have you had a reply to either of those messages?"

"Just the coast watcher's reply. It's on its way to your office, sir."

"Any chance you can remember what it said?"

"No problem, Commander. Don't get many like that."

Cullison looked at Harry who rolled his eyes in anticipation.

Gradzinski closed his eyes and recited the short message.

> **What is the name of the son of a whore running this war? No Japs on this island. There better not be any shooting or we'll haunt you from the grave.**

Harry held his arm up so Cullison could see the time, 0527.

Three minutes remained before the destroyers began shelling the island a thousand miles to the north.

"All we can do is hope."

"Bill, it's not your fault. They were supposed to go back to Limasawa. If they live through this, maybe following orders will sink into those thick skulls."

Cullison shook his head. "I don't know. I never should have sent those two near a battle zone. When they smell gunpowder, they act like bull elephants in a herd of cows."

"No point in beating yourself up over this. Whatever happens, they brought it on themselves. Now come on, let's grab some breakfast. By the time we get done, the Army will be on the island. After that…well, someone is sure to let us know."

* * *

Hurriedly closing up the transmitter, Clyde glanced over at Neville madly throwing things into backpacks and duffel bags. He stooped, put his arms through the radio's harness and hoisted it onto his back and bounced up and down to settle it in place. "Time's up old sport. Let's get our arses out of here. Didn't I tell you that you can't trust the Yanks. They make all nice and friendly and then when you think they're your friends, they stab you in the back."

Neville handed two bundles to Clyde and picked up the rest. "I know, but let's face it, this is our fault, we should have sent off a message when we first got here. Of course, that young man on the PT Boat is mostly to blame. He should have let someone know that he violated his orders by dropping us off."

"You have the right of it. Can't make a man an officer and expect him to act like one without a couple of years training. Good thing we never let them make us officers."

Neville shook his head disapprovingly. "Someone needs to talk with that Boat commander. Not the way an officer and a gentleman should act, not at all."

The two men hurried down to the beach. When they reached firm wet sand, they started jogging around to the other side of the island, as far from the Strait as possible. They passed the spot where they had buried their rubber boat under a pile of rocks without giving it a thought. By the time they could have uncovered it and filled its sides with air, the destroyers would have completed their assignment–creating little rocks out of big ones.

Chapter 22

Scrambled

October 22, 1944
Daylight

A response to Cullison's request to the seventh fleet finally arrived.

> **Information insufficient to alter Danawan assault. Change in plan must be authorized by TF-7.45.**

Harry handed the message back to Cullison. "There isn't anything we can do now, but wait. The decision has been passed up to the Admiral, and you know how long it will take before he even finds out about our problem."

Harry looked at his watch. The bombardment had already been in progress for more than ten minutes. He felt as bad as Cullison and tried to put a positive spin to things. "It is a really small island, and remember, the destroyers only have five-inch guns, isn't that right? They only have another twenty minutes to go. How much damage can six destroyers do in a half-hour?"

Cullison barely acknowledged Harry's effort to allay his feeling of guilt. He knew Clyde and Neville were responsible for putting themselves in harms way, but so what? Since the day he entered the Academy, his training taught him that he was responsible for the safety of the men under his command. Navy personnel were trained to follow their commander's orders. He was trained to take care of them. Even though, in this case, his men were not in the Navy and following orders only happened on rare occasions, he could not justify ignoring the situation. Even as he sat down to write out a message to the Admiral commanding TF-7.45, he knew that watching the tide come in would be just as useful.

* * *

While they ran down the beach, Clyde looked back. "Got to hand it to the Yanks. They're spot on time."

Neville shook his head in amazement. "I'm glad you approve of how they're trying to kill us. Now get your arse moving."

The first three high-explosive shells landed on the far side of the island almost exactly where they had slept through the previous day. The scream of a dozen or more shells following right behind did not allow them any time to discuss their impromptu plan. They ran off the beach into knee-deep water and up the open ramp of the patrol barge, the Japanese lookouts arrived in.

Neville found the hand crank designed for use by two men and rotated it as hard as he could. His muscles quivered with the effort to free the barge from the exploding island. Slowly, the ramp moved rising off the sandy bottom.

Clyde ran to the raised steering platform at the rear, slipped the radio transmitter off his back and hunted for the barge's ignition key. He frantically looked all around the small console covered with dials, switches, and rows of Japanese characters. He could not find the key or even a keyway to put it in. He slammed his hand against the console in frustration before randomly flipping switches and hitting buttons, all to no avail.

The ramp stopped its movement just past the halfway point. Neville bent over double, hands on his knees, he needed a break. As soon as he had some air in his lungs, he tried to call to Clyde. His shout came out as vowels interspersed with grunts and a wheeze. "Get this bloody thing moving. Those Yanks are walking their fire across the island. They'll be here in a few minutes and I would really prefer being somewhere else."

"Do you think I'm stupid? I know what's happening." In frustration, Clyde again slammed the console. The engine sputtered until he pulled his hand away. He pushed on the button he had hit by accident and kept it depressed. The engine made hopeful sounds, but did not start. He kept the button depressed and one switch at a time flipped the others on and off. The fourth switch energized the ignition system and the motor roared to life. The noise startled Clyde, making him pull his hands away from the console. The engine died before he could recover. He pushed the button–nothing.

On the verge of grabbing his carbine and shooting the console, he could barely contain his temper. Instead, he flipped the switch off, pushed the button and then moved it to on. The engine turned over. This time he kept the button depressed until the engine settled into its regular rhythm. Carefully, while holding his breath, he took his hand off the button. The deep rumble continued without missing a beat.

Clyde pushed the propeller control into reverse and the engine speed to maximum. Neville stopped cranking the ramp up. Three-quarters would have to do. At full speed, the barge leisurely backed away from the island while the beach in front of them erupted in geysers of sand and shrapnel.

For the moment, they were safe from the bombardment. They only needed to do one thing to stay that way, stay invisible from both friend and foe since at the moment, they didn't have any friends, American or Japanese. The plain truth of the matter was simple. Anyone who saw them would have little difficulty in sinking the ungainly metal box. A small naval flag flew from a short pole at the stern. Neville scrambled up behind Clyde and ripped it down. At least they wouldn't die under the wrong flag.

"Oh Captain, my captain," sang out Clyde in a happy voice that showed how proud he felt at getting their ship safely away from danger. "Where do you think we should go? I vote for Dinigat. We know all the Japs are gone."

Neville took a quick look around. In front of them sat Danawan, explosions occurring every few seconds, while Dinigat only two miles away looked quiet and welcoming. He pointed at the green island. "At least we think they're all gone, but that's good enough for me. As they say, 'Any port in a storm, natural or man made.' Find us a quiet piece of water along the shoreline under some grand trees where we can relax. After that, we'll see what our rude neighbors have to say for themselves."

With the barge on its new course, Neville took over the controls and Clyde set up his transmitter. They motored toward Dinigat at their maximum speed of eight knots. For a short time neither of them bothered to look down at the well-deck. Water that had been only a few inches deep had risen to almost two-feet. There seemed to be a reason why the barge's bow ramp was fitted with a watertight gasket around its edge.

Neville moved the gearshift to neutral before tapping his partner on the shoulder and pointing at the water sloshing around in front of them. "Come on. I'm going to need your help."

By the time they reached the ramp crank, the barge seemed more sluggish and the water reached above their knees. By the time the two of them finished cranking the ramp up, the water was up to Clyde's waist. With the water inside the barge almost as deep as that outside, Neville felt it would be best if they pumped dry their impromptu swimming pool. He slowly wadded around hoping to stub a foot on a discharge pump remembering once having seen such a thing on an American barge. Maybe the Japanese built theirs the same way. With water waist high, Clyde decided Neville didn't need his help and sent another message to Cullison.

With perverse pleasure, Clyde smiled as his words leaped into the ether.

> **Danawan being shelled. Original campsite destroyed. No injuries-yet. Escaped island in captured Jap barge. Destination-Dinigat. Inform trigger-happy ships we are NOT a target. All Japs eliminated prior to invasion by unnecessary troops. Will return and assume control of Danawan 1200 local time today.**

Neville patted Clyde on the shoulder when told what the message said. "Good show. Make the blighter sweat. He's old enough to have known better. It's bad form to shoot at one's own troops and then expect them to perform at peak efficiency."

Neville's search was successful and they were soon on their way. Clyde pointed at a place along the coast of the rapidly approaching island thickly covered with its mantle of green jungle. "That looks like a good place over there. We can tie this thing to a tree and relax until it's time to go back. With all the activity going on in the Strait, they'll need us more than ever."

"Of course they will. Why else would we be here?"

* * *

> **...Danawan ... campsite destroyed ... Jap ... destination Dinigat ... Not a target ... Danawan 1200 local...**

The incomplete message handed to Cullison raised more questions than it answered. He read it over again and handed it to Harry.

"Bill, this doesn't make any sense. Are they still on Danawan or are they fighting Japs on Dinigat and if they are, how did they get there? Besides, who's 'not a target' and what do they want to happen on Danawan at noon?"

Cullison shrugged his shoulders. "The message center doesn't know what's causing the problem. They don't think it's atmospherics. They're getting good reception of everything else coming from that area.

"One of the radio specialists thought the problem could be the result of a bad connection or them moving while transmitting, although that doesn't make any sense. The island is too small for them to have found a vehicle. That means, until they can reestablish contact, any decision made based on this piece of paper has a ninety-nine percent chance of being wrong. Damn it, I don't like having to wait, but until we get better info, that's all we can do. Besides, I still haven't heard from the Admiral. I don't know if he ordered a halt to the Danawan operation or not."

Harry looked out at the clear blue sky with only a few puffy clouds artfully arranged to provide the feeling of an unlimited horizon. "You know, when things don't go right, people in the operations office always mention the 'fog of war.' I guess this is what they're talking about."

* * *

Four assault craft, their tank-like treads churning the water hit their departure line at five-minutes before the hour. Their timing was exquisite and they touched the beach as echoes of the final bombardment died away. The vehicles, a cross between a boat and a light-tank surged out of the water, ran up the beach and kept going for another fifty yards. As soon as they stopped, Army troops spilled out of the rear and over the sides to take positions in the sand. Each vehicle carried a thirty-caliber machine gun. The gunners kept rotating their weapons, looking for something to shoot.

The company commander made an arm signal. In response, sergeants began yelling and several squads jumped forward to take new positions. In turn, other squads leapfrogged over them moving to take the lead. With the lack of resistance, the drivers of the landing vehicles turned off their engines. The quiet, broken only by the gentle surf and a light wind increased the gut-churning tension everyone felt.

Where were the Japanese troops they knew were here? The many stories of how Japanese defenders would lie in wait until everyone relaxed, were told and retold while the sun rose higher in the sky. Sergeants and officers continued to urge their men to be ready for anything as they moved forward. Contact with the enemy could be expected at any moment. The soldiers, ever mindful of booby traps, slowly moved up the island's one significant hill, and then, down the far side.

By eleven, they declared the place secure. The bodies of several enemy soldiers were found and reported up the chain of command. The mutilated remains were attributed to the accurate naval bombardment. The enemy had been met, and soundly beaten.

One private in a search party found an out-of-the-way spot to use as an outhouse and made an unexpected discovery. He ran over to his Lieutenant. He held up a U.S. Army web belt. "Sir, I found a stash of Army gear around the other side, hidden in some bushes."

The Lieutenant took several men and followed the Private to the pile of material. After searching the area, they brought it all back to the beach.

"I thought we were the first friendly troops on this island, sir," the Lieutenant stated to his company Captain.

"As far as I know, we are, but that stuff doesn't even look used. Maybe some Japs stole it from us." He shook his head, as he realized what he had said. "No, that doesn't make any sense does it, Lieutenant? This is only the third day we've been in the

Philippines." He looked through the items one more time, then said, "Take some men and do a search of that area. Someone could be hiding under those rocks waiting to hit us after dark."

* * *

Clyde and Neville took naps in between watching for some sign of movement from across the water as the sun crept towards its zenith.

"All right Captain," Neville, said to his accomplice, "I think it's time for us to take our flagship back home."

"Sounds like a good idea, but if I'm the captain of this ship, why are you trying to tell me what to do?"

"It's quite logical. You're the Captain of this ship, and I'm the Admiral in charge of our Navy."

Clyde climbed the ladder to the barge's control station and looked out at the surrounding water. "What Navy?"

"Have faith. This is the first of many mighty vessels. Now, untie us, it's time we took back possession of our island from those adventurers. And by-the-by, would you have a flag on you? Don't want to get our first ship damaged by friendly fire, now do we?"

"No, but there is some chalk in our survival pack."

Neville set the record straight as to what he thought of the intelligence of someone packing chalk in a jungle survival kit. "Brilliant. Only an idiot would do that. What good is chalk going to do us in a boat?"

A dispirited Clyde, replied, "It seemed like a good idea, and it comes with instructions."

Chapter 23

He Was Here

October 22, 1944
Noon

"Hey Sarge, isn't it time for our relief?"

"What's the matter, Smith? Don't you like the rock you're sitting on?"

"I just figured our time was up, that's all."

The Sergeant stood and looked down toward the unit's main camp near the beach. He saw four men slowly picking their way up the hill. "Okay you guys, get your gear together. I can see our relief on its way up, but I don't know why you're in such a hurry. There ain't nothing to do on this collection of rocks, except go and sit on some smaller rocks near the water."

The Sergeant's detail gathered their gear together in anticipation of turning over the lookout post to another group. After policing his area for trash and personal items, Smith used his binoculars for one more sweep of the Strait. Every time he did so, the only thing of interest to look at was their LST and one destroyer anchored a half-mile off shore. This time, he saw the destroyer had hauled in its anchor and appeared to be several miles away, heading north. After briefly dreaming that he was on the destroyer rather than stuck in an exposed position on a naked little island, he continued his scan of the area. He suddenly stopped when he swung far enough around to see the island to their east.

"What the hell?" He exclaimed, standing up straight and pointing. "Sarge, there's a Jap barge leaving that island over there. I think its coming this way."

"If this is another of your sick jokes…" said the Sergeant as he raised his binoculars. He brought the image into focus. "Aw shit. That's one of them large patrol barges. It can hold more than fifty men. I knew this was too good to last. Smith, keep an eye on them. Let me know if anything changes." He picked up his walkie-talkie and reported the sighting.

The main camp quickly took on the appearance of a highly disturbed ants nest. The entire company switched from being an assault force to playing defense. The few good gun positions were manned and new ones established along with the guns on their amphibious vehicles. In minutes, the area that had swarmed with men looked like a ghost town. Everyone settled into protected positions, waiting to surprise the enemy.

The Captain grabbed the handset of his walkie-talkie and tried to raise the destroyer disappearing into the haze. Frustrated, after trying several times, he handed the walki-talkie back to the radioman. He called another radio operator over. "Send a message to battalion. Tell them we have enemy approaching in a barge and need a destroyer for covering fire. Expect enemy to arrive in," he took a quick look toward Dinigat, "fifteen-minutes, strength unknown."

* * *

The two men stood next to each other–Clyde steering, and Neville trying to see what Danawan's temporary occupiers were doing.

"I'm getting nervous," said Neville as he stared through his binoculars trying to find someone…anyone, on the island. He looked at Clyde. "You're sure you don't have a flag? I don't think those boys are going to accept that we want to be friends on good faith alone."

Clyde tried to dry his hands on his tattered shorts, before wiping sweat away from his eyes. Nerves, heat, and humidity made for a bad combination. "If you think those blokes are going to act unfriendly, why don't you get on top of that ramp up front and wave to them?"

Neville gave his friend a dirty look. "How long have you been trying to find a way to get me eliminated so you'll have both our places? One good shot and I'm in the water."

"You don't say…and me leaving my lifeguard certificate at home. You'll have to be careful."

"That I will. In fact I'm going to be so careful I'm going to get down *behind* that ramp. No sense in staying up here in the open and being a target when you're already doing such a good job of it."

The hint of smile normally on Clyde's face disappeared as he tried to appear as if his feelings had been hurt.

When the barge reached the mid-point of the channel separating the two islands, he reduced speed to four-knots. "No sense in scaring those boys into doing something they'll regret."

Neville looked up from the cargo area when he heard the engine slow down. Turning serious, he said, "They start shooting, you drop behind that panel like you've been shot. A sore elbow or knee is better than a hole in the head, although, ain't nothin' going to leak out if they do get lucky."

Both men were concerned and the closer they got to Danawan, the more it showed. They didn't know how experienced or well-led the unknown troops were. They had to assume the worst and needed to find out what type of reception they were going to get before reaching point-blank-range. That necessity made Neville say a quick prayer, climb the inside of the eight-foot high ramp, stick his head up and wave at anyone on shore.

A response wasn't long in coming. It seemed the entire island shot at them with smoke blossoming from behind fifty different rocks. Fifteen or more bullets whizzed by, while others clanged off the bow or splashed into the water alongside. The two Englishmen dropped like sacks of cement followed by Clyde reaching up to the steering control and turning the barge back toward Dinigat.

It wasn't until the barge was safely back to mid-channel that either of the men dared poke his head up. "I guess that answers the question about who's the most scared, them or us," Neville said, as he and Clyde tried to figure out their next move.

"We can send a message to Cullison and have him contact those trigger-happy Yanks. Here we are, two old…"

"Two what?" Neville looked askance at his partner who didn't need to be told to correct his language.

"Sorry, two middle-aged white men, all by themselves facing a whole army, and they start shooting at us. You'd think we were going to let King-Kong loose on the island."

"Who knows? Maybe we are," suggested Clyde. "They can't see if this boat is full of crack troops, or not. We need to show them we're friends. Maybe we could lower the ramp and show them the boat is empty?"

"Sure we can, except this thing don't float with the front door open. Of course, we can swim the rest of the way. Oh, wait a minute…you can't swim, can you?"

"You bloody well know I can't. But you could go out and convince one of those friendly sharks to give me a lift. With your gift of gab it shouldn't be any trouble at all."

Neville held up his hands. "All right, I give up. You won that round. Now, what do we do?"

"Don't know and don't care. I ain't getting near them Yanks until they know we're allies.

"I…" Neville stopped, in mid-thought. The silence made Clyde look at his mate, who appeared to have gone into a trance.

Without saying a word, Neville started rummaging through all of their possessions. When he found what he needed he motioned for Clyde to follow him forward to the bow ramp.

"Once I get settled out there, you head us toward the beach. If those Yanks shoot at us this time…well, then they ain't smart enough to carry guns."

"Talk about not being smart. Where did you leave your brains?"

"This will work, and if it don't, it won't matter. Either those Yanks let us get to Danawan or they shoot us, or the ones on that destroyer coming this way will sink us. Which do you prefer?"

Clyde looked north where he could see the destroyer reappearing out of the haze.

They quickly created a sling in one end of a piece of rope and hung it over the front of the barge ramp. The free end they tied off to a deck cleat. Neville climbed up and over the top. When he felt secure in the sling, he motioned Clyde back to the control console.

Neville used his amateur artist's eye to visualize what he wanted to achieve. He worked quickly, if not artistically, and an image seen by Yank troops all over the world took shape on the dark gray metal.

* * *

Yelling to his men, the Captain said, "Get ready men, they're coming back." He looked around to make sure everyone had taken cover and then focused his binoculars on the enemy barge. He stared at the vessel for a moment, checked that his lenses were clean, refocused and stared at it again.

"I don't believe it," he said to himself. Then, louder, "I'll be Goddamned! Never heard of the Japs trying a trick like this. Either the guys on that barge have the biggest set of balls in the universe, or they're on our side." He turned to make sure his voice carried to all his men. "I don't want to shoot some of our own boys, but be ready. Safety's on. No shooting unless I say so."

He turned to shout to the men closest to the beach. "Nobody shoots unless I say to."

*　　*　　*

The barge's small bow wave lapped at the ubiquitous *Kilroy's* nose as Clyde and Neville's private yacht approached the beach. When its keel hit the sandy bottom, its ramp dropped with a crash. A scrawny civilian appeared to be the only occupant other than the driver. He stood with hands raised, one of them still holding a piece of chalk. At the control console stood a slightly rounder civilian, whose clothes were in desperate need of a landfill.

The Captain made a come-to-me gesture and the original liberators stepped onto Danawan soil, returning to the site of the previous night's victory.

Captain Albert Skidmore, U.S. Army Reserve didn't want to believe a word either of the two disreputable looking Englishman said. Even after thirty minutes of discussion, often heated, the basic fact and its results were still in dispute–who had captured the island and liberated its non-existent residents, fought the enemy, and could exercise all rights normally devolving to liberators.

Secure in their knowledge that for once, they had the law on their side–a rare occassion–Clyde and Neville maintained a calmness few would have believed possible. Skidmore, on the other hand became more upset every time he repeated himself. His large blue eyes bulging, his face color changing to a deep red, he wanted the interlopers gone.

"By God, we're fighting a war here. We can't fight and take care of helpless civilians at the same time. You say you came here from Limasawa. I don't know if that's true or not and I really don't care, as long as you take that barge and go back where you came from. This island is the property of the U.S. Army, until General MacArthur says otherwise."

Neville bit into a hard cookie and washed it down with some fresh made coffee. The Yanks could always be counted on to travel in style. "Here are the facts, Captain." Keeping his voice calm, his words measured, Neville ran through his list, ticking them off on his fingers. "Did you kill any Japs on this island? No. We killed six of them. Did you have lookouts posted on the hilltop all day yesterday? No. We did. Did you leave a cache of supplies here yesterday? No. We did. Are your men qualified to report on enemy troop and ship movements? No. We are, and, if the Japs come back, can your men keep headquarters up to date on enemy movements in the area while living behind enemy lines? No they can't−but we can. We've been doing this for three years without losing our scalps, so why don't you bugger off?"

"Bugger off? I'll show you, bugger off." Skidmore called to the Lieutenant who hoped he had been forgotten. "Bring a squad over here and take these men into custody. I want them put in a cell as soon as you can get them out to the LST."

"Yes Sir," he answered, and chose eight men. Ready to do his duty, he approached the two civilians who, standing with arms folded, dared anyone to touch them.

"If you touch us, the British Consul General will hear of this. Once he tells Winnie, you'll be lucky if they let you command a garbage dump."

Skidmore felt tempted to reach out and grab Neville by his scrawny neck, when a corporal yelled, "Captain," and waved a piece of paper as he approached. "I have a message from the Task Force commander, sir."

Whatever the message said, Skidmore deflated like a burst balloon. Clyde and Neville sat on the small, shaded lookout platform Skidmore's troops had already put together in expectation of being there awhile. The Strait was quiet as the few ships they had seen were gone. All of the Naval vessels had been pulled back in preparation for the battle everyone knew to be coming.

"Ain't the water beautiful. It's such a nice shade of green close to shore. Almost as good as back on Pyramid."

"And a lot quieter," added Neville. "After all the noise them Yanks made about this being their island. The nerve of them. Think they own the whole world. Well, we showed 'em."

"That we did and it certainly was nice of that Lieutenant to give us a flag. Might come in handy if we need to go anywhere for groceries."

Chapter 24

Messages

October 24, 1944

At times Cullison and Harry seemed as inseparable as Siamese twins. They slept, ate and worked next to each other on Morotai, even though the word *work*, seemed a bit out of place for what Harry did. His job description was topography consultant, although now that the war was moving away from the forbidding and little known island terrains of the Southwest Pacific to well-mapped areas, he chose to do whatever he could to be useful while staying away from the big brass.

His other choice was to go home to Melbourne, his wife Marieke whom he loved, and teach first year students who he tolerated. He didn't do that simply because he needed to be involved. In a war where his age prevented him from making any other direct contribution–he needed to do his "bit." Marieke agreed with and supported his decision. She had first-hand knowledge of the horror known, as the Japanese Greater East-Asia Co-Prosperity Sphere. She met Harry in the jungles of Sumatra while running for her life to escape Japan's conquering army. She saw the Emperor's troops execute her first husband as he tried to steal medical supplies for other civilians. She and

Harry, thrown together by circumstances, had been together ever since.

Where, a month ago, the small island of Morotai had been in the center of the fight, it now felt far removed from the combat zone–at least most of the time. Morotai happened to be an island of halves. One part with terrain ideal for use as an airbase, the other–all mountains. The Japanese had been chased into the mountains where MacArthur saw little reason to follow, content to leave them to their own devices.

With the Japanese Navy starting to show its hand, the two men made a habit of stopping by their Quonset hut office every night before hitting the sack. A frustrated Cullison slapped a radio message down on his desk.

Harry looked up, "What's wrong, Bill? You don't look very happy–maybe you should get a little more sleep?"

"No, it's not the lack of sleep that has me upset. It's all these messages coming in from up north. I should be up there, not here, pushing paper around all day." He pointed at his heavily laden desk. "I'm a submarine commander, I should be out there, in the hunt, like these fellas." He picked up two radio messages and shoved them at Harry.

"Wow, the Darter and the Dace. They each sank a Jap cruiser, almost at the same time." The messages detailed the action and coordinates, which Harry's mind had difficulty placing. He was a whiz with anything involving dry land, but figuring out where things were located in the vast Pacific Ocean always gave him a problem. "Where…"

"The Palawan Passage, this side of Formosa. Those cruisers were part of a large Jap task force under Admiral Kurita heading for the Philippines. They came out of Cam Ranh Bay."

"Two cruisers sunk. That ought to make a difference."

"Not hardly. Both reports could be off however, it looks as if the Japs have four or five battleships plus ten to twelve cruisers and more destroyers than the subs could count. We think both the

Yamato and the Musashi are with him. They're the two largest battleships in the world."

"My God, that must be all of their capital ships."

Cullison shook his head as he rooted through message copies littering his desk. He found the one he wanted and tossed it over to Harry. "I wish. The Japs are going to try for a knockout blow. They have two more groups coming up from the south, each one almost as big as Kurita's, and maybe another from the north, although info on that one is still mostly guesswork."

"Can we stop them? If they get through to the landing support ships…"

"It'll be a massacre. Both the Seventh fleet under Kinkaid and Halsey's Third fleet are there. My money is on the Japs losing a lot of ships." Wistfully he added, "What I'd give to be there."

Harry handed the message back to Cullison. "I guess we really didn't need to send Clyde and Neville up there, after all."

Caught by surprise, Cullison said, "Why? We'll need every set of eyes we can get."

"Well…we seem to know so much already, I'd think any information those two send in won't make a difference."

"Maybe you're right. Although, who knows how things will go. My money is on those two juvenile delinquents. Somehow, they always manage to blunder into the middle of everything and finally do the right thing, usually by mistake. We could probably send them to the Aleutians and they would end up saving all of Hawaii. I don't know how they do it, but mark my words…"

"If the Japs don't capture or kill them."

Harry's comment triggered a thought and Cullison started to chuckle. "The best thing that can happen is for the Japs to make a mistake and *take* them prisoner. That will be the end of the war. The Japs will have to surrender to get those two to stop talking."

Cullison gave himself a shake, mentally to get back to business. "Come on, let's neaten up our desks and see if the donuts are ready before we hit the sack." After going through the latest dispatches, they always stopped by the mess tent to see if the cooks had put out the next mornings' donuts. They fully understood the relationship between the arrival of a supply ship and the quality of their meals.

Thinking of one or two fresh donuts to help him fall asleep, Harry looked up when the hut's screen door slammed shut. "Better wait a minute, Bill." He pointed to a messenger walking down the hut's center aisle with several messages in his hand.

Harry walked over to stand behind Cullison and read over his shoulder. "Another problem?"

Cullison didn't answer as he pulled out a chart of the southern Philippine islands. He reread one message and then found the referenced area on his map. "We have a report from guerilla's on the coast of Mindanao. They spotted another Jap task force coming up from the south just off the coast. I guess I was right. The Japs are going to throw everything they have at our ships and try to force their way through the Surigao Strait while Kurita is heading for the San Bernadino. I sure hope Halsey and Kinkaid are working from the same playbook, but I doubt it. One takes his orders from MacArthur and the other from Nimitz. Divided commands can get messy."

Harry thought of the coming battle in a more personal way. He pointed to a spot on the chart. "And there is little Danawan, with Clyde and Neville enjoying a quiet night under the stars. They'll be right in the thick of things, just as you predicted."

"I hope they're getting some sleep tonight, I doubt they will tomorrow. In fact, I think I'll write up a short message to alert them." Cullison pulled a message pad out of his desk drawer. With a pen in his hand, he stopped and looked over his shoulder at Harry. "There is one good thing about them being where they are. Clyde shouldn't have to worry about being forced to take a saltwater bath. The Japs can't shoot them down or sink the island."

"True, but sixteen-inch guns could significantly alter its shape."

*   *   *

Neville gave Clyde a kick to wake him up at a little before five in the morning. On the hour, Clyde received the message from Bill and Harry. For a change, thought Neville as he read the information, *someone is telling us what might happen, before, rather than after the fact.* The final line of Cullison's heads-up message to them contained a greeting and warning from Harry.

> **...Glad hear both doing well-enjoying scenery. Do not invite boisterous guests who pass by to join you for drink. See you soon.**

Neville laughed at the words while Clyde found it an insult. Harry needed to choose his words more carefully. He made it sound like they were unable to tell friend from foe. Clyde's personal criteria for picking his friends had not failed him in over twenty years. Friends got drunk with you and paid your bar bill. Enemies stayed sober, got you drunk, stole your money, offered to pay for everyone in the pub, and stuck you with the tab.

The two Englishmen soon let the warning slip to the back of their minds as they went about their morning routine. Neither of them ever had any difficulty finding a reason to do, or not do something. In this case, being on a dry, almost treeless island provided more than enough reason to skip bathing or shaving. However, Neville did take the time to walk into the ocean with his clothes on for a quick rinse. Clyde thought such an activity could be hazardous to his health, there might be a hungry shark out there. Besides, he needed a few more hours' beauty sleep.

The morning crept by as did most of the afternoon without any ships cluttering the Strait. It seemed everyone had decided to stay close to home. This changed a little before four when three PT Boats, motors roaring, sped by heading west. The tip of the spear needed to be in position to greet Admiral Nishimura coming up from the south. No sooner did the PT Boats disappear in the haze than two American destroyers barreled through the Strait heading east.

Another update from Cullison, received during the evening fleshed out their picture of opposing forces. A third enemy force under Admiral Shima had been spotted steaming south between Cebu and Negros. The Intelligence people were trying to figure out how big a force Shima had and whether he and Nishimura were going to combine into one huge fleet or attack separately.

Refreshed by an afternoon thunderstorm, the coast watchers were ready to do their job. The rain refilled their canteens and washed the dried salt out of Neville's clothes. After some animated discussion, Clyde gave in to his partner's comments about his personal hygiene. He grudgingly agreed that he might be able to reduce the wildlife exclusion zone floating on the air surrounding him, and stood out in the rain sparingly using a bar of soap.

The day was coming to a close as they sat eating their dinner on the lookout platform Captain Skidmore's people had been so considerate to build. Neville raised his head, sniffed the air, and commented, "This food smells different. I wonder what those people in Kansas did to it?"

"Kansas? Are you sure? I thought this stuff came from Texas."

"No. It's definitely from Kansas, wherever that is. Why would you think Texas?"

"Every other Yank we meet seems to be from there. To listen to them makes a bloke think that the other states are hangers-on, and that anything good only comes from Texas."

Neville pointed at his food. "Are you saying this is good?"

"What I'm saying is that it's better than getting hit in the head by a cricket ball."

"On that, I agree, but what food isn't? I was simply saying it smells different, and now I know why. Since you took your shower, I can smell things other than you."

Clyde pointed a finger at his mate. "Careful there, or I'll tie a rope around your waist and use you as *Kilroy's* anchor."

"Ahh, I knew I forgot something. Thanks for reminding me. We need to get back over to our ship, raise the ramp and redraw our patron saint's face, *Mr. Kilroy*, on the bow. I'm sure the drawing disappeared yesterday when we dropped the ramp in the water."

"Why? We have a flag now. Too bad it ain't one of ours, but at least the Yanks won't shoot at it."

Neville stood up and put his kit away. "Let's just say, I like insurance. Too many people are going to be in our neighborhood trying to kill each other. They might make a mistake. Do you want the papers to list you as a casualty of someone's mistake? What will people think?"

"I don't care, as long as I'm around to hear them."

Neville reached out his hand to encourage Clyde to get up. "Come on. It'll be dark soon. Now that you smell better, you don't want to be walking around on a dark night and get bitten by a love-sick vampire, now do you?"

"Blimey, it wouldn't be a fair fight. I still have most of my teeth."

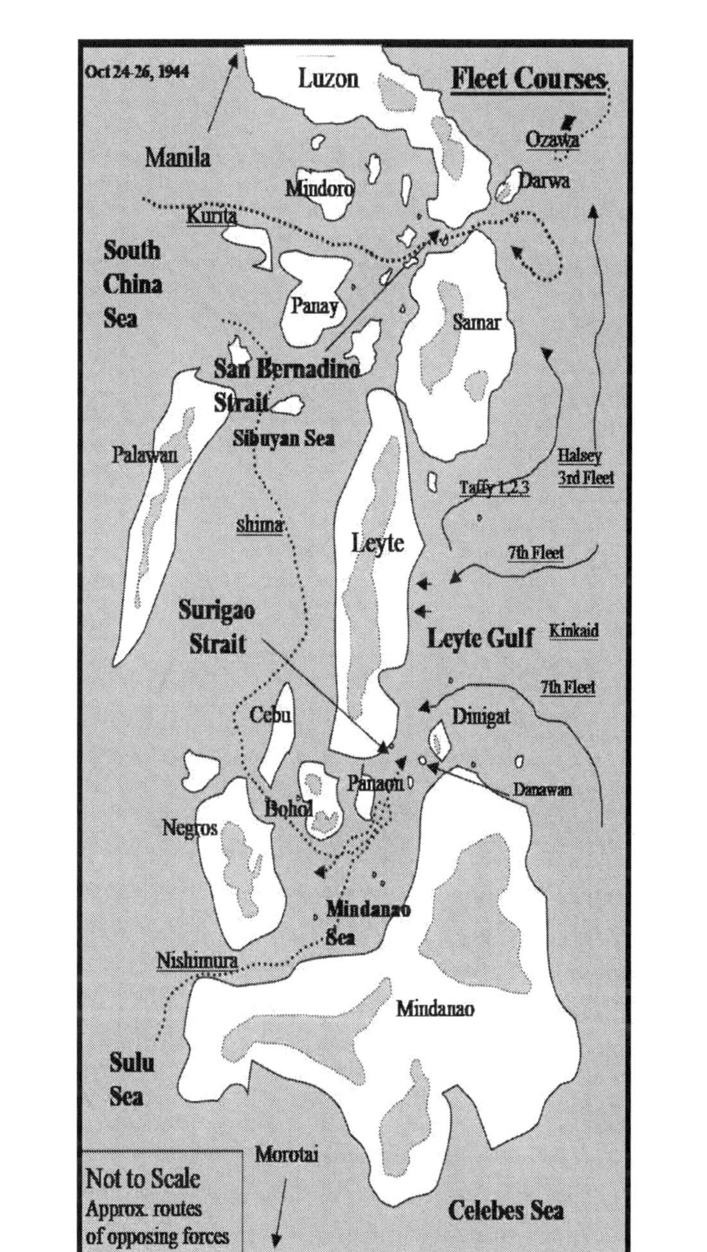
Oct 24-26, 1944
Luzon
Fleet Courses
Ozawa
Manila
Mindoro
Darwa
Kurita
South
China
Sea
Panay
Samar
San Bernadino
Strait
Sibuyan Sea
Palawan
Halsey
3rd Fleet
Taffy 1,2,3
shima
Leyte
7th Fleet
Surigao
Strait
Leyte Gulf
Kinkaid
7th Fleet
Cebu
Dinigat
Panaon
Danawan
Bohol
Negros
Mindanao
Sea
Nishimura
Mindanao
Sulu
Sea
Morotai
Not to Scale
Approx. routes
of opposing forces
Celebes Sea

Chapter 25

Voices

October 25, 1944

The morning's radio message Clyde received and Neville decrypted alerted them to coming events. The Japanese plan had been unmasked. It sounded as if a good portion of the coming operation would be occurring in the area the two Englishmen thought of as their, new neighborhood. With a little bad luck, Danawan's liberators could expect to receive some more unwanted attention.

Each of the four Japanese task forces were identified in American messages by the names of their commanding Admirals. The brainy fellows in Intelligence must have been working overtime. Kurita and his force with several battleships had been sighted heading for the San Bernadino Strait several hundred miles north of Clyde and Neville. At the same time, reports said Ozawa and a strong group of aircraft carriers had been sighted coming south along the east coast of Luzon. If the two groups came together, a swarm of carrier-based planes supporting cruisers and battleships might be able to break through Halsey's Third Fleet and threaten the landing force from the north.

A danger to the Leyte landings from the south came from Nishimura, along with a smaller force commanded by Shima.

They were aiming to break through the Surigao Strait. If any of this southern force made it through the Strait, the landings would be a disaster The obvious conclusion–the Japanese intended the upcoming fight to be the decisive naval battle of the war. In essence, their orders were win, or die with honor–Japanese warriors do not surrender.

After getting approval from higher up, Cullison sent a second message. He provided the two inhabitants of Danawan with the fleet-wide general-signals radio frequency, and the short-range voice, ship-to-ship, communications circuit. To save their batteries, Clyde and Neville decided to only tune in to these frequencies every two hours, at least until things got interesting.

Through the morning they took turns, one watching the Strait from their lookout post, while the other carried items they might need down the hill to their backup command post and mobile hideaway, the newly christened, HMB-CW1/*Kilroy*. After much thought, they officially designated their fleet's only vessel, *His Majesty's Barge-Coast Watcher 1*. Unofficially, its name remained, *Kilroy*.

A light breeze from the north threatened to push the clouds hanging around Leyte's mountaintops south across the Strait. Every so often, the haze thickened bringing visibility down to less than two miles and then, miraculously, disappeared. During one of the times when they had good visibility, Neville saw the distinctive towers of several American battleships in deep water at the east end of the Strait. Peeking over the horizon, the Seventh Fleet stood ready, in position to block the Strait with six battleships and twice as many cruisers. If Nishimura got as far as Danawan, it opened the possibility, for only the second time in the war, of battleships fighting battleships. The spirit of John Paul Jones could hardly contain itself in anticipation of the coming event.

Neville stepped onto their lookout platform, carefully balancing two tin mugs of freshly brewed tea. He set one down next to Clyde. "Be careful with that, it's hot."

Clyde ignored the caution and wrapped his hand around the body of the metal cup instead of grabbing it by the handle. He didn't raise it more than a few inches when he screeched, "Yeow," and quickly set it down, blowing on his fingers.

Neville simply shook his head. "What did I tell you? Still can't do two things at the same time, can you?"

"I can do a lot of things. Right now, I've been thinking about how far those ships out there can shoot."

"I remember someone saying over twenty miles."

"Twenty miles? Blimey, you've got to be joking. They can't see that far to know what to aim at. Someone's been pulling your leg."

"You ever hear about a new fangled invention, Radio Detection and Ranging?"

After taking a cautious sip of tea, Clyde shook his head. "Don't think so."

Although he knew Clyde since childhood, the man's ability to not be aware of the world around him still had Neville shaking his head. "Why does your ignorance not surprise me? The Yanks have it on all their ships, but *we* invented it. Those sailors don't have to be able to see something to blow it out of the water."

"Bloody hell. You're foolin', ain't you?"

"I knew it was time to go home after that New Guinea job. You've been in the jungle so long, your brain has turned green, along with your feet.

"Now tell me, you've heard of radar, right?" Neville waited for his mate's acknowledgement. "I knew you couldn't be that numb between the ears."

His voice full of false bravado, Clyde said, "Well of course I've heard of radar." In a less confrontational way, he continued, "Only, ain't no one ever explained what the bloomin' thing does."

Neville stood and walked around the platform, flapping his arms in frustration. "Thank the Good Lord no one else is around to hear you. You are aware, I hope, that this is the twentieth century. We have radar, we have asdic, why–we even have radios. When we get back to Brisbane, you need to learn about what the world has been doing without you, instead of sitting in a pub getting drunk."

Clyde lowered his binoculars, to ponder what Neville said, before shaking his head, no. "Don't sound like much fun, but you go ahead and learn whatever I need to know, then I can ask you, if you ain't already passed out drunk."

Satisfied that he had properly dealt with the problem, Clyde brought the binoculars up to his eyes. "Take a look out there. Somebody's getting serious about them Nips coming this way."

Neville focused his own binoculars on a group of ships coming straight at them. A force of ten destroyers and three cruisers separated itself from the American Seventh Fleet and sailed west into the Strait. Soon after they passed Danawan, the group split in two. Both sailed as close to the north and south shores as they could. They patrolled along the sides of the Strait in water hardly deep enough to keep them afloat, as the setting sun turned their gray hulls pink.

Clyde reached over and picked up their walkie-talkie. The tactical radio only worked over short distances. He figured that with some of the destroyers less than a mile distant, he might be able to talk to them. He took one more look at the ships and wrote several of their hull numbers on the palm of his hand.

"Destroyer number four-five-one, this is Clyde, over." He repeated the message three more times. All he received was static. He looked up at Neville standing next to him, and shrugged. "Must be too far away."

Silence suddenly replaced the static, followed by, "Four-five-one to Clyde?" The friendly voice from the American South responded.

Clyde's face broke out in a wide grin, telling Neville, without any words, "*I told you so*."

"Clyde to the Yank Navy. Are the Nips on the way?"

A pleasant voice, answered, "This is the Yank Navy."

"Certainly is a friendly chap," said Neville.

Without warning, the voice changed into that of a sleep deprived grizzly after the spring thaw. "Who the hell are you? Get off this radio net."

"Now there isn't any need to be rude. This is the island to your left. You want us to let you know when the Jap fleet shows up? That's why we're up here. Otherwise, we'll simply sit here and watch. We're glad to help you find the blighters if you think you can hurt them with your little destroyers."

"I repeat, who are you?"

Emphasizing his British accent, Clyde answered. "This is the Australian Coast Watcher Service, Danawan Station, Surigao Strait, old chap. Can we be of assistance?"

Neville whispered, "Good show, Mate. Make us sound official."

There was nothing coming in but static for more than a minute. It disappeared when the Grizzly Bear said, "This is Commodore Sherman, TF seven-four-one. Suggest you jump in a deep hole and pull the top in over you. Enemy forces expected at this location, zero-two-hundred hours. TF seven-four-one, out."

Clyde answered, "We'll be here if you need us. Danawan, out." He put down the portable radio and yawned. "The man sounds like he knows what's going on. He might even have made me a bit nervous, if it weren't for us having our own floating foxhole. This hunk of rock we're on ain't exactly the garden spot of the Pacific–hate to think what it would be like if somebody starts shooting at it. But, since there ain't anything to do except wait… I think I'll take a nap. Don't want to miss tonight's fireworks."

"Go ahead. It's probably a good idea to be well-rested with the end of the world coming along in a few hours. I'll stay up for awhile, and I'm going to leave the radios on. We have plenty of batteries."

After dark, several reports came in about activity north of Leyte. Halsey reported that his aircraft hit Kurita's fleet west of the San Bernadino Strait with over two-hundred sorties doing significant damage. With only a few aircraft of his own to provide him protection from the air, Kurita's ships turned tail and headed back west.

With the Kurita problem solved, Halsey decided to move most of the Third Fleet north and try to intercept Ozawa's ships, which included most of the Japanese fleet's large aircraft carriers. Kill the carriers and the U.S. could stop worrying about surprise attacks on their land-based facilities anywhere in the Pacific.

Lookouts on the destroyers in the Strait stood down as their replacements took over when the clock struck ten. Small, quick rain showers moved across the area. Several times visibility changed from very good to lousy and back again in the span of minutes. Most of the men preferred getting soaked, and cooled, by the rain rather than endure the sticky, soggy feeling of wearing sweat soaked clothing. The hoped for relief from the heat however, did not come with darkness.

Late in the evening, Neville gazed out at the dark shapes that formed the Strait and its islands. "What do you think? Maybe that Commodore fella didn't get the word?"

"Why?"

"Why? It's too bloody quiet, that's why. Somebody should have spotted the Japs by now…if they're coming."

"Maybe the radios ain't working. How long has it been since you changed the batteries?"

"Didn't have to. You changed them when the sun went down, right?"

Clyde hesitated before answering. He needed to take time to remember if that was true. "Getting old can be hard on a bloke and I forgive you if your memory ain't what it has been. However, I did not change the batteries."

"You didn't? You're sure?"

"Positive, which means…"

"Stop talking and give me a fresh pack. Who knows what we've been missing. You shouldn't mislead me like that."

"I shouldn't…?" Clyde sputtered, and grabbed for the voice radio but missed as he ducked away from Neville. His quick move prevented Neville from hitting him in the head with a pack of dead batteries. Solid contact might have done some good, and then again… maybe not.

Both radios quickly returned to service, and yet, everything remained quiet. They felt as if they were in a cowboy and Indian movie where someone always said, "It's too darn quiet." The only sound they heard was that of waves dying against Danawan's shoreline.

Finally, their long-distance radio started making its familiar clicking sound as a message came in. The sender knew his business. Dots and dashes spilled out, as if trying to push each other out of the way in the sender's hurry to tell everyone–something.

"Plain language," Clyde concentrated on understanding the message the sender didn't have time to encrypt. As soon as the sender signed off, he quickly removed his headphones.

"Well?" said an expectant Neville. "What did he say?"

Clyde hesitated, first looking at his watch–10:30. He looked up at Neville. "The PT Boats have been ordered to attack Nishimura's fleet. They expect contact in about five minutes."

"How many Yank boats are going in. If they only send a couple against that kind of fire power it'll be suicide."

"Every one of those little boats is going."

"How many is that?" Neville's voice said it all. He felt anxious for the brave young men. PT Boats were fragile things, made of plywood, meant to sting and skedaddle. They relied on their speed and maneuverability rather than armament.

"Thirty-nine boats are going to attack from behind Bohol Island."

Instead of looking to the west, Neville looked in the opposite direction. Low on the eastern horizon, a whitish glow lit the sky. "Good thing they're going in now. The moon will be up in twenty minutes."

Clyde sat glued to his radio receiver waiting to hear how much damage the young men, well-known for their daring, would inflict on the Japanese–especially the two large battleships. The minutes ticked by with an occasional flash in the western sky. With small rain cells traveling across the water, they couldn't tell if the flashes were lightning or exploding torpedoes.

During the attack, the PT Boats communicated through their short-range voice radios. They were too far away for the two coast watchers to hear any of the excited, scared, and determined voices on the short-range radio system. Each boat bobbed and weaved through the enemy's protective screen of destroyers, and then the cruisers in their rush to claim the battleships. Water boiled up all around them as the ocean came alive with shells of all sizes landing in their midst. Boats disappeared under tons of water thrown skyward by exploding near misses before reappearing with the crews looking like drowned rats. Against the dark sky, tracers created a seemingly solid wall of streaking light in front of them. The threat of death was everywhere. Some tracers even looked to be moving in slow motion. They were the worst, since they were coming directly toward them.

The brave crews launched their deadly cargo, some with skill, many with little more than a prayer's chance of hitting a target. The attack continued in fits and starts for almost an hour. The daring sailors pressed their advantage of stealth and speed to the breaking point. They reported several torpedoes exploding against the hulls of the two largest battleships while others simply exploded against whatever was in their way, primarily coral outcroppings or island beaches. The big ships were equipped with up to two-feet of armor along the waterline, but that didn't stop the little boats from trying. No one knew if a torpedo could inflict more than superficial damage to the largest warships in the world. It seemed like a good time to find out.

Near midnight, Clyde received the first after-action report. All of the PT Boats reported in after the attack, a testament to the skill of their commanders, as well as the poor training of the Japanese gunners. Even so, several boats might yet succumb to the damage they received. Many of the boat crews working on the open decks were missing, killed, or wounded. The two primary targets had been damaged, although no one knew to what extent. To their disappointment the Japanese fleet did not turn back. In fact, it didn't even change speed–not a good sign. At their current rate of advance, Nishimura's fleet would be at the Surigao in less than two hours.

Clyde and Neville didn't say anything, each showing with their tense body language how concerned they were while unable to help. They had met the enemy on any number of occasions on islands of the South Pacific. Frequently they emerged victorious, while on a few occasions they escaped with little but their sun-burned skins. This time would be different. Never before had they faced the enemy on an island so small.

Neville looked at his mate. "Stay or go? There ain't any good place to hide."

"We were hired to do a job. Once we're done, we take HMB-*Kilroy* and see what else we can do. Agreed?"

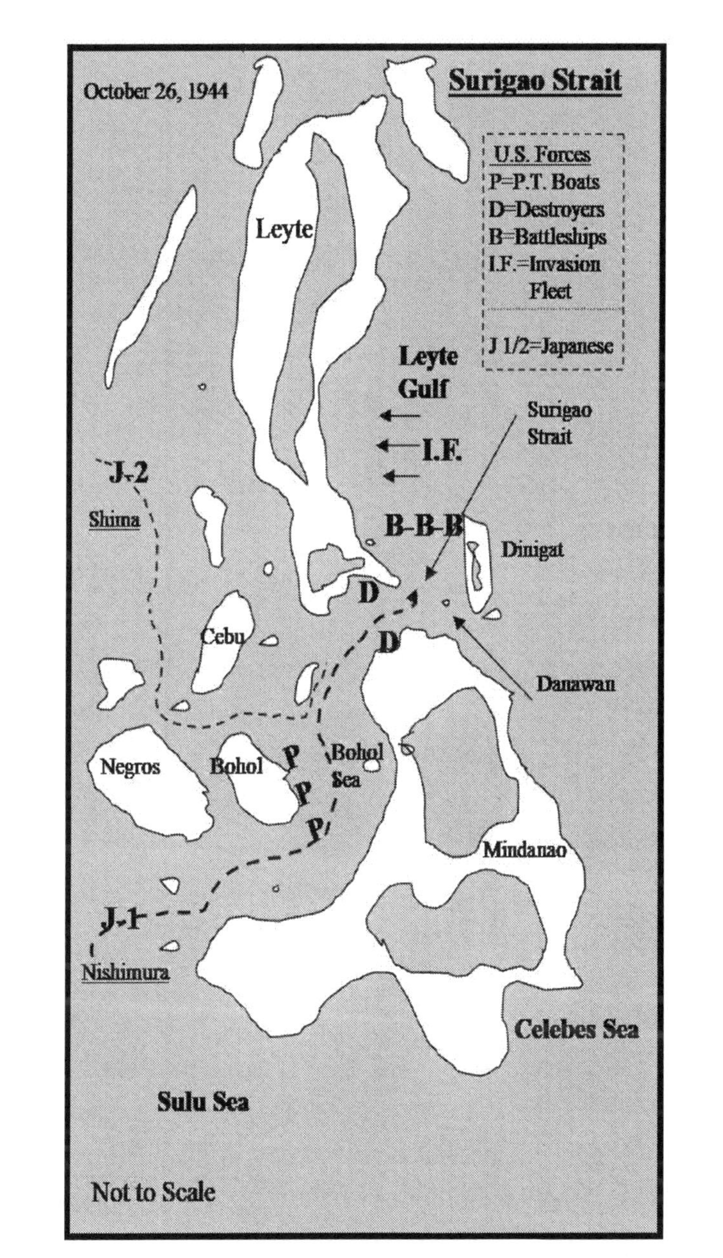
October 26, 1944
Surigao Strait
U.S. Forces
P=P.T. Boats
D=Destroyers
B=Battleships
I.F.=Invasion Fleet
J 1/2=Japanese
Leyte
Leyte Gulf
I.F.
Surigao Strait
J-2
Shima
B-B-B
Dinigat
D
D
Cebu
Danawan
Negros
Bohol
P
P
P
Bohol Sea
Mindanao
J-1
Nishimura
Celebes Sea
Sulu Sea
Not to Scale

Chapter 26

Black on Black

October 26, 1944
Time – 0130

Clyde looked at the glowing numbers on his watch and then the open waters of the Strait. "Where are they?" He said to Neville, "Maybe they ain't coming. Maybe those little boats sank some of them and they turned around."

Neville held up the walkie-talkie. "Sure they did, and everyone got so excited they forgot to let us know before getting drunk."

"You know they can't do that. No liquor on Yank ships."

"That's my point. Only they…"

When his mate didn't finish his comment, Clyde said, "What? What smart thing are you trying to think up?"

Neville waved for Clyde to be quiet. He needed to concentrate on what was visible, or almost visible. The enemy had to be out there and he needed to find them. Slowly he turned, binoculars glued to his eyes. He stopped and held his position for a moment before starting back. There was something out there, he knew it, but where?

The Japanese had earned a reputation for their night-fighting skills and it was well deserved. Everyone said that either their excellent night-vision or the superior optics of their binoculars gave them an edge at night. Even with superior firepower, the Allies could not afford to be surprised by a tenacious enemy.

The Japanese were somewhere in the waterways between Mindanao and Leyte. The fact that they could only go west or east, didn't prevent self-doubt from creeping into the back of Neville's mind. He and Clyde had used their mouths to put themselves in the middle of the action, so where was everyone?

A bolt of lightning ran along the underside of a cloud, creating an eerie black and white seascape of waves frozen in place for the blink of an eye. However, Neville did not blink. He saw the Japanese fleet in stark relief, ghost ships heading straight for them from behind a bend in the Mindanao shoreline. He looked down to where he thought the American Navy should be. Although, at that moment, he could not see them, he knew, without a doubt, that what he had seen from his position atop the island remained invisible to the ships of TF 7.41.

Neville let his binoculars drop to his chest and picked up the voice radio. Trying with only moderate success not to rush his words, he said, "Coast Watchers, Danawan, calling TF seven-four-one, are you there?"

He waited five seconds and repeated the call. Colonials, he thought. Can't trust 'em to be where they're supposed to be, when the balloon goes up. Well chosen words were about to escape his lips when he heard, "Seven-four-one, over."

Without knowing it, Neville had been holding his breath. He exhaled and then filled his lungs. "Jap task force sighted coming out from behind peninsula on Mindanao, over."

"How far from you, over."

"Hard to say. Only saw them for a moment. Less than ten miles, Mate."

"Thank you, Danawan. Don't forget about that hole. TF seven-four-one, out. Break, break. Seven-four-one, to all units. Initiate plan Able on my command. Northern force. Initial course, two-four-zero. Southern force. Initial course, three-one-five. Acknowledge, over."

One after the other, each of the ships patrolling along both sides of the Strait responded. Another voice, excited but trying not to show it came through the radio. "North leader. Radar contact. Multiple targets bearing two-five-zero, speed twenty-plus, distance nine-six-double-zero, over."

"Roger. Seven-four-one to command, initiate. Good luck."

Clyde and Neville's work was done. The time had come for them to be spectators. From their hilltop post, they had difficulty separating the gray ships from the dark water below. The moon casting its light through holes in the clouds didn't help. It created moving shadows that only fed their imaginations.

Alerted to the advancing enemy by the Danawan lookouts, the ships reacted swiftly to the attack order. They surged ahead increasing to flank speed on courses calculated to bring them in at oblique angles. Aware of the danger of being hit by torpedoes released by the destroyers attacking from the opposite side, each ship remained within its assigned lane, while still making seemingly erratic changes in direction and speed. For the next hour, destroyer captains acted like PT Boat commanders on their first day in command. Each ship weaved and bobbed like a halfback trying to reach his opponent's goal line.

While the destroyers were still some distance from the optimum release points for their torpedoes, a Japanese gun fired and the harsh light of a flare exposed them. The world stood still as hundreds of guns fired at the same moment. Mayhem and death reached out in both directions as the American ships opened fire using their five and eight-inch guns and even their anti-aircraft batteries. The relatively small caliber guns they fired were all they had while the Japanese fired eight, fourteen and even the huge sixteen-inch guns on the battleships. The American ships continued steaming into the oncoming barrage until each captain felt he had reached a satisfactory firing position. The destroyers released half their torpedoes, changed course and fired the remainder.

Freed of the threat of being sunk by their own torpedoes, commanders took independent action against an enemy that doggedly maintained its course. The attack continued with the destroyers sailing as close to the large Japanese ships as possible, guns of all calibers firing as quickly as they could be loaded. The destroyers, often found themselves so close, the Japanese guns could not be aimed low enough to hit them. In one case, a shell that measured sixteen-inches in diameter and five-feet in length entered the thin front wall of a destroyer's bridge and exited the other end before exploding. The damage caused by the two-thousand pound shell exploding close to the ship was beyond comprehension, but preferable to it exploding inside. If that had happened, the vessel would have ceased to exist.

From their island vantage point, the Strait looked like a fireworks display gone haywire. "Who's winning?" said Clyde.

"Haven't the foggiest," answered Neville. "Can't tell if we're seeing explosions caused by torpedoes or gunfire and even, if we could, still wouldn't know who's winning."

The relative position of each ship to the overall battle meant nothing. Each captain made decisions based on, first, stopping the enemy, and second, preserving his ship and crew. From above, in the darkness, it would have appeared more like a street riot of mammoth proportions, than a historic naval battle.

The melee continued with the Japanese fleet firing fire its guns in all directions while never deviating from its course, heading straight at Danawan. Fires burned on the water providing enough light for Clyde and Neville to see who might be winning as two ships, only minutes apart, blew up with cataclysmic explosions. Each one produced a blast wave that expanded out to wreak havoc on other units close by. While most ships that sank, did so due to multiple hits, a Japanese cruiser, dramatically disappeared, caused by a direct hit on its forward magazine. The ocean surface appeared to split open and the ship disappeared in the hole. Nothing remained on the surface but some life jackets and a few pieces of fresh meat for the sharks.

An errant shell, fired by the Japanese, exploded on Danawan. Large rocks became newly minted pebbles filling the air. The two men, like scared sand-crabs, ducked under a rock slab. When a second shot did not follow, they climbed out and brushed themselves off.

Not yet finished removing the grit from both the inside and outside of their clothes they didn't hear another shell screaming down toward them until, at the last second, Clyde grabbed Neville by the back of his collar and dragged him back down into their hole. The explosion threw up a huge cloud of choking dust, dirt, and stones. The only part of Neville not protected by their makeshift cave were his legs below mid-thigh. Hundreds of pounds of debris thrown into the air landed on exposed flesh. Suddenly, he could not move them.

Several times, Neville tried to raise his legs without success. He arched his back, grunted with the effort, and tried again, without success. In the blink of an eye, the island had taken ownership of his lower limbs. His body sagged as he acknowledged his fate. He turned his head toward Clyde. "I think they got me. Can't move my legs. You know…didn't want to think they'd ever get me." His love of life sucked from him, Neville's voice grew softer. "Take care of my place and, if my wife ever shows up on Pyramid, make sure she gets some money. It's the least I can do, even if she did leave me. Never did go before a minister or anything."

Clyde leaned over his mate to see what he could do. The flashes of light from all the guns firing helped a little, but he couldn't see any damage. He ran his hands along Neville's body feeling for broken bones or sticky liquid. His mind couldn't comprehend what his hands were touching when he felt Neville's legs ending in a mound of dirt. He latched onto the only logical thing he could think of–*he's lost his legs*. But, where's the blood? There should be a lot of blood. As much as he wanted to take his hands away, he knew he had to keep going and find out how much of his mate's legs were left and apply tourniquets.

"What's the bad news? Are my legs gone or am I paralyzed? Can't get anything down there to move?"

Clyde felt as bad as if his own body had been ripped apart. Their long association had changed them. Each of them had become one-half of a single being. Before Clyde could force himself to find out how much of his mate was missing, several five and eight-inch shells followed by one even larger exploded on the island in rapid succession. Clyde draped himself over Neville to protect him from further harm. The final explosion on Danawan knocked boulders loose from above their burrow. One rolled off the rock lip above, and dropped onto the dirt covering Neville's legs. The impact pushed much of the mound downhill and unlocked his temporary leg irons.

The automatic desire to protect himself made Neville curl up, drawing his knees up to his chest. He stunned himself by hitting himself in the jaw with his knees. Amazed at his sudden recovery, he didn't waste any time trying to figure out what had happened. Instead, he took advantage of the situation, and jumped to his feet. "Come on, let's get off this bloody island while we can."

An amazed Clyde sat there, his mouth wide open, unable to say anything, stunned by his legless friend scrambling to his feet as if nothing had happened. It was one of the few times in his life when his mouth did not react as fast as the rest of his body.

Neville looked down at Clyde. "Well come on, ain't got all day. Let's get our arses out of here before the blighters learn how to aim."

Neville had to climb over a number of boulders before being able to head toward HMB-Kilroy. Clyde followed, several feet behind. Without warning, Clyde found himself knocked off his feet with Neville laying on top of him. Another errant shell, origin unknown, exploded blowing Neville back into Clyde.

"What happened?" said Clyde, trying to make sense of the situation. Neville didn't answer. Clyde shook his partner without getting a response. He pulled out from under Neville's inert body and started another examination. Twice in the span of a few minutes, Neville had come within a hair's breadth of meeting his maker. Either his unknown patron saint was working overtime or he needed to start sending the Church of England some of the donations he had promised.

A quick examination in the dark did not reveal any physical damage. The shell exploded just close enough to catch Neville in its blast zone knocking him out. Clyde pulled out his canteen and wet Neville's face. He sighed a breath of relief when his partner moved and then moaned. Neville's eyes opened to see Clyde staring down at him.

"How do you feel?"

"What happened?"

"One of those ships tried to kill us. Knocked you out, but not a scratch on you."

"Um, maybe no scratches, but I can feel some sore spots. How long was I out?"

"Only a minute or two, but I've decided we're going to stay right here until we can be sure it's safe to get to Kilroy. Walking around in the open is the same as committing suicide."

"I'll take your word on that–certainly don't want to get bounced around again." Neville pushed himself up to a sitting position and took a quick look around. "Are the Nip ships still here?"

"Sort of," answered Clyde. "The Yanks are still shooting at them, but everyone is almost past the island."

"Then we couldn't stop them. That means they're going to get at our invasion fleet."

"If that happens, the war ain't going to end till next century."

Without any warning, the entire eastern sky lit up. It was like nothing they had ever seen. "Holy shit," the two men said in unison.

The main battle line of the Seventh Fleet acknowledged Admiral Kinkaid's order to engage the enemy. For only the second time in the war, capital ships were firing at each other. Six battleships arranged across the Strait in a classic "Crossing of their opponent's T" formation, fired all fifty-four of their fourteen and sixteen-inch guns at one time. The sound reached the two volunteers several seconds later.

Swift allied advances in radar technology nullified the advantage Japanese ships always had fighting at night due to their extensive night-raid training. The largest artillery shells in the American arsenal fell out of the sky. The sound tore the air apart like nothing they had ever heard. Tremendous geysers sprang up all around the Japanese fleet. Explosions caused by targets being hit were hard to distinguish from others occurring in the water around them. Even the misses caused horrendous damage as pressure waves transmitted through the water damaged Japanese light cruisers and destroyers. Superstructures were shredded and hull seams split open. The cohesiveness of the attacking fleet came apart as damaged ships dropped out of line. One destroyer, a fire raging amidships, headed for the north side of the Strait. Another, missing fifty-feet of its bow tried to do the same, only to appear to emulate a submarine when the water pressure caused the internal bulkheads to collapse. Ships that remained unscathed had to change course to avoid colliding with those less fortunate.

Destroyers and destroyer escorts assigned to the American battleship's protective screen approached the enemy fleet while death and destruction from their own guns rained down indiscriminately. Playing a daring game and working the odds, several American destroyer captains pressed home their attack with torpedoes and guns. The primary targets of the Seventh Fleet's big guns, the Japanese battleships and cruisers, sustained significant damage even with their thick protection. Armor piercing shells might not penetrate the thick steel of the gun turrets, but they could plunge through the decks and detonate deep in a ship's bowels. It would be enough. The most heavily damaged ships stopped dead in the water. They provided unparalleled targets for the gunners on battleships, which a few years earlier, had been sitting on the mud bottom of Pearl Harbor.

The big Japanese ships continued to be the primary targets as American radar fed accurate fire control information to their guns. The older battleship Fusō and then the Yamashiro disappeared under the blood stained waters. Many thousands of Japanese sailors died in a futile effort to provide the Emperor's Navy with the victory Japan so desperately needed. After ordering his remaining units to retreat, Admiral Nishimura, chose a warrior's death. He went down with his ship. The Japanese, in total disarray, retreated west, passing Negros as the sun came up. They had not violated the warrior's code, they had not surrendered, but what remained of Nishimura's fleet would be of little use in defending the home islands.

Never forgetting the Seventh Fleet's primary mission "at all costs, protect the landings," Admiral Kinkaid held his ships back, content to allow the few remaining units of the Japanese fleet to escape. The American and Australian Navies had achieved a stunning victory, but there had been losses as well. The victory came with a bill as the narrow waters of the Strait turned red. Victory had been achieved–at a price.

Chapter 27

One Too Many

October 26, 1944
Time – 0445

Clyde and Neville remained curled up between several boulders as brave men from each navy tried to sink each other's ships. Since the explosive beginning of the battle several hours earlier, shells of all caliber detonated one after the other, until the past half-hour, when things changed. The sounds of death came less frequently, and farther away.

"Which one do you want to be?" asked Neville.

Without batting an eye at the off-the-wall question, Clyde answered with a question of his own. "I'll give you a straight answer when you ask a serious question. Which one? What kind of a question is that? You know I can't read your mind. At least, not until you decide to turn it on. Now, what are you talking about?"

"I'm talking about us. Are we going to act like a hare or a tortoise. Do you want us to stay in our burrow like a tortoise or get out of here fast like a hare? The Yanks seem to have scared away the Nips, but…"

"Why is it, you always have a, but? You think those fellows are going to turn around and try it again?"

"What would you do if you had the choice of sailing back to Tokyo with your tail between your legs, or surprising your enemy like a true warrior and win the day?"

"Me? I'd go home and learn to grow flowers. Thing is, I ain't them."

"Exactly. They might want to take another ride on the carousel and make a fresh stab at grabbing that shiny gold ring. Personally, I'd prefer not to be here, if they do. I've had enough of living at the wrong end of a firing range. Let's get Kilroy and putt-putt away before someone shoots at us on purpose."

True to form, if Neville wanted to do something, Clyde simply had to go in the opposite direction. However, if Clyde made the proposal Neville always found a reason to disagree. Their ability–their need to disagree about almost everything–was the glue that kept them together. It drove others mad. How could two men argue so much and still be lonely when they were not together? No one knew the answer, but in this case, Neville's suggestion grudgingly won Clyde's agreement. Staying alive sounded better than winning the argument.

With a new day about to start, they easily picked their way down to the water through the rock field they called Danawan. Kilroy, their ace in the hole, sat there, waiting for them, unscathed by the night's activities. With its bow-ramp closed, the freshly drawn face of Mr. Kilroy with his big white-chalk eyes peered at them from the semi-darkness. Neville went directly to a group of large boulders and untied the three ropes holding the barge in place. Clyde headed for the steering console and started the engine.

Neville joined his mate and leaned on the railing to watch as Clyde backed the boat away from shore. A hundred yards from land, he changed from reverse to neutral. "Alright, we are now officially off that island. Where do you want to go? Follow the buggers who made a mess of the place or go east toward our friends with the big guns?"

"I'm tempted to go see how the Japs are doing, but I don't think we'd be welcome. What do you think?"

"Let's go talk to the Yank battleships and see how the other half lives. Maybe they'll have something to drink."

"The other half? Hope you're planning on a short visit. No alcohol, remember?"

Clyde put the engine in gear, spun the steering wheel, and sent Kilroy out from behind their island. He aimed their flagship for where he thought the big ships might be. He happily whistled a non-existent tune, feeling good about not being in someone's line of fire.

The morning haze was up to its normal tricks making a joke of the word, visibility. Kilroy's movement made the heavy air tolerable as Neville stretched out on the engine hatch and let his mind drift as the barge rose and fell in time with the waves. His thoughts were getting fuzzier with each wave they went over until Clyde said, "When we were back on Los Negros, I remember some sailors talking about rules-of-the-road."

"What? What did you say?" Neville's voice carried his annoyance in every word. "Are you talking to me?"

"Who else? We ain't picked up any passengers lately."

"Were you talking about slow drivers having to stay to the left. How is that important?"

"I'll ignore that last comment." Clyde pointed straight ahead. "I think there are some ships coming our way. If somebody doesn't move, we might get wet. Should we go right or left?"

Neville stood up and looked at a group of destroyers heading right at them. "The Nips didn't get us. That means the good Lord saw fit to save us for something important. I vote for getting out of the way since I don't float and you don't swim. Go right."

"Save us for something important? You?"

"Of course, me."

The destroyers, were only a mile or two away–the distance was hard to ascertain with such poor visibility. Being so close, they had Neville fully alert and nervous at Clyde's lack of concern for their exposed position. "I think its time for you to turn our little ship north. Those fellows don't seem inclined to go around us. We could even go ashore and pick some fruit as a peace offering to whoever's in charge of the battleships."

Reluctantly Clyde agreed, and turned Kilroy toward the Leyte shore. Before they had time to relax, a familiar ripping sound occurred. They both dropped down into the well of the barge as a large caliber shell exploded close to where Kilroy would have been. The explosion violently rocked their little ship and shrapnel, ricocheted off its side.

Neville stuck his head up over the railing, turned left and then right. "Where the bloody hell did that come from?" He looked out at the disturbed water, then at Clyde. "Can't you get this thing moving any faster?"

Clyde reached up and shoved on the controls before shaking his head. "Next time we need to put in our transportation request before, not after we need it."

Several more shells exploded in the water at the same time that one scored a direct hit on an American destroyer. The ship suddenly had a smoking hole in its forward deck taking the place of a five-inch gun blown into the air. The gun and its complete rotating mount pirouetted in the air and sank alongside the ship with all of its crew still locked inside. Each of the ships in the group executed radical turns to throw off the unexpected newcomers' aim.

Clyde Looked to their left trying to see where the shots were coming from. "There they are," he shouted, pointing at several large ships. "I thought I saw them a minute ago. Looked like they were Yanks."

"They damn well should be." Neville grabbed his binoculars and took a good long look at the intruders. "Damn."

He pounded the handrail. "I'll be damned." What he saw stunned him. "They're Nips, but *not* the same ones that were shooting at us before."

Questions quickly tumbled out of Clyde's mouth. "New Nips? I thought they all went home. How do you know they're new? Where'd they come from?"

"No damage, that's how. They look like they just came out of dry dock. Haven't the foggiest idea where these fellows came from, old chap. Maybe somebody else does?" Neville grabbed the walkie-talkie. "Coast watchers calling…anyone, over."

"DD three-four-nine, over," came back at them.

"The Japs that are shooting are new to the game. They are *not* the same ships from before, over."

"Acknowledged. We think these are from Shima's task force. Hope you can find another hole to hide in. Heavy hitter is at the plate. Three-four-nine, out."

Neville looked at Clyde. "Shima? Who's he?"

Clyde shrugged his shoulders. "I'm just glad there are some ships out here for Mr. Shima to shoot at besides us."

Neville took another worried look at the Japanese ships. "You sure this thing won't go any faster? They're coming straight at us and I don't think we have the right of way."

"This is as fast as she will go. Of course, you could lighten the load."

Neville looked down at the well area where the load would be. The area was empty, except for a small pile of used building material. "What load?"

"Jump overboard. That's sure to help, but if you don't want to do that, you could take down that Yank flag. No sense waving a red flag in front of a bull."

High-pitched screams of American naval artillery shells stepping on each other filled the air with more sound than it could hold. It seemed like a train of shells was parading nose to tail from right to left across the sky. The deeper throated roar and less frequent shots from the Japanese ships went the other way. Once Clyde and Neville realized they were spectators and not the main event, they were able to take their hearts out of their mouths. The opposing salvoes were loud, but no worse than several high speed express trains roaring through a station at the same time. Fired from fifteen miles away by Heavy Hitter, the American battleships, the shells plunged down toward the Japanese.

Unlike the previous fight, the first salvo from the big guns missed. The shells fell short by several hundred yards.

At the sound of the arriving shells, Clyde dropped down on the floor of his pilot's station. Even though the huge waterspouts occurred several miles away, both men remained flat on the raised deck until the spouts collapsed on themselves. Cautiously they got up to see what had happened. They looked at one fleet, turned and looked at the other group of ships, trying to gauge who was closest.

Neville swiveled his head back and forth several more times. "Remember that pinball machine we played with back in thirty-eight? I think we're about to find out how that ball felt."

"No need to worry, Mate. You and me, we've always been lucky. I bet the Yank ships miss us by at least a hundred yards, and then Kilroy will be in the shallows."

"That would be nice, only the thing is, that slant eyed fella is a bit closer."

Admiral Shima's task force was not only late to the party, it was smaller than its predecessor, Nishimura. The two probably had meant to conduct a joint attack. Yet again, fortune smiled on the American Navy. The barge, too small to be bothered with, continued north toward Leyte's southern shore while the two navies pounded away at each other. Since the Japanese ships had gotten so close to Clyde and Neville, it didn't hurt being in a Japanese barge.

The enemy destroyer closest to them fired its torpedoes, giving the two Englishmen a scare. One of the deadly weapons was tracking right at them. By the time they saw its wake, they didn't have time to do anything. The faint white line in the water pointed right at Kilroy. Things were happening too fast for them to do anything but hold on to the railing, close their eyes and offer a very short prayer. Death was only a few feet away and they did not expect to be greeted by trumpets and angels.

Neville started counting. At five, he opened his eyes wondering what was taking so long. They were still in the land of the living. Pleasantly surprised, he turned around and saw the white line disappearing to the east. Their private barge only drew two feet of water. The Japanese Long Lance torpedo, designed to kill large ships, not barges, was set to run several feet deeper.

The battle between Shima's ships and the Americans was getting louder as destroyers from both groups approached each other. It looked like the most northern Japanese destroyer and Kilroy were aiming for the same patch of water close to the coast. Clyde and Neville knew a tie was not to their benefit.

"Slow down," said Neville. "Let him pass us, then head for shore."

As if the Japanese Captain had heard him, machine guns near the ship's bow, meant to protect against aircraft, fired at them. He needed to make sure the men dressed in a hodgepodge of clothes, not the Emperor's uniform, in possession of his Emperor's property did not escape their fate. The machine guns created several lines of jumping waterspouts drawing a line toward the barge. The distance, however, was too great for accurate fire by the fifty-caliber guns, but it wouldn't be that way for long. Clyde frantically spun the steering wheel. He needed to turn the slow, maneuverable barge away from the destroyer who swung to its right to follow them.

The fast approaching destroyer's bow stayed lined up on Kilroy's mid-section. Moving at better than twenty-knots, the ship heeled to its left as it swung to its right. Even with the gunners getting better, only a handful of shots actually hit.

Keeping lined up on their small target from an unstable platform required skill and luck. It also required the gunners to remain exposed as large shells fired at their ship from miles away, exploded close by throwing up waterspouts and drenching the ship with seawater and shrapnel. Men exposed on deck firing at the barge were eviscerated by small and large pieces of flying metal only to be quickly replaced by others.

Clyde kept his eye on their adversary. When he saw the ship leaning to its left, he changed course back toward land. Replacement gunners could not compensate for the changing angle quickly enough. Other gunners positioned farther back along the ship's waist took valuable seconds finding the range. Clyde and Neville, a modern day David, tried to stay out of Goliath's reach, while men on the distant American cruisers and battleships, using improved fire-control radar were also trying to hit their targets.

* * *

The American captains, well aware of the Japanese habit of sending off torpedoes in the middle of a surface action kept a sharp watch. They guided their ships around several of the deadly weapons, but not all of them. DD three-four-nine moved to its right so quickly to avoid one, it looked like it skipped sideways. Unfortunately, it could not do it a second time. A torpedo penetrated the hull under turret number one and exploded just behind the magazine. The forward half of the ship erupted with flames. Smoke climbed hundreds of feet in the air. Water poured in, flooding the magazine and drowning more than fifty members of the crew in the forward section of the ship.

Even with all compartments sealed against flooding, the intense heat caused the fires to spread quickly. It was a mortal wound. The Captain found himself thrown to the deck by the explosion. As soon as he could get up, he ordered "All stop." The ship's forward motion slowed, but not fast enough. Its movement continued to push water through the gaping hole in the hull collapsing internal bulkheads. By the time he could think clearly, there was only one more order for the Captain to give. "Abandon ship."

*   *   *

The Commander of the Japanese destroyer smiled. He ordered speed reduced and the helm hard-a-port to line up on the pesky barge that should already have been sunk. Being kept in port to conserve valuable fuel oil had reduced his crew's gunnery skills. No matter–this was good practice for them.

Large caliber shells crossed the sky. The sound they dragged behind assaulted ears with a heart-stopping roar. Hidden under the roar were several other sounds as smaller caliber shells fell out of the sky. The Commander grabbed onto his ship and held his breath.

The shells, as tall as a well-built man landed closer to Kilroy than the destroyer. The explosions generating large waves grabbed the insignificant barge and flung it toward the nearby Leyte shoreline. Kilroy and its crew of two was sent surfing toward a peaceful looking beach. Abruptly, it stopped when the vessel was shoved onto a coral outcropping. The boat bumped and scraped over the rock-hard organism. It finally came to rest with its stern in the water, its bow in the air, hung up on an exposed portion of the reef.

An instant later, an eight-inch shell fired by a cruiser, slammed down through the roof of the Japanese destroyer's radio shack, exploding in the officer's wardroom. The entire superstructure and lower decks amidships disintegrated. In a flash, half the officers and one-third of the ship's sailors disappeared. No one remained to issue orders. The bridge became a tangled mass of smoking metal smeared with blood. Several hull seams below the waterline blew open and fires raged out of control all the way down to the keel. Forcibly separated into two groups, the crew fought the fire and flooding from the bow and stern. The undamaged engines kept the ship moving until the engineer, the most senior of the remaining officers, received the damage reports and shut down his boilers. The ship slowly lost headway as it approached shallow water. With heroic efforts by some of the crew, the fires came under control, while flooding continued until the ship came to a halt, down by the bow, stuck in mud near the shore.

* * *

The second battle of the Surigao Strait soon became a one-sided affair. Admiral Shima's late-arriving fleet was all but annihilated by the American fleet's overwhelming firepower. Even Japan's superior torpedoes could not save a fleet so badly outmatched. The engineer of the Japanese destroyer sinking into the mud made a quick assessment of the ship he now commanded. He ended one of the shortest commands in history by ordering the crew to abandon ship. A nearby cruiser, badly damaged, but still seaworthy picked up survivors trapped on the stern. Caught without a lifeboat, the men on the bow jumped into the water and made their way ashore, to be picked up by one of the cruiser's boats. Following orders, the American ships did not pursue their mortally wounded enemy. There was still danger out there and the landings, above all else, had to be protected.

By 0800 the only Japanese remaining in the Strait were long past caring as their bodies floated west with the current.

* * *

With their barge stuck on the coral reef, Clyde and Neville happily discovered they were being ignored by both navies. Clyde looked down at the water and then at the beach several hundred yards away. "What do we do now? I ain't never learned to walk on water."

Neville pointed behind his friend. "Hand me that rope. I'll climb down and see what's holding us here."

After carefully planting his feet on the uneven coral, he found that, in between waves, the water only came up to his thighs. He held on to the rope getting a feel for the pull and surge as water spilled across the reef. After the third wave, he let go of the rope. He had a good idea of how long he could be away from his lifeline before another surge tried to sweep him away.

Neville cautiously bent down, and looked at the underside of the barge. His internal clock got him to stand up and hold on before another wave hit him. The center of the hull near the bow rested on a finger of coral. The barge wasn't about to go anywhere until they found a way to break free of the coral.

No thicker than a man's arm, the coral had them at its mercy. Neville shook his head in disgust and climbed back up. It appeared Kilroy might be stuck on the reef for the duration. The situation was going to take a lot of thinking. Confident that eventually he would come up with a solution to their predicament, he thought about their much-delayed breakfast and the restorative powers of a nap on their open-air, ocean-view balcony as, in the distance, the war continued.

Chapter 28

Why Not?

October 26, 1944
Time – 0900

At some point in its recent past, the barge had been used as a workboat. Piled against the rear bulkhead under where the control station extended out over the well deck, were various items used in constructing buildings out of local materials. Clyde rooted through the pile pulling out material he planned to use to construct a sunshade over part of the vessel. A resident of the tropics for almost twenty-five years, he placed a high priority on having protection from the sun.

He carried several armfuls of material up to the control station. Bamboo poles, mosquito netting, and rope were the primary ingredients he used to construct a shelter. With their living quarters assembled, Clyde piled some pieces of thatching against the short forward wall of the control station and sat down to enjoy the view while Neville slept or did a good job of faking it.

The only thing marring the peaceful scene was the smoking hull of the Japanese destroyer stuck in the mud less than a mile away. The Strait, so violent only hours before, went about its task of cleaning up, carrying off the less permanent bits and pieces of the battle for ocean burial.

Clyde chastised himself for thinking of the occasional body parts floating among the debris, as bits and pieces. He knew it was wrong, but three years of war had hardened him to what it did to people. Staring at the water flowing by, his vision blurred…eyelids drooped. Starting to nod off, he realized something wasn't right. His eyes opened wide, searching to find what his brain said he should look at.

A head, surrounded by the collar of a life jacket moved. The face turned toward him. A hand came out of the water, feebly waved, and fell back. Whoever the desperate man might be, American or Japanese, officer or enlisted–he had not given up his tenuous grip on life. From his comfortable spot on the damaged barge, Clyde might be the man's last chance, his only chance at survival.

Clyde stood helpless and watched, unable to reach the man floating by on the current. Frantically he looked for something to throw to the lad, more than a hundred yards away. His own fear of drowning helped him understand what the fellow was feeling. Where only moments before, Clyde had been prepared to accept *Kilroy's* condition as a permanent reef ornament, he now rooted through the materials on board looking for something he could use to free the barge and rescue that one man. He had a mission–to save the life of a man he had never met.

Neville turned his head to escape being disturbed by Clyde's digging. When the problem didn't go away, he said, "What are you banging around in that rubbish for? We had a long night and I need a nap."

Clyde stopped pushing things around and looked at the almost inert body of his partner. "Get over here, Mate. I need that brain you say is so wonderful."

Neville humored Clyde by getting up and moving close to him. "What's gotten into you?"

Clyde looked up. "It ain't all rubbish, not all of it. We need to get this thing off this reef. A minute ago, the current swept a lad by. He was too weak to swim over. We can save him, if…"

"That's a big if, Mate. What exactly do you think we can use to get our front–end back in the water?"

Clyde shrugged. "That's why I called you. You have ideas all the time."

"Coming up with a way out of this situation would be simple if that radio had been built better."

"Forget the radio. It ain't going to be any different than when we tried it an hour ago. It got knocked about when that wave hit. Probably broke a couple of tubes, or whatever. Nothing we could do about it. But, we need to get *Kilroy* moving. That lad won't last very long, even if the water is hot enough to take a bath."

"Will you please calm down. I can see getting off of here is important to you, but just how important? Would you still want to get off, even if it might be a wee bit dangerous?"

Clyde frowned. "How dangerous? No…never you mind. No one deserves to die like that."

Neville took a moment to gather his thoughts before telling Clyde his idea. He had thought about one way that might work−if it didn't kill them, which was why he hadn't mentioned it before. Staying alive seemed to be a full-time job and this might be a step too far, but then, none of his other ideas had killed them.

With thick pieces of roof thatching tied to their legs as protection against the sharp coral, both men worked under the barge, kneeling on the sharp living rock. They alternated between drowning and almost drowning as waves swept across the reef.

"How many of these do we have?" asked Clyde as he held up a hand grenade.

"Nine."

"You going to save any for later?"

Neville shook his head. “It’s all or nothing, Mate. We tie them on around the coral, get as far away as we can, and shoot at them.”

“How far away is far enough?”

“Just as far away as you can be and still hit one of them with your pistol.”

“Why not use a carbine? We have a better chance of hitting one and we can be farther away.”

“Think you can keep yourself steady lying in the water bobbing up and down on top of some bamboo, hold the rifle with two hands, and hit your target from a distance of more than a hundred feet? Personally, I doubt it.”

“All right. You win. Pass me some more rope and I’ll finish tying these things on.”

They tied the last of the hand grenades on as close to the base of the coral shaft as possible. By the time he finished, Clyde’s hands were raw from both handling the native rope and touching the coral. Neville’s job was to keep Clyde from being swept off the reef by the waves while he tied the explosives onto one side of the coral shaft.

“You hold on to our climbing rope while I put your raft together.”

“My raft? What about you?” The way Clyde felt about water, there wasn’t any way he would go out alone, even with a rope to pull himself back. The very last place he intended to be was in deep water without a boat.

“I’ll be in the water right alongside wearing a life vest ready to catch you, if you start to slide off.”

“Brilliant. Me and my big mouth. I had to ask you to come up with an idea. Next time I do that, please hit me.”

“It will be my pleasure. Now, let’s get going. The tide is coming in. Pretty soon those grenades will be totally submerged and there ain’t any way you can hit them if they’re underwater.”

Clyde held onto the bamboo pole raft with a death grip, even though he wore a life vest. He tried not to move as Neville towed him away from *Kilroy*. The farther out they went, the harder the current pushed them to the west. It made Neville's work a lot more tiring, but they needed to keep the hand grenades in view.

"All right now. I'm going to the other end of the raft and try to keep us from drifting away. Get your artillery ready." Neville got into position and started kicking to push against the raft and hold it in place.

"I'm ready. Just get your arse around there and keep me steady. We've taken too long with this already." Clyde pulled his pistol out from inside his shirt, held the weapon in both hands, aimed, and fired.

Neville flinched with each shot. He fully expected to be hit with flying…whatever, if Clyde ever managed to hit the explosives.

"That's your fifth shot, Mate. Think you've got those things scared yet? How about hitting one before my legs give out."

Stung by Neville's disparaging remark, Clyde took his time, steadied his breathing, brought his handgun on target, waited until the grenades were centered in a wave trough and pulled the trigger. With Clyde's fear of water, Neville knew his partner wasn't going to willingly get off his raft when the grenades blew. They were a little over fifty-feet from the reef when the bullet hit one of the grenades. The blast started out loud and got worse from there. The little bombs exploded one, two, and three at a time.

Neville didn't react as quickly as he thought he would, but he still pulled Clyde into the water before any projectiles hit him. Small and large pieces of coral flew in all directions. The barge jumped like a bucking horse with each explosion. A number of coral pieces embedded themselves deep into the bamboo of the raft. Neville had saved Clyde from some serious injuries and infections, which didn't earn him any thanks as Clyde's arms wind-milled, slapping at the water. The instant the explosions stopped, Neville pushed his mate up against the raft.

Clyde spit out the last of the saltwater, turned and looked at *Kilroy*. He expected to see it quietly floating alongside the reef. Neville's face showed his surprise. The finger of coral, pitted, gouged, and scorched, but still vertical, held the barge in the air, even if it did seem to be leaning ever-so-slightly to its right.

"You said it would work."

Neville shook his head. "I did not say that. You're trying to put words in my mouth. I said I had an idea that I thought *might* work."

"Well, it didn't. So, what are you going to do now? That lad is floating farther away every minute."

"I know he is, but I don't have any more ideas–at least not right this second. So, what am *I* going to do? I'm going to climb that rope, then hang *my* clothes out to dry, and find something for *me* to eat. And…if you want me to help you back onboard, don't say another word. Understand?"

"But…"

Neville held a hand up. "Stop. Not a word and I mean it. That was the only way I thought might get us free with what little we have. Thank goodness, it didn't work."

"What do you mean? Don't you want to save that man from drowning and get out of here?"

"Of course I do. What I mean is, all the hand grenades would have had to explode at one time to blast through that coral. We would have been successful *and dead.* We weren't far enough away to survive, if they all went off at the same time."

Clyde needed time to think through what his friend said, hating the idea that he might be right.

They climbed back onto *Kilroy's* deck in silence and stripped out of their clothes, laying them out to dry. With the humidity over eighty percent it was going to take awhile.

With his arms crossed, Clyde walked around the well deck wearing only his shorts until he stood near Neville. "When you lay things out all neat like… I can live with the fact that your idea didn't work, but I still have faith in you. Just keep thinking. You'll figure out something that does, and if you don't take too long we can still save that fellow. However, he is getting farther away every minute."

Clyde leaned back against the right side of the barge to give Neville the space needed to think up another idea. As soon as his back touched the wall, he found himself sliding sideways. He reached out to a cleat to steady himself and missed. He ended up on his left side on the deck.

"What happened?" he said from the floor, immediately after a grinding crunch stopped. The barge shifted, and leaned even more to its right. The deck slanting at least thirty degrees. They crawled across to the short ladder up to the control station and then to the rope hanging over the side.

Neville got in position to go down and see what had changed. "You stay up here. I may need you to get something for me."

"Be careful, Mate. Don't let this thing drop on you. I'm too old to start looking for another partner."

Neville had already started down the rope, hand over hand. He stopped, looked up and opened his mouth ready to say something and thought better of it. He simply smirked and shook his head at his best friend trying to hide how much he really cared.

Leaning under the barge, Neville yelled, "A piece of the coral broke away. ain't much holding the old girl up. Pass me one of the carbines and I'll try and shoot the rest of it loose."

With the weapon in one hand, Neville picked his way across the reef as far as he could go and still keep the obstinate finger of coral in view. "Hold on," he yelled, and shot an entire clip of ammunition. Dime sized pieces of the living rock sprayed out with the impact of each shot. He inserted the spare clip they always kept attached to the stocks of their weapons. Frustrated at the coral finger not breaking he used the second magazine without stopping to check the results.

With his feet braced and knees bent, Neville fought the waves flowing across the reef. The coral was definitely the worse for his assault, but so what? It still held the barge out of the water. He debated whether he should use up the rest of their limited amount of ammunition or admit defeat. Hitting his head against a wall wasn't new to him and over the years he had accumulated the bruises to show for it. None of that made him feel any better as he picked his way back to Kilroy.

He grabbed the rope. As soon as his feet came out of the water, there was a loud crack. Kilroy trembled, acting as if it was a living being and had been shot.

Neville's hands slipped. He fell into the water on his back and went under, having barely enough time to close his mouth. Clyde was leaning over the side ready to help his friend up. *Kilroy* moved again. This time it was a sliding motion as the barge tilted to its left. The entire left side was in the water when the movement stopped. Clyde, holding on for dear life kept yelling Neville's name as he peered down at the disturbed water.

The left side was in the water, but the right side was still in the air, stubbornly held in place by the coral finger. Neville's head reappeared, his coughing announcing his great desire to take his place among the world's land-dwelling, two-legged, air breathing mammals.

Neville once again grabbed the rope and started up. With several feet to go, he stopped when Clyde pointed out toward the Strait and yelled, "Hold on. There's a big wave coming in."

This time, he held on for his life as the foaming water surged around and under the barge. He tightened his grip on the rope an instant before being buried under water. Shoved against the side of the barge, the water spun Neville around and dragged him back and forth, bouncing along the hull like a bent metronome. He didn't dare let go and managed to get his legs wrapped around the rope. The wave lifted *Kilroy* and shoved it across the reef toward shore as if it was a child's rubber duck in a bathtub.

The receding wave tried to pull the barge back across the reef but failed. Kilroy settled down, drifting quietly on the small waves inside the reef line. Neville ended up too weak and battered to realize his arms and legs had become entwined in the rope. Had they not, he would have been thrown onto the reef and drowned. He waited for his lungs to resume functioning before finding the strength to loosen himself from the rope's rough embrace.

With Clyde looking on from above, he pulled himself out of the water and onto *Kilroy's* control platform, still spitting and coughing. His shorts had been reduced to nothing more than a cloth waistband and his body was covered with scrapes and cuts. When his eyes could finally focus, he saw Clyde's concerned and grinning face only inches away.

"Brilliant. You did it, Mate. You broke us free."

"Not me, that wave did it."

"All right. If that's the way you want it, I won't make you out to be a hero." Clyde turned and looked down into the well deck to see if it was still dry. It wasn't. "Come along, then. Let's check this thing for leaks and get after that bloke. It's been almost three hours since I saw him."

Chapter 29

The Wave

October 26, 1944
Time – 1200

Clyde pointed at his partner's state of un-dress. "If I was a woman in need of servicing, I might be impressed with your lack of high fashion clothing. But, since I ain't–go find yourself something to wear. After that you can help me stuff things in all the places where you allowed *Kilroy* to hurt herself."

"Himself."

"What?"

"*Kilroy* is a man's name." Neville spread his arms. "And now all of *this* is my fault? Blaming someone else isn't very sporting, ol' boy. Not sporting at all."

Clyde opened his mouth to present a counter-argument. Before any sound came out, Neville held up a hand. "Ah-ah, now don't say anything you'll regret, since I've already forgiven you. After all, you haven't been living with civilized society for some time."

"Too right. I've been living with you. Now go make yourself decent. While we're talking, our private yacht is sinking."

Pieces of roof thatching made from woven palm fronds, liberally soaked in engine oil and cut to size worked well as plugs in a dozen or more places. The floor of the barge looked as if someone had used it for target practice–dimpled, punctured, and torn where it slammed down on to the reef. Even a few seams where the floor plates came together had separated under the pounding. There wasn't anything they could do to repair the hairline thin gaps since they needed to be welded or filled with some old-fashioned tar caulking. The pump they used earlier was going to have to see them through. If not…well, then they would need to see if option number two, what ever that might be, worked. Only time would tell.

"All right. It's time for you to start praying," said Clyde an hour later when he put his hand on the control console, turned on the ignition and held his finger over the starter button.

"You want me to pray? You were the one that almost made it to altar boy."

"That's why I didn't. They caught me faking my prayers." To prevent any more discussion on the subject or his fall from grace, Neville pointed at Clyde's hand. "Push the bloomin' button!"

The engine made all the proper sounds without ever actually starting. After several tries, Clyde turned the switch off and announced to his audience of one, "Maybe it's flooded. I'll give it fifteen minutes and then try again."

Neville nodded. "Come on. We can dig through our bags in the meantime and find something to eat. I know you want to get after that bloke, but not eating isn't going to help. We missed lunch, and I don't remember breakfast, do you?"

They each wolfed down a can of spam before returning to the problem at hand. They owned a reasonably buoyant boat, the water was calm, and the enemy was nowhere in sight. *Kilroy's* engine making a putt-putt sound was all they needed to take up the chase. Clyde turned the switch, Neville hit the button and the engine started without a single complaint. Neville smiled at his mate. "See, all you have to do is treat it with respect."

Clyde held up a fist. "I could show you some respect, but I want to find that sailor."

"It ain't going to be easy, but I'm with you. Put this thing in gear and get going."

Moving with the current, *Kilroy* was able to exceed its maximum speed. Clyde steered and Neville patrolled the well deck repairing their patchwork where necessary. After traveling west for almost an hour, Neville rejoined Clyde and the two of them began scanning the water and shoreline. In the scheme of things, saving one life after a battle of such ferocity would go without notice, but to Clyde and Neville, a successful rescue would help them justify many of the unpleasant things they'd done during the course of the war.

Neville took his eyes off the water and looked up at the sky. "If we don't find him in the next hour or so…"

"I know. It'll be too dark." Clyde gave an involuntary shiver. "Don't know which way I'd prefer to go, drowning or a shark. What about you?"

"It ain't something you can choose. In a situation like this, either one can happen and that's the end of it. Hey. You're drifting out of the middle."

"I know. The Strait bends to the right. I'm going to get us closer to the left side. He might have gotten pushed that way by the current and been able to get ashore."

"Good thinking. Who gave you the idea?"

The barge's engine was the only sound they heard other than the shrill squeal of a few birds flying low scanning the water for dinner. The closer the barge got to shore and the bend in the Strait, the more floating debris they encountered. Clyde's idea was bearing fruit, but they had not found the one man who had given them a life-or-death mission. His young face, smeared with diesel fuel had looked so lonely and scared staring back at him, his hair plastered to his scalp–a result of the fuel oil. Clyde needed to find him as a way of saving himself–providing some personal justification for the life he led.

Neville used his binoculars to scan the muddy shoreline for anything that looked like a floating body. He concentrated so hard on trying to find that one sailor, he at first missed a group of them on shore sitting on logs where the mud changed to green jungle. Only when some of them jumped up and started waving did he realize who they were. While looking for one man, they had found more than fifty, suddenly happy Yanks.

Clyde steered toward shore. When the barge's bottom touched the mud, Neville dropped the ramp. The last vestiges of *Kilroy's* face on the bow disappeared in the mud. The men, all Americans, were in every condition imaginable. Clothed or unclothed–injured or totally unscathed–mentally alert, in a daze, or unconscious. They were all survivors of the battle and almost all from DD349, the destroyer that had been sunk with a hit under its forward gun mount. A Lieutenant, j.g. was the senior of the two officers. The other was a freshly minted Ensign. The Lieutenant tried to sit up. His right leg, wrapped with living vines to hold a pair of makeshift splints in place restricted his movement.

When they stepped off the barge's ramp, Neville gave his hurriedly prepared speech. "Welcome aboard Yanks. The Australian Coast Watcher Service and its Philippine island commuter barge are happy to provide you with transportation back to your fleet." A few of the men, who decided to slip into the jungle to escape what they thought might be a boatload of Japanese soldiers, turned around and stumbled toward the water. Neville had forgotten that they were in an enemy barge. He also forgot about raising their flag until he concluded his little speech.

The water that continued to seep into the barge had gotten over a foot deep, by the time Neville dropped the ramp. Most of it ran down the ramp, the remainder would be pumped over the side with the help of the barge's new crew, as long as the pump continued to work.

While Clyde scanned the group, searching for the face that had begun to haunt him, he looked hard at anyone who might be smeared with fuel oil, Neville greeted the men streaming aboard. He tried to distribute them according to their condition. The injured or weak were given spots where they could lean against a sidewall.

"What ship are you attached to?" asked Lieutenant Flynn, as two men carried him to a place along the rear wall.

"The *Kilroy*," answered Neville.

"Never heard of it. Australian?"

"I guess you might say that."

"How far away is the *Kilroy.* Some of these men need medical attention."

"This is the *Kilroy*, Lieutenant. I'm the Captain, and that," he pointed at Clyde, "is my crew. Our radio ain't working, so the closest ships we know about are at the invasion beach, the other end of the Strait. Don't know how long it will take to get there–maybe all night."

"That's going to be hard on the men. Some of them were in the water for over eight hours, scared of being torn apart by sharks. In fact, we know of at least three that were."

"Sorry to hear that and of course, we'll do what we can, but *Kilroy* wasn't built to win any races."

"You finding us is a miracle so all I can ask is for you to do your best. These men need rest and medical attention."

Neville called to Clyde. "Hey, Mate. How we doing. Ready to get going?"

Clyde stood on the lip of the ramp helping men aboard, still examining each one to see if he might be the sailor seen floating a few hours ago. Almost everyone was on board when the last six men lifted three bodies from the beach, carried them up the ramp and laid them out near the bow. Instantly, Clyde knew where his missing sailor was. His excitement at finding the men evaporated. He was too late. In a subdued voice, he set several men to work raising the bow ramp.

With Clyde once again at the helm, *Kilroy* plowed through the water toward their fleet somewhere to the east. The passengers they had acquired came from every specialty on the destroyer. The signalman dived into the radio, but soon learned that it wouldn't work without new tubes. The lone corpsman, without any medical supplies still tried to minister to the injured. The rest of the survivors stayed out of the way, while hoping to see another naval vessel around every bend or point of land.

The two Englishmen stood together watching the shoreline slowly slide by. "I finally worked it out."

"Worked what out?" asked Neville, "How old you are?"

"Don't be silly. I know how old I am. The same as you. What I figured out is, it's going to take us a lot longer to get back to where we came from than it did to get here. We're going against the current. I was hoping, for the sake of all these boys, that we'd come across a big ship real soon."

"I was thinking the same thing. Wish we had more to give them."

"My sentiments, exactly. That's why I think we shouldn't try to find a friendly ship tonight."

Neville looked at his partner in surprise. "But they need help, now."

"Brilliant. Of course they do. That's why we should stop at that Japanese destroyer stuck in the mud near the reef we were on. A lot of it is burned out, but there are still some usable areas and we might be able to find some food and water."

Their shadows had gotten longer, extending out over the water. Night in the tropics came fast, unlike the higher latitudes. Clyde flipped a switch for the barge's spotlight. He alternated lighting the main channel looking for obstructions and the northern shoreline looking for the abandoned destroyer. The light showed an unbroken wall of greenery along their left side, until an hour later, it changed to the unnaturally straight lines of a warship tilted onto its port side. All of his worries disappeared, as if missing the disabled ship had never occurred to him.

Their large crew tied the barge to the nets hanging from the starboard side of the abandoned ship, near the stern. The most able bodied of the crew climbed the nets first and with a few emergency flashlights started to explore. One man borrowed Clyde's pistol and another carried his carbine, although the only danger they encountered were some confused rats. Their search quickly turned up a dozen emergency battle lanterns inside the ship. The lights not only allowed everyone to get involved in setting up housekeeping on the open rear deck, it raised their spirits and brought them a unity of purpose.

All of a sudden, Clyde and Neville felt unnecessary. The Lieutenant, from his position propped up against the base of a gun tub, called sailors to him in groups of two or three. They listened a minute and then scurried off, disappearing through various openings in the ship. Two sailors popped out of a hatch and called out "Doc." The medical corpsman quickly finished what he was doing, jumped up and followed them back into the ship.

The majority of the sailors were from the engineering department, but there were enough naval specialties represented to provide a large base of knowledge. Unfortunately, one of the departments not represented, was damage control. They were the jack-of-all-trades men, who had to think fast in an emergency.

The corpsman set up his open-air hospital ward with supplies found in the ship's sickbay. The engineers started exploring the engine room, the cooks found the galley, the electricians located the auxiliary generator, and the gunners made sure some of the fifty caliber machine guns were operational. No longer survivors, they were winners. Their voices exhibited their optimism–their renewed self-confidence. They had established a beachhead–of sorts, on the southern shore of Leyte. Anyone who challenged them, would do so at their peril.

With Neville leading, the two coast watchers waited for a break in the line of men getting instructions from or reporting to Flynn. They walked over and stooped. “Lieutenant, Clyde and I want you to know how much we appreciate what your men are doing, after being in the water for so long. If this ship wasn’t sitting on the bottom, I think you’d be getting up steam to chase after those Nips.”

“Mister Arnold, Mister…Saunders. That’s right, isn’t it?” Neville nodded. “You two are the ones *we* need to thank. If you hadn’t come after us…” The Lieutenant’s face twisted as a pain from his badly broken leg made him grimace.

Neville moved a little closer. “Is there anything we can do for you?”

“Thank you for asking, but no, I’ll survive.” All three men looked up at the same time. One after another, different sections of deck lights came on. For an instant, everyone felt exposed, naked–vulnerable. They knew being in a well-lit area could be deadly. Darkness was synonymous with safety. War had reversed their perceptions of reality and as nice as it was to be able to clearly see what they were doing, they did not feel safe, but for the moment, the light was welcome. “Things are looking up. It seems, gentlemen, my engineers and electricians found the auxiliary generator.”

The disabled and abandoned enemy destroyer had become an island of light in a world otherwise devoid of it. The borders of their world expanded to the edges of the pool of light surrounding them. Within that world, the only movement was the water flowing around the hull. Outside of it, the enemy lurked, fighting to retain his control over a hostile land and its people.

The operating generator opened up new possibilities. The lieutenant called together a fire fighting crew. They began probing through the destroyed sections of the ship, finding and extinguishing areas still smoldering. One area where the heat kept getting worse was located deep in the hull at the forward end of the damaged area. Even when all evidence of a fire had been dealt with, the place still remained too hot to tolerate for more than a few minutes. Things got exciting when one crewmember opened a hatch into the next compartment and found it stacked head-high with ammunition. Suddenly, no one felt tired. Their new home was in danger of being snatched out from under them. More than half the crew took their positions and established an assembly line, dumping the forty and sixty pound cases of small arms ammunition into the water.

Having electric power made other things possible. The two cooks, with an entire galley at their disposal put together a meal. Many of the food items were more foreign to them than the equipment they used, but the men pronounced it edible and filling. Pumps activated by electric power, pressurized the fresh water system. Once isolation valves were located to shut off flow to the damaged areas of the ship, showers were rigged on deck and each man had a two-minute shower. Feeling clean, with full stomachs and no one shooting at them, they prepared to sack out.

Six injured men still needed a doctor, but even they were in better shape than a few hours earlier. The corpsman made one last circuit of his patients before the deck lights were turned off.

"Time to put our heads down, ol' boy." Neville, hands on hips, said to Clyde as they looked around at the men spread over the ship's rear deck. "We did some grand work today without much effort. What do you think we can do tomorrow?"

"It all depends on the Admirals."

"How do they figure into anything?"

"The more orders they give, the more difficult it is for us to get anything done."

"In your quaint, uneducated way, I think what you mean is, as long as we have a busted radio, the big men can't tell us what to do."

"Can't deny the uneducated part. Never had much use for books, but that don't mean I ain't the smart one here. And just to prove it, I'm going back to *Kilroy* for a moment."

Clyde swung his legs over the railing and climbed down to their barge. He quickly returned with their somewhat battered Yank flag, which he held up for Neville to see. "I think we need to put our claim in for salvage rights before anyone else steps up. But, I have a question. Let's see who the smart one is."

Neville's eyebrows went up. "You sure you want to do this? I win every time."

"Maybe… Tell me, mister brains, what is the proper way for me to hang this flag on this ship?"

"Oh, come on now. Everybody knows that. The section with the stars is the top."

"Anything else?"

"You're trying to trick me, ain't you? No there ain't anything else."

Clyde smiled knowingly. He walked to the rear of the deck and lowered the Japanese flag still hanging there. He replaced it with the American flag and then clipped the Japanese flag on under it, before raising them both.

"What did you put the Nip flag back on for?"

"I thought you were smart. That shows that we captured a Jap ship, although I would prefer if we had an Aussie flag."

"I salute you. I never knew about that critical piece of naval etiquette. Now let's get some sleep. Soon as its daylight we need to get these fellows to a proper ship."

With so many men available, no one had to stand guard for longer than an hour. Near midnight, the man on duty woke Clyde and Neville.

Clyde batted away the man's hand. "Go away. I'll wake up when the sun decides to come up."

The seaman whispered to the pair. “You need to get up. Something is moving out there in the Strait and I didn’t want to wake Lieutenant Flynn.”

“More survivors?” Neville came awake, the idea of being looked upon as someone’s savior was new to him, but it felt good. The possibility of being able to save some more sailors from the growing number of fins slicing through the black water off their stern made him perk up.

Without taking his eyes off the *something* he sensed more than saw, the sailor, hesitantly said, “No-o. Don’t think so.”

Clyde grabbed hold of Neville’s pants waist and dragged himself up. His blood pressure was still in sleep mode when a blinding flash occurred only a mile away. “Blimey…” was the only word he could get out before the crash of gunfire hit their ears. A shell exploded in the water a hundred feet from the stern. Water cascaded over many of the survivors. Hopefully, the shot had been a warning. It couldn’t have landed any closer.

The force of the explosion made Clyde stumble. He fell to his knees, dragging Neville with him. Before he could get up, a spotlight from the intruder snapped on nailing everyone to the deck. They couldn’t run and they couldn’t fight.

The same thought ran through everyone’s mind–their enemy had returned to salvage the stuck-in-the-mud destroyer. Their fear of being captured had been realized.

A voice boomed through a loudspeaker from across the water. The distance and the sudden turn of events made the words unintelligible. The searchlight moved back and forth across the ship’s stern. At the end of one of its passes, the two flags, one over the other, became visible. The light moved away, stopped, and then jerked back. It stayed there as the voice, asked, “Friend or foe? This is the USS *Timberon.* Who’s in command?”

Neville didn’t wait for a committee to figure that out. Delay might be fatal. He yelled back, “Lieutenant Flynn, US Navy.”

One of the engineering crew survivors ducked into a passageway. A moment later, all of the deck lights came on. Fifty pairs of hands frantically waved and throats became raw from shouting until the *Timberon's* searchlight was turned off.

While waiting for a motorboat to arrive from the cruiser, Clyde and Neville moved to an isolated part of the deck where they could talk without being overheard. They needed to think about the future and make some decisions. Rarely, in their day-to-day lifestyle did they ever plan for the future. It was, in fact, something that usually got in the way of having a good time. They believed planning to be highly overrated and detrimental to the enjoyment of a good hangover. Of course, *mornings after* were looked forward to with great anticipation. Without a good hangover, there wouldn't be an excuse, if one ever needed an excuse, for consuming some *hair-of-the-dog*...

Chapter 30

Two Flags

October 27, 1944

Like the rest of the crew, Clyde was curious about their intruder. He watched as the launch's coxswain settled the boat into place alongside *Kilroy* without a scratch. A half-dozen armed sailors climbed across the barge and up the net to the destroyer's deck. They formed a protective ring around their captain when he climbed over the railing.

Ensign Miller, Flynn's "go-fer," came forward and saluted. Until now, he had managed to stay in the background. He was a small man, who after a large meal might weigh 120 pounds. He had been commissioned in the Navy immediately after graduating from college at the end of the winter term, with a major in English Literature. On his first assignment, crewmembers of DD349 were still making jokes about how he always managed to get lost on the ship. One of his duties while on temporary assignment was to act as the morale officer. If a crew's morale was judged by its laughter, primarily at Miller, he had done a bang up job.

The *Timberon's* Captain, a full Commander, turned to the stern, saluted the flag and then turned to Lieutenant Flynn and returned his salute.

"Are you the senior officer, Lieutenant?"

"Yes sir."

"What's your situation, here? How can I help? I don't have much time. We've been attached to the Seventh Fleet and need to take our place in the invasion beach's protective screen by dawn."

Flynn provided a bare bones explanation of what happened.

"That's quite a story. Where are these Coast Watchers? I'd like to thank them."

"Here we be, Captain." Clyde and Neville stepped out from behind Miller. A silent message passed between them. *Don't let this fella get in our way. We were doing just fine, thank you.*

"Welcome to the Coast Watcher Navy," Clyde said with more of a smile than he intended. "What can we do for you?"

"Not a thing. I simply need to get underway as soon as possible, but I'm the one offering assistance."

Not wanting Clyde to hog the conversation, Neville said, "You know, for a navy that beat the living hell out of the Japs, you sure seem to be in a hurry. You missed a rare sight with all those ships on fire or sinking. However, we do have a radio that needs to be repaired. We can't do a very good job of watching, if we can't report what we see."

The Commander turned to one of his sailors and motioned with his hand. One of the survivor crew came forward and led the man to the radio aboard the barge.

Clyde slipped back into the conversation. "You say you're in a hurry to get to the landing area. You expecting more Japs?"

"Maybe. All I can tell you is, don't count them out. At least, not yet. Admiral Kinkaid's escort carrier groups, Taffy one, two and three were up north to protect the landing beaches. They took a hell of a beating when the Japs broke through the San Bernadino Strait yesterday. It should never have happened, but someone screwed up, real bad. The Jap battleships came through at dawn. Before we knew it, those ships along with their cruisers were firing on our small carriers at point-blank range. We didn't have the speed to get away. Our boys were launching planes and trying to dodge broadsides from sixteen-inch guns at the same time. Shells were landing all around. We lost three carriers before the destroyer screen was ordered to attack the Japs. To their credit, they did. We lost a few but it scared that Jap Admiral, Kurita. He almost had our number, but without planes of his own, he finally bugged out before Halsey's boys could get there. Battleships chasing carriers has never happened before. Someone's head is going to roll."

"Sounds like it was a good thing we were here and not there." Clyde looked around for a moment, trying to remember if they needed anything. "As far as needing anything, we're in good shape, Commander. But the Lieutenant here, and some of his men, need medical care. It would be grand, if you could take them with you and get them to a hospital ship. The rest of the men can come with us in the morning. Of course, if any of the others want to leave now or if you're short-handed, you can take as many as you need."

"I'm not short-handed, but I can take any that are willing."

"Ensign?" Flynn said with a smile on his face. "I want you to stay with the men who decide they want to rest awhile with the coast watcher navy before they get their mandatory thirty-day survivor's leave. These gentlemen might need some additional firepower, and we owe them. Follow their lead."

With two senior officers looking over his shoulder, Miller didn't waste any time taking charge. He detailed a group of men to carefully move the injured across to the *Timberon*. While this was happening, the Commander walked around the deck looking at how the Japanese mounted their guns and where, in a fight, the ship might be most vulnerable. When he finished his tour, without addressing any specific person, he asked, "Who hoisted your flags?"

Neville looked at Clyde, ready to enjoy hearing what his mate had done wrong, and at the same time, ready to defend him.

"I did. Anything wrong?" said Clyde.

"Not a thing. No…not a thing. The last time I heard of flags being flown like that on a captured ship was when I read the account of Nelson's victory at the Battle of the Nile almost a hundred and fifty years ago. You must come from a long line of deep sea sailors."

Clyde puffed up with the complement. "Can't say it's a long line, but we know a thing or two."

Neville controlled his desire to laugh and simply rolled his eyes.

Thirty-one survivors remained behind after all the injured, and a few others transferred to the *Timberon.* On one of the shuttle trips, a sailor returned their repaired radio to its position on *Kilroy.* The Commander looked around, before shaking hands with Clyde and Neville. He followed this by saluting the flag and stepped over the railing. It was time for him to get on with the war.

Clyde ordered the deck lights turned off and the two men stood by the railing imagining they could still see the *Timberon* heading east to its assigned position. After a yawn loud enough to startle a nearby sailor, Clyde said, "These fellows have done a bang-up job getting things working on this wreck. Almost seems a shame to leave it here."

"You want to take it with us?" Neville turned and put his face in front of Clyde's. "I'm all for that, just as soon as you tell me how you're going to strap it to your back."

"Don't be daft. I was simply trying to say, why not use this as our watch station instead of going back to one of the islands? We could do the job the same way and be more comfortable."

"What about our crew? It appears to me they might like to get started with their survivor's leave. What do you think?"

"It can't hurt to ask. In any case, once we check in with Cullison, we may be told to move on."

Neville kept silent for a moment. He had to agree that having all the amenities made a difference in the way a bloke approached his work. For once, Clyde made sense. "All right. Let's see what Cullison says. If he says to stay, I don't think we'll have any trouble with the young Ensign.'

"I'm sure Commander Cullison will be happy to know we're still among the living." Clyde glanced at his watch. "You better get a shake on. You need to write and encode it in time for me to get on the air at five."

Neville turned to look for paper and a pencil, as Clyde added, "Write it up good. Make us sound like bloomin' heroes and he'll have to agree."

"And if he doesn't?"

"We'll think of something. *You* always do."

* * *

The day hadn't started well for Cullison. The large tent he slept in developed a leak directly over his pillow. In addition, one of the cooks was sick and the chow line was all screwed up. To add to his misery, an instantaneous downpour caught him between the mess tent and his Quonset hut office. And now–this. For the second time, he read the message, before slamming it down on his desk. Trying for some self-control, instead of screaming, he groaned, while under his breath he cursed McCulloch for getting transferred to Burma. Why did he keep thinking his Englishmen would follow orders?

He stood up and sailed the thin piece of paper across to Harry. As soon as he understood, his Clyde and Neville warning light started to flash.

Harry took his time reading the long message, occasionally shaking his head in wonder while trying not to laugh. "You have to hand it to them, they are the only people I know that, if they were in the army, could win a medal and qualify for a court martial at the same time."

"Don't I know it. On the one hand, they somehow talk the Navy into dropping them on the wrong island, while on the other they eliminate an enemy position, give our ships a heads-up on the Jap fleet and rescue a stranded crew. I should pull them out of there, but I think it would be better to let all of this settle out for a couple of days. Otherwise, some good people are going to get hurt. There's nothing an Admiral likes more than to find fault with subordinates."

"You mean you're going to tell Clyde and Neville to stay on that ship?"

"I think that makes the most sense. Who knows, they actually might surprise me, and do something right, but odds are, they won't. I know, as sure as we're sitting here, something is going to happen. I have no idea what or where, but I'm positive neither one of us will want to know about it until they're finished. Hopefully, they won't get themselves killed."

"Do you want me to write the message, Bill?"

"Thanks, Harry. No, I'll do it. It's got to be simple and to the point." Cullison reached into a drawer and pulled out a message pad. He wrote–

> **Stay where you are until relieved. Report enemy activity.**

"I'm sure they'll find a way to create an incident and come out smelling like a…"

"Like what?"

"Haven't made up my mind, although I'm sure it won't be a rose."

Chapter 31

Beginnings

October 28, 1944

With a wistful sigh, Neville said, "If only we had..."

Clyde turned his head, careful not to affect the way he lay in one of the two hammocks. Their open-air beds hung from the depth charge racks on the destroyer's rear deck. "If only, what? We already have everything we could want."

"Not quite, my good friend, not quite. Granted, we have a comfortable place to do an easy job, with more people to do our bidding than we have any right to expect, but still…"

"Come on, out with it. You've got my curiosity up–which is exactly what you planned to do. Tell me about this thing we're missing."

"Beer, booze, alcohol, even wine. The fact is, we ain't got anything decent to drink. That stuff the Japs drink–that Sake–ain't fit for humans."

"Why is it, you're always right…once a day? Here, I thought we had it so good and you have to ruin it. You know, we wouldn't have this problem if it wasn't for the Yank Navy."

"How so?"

"They let the Nips sink their destroyer and put all these nice lads in the water. And that includes that Ensign, even if he is an officer, who, we of course saved from... Well, you know…"

"I know. We're always saving people. It's getting to be a habit. People need to learn to take care of themselves. We won't always be around, now will we?"

Ensign Miller heard them and walked over. "Gentlemen, did you call me? Do you need something fixed?"

Clyde shook his head. "The only thing that needs fixing is the lack of alcohol. Can you fix that?"

"No, sir. Although, technically, that does come under my responsibility as morale officer. However, I doubt the Navy ever expected me to have to solve a problem like that. But, if we had any alcohol, I'd be happy to sample the supplies for you."

Neville carefully turned around. "He's brighter than he looks."

"Thanks." Miller pointed toward the water. "It sure is quiet out there. We've been here a full day without seeing any activity. I know you two are probably accustomed to the quiet, but my men are having trouble adapting. They're getting restless without specific duties to perform or women to chase."

Clyde understood the woman chasing problem, but not having anything to do? That had never been a problem for him. It was one of his greatest skills. Clyde carefully raised up on one elbow. "What's your solution, Mr. Miller? Want to take the barge east and find our fleet?"

"No, sir. I don't see any need to rush things. What we need to do is keep the men occupied. I've heard both of you talking about claiming this ship as your prize, and that's fine with me, if you're serious. What I'd like to do though, is set the men some chores, cleaning and repairing."

Neville smiled. "Really? You're sure you aren't planning a mutiny to steal our ship?"

"Of course not. Working on foreign equipment will be a challenge for them, or at least, it should be, that's all."

"You want your men to start repairing this ship?" Neville thought about it for at least five seconds before waving his hand. "Go ahead. Only tell them to be careful. Don't want anyone getting hurt on our ship and make our insurance rates go up."

"That's right," Clyde chimed in. "Do you have any idea how difficult it is to find a decent insurance agent out here? And, don't forget to tell us where they're working. Right? Don't want to lose any of them."

Miller brought all of the survivors together in what remained of the crew's mess. "If this was our ship, it seems to me the first thing to do would be to find the hull damage, seal it up and then pump her dry. If we can't stop the leaks, there isn't any point in fixing anything else." He tried to make it sound as if he knew what he was doing. When no one said any different, he decided he must be on the right track.

The men were listening to him without a smirk on their faces. For the first time since he joined the crew two weeks ago to help the Captain transition into being the Commodore of their squadron he was their commanding officer–sort of–and for the time being they acted as if he really was.

He broke the group into work teams to locate the damage and figure out what needed to be done. Assuming the ship would float, the next problems to be solved would be propulsion and steering. He told his three engine room men to figure out how the Japanese engines worked and what they needed to do to get steam up. From his miniscule knowledge of a ship's propulsion system, he knew that starting a ship's engine was a lot more complicated than starting an outboard motor.

The Strait remained quiet and the men stayed busy. Things were looking up. If they actually fixed anything, it would be a bonus. The only real griping the Ensign heard was about the food. At every meal, the cooks served rice and something they said was fish.

* * *

Clyde and Neville, refreshed from their afternoon naps perked up when they saw a small group of locals paddle by in an outrigger canoe. They waved to the group. No one returned their greeting. It was as if they weren't even there. Several more canoes came south from somewhere along the Leyte coast. In one, some of the people appeared injured, but just like the other groups, no one waved back.

Neville looked up at the remains of the signal flag mast mounted on the ship's burned out bridge.

Clyde saw what his partner was doing. "What're you looking at?"

"The way these people are ignoring us, I was wondering if we had raised the quarantine flag."

"Well we raised our flags on the rear of the ship, not up there. But flag or not, we're quarantined just the same. These people have been ruled by the Nips for three years, and here we are on a Nip ship along with a Nip barge. And, as you may remember, the Jap Army ain't the nicest of fellows, even when they're friendly. With our boys kicking them out of their comfortable houses and their officers telling 'em it's time to die for the Emperor, I'll bet their taking it out on the locals. If I was these people, I'd keep as far away from this ship as I could."

"But we have a Yank flag flying." Neville turned and pointed at it. His arm still raised, he said, "Oh! We still have both flags up. Maybe they can't tell who beat who."

"Maybe–but I'll bet they live by the rule, 'Better safe than sorry.' Besides, what would you do if some of them came aboard? Good Samaritan that you are, you might have noticed that every one of them canoes had more men in them than women."

Neville stepped back and looked at Clyde. "Are you saying that I would try to take advantage of some innocent woman?"

"You might, but you wouldn't get very far. Every one of the men has a machete hanging from his belt, and I'd be bloody careful as well, turning my back on any of their women."

"Very nicely done, old chap. Now that you've convinced me to remain a bachelor tonight, why not go downstairs…"

"You mean, go below?"

"That, too, and get us some tea."

The setting sun changed the color of everything to different shades of orange and pink. It was the second most dangerous time of day on a warship in enemy waters. Even though the ship was non-mobile, that rule still applied.

A small boat holding a man, three children and two women, one quite old, came into view. Unlike all the other locals, this group changed course and paddled toward them when they saw the American flag.

"Look smart, old chap, we're about to have some visitors." Clyde pointed at the small boat.

The man tied the boat up to Kilroy and after an animated discussion, he came across and climbed the boarding net. He removed his straw hat, clutched it to his chest and bowed, deeply. His knees locked, he bent his body into an "L," his face pointed at the deck and stayed that way, long after he should have returned to a normal position.

Clyde looked to Neville, who, in return, shrugged *I don't know*. "Maybe he's from the backcountry and to him, any foreigner is a Nip."

Several of the sailors saw the unusual encounter and walked over. One of them, an old timer who had served in the Yangtze River Patrol said, "You need to tell him to stand up, Mister Arnold, otherwise he won't ever move. The Japs make them do that. If your bow ain't proper like, they might take your head off with one of them fancy swords."

Clyde nodded to the sailor. He walked over to the local man, put his hands on the man's shoulders, and pulled him up. When he stood upright, words flooded out, non-stop. Finished with his tale, he looked around, expectantly. No one responded, so he repeated himself, accompanying his words with frantic gestures, pointing at his boat.

"Can't make any sense out of what he said, but I think the fellow has a problem. Let's take a look-see." Clyde made an, "after you" gesture, and the three of them climbed down to the boat. One look was all it took for Neville to stand up in the rocking boat and yell toward the ship. "Get that corpsman down here. One of the ladies is having a baby."

* * *

At that moment, the corpsman on his knees, was head and shoulders deep in the medical supply cabinet, adding English labels to everything he recognized. He wasn't a doctor, although he had taken pre-med in college. Doc, as everyone called him worked hard at his job, preparing for the day when he could go to medical school.

A rough hand grabbed his shoulder and shook him. "Doc, they got a lady up top about to have a baby. They need you right now."

Doc, fell back on his ass, a blank look on his face. The sailor repeated the message and tried to pull him up. "Okay, okay. I got it." He looked around at his own personal surgical suite. "Can they carry her down here?"

The sailor shook his head. "The way they were yelling for you, I don't think so. You better get up there."

Doc hurriedly filled a bag with some basic instruments, a gown, and towels and handed it to the sailor. "Get this up there. I'll be right behind."

The sailor charged out of the compartment. Doc suddenly felt the sweat pouring off him. He took one more hurried look around, grabbed a few more items, and ran to take care of his first female patient, praying that he would simply stand by and watch a delivery free of complications.

As soon as he stepped into the boat he knew things were going to be difficult. His prayers had fallen on deaf ears. This was the woman's third childbirth and should have been simple, but the baby was in the wrong position and her contractions were almost constant. She screamed with the pain of trying to force the baby out. Doc worked for almost an hour to get it turned. No sooner than he finally had the baby maneuvered into position head down, it started to appear.

The woman struggled, thrashing around. At one point, she changed position so abruptly, her husband was almost thrown out of the boat. The corpsman and the woman both seemed about to drown in their own sweat. No sooner than the baby's shoulders appeared, she passed out. The hard work was done and Doc kept out of the way as nature finished the job.

Doc held her crying baby up in front of her, wrapped in a clean towel. His ambition to be a real doctor got a boost when he took a moment to think about what he had done. Helping to save a woman's life and bring a new person into the world–it couldn't get any better than that. He gave himself a pat on the back and then went about finishing up, as the entire crew cheered, watching from anywhere they could get a view.

As soon as he cleaned up both his first and second ever female patients, he tried to have the crew move them to the ship. Up until then, the father had been jittery and upset, but quiet. Now however, he yelled and drew his machete threatening anyone who came near his wife. He pointed at the flags visible in the deck lights, which had been on for some time.

Clyde looked from the man to the flags and back again. "What's he trying to say?"

Neville scrunched up his shoulders, and shook his head. He opened his mouth, and then stopped a quizzical look on his face.

It dawned on him. “He’s afraid of the Japs. He must think they’re going to come in this direction.”

“If he’s right…”

“I know. If he’s right, we have ourselves a problem, but first things, first. This fellow wants to get going. Doc, is the lady fit to travel?”

“Uh, I guess so. As long as she can lie like she is for a while. She’s wore out, but I don’t see any hemorrhaging. Make sure he understands that she should stay like this, at least till morning.”

“Think he can manage?” said one of the sailors. “That boat needs two people paddling to make any kind of speed.”

Ensign Miller, quiet until now, said, “They can stay here and we’ll protect them, but if they leave, no one goes with them.” He said his words so forcefully, everyone acted as if he might actually be in charge.

While the family’s desire to get moving was discussed, a large outrigger canoe sat quietly in the darkness nearby drifting on the current, unseen and unheard–invisible to everyone involved in the family drama. It remained stationary, just outside the pool of light cast by the ship’s deck lights. No one took notice of it when it silently approached. Not until two ropes landed, bow and stern on the smaller boat did anyone become aware of its arrival. It carried twelve people, each one holding a rifle or shotgun.

The man closest to the stern, large by Philippine standards, pointed to the ropes, and said to the small group helping the family get ready to leave. “Tie us up and step back. I’m coming over.”

He stepped across the small gap between the two boats making both of them rock. He worked his way around the family, careful not to disturb the prostrate mother. When he reached Neville and Clyde, he looked them up and down, his small dark eyes seeming to catch everything. Unlike the rest of his men who were dressed in white field-hand clothes, he wore dark pants and a black shirt.

In perfect English with a New England accent, he said, "Why are you keeping these people from leaving?"

Clyde was upset, but outwardly looked unfazed by the newcomer's arrival. "Keeping them? We were helping them get away. Now who the bloody hell are you?"

The man ignored Clyde's question as he asked his own. "Everyone here is in uniform except you two." He pointed at the Englishmen. "What are you, military or civilian–friend or foe? Come on, out with it. I haven't got all day."

Neville stood as tall as he could, with a moving boat under his feet. "I believe, old chap, you mean, all night." He waved his hand dismissing any comment the man in black might be about to make. "But, never mind that. We are part of His Majesty's Australian Coast Watcher Service, working with the American Navy to free this country from the Japs. Please identify yourself and tell your men to lower their guns, someone might get hurt."

The man in black nodded and told his men to lower their weapons. "I'm Rodger Sicone, Captain, US Army, Commander, District Six of the Leyte Division, Free Philippine Resistance Force. We have orders to sabotage Japanese installations farther west along the Strait."

"Any news on how the invasion is going, Captain?"

"The landing beaches are secure, and our boys are back on schedule after that Jap fleet tried to break through." Sicone pointed at the man still holding a machete in the canoe. "You were right about these people. They're afraid of the Japs. As our boys advance, some of their forces are being forced in this direction. I'd take these people with us, but they won't be able to keep up."

At this comment, Ensign Miller didn't hold back. "Sir, we could protect them but they don't seem to think that is a good idea. If the Japs do come this way…"

"You have a point there, Ensign. I'll leave one man to assist them. With his help, they should be able to stay out of the way. The rest of my people will come with me. We need to be in our new position by tomorrow."

Sicone took a moment to look at the destroyer, down by the bow, and still stuck in the mud, its bridge structure twisted into the caricature of a child's jungle gym. "If the Japs get this far, you're situation isn't going to look too good. Why don't you join us? With your men added to my group, and the other units we're going to meet up with, we could eliminate the enemy from western Leyte in no time at all."

Neville turned to face Clyde. Once again, their thoughts were as one, sharing the invisible message that flashed between them. Helping the guerillas could have been a real possibility. However, working *for* the guerillas instead of *with* them, was a non-starter. "Sorry ol' boy, we have to keep watch over the Strait. Wish you good hunting, and all that, but our orders have us sitting right here until we're relieved. If the Nips gain control of this waterway, we might not be able to pry them loose from Leyte. And without Leyte, we won't be able to pry them loose from the rest of the country."

"Well, that's your call. Wish you luck. Anything I can do before we shove off?"

Neville shook his head. Miller said, "No sir." Clyde raised his hand. "We're fine, although, I was wondering, is there any place close by where a bloke could find himself a drink?"

Ensign Miller looked embarrassed. Neville's face lit up. "Capital idea, ol' boy."

The Captain laughed and turned to one of his men. After a few quiet words, six bottles of beer passed from one boat to the other. "This is a local brew from Tampong, about fifty miles north along the coast."

In his normal, undiplomatic manner, Clyde asked, "Is it any good?"

Sicone's reply was quick and emphatic. "You bet it is. I'd rate it even better than San Miguel Dark Horse, Extra Strong. Sorry this is all I can give you. If you want more, you'll need to get to Tampong before the Nips decide to torch the place. They're destroying whatever they can in every town they're forced out of."

The bow and stern ropes were thrown back to the guerillas, Sicone waved goodbye, and his outrigger disappeared into the dark. The newly enlarged family followed in their wake at a slower pace. As the outrigger gained speed, Neville tried to soften Clyde's previous remark. He called after them, "Thanks for the beer, Captain. Next time we see you, we'll let you know what we think."

A minute later, the destroyer's deck lights blinked off and the ship settled down for a quiet night. The only natural sound to be heard was that of night birds squawking in the distance. They couldn't come close to competing with the beautiful and unnatural sound of bottle caps being hurriedly pried off, followed by sighs of contentment. For the moment–all was right with the world.

Chapter 32

Decisions

October 29, 1944

"Neville...Neville, you awake?" said Clyde in a throaty whisper. They were in their hammocks on the destroyer's rear deck with some members of *their* crew sleeping close by. An evening storm had chased everyone below for a short time and they had only just settled down again.

"What do you think, I'm talking, ain't I?"

"Brilliant. I got an idea."

"You couldn't hold it till daylight? It's one in the morning. If you work at it, you might be able to remember it all by yourself and then you can tell me about it when we have breakfast."

Clyde stifled his normally cutting reply. In its place, he said, "No, really, this is a good one."

"Right. Just like the last one. I almost strangled you for that good idea. Besides, you ain't likely to lose what ever it is by mixing it in with the other two ideas you've had this year?"

"Oh come on now. Just shut your mouth and listen for a minute."

Neville squirmed around in his hammock without saying anything. The creaking of the ropes holding it up told Clyde his audience was still awake, and possibly listening.

"First, did you like that beer?"

"You know I did. It was the best brew we've had since…I don't know when."

"I agree. Second, would you like to get some more?"

"You're wasting your minute. Of course I would, only that Yank Captain ain't coming back to give us some more. Did you see the way the others in his boat looked at him when he handed over those bottles?"

"I agree."

"Come on now. Your sounding like a broken record ain't helping me get to sleep. What's your brilliant idea?"

"All right. It's really quite simple. We like the beer. We know where there's more of it." On his fingers he ticked off each item on his list. "We have transportation, and finally, we have all the help we need."

Neville was so startled by Clyde's idea, he forgot he was in a hammock and tried to sit up. He fell out and landed on his hands and knees. "Bloody hell, that hurt."

"I knew you'd be excited. I almost did the same thing when the idea came to me. That beer is way too good to let the Japs run off with it."

Neville grabbed the edge of his swinging bed and got to his feet, then settled his rear end down into it with his feet still on the deck. "Let me get this straight. You want to take Kilroy and some of these Yanks, and go fifty miles into enemy held territory to steal a few cases of beer?" Neville's voice went up in volume. "Are you insane?"

"You got me wrong. That's not what I said."

"It certainly sounded that way. What are you saying we should do?"

"We don't steal a few cases of beer, we steal a boat load. There must be hundreds, maybe thousands of cases of beer, and who knows, maybe some kegs as well. Think how much we could make selling it to the Yanks."

"And the Nips? What are they going to think of your brilliant idea?"

Clyde heard his partner's words *brilliant idea,* without listening to his tone of voice. Thinking Neville agreed with the idea, he said, "It is brilliant, isn't it? I knew you'd like it."

"No, it is *not* brilliant. It's the stupidest idea you've had in a long time and, even if you could get past the Japs, what about the locals? You'd be stealing their beer. Not the thing to do when you're trying to make friends."

"Don't worry about that. We do it at night−tomorrow night. If they don't know we did it, they'll blame it on the Nips. See? My plan is fool-proof."

Neville worked his way back into a comfortable position in his hammock. "No it ain't."

"It ain't, what?"

"You thought of it, so it ain't fool-proof. Now let me get some sleep. If you have any more ideas, go tell them to the Ensign."

The night was dark, the Strait was quiet, and time passed at the speed of a glacier sliding down a New Zealand mountain. Clyde knew they were passing up the opportunity of a lifetime. He stayed awake as long as he could, thinking up arguments to make Neville change his mind. He catalogued them, from the most likely to work to the least plausible, although most of those still made sense to him.

He thought all night about their problem, *his problem*, and decided the time had come to follow his instincts, with or without his shadow. At first light, he went into the ship and checked each of the cabins that had not been destroyed. He needed a map.

He found several naval charts, which were fine as far as locating things along the coast. Tampong and its harbor were neatly displayed. However, almost nothing about the city itself was shown. The charts showed how deep the water was, where underwater hazards were, and the location of channel markers, but nothing on land other than a few roads. After another half-hour of searching, he accepted the fact that what he had found would have to do.

Clyde sat down at a table in the crew's mess area to study his newly acquired information. A cook handed him a cup of weak tea with an apologetic shrug of his shoulders.

With little to do until breakfast, the sailor leaned over Clyde's shoulder. "What-cha got there, Mr. Arnold?"

Clyde pointed at Tampong. "This is where the best beer in the entire Pacific is brewed."

"Ya don't say. We're not that far away from there, are we?"

"Exactly. We're only a few easy hours travel from this lovely place."

"You planning on liberating some of it after the Japs pull out?"

"Good idea, but no. The Nips will either take it or destroy it."

"So, why are you looking at that map?"

"Because I need some beer, and this," Clyde pointed to Tampong, "is where it's at."

"But you said…"

"Correct, young man. From what I've seen, this country doesn't have many things that can be called special or different from any other jungle island. Tampong and its beer are. We need to do something to prevent the Japs from burning down that brewery…"

"And stealing the beer."

"Yes. And stealing the beer. That simply means I've got to get up there before anyone harms those buildings." Clyde looked over his shoulder at the cook. "Care to come along?"

"Sounds kind'a dangerous."

"Not likely. Those people will be so disorganized we can simply sail in there in our Japanese barge, wearing Japanese uniforms, and take what we want. Breweries need large shipments of grain and stuff. Seeing that this is an island, I'll bet you the place is close to the harbor. Might even have its own dock. Can you use a rifle?"

The cook pulled away. "I thought you said it would be a cake-walk."

"I've lived too long not to expect a surprise or two. If you want to go, get a half-dozen of your friends and meet me on deck in two hours."

Before the cook turned away, Clyde added, "The smaller the better."

"What? What do you mean the smaller, the better?"

"Your volunteers. We have all the uniforms the Nip crew left behind, but some of our men might not fit into them." He was about to say something else when he heard several loud bangs. On a ship, otherwise as quiet as a tomb, he knew the sound had to be a problem. "Did you hear that?"

The cook appeared not to have taken notice of the noise. "What? Oh, you mean the banging. Those guys have been at it since early evening. I guess you can't hear it up on deck."

"What are they doing?"

"Mr. Miller told the guys to get the ship seaworthy. They've been building a coffer dam in the bow where the worst hull damage is located. I think some of those guys must have been carpenters. You should see what they built."

Exploring the ship wasn't high on Clyde's list, but he wanted to get the cook's cooperation in his quest for a beer fit for the Gods. "I think I will," Clyde said, and walked toward the bow. His parting comment as he left the mess area was, "Don't forget about those volunteers."

Clyde had never bothered to examine the front of the ship. Given his lack of knowledge when it came to how a ship was built, he hadn't seen any reason–until now. He followed the banging, walking down the slanted deck until he was slogging through water that quickly changed from ankle deep, to knee deep, and finally it was almost up to his armpits. He became less curios about the noise with each step as he pushed a small wave ahead of him. He was in water deeper than he thought safe and started to turn around when he heard voices coming from the next compartment.

The entry hatch was only a few feet away. He talked himself into carefully stepping through the hatch, holding on to some fittings while feeling ahead with a foot. Portable floodlights lit the compartment in the very bow of the ship. Without being aware of it, he had been following an air hose all the way to this compartment where it dropped down into the water. Bubbles surrounded two men floating, their faces in the water near the ship's outer skin.

Two welder's helmets modified to act as diver's masks, with air hoses attached, came out of the water. Using a rope, the men pulled themselves over to a metal ladder and climbed up to where Clyde stood.

One man turned and said to his partner, "I think that does it, Joe. What do you think?"

"Won't know till we try and pump her dry, but I think maybe this old girl will float as long as we keep the pumps around."

The first man looked up. "Hi there, Mr. Arnold. What cha' think?" He pointed at a ten by thirty foot wall of wood planks and beams covering the damaged area of the hull with mattresses sticking out around the edges.

Amazed that a few men could build something that big, with most of it under water in less than a day, Clyde said, "You really think you'll be able to get this ship up out of the mud?"

"Won't know till we start the pumps, but we think so."

"We can sail the ship back to Morotai." Clyde's words sounded like a question hidden inside a statement.

"Maybe. All depends on the fellas in the engine room, but I'm betting they'll get her running. We'll know later today."

"When I bring the beer back from Tampong, you men can have as much as you want." It was the most generous thing Clyde could offer them. The idea of getting the ship out of the mud created an unexpected opportunity. A vision popped into his head. Piles of money being offered in exchange for salvage rights to the Jap destroyer. The money, sitting on a table competed for his attention with the thought of a boatload of Grade AAA beer.

* * *

Clyde quietly returned to his hammock and stripped out of his wet clothes. After he stretched out, Neville raised his head. "Been all the way to Tampong and back already, have you?"

A self-satisfied Clyde, responded. "Not yet, Mate, but things are looking up. Made myself a preliminary reconnaissance and did some recruiting, now didn't I?"

"You found some men as crazy as yourself? We've done some idiotic things in our lives, ol' boy, but seldom have we done anything this stupid. Raiding a city behind enemy lines for a good pint of beer–you have to know what is likely to happen."

"I think you're wrong. Something *might* happen, but I don't think it's *likely* to happen. You ever heard of the fog-of-war? We'll go in at night. The Nips will be concentratin' on saving their skins, not on a small group of men loading packing cases on a barge. An hour or two and we'll be on our way back, and think of the fun we'll have afterward."

"If there is an afterward."

Clyde tried to act hurt by Neville's comment. "As I was saying, we'll have fun telling people about it. Besides," a spur of the moment idea popped up, "we'll be saving a national landmark from destruction."

"What landmark?"

"The brewery, of course. A place that makes beer like that–people must come from all over to see it. We might even get a reward from the government."

Neville grunted signaling his disbelief. "Don't forget to leave me a copy of your will. I'm looking forward to being the largest landowner on Pyramid."

Clyde woke up well rested to see a line of twenty sailors waiting to volunteer for beer retrieval duty. He told the first five in line to bring up all the Japanese uniforms from the crew berthing areas. While that was being done, he questioned the men about naval experience and their weapons knowledge, quickly eliminating a half-dozen men. After the uniforms were brought on deck, four more were eliminated–nothing fit their too wide or too tall shapes.

Clyde felt good about his idea. He had ten men facing him in two rows, who looked as if they could handle themselves in a fight. "All right, you lot, the next thing a proper soldier needs are weapons. There are two small arms lockers downstairs. Get whatever you think you can handle, without shooting each other."

A voice from the back row called out, "What about a machine gun–you know…just in case."

"Right you are. More is better than less. Now…off you go." Clyde said, pointing toward a hatch near the after-gun mount.

While Clyde recruited and outfitted his personal army of amateur alcoholics, Neville sat close by on the seat of an anti-aircraft gun. He tried to keep his thoughts to himself, and for the most part, was successful. However, there were a few instances when crewmembers saw him shaking his head or grimacing at what he felt sure would happen. The more he looked at Clyde's armed to the teeth rag-tag army, the more he wanted to shake some sense into his best friend's empty head.

Ensign Miller walked over to Neville. "You're not going to let him go without you, are you?"

"Do I look crazy?" Neville quickly said, "Don't answer that. There ain't any way I'm going fifty miles into enemy territory for some beer. I've been accused of doing a lot of crazy things in my life, and most of them are true. But, to do this for some beer, which, God knows I dearly love, is…" He shook his head. "He has to be barmy, even if that stuff is the best brew this side of the GMT." Neville licked his lips as the memory of its taste came back to him. "If that place was a little closer, like two or three miles away, I'd be on my way. As it is, I'm upset that Clyde is being so bull-headed. It ain't like him to go off without me."

A new thought broke through Neville's irritation. "Say, you're an officer. You can stop these idiots."

"You're right, only this is my first assignment and we both know they won't listen. Lieutenant Flynn told me to follow your orders. Both of you, and most of the men heard him. With the two of you split on what to do, they're going to follow the one who says what they want to hear.

"Besides, I'll be the first to admit that I don't belong here. I should be in an office on some naval base. I was temporarily posted to the ship to assist the Captain. He's going to be…I mean, was going to be promoted to Squadron Commander. I was supposed to help him get up to speed with the administrative paperwork."

Neville started to hit a bulkhead next to him in frustration. At the last moment, he realized it was solid steel, not thatch or even bamboo. He changed his motion from a punch to a simple swipe. "How does it feel being ignored? Personally, I don't care for it."

"Most of the time it doesn't bother me. Other men crave to be in command, but being responsible for someone else's life is something I can do without."

The noise of Clyde's army climbing down into Kilroy, drew their attention. Neville got out of his seat and started to pace along the railing, not knowing how to stop the madness.

Some men went down to the barge and waited for those above to pass machine guns and ammunition down to them. It seemed a miracle that none of them, weighted down as they were with weapons, didn't fall and break their neck.

Kilroy's engine sputtered a few times before roaring to life. Clyde's men took positions around the well deck where they could mount their weapons. The four thirty-caliber machine guns they brought with them were equipped with snap mounts that mated with fittings in the bulkheads.

One of the men untied the rope holding Kilroy's bow in place. The front of the barge slowly swung away from the destroyer. From above, Neville watched these preparations with increasing agitation. He slammed his hand down on the railing, first in frustration and then in defeat. He muttered to himself, wishing for the worst possible things to rain down on his headstrong partner before giving up and throwing one leg over the railing. To Miller, he said, "Ensign, if a ship comes by, get your men back to the fleet."

"But…but," sputtered Miller.

After everything he had said to the contrary, Neville didn't try to explain why he suddenly changed his mind. Only one thing mattered–Clyde was his mate. He shut out Miller's voice and concentrated on where to place his hands and feet going down the netting. Halfway down, he stopped long enough to yell at Clyde, "You better not go until I get down there. You ain't going to take our little Kilroy without me on board to tell you where to go."

No sooner than his feet hit the deck than a pile of clothes hit Neville on the head. He looked up to see Miller smiling. "Don't forget which army you're in when you get back."

Kilroy pulled away from the destroyer as Neville cupped his hands and yelled back to Miller, "Make sure your Navy don't take our ship. Yank flag or no, it's ours. Your Navy don't allow alcohol and we're going to need a place where we can get drunk–proper like."

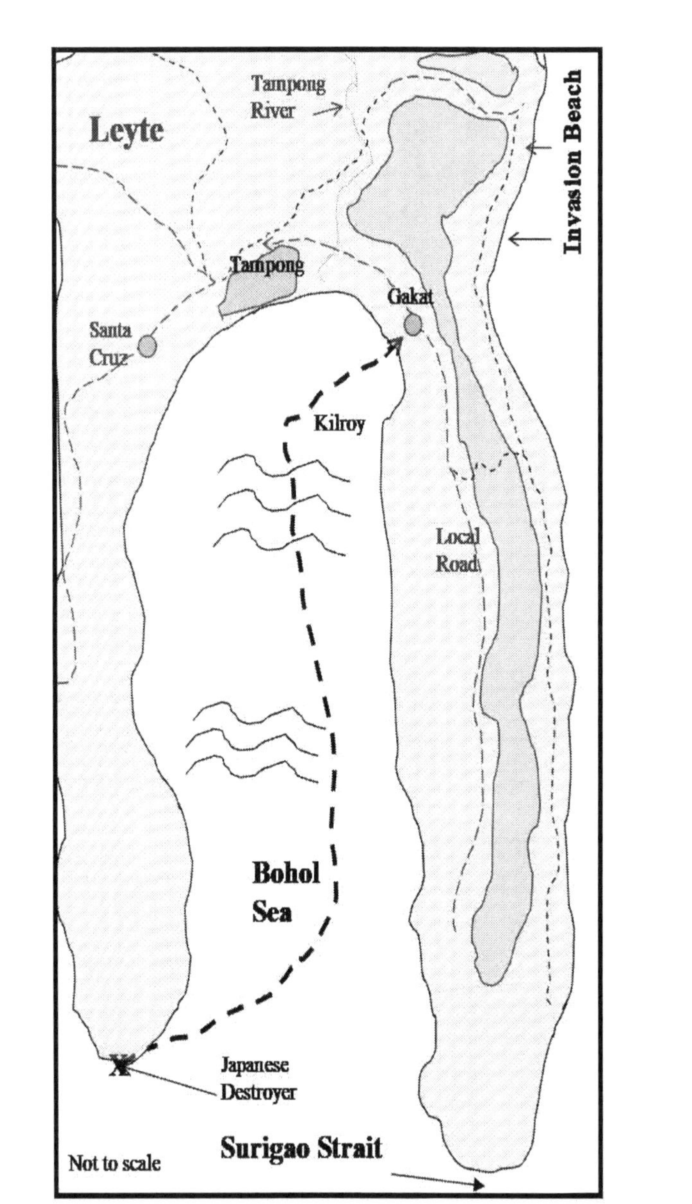
Tampong
River
Leyte
Invasion Beach
Tampong
Gakat
Santa
Cruz
Kilroy
Local
Road
Bohol
Sea
Japanese
Destroyer
Surigao Strait
Not to scale

Chapter 33

The Voyage

October 29, 1944
Sunset

The first thing Neville did after making peace with Clyde was to check their fuel level. Satisfied that they had enough for a round trip to Tampong, he went around the well deck talking to each of the men, quietly asserting his position with the crew as co-commander of the beer retrieval expedition. A few of them were having second thoughts. Clyde had quickly bonded with the sailors, but having the *level-headed* Neville around made them feel better about joining such a hair-brained scheme. They needed to celebrate surviving the sinking of their ship and to remember those who had been lost. Remembering and forgetting, two sides of the same experience needed alcohol. They needed to get blindingly drunk and Clyde offered them the opportunity. They believed, or at least hoped, this would be a lot of fun without any real danger.

Clyde split the sailors into two squads that rotated every two-hour. Whichever group stood watch did it with weapons at the ready, trying to imitate Japanese soldiers. No one bothered to explain the finer points of international law governing combatants, but now, even the densest of them understood their position. Without actually saying the words, everyone accepted the fact that by not wearing their own uniforms, they had given up any protection afforded by the laws of war and, if captured, could expect to be treated as spies. When each man appeared for the first time in his Imperial Army uniform, the jokes some made back on the ship were in good humor. Now their fate was no longer a joking matter. The longer it took to get to Tampong the more serious their spur of the moment decision seemed. Clyde and Neville, who never wore a uniform, were well aware of their fate should they get caught. It was an accepted hazard of the Coast Watcher profession.

For hours on end, they heard the steady throb of the loud diesel engine. It made staying alert difficult. Even for the most motivated of the group, sleep was only a few feet away. Their course, ten degrees west of north, did not vary as they motored through the smooth water. Their destination was where the large peninsula, occasionally visible to their east, merged with the main underbelly of the island. Tampong sat at that juncture, nestled beside its namesake river. The waterway drained the torrential rains that frequently drenched the central mountains of Leyte. Wide and shallow where it entered the bay, it experienced wild fluctuations in depth where it flowed out of its canyon farther north that the Japanese had fortified as a major defensive position.

Neville moved closer to Clyde to overcome the noise from Kilroy's engine. "If we have this thing figured right, we've been on the water for six hours. At eight miles an hour, we should almost be there, and we still have a little daylight. Think maybe we should stay right here until full dark?"

"Let's keep going until we can see some buildings. Remember that brewery in Melbourne. The beer was horrible, but the locals couldn't get enough of it. It had several large buildings. This place must be as large. Maybe we'll be able to pick it out and still be far enough away not to be seen. It only stands to reason, a place making beer that good ought to be quite large."

"You're the Captain. I'll just go around and talk with the men again, make sure they are ready."

Clyde shrugged his shoulders. "Go ahead if you want, but it ain't necessary, so don't start making them nervous for no reason. Don't want anybody shooting at their shadow."

Neville hoped his partner was right, but knew better than to simply hope things went smoothly. He slowly worked his way around the barge, talking and joking with each man, helping them to relax, but stay alert. The first part of this adventure–or was it insanity–had gone according to Clyde's plan. That, in itself, was unusual. Also unusual, the lack of any Japanese patrol craft, especially with the large number of small boats they continued to encounter–every one of them heading south, away from Tampong. He couldn't help thinking they knew something he should be aware of.

"We're five miles from Tampax," announced Clyde laughing at the new name he gave their destination. He looked first at a red and white buoy bobbing in their wake and then at his chart. He knew exactly where they were or, at least, he sounded like he did. "We're in the main channel." He made a production of seeming to sniff the air. "Do you smell it? I do believe I can smell the beer from here."

Neville, standing behind Clyde, didn't respond. For the last thirty seconds, he had been silent, as he looked behind them with his binoculars. It was a normal part of his routine search of the horizon, only this time there seemed to be something back there. The gray-blue humidity laden air appeared to be changing. He patiently watched the area until the haze solidified into a discernable object, before calmly lowering his binoculars.

Keeping his voice normal, he said in a matter-of-fact way, "Good work and I certainly agree that we're in the channel. In fact, everyone agrees, including that Jap patrol boat on our ass. Wonder what he will do when he gets close enough to take a look up our skirt?"

Clyde's head snapped around so hard Neville thought his partner's head would twist off.

Trying to maintain a calm exterior, Neville mused, "Do you think if we stay in the middle of the channel he'll know on which side to pass?"

"How the bloody hell did he get there?" Clyde's head jerked from one side to the other looking for a way out. To the east, land and deep dark jungle stood at least six or seven miles away. The bulk of the island, not yet in view, lay in front and to their left. The problem, as Clyde saw it, was simple, being in a boat on the water, there weren't any caves to hide in or trees to disappear behind. The ocean reduced his options. He felt naked. It was one more reason why he didn't like water. "How long till he gets close?"

"Ten, maybe fifteen minutes," said Neville, who tore his eyes away from their death sentence and looked at the chart. Clyde had already identified the beginning of the channel as they entered the shallow water at the top of the fifty-mile long bay, which was one finger of the Bohol Sea. Neville looked up in time to see the next buoy slide by. In another mile, a side channel intersected theirs. He glanced back at the large patrol boat equipped with a three-inch gun prominently positioned near the bow. "Which side of the channel is he staying close to?"

"The left. Why?"

"There's a side channel up ahead. It goes to another town and gives us a logical reason to get out of his way without appearing to be running away. If he stays left, turn right."

"If we choose wrong…?"

"We'll be the first and last to know."

Tight nerves were on the verge of breaking. Even though everyone wore Japanese uniforms, Neville made sure the men stayed out of sight in the well of the barge. It took a long five minutes for them to reach the buoy marking the side channel. By then, the patrol boat was no more than a mile away. "He's staying to the left," said Neville.

Clyde aimed the barge to the right. "Here's hoping we made the right choice, otherwise I'm going to need a swimming lesson."

Neville pulled the bill of his army cap lower to hide his face and turned to see what fate had in store for them. Without knowing it, he held his breath in anticipation of things going from bad to worse, the way they frequently did. He raised his arm to wave farewell to the patrol boat when he saw it heel over and follow Kilroy into the side channel. "I don't believe it. They're still following us."

"Brilliant. We're on our way to Gakat, and all *our* beer is in Tampax. Next time, don't tell me which way to go. I wasn't going to turn, until you told me to."

"I'm sorry you feel so bad about our choice of destination, ol' boy. When we get to Gakat you can let me off. Then, you challenge them to an arm wrestling match. The winner gets the beer."

Clyde thought about the beer waiting for them in Tampong, and felt as if he'd lost a close relative. His great idea gone up in smoke. His only response to Neville's verbal jab was, "Oh..., shut yer' trap. It ain't nice to bother a person when he's in mourning."

"Being a little dramatic, are we? Go ahead and mourn, I'm going to get the men ready."

Neville moved from man to man, checking weapons. He made sure his troops were aware of the situation, ready for whatever might happen, and knew how to unsafe their weapons. He told each man, "Don't try to be a hero. Stick with your buddies. If we can get to shore, we'll have the advantage. They can't haul their heavy weapons ashore."

As much as Neville preached the idea of, being ready, he was as surprised as anyone when he heard several machine guns firing, and the roar of an airplane flying a few feet off the water. The plane got everyone's undivided attention right after they ducked below the sides of the barge.

A line of splashes occurred near the rear and to either side of the patrol boat behind them, but they all seemed to miss. Then, it was their turn to pray. The fifty-caliber bullets created a wavy line of waterspouts down Kilroy's left side less than five feet away. By shooting at both vessels along their length, the pilot had tried for maximum damage instead of a sure hit by shooting at them from the side. Neville's heart skipped several beats as he looked up. He knew a one-foot miss was as good as a mile, but he definitely preferred the mile.

Clyde spun the wheel to change course. The ungainly barge continued straight for several heart-stopping seconds before it answered his command and turned to its left. A carrier based US Navy Hellcat fighter plane had shot at a target of opportunity, and missed. Before a single shot was fired in return, the plane swooped back up into the sky and disappeared into a cloud, contrails of moisture swirling off its wingtips. Clyde spun the wheel in the opposite direction to get the barge back on course, while eleven sets of eyes scanned the darkening sky for danger.

"Did you get his tail number?" Clyde asked.

"Did I…? Why? You want me to call him back to finish us off after he goes home for dinner? Or, maybe you want to write him up for missing us?"

"Maybe. How else are those fellows going to get better?"

Neville shook his head in disgust. "Here we are, running for our lives and you're concerned that the fellow who attacked us…missed? I certainly am glad that you haven't lost your sense of priorities."

"No, I haven't, but the lad ought to be told to watch who he's shooting at. *That* is important, but the boat behind us, is *really* important." Clyde took a moment to see what it was doing. Pleasantly surprised, he saw it dropping farther astern. "I think that flyboy might have done us some good." He pointed behind them. "Look."

The patrol boat no longer had a large bow wave. It had slowed down, but no matter how hard they tried, telepathically, to get it to stop, it kept limping after them. With all of the shallow water and coral outcroppings lurking just beneath the surface, they didn't dare leave the channel to get around their *escort* and reach the target of their voyage. For better or worse, their next port of call would be the beer-free zone and bustling wanna-be metropolis of Gakat.

* * *

The sailors still on the disabled destroyer had taken up the challenge of making the ship seaworthy. To coordinate the various groups of sailors Ensign Miller felt as if he was in a track race. All afternoon he shuttled between the pump room near the destroyer's stern and the bow compartment. As the only officer onboard, he needed to keep notes on how the pumping was going, what was happening and how close it mirrored what they expected to happen.

Water depth in the bow was down to less than two feet and yet the ship had not moved. The bow remained stuck. More pressure than expected was being placed on the patch. Beads of moisture appeared from under the edges of the mattress gaskets. The lower the water level sank the quicker the individual beads changed to seeps, and then to rivulets. The repair crew in the bow was worried. They feared the cofferdam would give way under the added pressure.

Miller relayed their concern and had the engineering crew stop the pumping. As soon as the pumps were silent, he asked, "How long till you get the engines working? The men up front believe the bow will float as soon as you can make the engines pull us back a little. All we need is a couple of feet to break free of the mud's suction."

"It's all the same Ensign, a foot or a mile," said the Senior Chief, who appeared to have more oil on him than either of the engines. "We finally figured out how to light off the boilers, but we're taking it slow, don't want anything to blow up. Give us an hour or so. We'll let you know when we're ready. In the meantime, I'd get everybody to move toward the bow, you know, just in case."

"You got it Chief. I'll get everyone moved. Good luck."

Chapter34

Gakat

October 29, 1944
A Little Later

The less than memorable town of Gakat appeared ahead of the Kilroy as the twilight sky quickly lost its color. The town, squeezed between the ocean and steep jungle covered mountains, sat on the main road serving the peninsula's west coast. With two or three other north-south streets and a dozen more going east and west, the area appeared capable of housing a thousand or so, although it was hard to be sure. Thick stands of Philippine Chestnut trees grew right to the beach obscuring a good deal of the town. What housing they could see, appeared to consist of small buildings, some with thatch walls, others with wood, facing in every direction. Each one, no matter the size, had a large porch affording protection from rain and sun.

Hoping for the best, Clyde reduced engine speed to an idle allowing the barge to come to a stop and then drift with the tide a quarter-mile from the beach. Both he and Clyde took their time scanning the visible parts of Gakat and the surrounding terrain for any indication of Japanese occupation.

Neville spoke first. “I can see a flagpole, no flag on it, near a building just to the right of that long pier. Wonder why a town this small needs such a long pier?”

“Never mind the pier, what about the building?”

Might be city hall, or…”

Clyde aimed his binoculars at the building. “Can you see anyone walking around, Mate? It’s that ‘or’ of yours that can get us killed.”

One of the sailors clung to a short ladder between the well deck and the motorman’s position relaying information to the rest of the men. “What about a truck, Mr. Arnold? Do ya’ see anything we can use to get to Tampax?”

“No-o. Too many trees. Everything is in shadows,” said Clyde as he continued his examination of the town. With the engine idling, Kilroy continued to slowly drift south with the outgoing tide. The change in their position affected their viewing angle. Clyde stopped his scan and concentrated his examination on one spot. “Wait a mo’. I do see something.”

“What? Where are you looking?” asked Neville. When Clyde didn’t answer, he repeated his question, more forcefully.

Irritation in his voice, Clyde said, “Hold on to your britches. I ain’t sure. We need to drift a little farther to our right.”

A tense couple of minutes passed in silence. The speeding darkness, intent on hiding important details, was racing the creeping Kilroy. Had Clyde found something important–life threatening, or simply an unexplained shadow? The answer finally emerged when someone with a lantern walked past the area in question. “It’s a truck and a motorcycle with sidecar parked behind the flagpole building. That means…”

Neville finished the thought. “It certainly does.”

“What? What does it mean?” asked the sailor, still hanging from the ladder.

“There’s a Nip detachment there. That building must be their headquarters. It might also be their bunkhouse.” Neville turned to his mate. "We can bring the barge up to the beach a couple hundred yards south of the building, take a gander and, as officers like to say, neutralize who ever is there. Can't be more than a handful in a place like this."

"But, what if there is?"

"We improvise, but if I'm right, we eliminate them. After that, we take the truck and get us a pint."

Clyde turned toward the sailor. "Any of you men good with a knife?"

One man who barely fit into his unauthorized uniform, said, "I can do a neat job dressing out a deer."

"Neat ain't important, but silence is. You need to keep your man quiet till he bleeds out. Can you do that?"

The sailor did not immediately respond. Clyde opened his mouth to repeat the question when the answer came. "Yes, Sir. I can do that." The man sounded more timid than a moment earlier.

"What's your name?"

"Distopolis, Sir."

"Right. You stay with Neville and me when we go ashore. Make sure you have a pistol and a sharp knife."

Seaman Second Class, Nathan Distopolis, a twenty-four year old deckhand, assigned as loader for a twenty-millimeter deck gun, enlisted a few months prior to Pearl Harbor. Born and raised in North Dakota, he wanted to see the world. So far, he'd seen a lot of water and survived multiple attacks against his ship by Japanese fighters. As far as he was concerned, he'd never done anything to actually win the war. Nervously, he looked forward to being the one who did something, rather than simply stuffing shells in a gun while others did the shooting.

"After we land, I want the lads in the first watch to approach that building from the ocean side. Keep low and near the water and make sure we ain't surprised by anyone on that pier. You other lot, get across the road and get as close as you can. Stay concealed and cover them vehicles. Clyde, Nathan, and me will head straight for the building. If you hear any shooting, you make sure no one gets away."

Clyde added, "Keep your safeties on unless you charge the place, or if you see anyone trying to escape, but make sure it ain't us. We need to keep this quiet if we can. We'd like to get this taken care of fast, but we have to wait for the right moment. Remember, quiet is good." Satisfied they were as ready as they were going to be, Clyde increased Kilroy's engine speed and started the short trip to the beach.

Neville took Distopolis aside to give him a quick lesson in how to use a knife on a two-legged animal. By the time he finished, the flat-bottomed barge had slid to a stop, its bow only a few feet from the beach.

They didn't lower the bow door in case they might need protection from enemy fire. Everyone climbed over the sides and silently dropped into less than two feet of water. Clyde and Neville waited a moment, watching, as the two groups of sailors scurried away intent on their mission. Then the two veterans and their trainee hurried toward their target keeping as low as possible.

The building used by the Japanese had walls made of vertical wood slats. There were several large window openings on each side of the building covered with mosquito screening, but no glass. Folding wood shutters lay back against the walls. Several gas lanterns cast an uneven yellow light across its three rooms. The room in the rear, closest to the ocean contained four cots, one of them barely visible behind a bamboo curtain. The central room had a table and chairs and a small cast-iron wood burning stove. The office, containing a desk and radio console was in the front.

The officer in charge, a young lieutenant, sat at his desk, writing while two enlisted men sat at the kitchen table playing a game of GO, using a board along with some black and white stones. It was a fast-paced game that appeared deceptively simple, but wasn't. It called for patience, strategy and concentration.

After peeking into each room through the window openings, Clyde and Neville moved away from the building to discuss their plan. Nathan acted as their silent shadow. Neville started the discussion. "All their weapons are stacked in the front room. If we control that area and keep the men in back bottled up, we can take care of this place in under a minute."

"What do you think?"

Clyde took a quick look toward the building. "That'll work. I'll take the back with Nathan. You okay handling the officer?"

Neville grunted his agreement. "Let's get this over with." He pulled his knife out from the sheath attached to his belt. It was only a third as long as a machete, but thrown by an educated hand, the newly sharpened blade could penetrate a man to its hilt. It was guaranteed to stop anything short of a gorilla. He held it by the blade knowing he might have a problem–his lack of recent knife throwing practice. To compensate, he removed his handgun from its holster and settled it under his belt where he could better reach it in a hurry.

Neville crept up the three steps to the porch, and crouching, approached the door. He got as low as possible and slowly peeked around the doorjamb. The young officer seemed to be slaving over a report, the bane of every officer's life. Neville stood, preparing to throw the knife with his right hand, if he got the chance, his left settled onto his American Army pistol.

He took a deep breath and stepped into the doorway as the officer's phone rang. The young man looked toward the phone. Out of the corner of his eye, he saw Neville appear in the doorway. The officer's automatic reaction, reaching for the phone, changed. His hand moved to the right where his pistol lay in its holster at the edge of the desk.

Neville hoped his Japanese uniform would give him a few seconds to reach the man before awareness set in. The distraction of the ringing phone should have helped, but it didn't. Neville took a step forward, assumed a throwing position and sent the knife on its way. As soon as he released the weapon, he drew the pistol and switched it to his right hand. He stepped to his right to get out of the doorway and throw off the aim of the officer whose hand was on the butt of his pistol. Neville's knife throwing skill had indeed deteriorated. The handle quivered as the blade embedded itself in the wood back of the officer's chair. A trickle of blood ran from the crease of the officer's neck where the knife barely touched him.

The sudden appearance of the knife and the loud thud announcing its arrival startled the officer. By the time the young man recovered, Neville stood in front of the desk, his pistol aimed at the man's head. The fight was over, until the sounds of furniture being overturned made Neville look toward the rear of the building. Shouts and a man's scream created more distraction.

The officer did not hesitate. He wrapped his hand around his pistol and shoved a finger onto the trigger while the weapon was still in its holster. He fired the gun while still in the process of aiming it.

Neville was slow to react, but his shot was accurate, hitting the man in the left eye. In contrast, the Japanese bullet scoured a groove in the desktop and exited through the wall next to Neville. The two gunshots sounded as one, with accuracy overcoming speed. Neville's bullet and a large part of the man's brain exited the back of his head, while a spray of blood hit Neville on the forehead. The force of the bullet threw the officer's body back into his chair making it tip over. He fell to the floor and lay in a growing pool of blood, his hand still gripping his pistol.

The irritating ring of the phone stopped before Neville could yank the cord loose. He automatically used the back of his sleeve to wipe the blood from his face as something moved in the doorway to the next room. Without thinking, he raised his pistol. His finger started to squeeze the trigger when he recognized Distopolis grinning at him. He lowered his weapon and took a deep breath. Upset that he almost shot one of his own men, he worked to regain his composure. Neville tried to conceal how he felt as he reached over and pulled his knife out of the chair back. The officer's reflexes and dedication had almost beaten Neville, and he knew it.

He swallowed hard, and asked, "What happened back there? Sounded like you had some trouble. Is Clyde all right?"

Neville needed a quick answer. Instead, Distopolis turned and looked back into the room where he could see Clyde. Before the young sailor could form an answer his legs gave way making him sag against the side of the doorway. Clyde rushed over and caught him before he fell over.

Distopolis mumbled, "Sorry, Sir. First time I ever killed a man," as he looked down at his hands covered with blood.

Clyde walked up behind him with a limp and helped Neville guide the sailor to a chair. "You did good, young man. Glad you were there."

"Both of them?" asked Neville.

Clyde nodded.

"Good on you, Mate. You all right?"

"One of them had a bayonet. Didn't see it till he stuck it in my leg."

Neville looked down to see Clyde's right pant leg streaked with blood from mid-thigh on down. "Sit down–let me take a gander." He helped his partner sit before going to the back room to verify the situation. Both soldiers were on the floor, eyes wide open. He went to a window, punched through the screen, leaned out and yelled for the rest of the men to come in.

As soon as the others arrived, he grabbed one man's medical kit and started working on Clyde. The wound turned out to be a simple puncture–painful, but not life threatening.

Ten minutes later, Clyde was on his feet ready to go, a thick bandage tightly wrapped around his thigh, when one of the sailors hunting for a souvenir said, "I've been looking around. We got us three bodies, but all four of them cots were in use."

Neville's head jerked around. "I missed that." He pointed at Distopolis and the souvenir hunter. "Take a look around outside. Be sure and check the outhouse. We need to get on the road, but we don't want to be looking over our shoulder if we don't have to. We're about five miles from Tampax, thirty minutes." He pointed at another of the men. "Grab all the weapons you can find and throw them in the lorry. It's bad form to be shot by a rifle we left behind. When you get outside, take a look and make sure that thing will run." Neville pointed at a board on the wall behind the desk. "Those are probably the keys over there, and make sure you disable the motorcycle."

Neville looked around the room and then at Clyde. "He stopped, snapped his fingers and called for another sailor to come over. "Almost forgot. Run back to Kilroy and get the radio." Talking to Clyde again, he said "Never know when… can you think of anything else?"

"We should leave a man with Kilroy, only if we leave one, we need to leave two. Then, what happens if we run into a problem? Two men can make a big difference."

"Agreed. We stick together. We can worry later about finding Kilroy or a yacht that better fits our station in life. Something more in keeping with our positions."

"Which are?"

Chapter 35

Tampong

October 29, 1944
Late Night

The abrasive grinding sound of a truck engine in dire need of a mechanic's tender hands broke through the tweets of the local night birds. The engine coughed, wheezed and even hiccupped before settling into an unsteady throb. The sound ended conversation inside the freshly liberated Japanese Imperial Army outpost. Everyone wanted–needed–to get on with their great adventure. Simply standing around provided too much time for them to question how they could have been so stupid as to volunteer for a mission behind enemy lines. The first thing each man learned in boot camp was still the most important–women didn't go out with volunteers for one simple reason. A man who volunteered, didn't live very long.

The sailor sent to get the radio out of Kilroy returned and placed it in the truck. A moment later, the two men out searching for the enemy soldier who had avoided being caught in their assault on the Japanese outpost appeared out of the trees.

"Sorry Mr. Arnold, he must have gotten away."

Clyde waved an acknowledgment and squeezed into the truck cab along Neville and the driver. “All right young man, it’s time to get on with this mission.”

“Hold on there, Clyde. We forgot something.”

“What? We killed every Nip we could find. Now its time to find that brewery.”

Neville shook his head. “Not quite. We need to go back to Kilroy and get a couple of those machine guns. This little town had four soldiers. I know you said the soldiers in Tampong will be running around like headless chickens, but how many do you think the place might have if this place had four?”

“That’s a fair question, I’ll grant you that, ol’ boy. I apologize. We’ve been in this war too long to die from an oversight.” He turned to the sailor next to him. “To Kilroy, young man, and then the beer.”

Fully equipped with one machine gun on top of the cab and two more pointing out from the cargo area, the truck rumbled through town and onto the tree lined road to Tampong. The vehicle’s poor excuse for headlights combined with the road’s two deep ruts required the driver to stay in second gear. Their speed, or lack thereof, increased the nervousness each man felt. Every tree they passed was a new and threatening form. Every bend in the road concealed a deadly ambush. The few buildings they passed, all dark, contained enemy lookouts, or so some believed. Even the two Englishmen had become unusually quiet, intently watching the road ahead.

A cough by the truck engine made several hearts skip a beat. A second and then a third cough, accompanied by the vehicle shuddering to a stop had them seeing all manner of movement in the trees. Neville made sure all the weapon safeties were on. It was a good decision. It kept them from shooting every imagined enemy soldier and vampire in the forest.

The driver repeatedly mashed the starter switch. The engine obediently revolved, but refused to start, even though the gas gauge read half-full. It took less than a minute for the battery to die.

Clyde was the first one out of the cab. "So much for that lads. Let's push it off the road. Tampong can't be more than one or two miles."

"How we going to get the beer back to the barge?" asked the driver.

In times of stress, people often fell back on their religion for support. Clyde's only religious belief was that nuns could swing a mean ruler, with the back of his head being their favorite target. Nevertheless, he made the others feel better, by saying, "We do our part–the good Lord will provide the means. Out of the truck," he called to the men in the rear. "Form lines on either side of the road. The longer we sit here, the thirstier I get and I don't mean water."

"What about the machine guns?" said Distopolis.

"One," said Neville, "and two boxes of ammunition, and don't forget the radio."

It only took them a few steps to realize how difficult it would be to walk at night on the deeply rutted and slippery road covered with decaying foliage. Their second choice was to walk on what would have been the road's shoulder except for the heavy growth blocking their way. Even so, they tried, but gave up after unseen branches and sharp edged palm fronds continually tried to find unsuspecting eyes. Accepting the reality of the situation, Neville said, "We can keep going at this pace or wait until morning. Then we can see where we're walking and be there quick as a rabbit. My ankles vote for a morning stroll, but the rest of me says to be cautious. Let's keep going and see what happens." He took a quick look at the luminous dial of his watch. "We have about an hour before we need to find a hidee-hole."

The area on either side of the road was jungle or thick forest. The description changed depending on a person's outlook and whether any of it was edible. Even if it had been daylight, the foliage was so dense they still would not have been able to see anything more than a few feet away.

* * *

Someone shoved the Ensign's shoulder several times. When he stopped snoring, the sailor said, "Mr. Miller, the Chief says the number two boiler lit off and pressure is building. He thinks we'll be able to get under way in a half-hour."

The sailor stood nearby enjoying being on deck compared to in the boiler room. The air was relatively cool although quite humid.

Miller rubbed his face in an effort to wake his body. He looked over at the sailor. "No chance of it blowing another hole in the deck like number one did, is there?"

"Well…Sir. The Chief didn't exactly sign any guarantee, but he thinks he knows what went wrong with the first boiler."

"Good. The Japs built this baby tougher than she looks, but I doubt she could survive another boiler blowing a hole up through two decks. We're damn lucky she blew up, rather than out.

"Tell the Chief I'll start hauling in the anchor in fifteen minutes. If that works and the auxiliary steering station works, and the bow doesn't collapse, we'll back out of here and head north. The ship's new owners would be pissed if we left them behind."

"Yes, Sir. Clyde and Neville would never forgive us, and I sure don't want to be on their bad side. No telling what those crazy bastards would do."

* * *

Neville heard the sailor two men behind him say something. His words passed on to the next man and then to Neville who called a halt. He and Clyde walked back to the sailor. After a brief discussion, he led them back down the road toward Gakat. They only walked a short distance before the sailor brushed a thick tree branch aside revealing a ramshackle building. "How did you see this place?" whispered Clyde.

"I didn't," replied the sailor. "I'm from Wisconsin. I smelled it. There were animals here not too long ago, but not now."

"I'll take a look," said Neville. "This might serve as a hidee-hole for the day."

With his pistol in one hand and a flashlight in the other, Neville found the door and slowly pushed it open. The rusty hinges protested all the way. He stuck his flashlight through the doorway and turned it on. Neville played the light around the fifteen-foot square shack, over the bare walls and empty windows. At first, all he saw was a dirt floor and some broken furniture. Then, something in a corner twinkled at him. He bent down to examine it. His tired face came alive, a smile transforming him into the friendly fellow his drinking buddies knew him to be.

He backed out, leaving the door open. "Ain't anything in there, but Tampong must be just ahead."

"If there ain't anything in there, how do you know we're close to Tampax?"

"We'll know for sure when it gets light, but there was one thing in there. It makes me think we're real close."

"What?"

"An empty beer bottle. It was the same brew that Captain gave us."

Clyde's dirty face, smeared with black earth and streaked with sweat mirrored his partner's. He felt the same as a hound smelling the strong scent of his prey close at hand. He placed his pistol back in its holster and waved to the sailors to head for the old building. "We'll make this our headquarters. The men can stay here, out of sight, while we 'suss' things out in town."

Neville didn't need to say anything in response. Clyde's words voiced his exact thoughts. Their mental-telepathy system was in perfect working order.

* * *

"For once, I'm glad not to be a tall Anglo-Saxon," said Clyde, as the two men tried to appear relaxed. They intended to look bored, leaning against the side of a small store in their Japanese uniforms while they watched activity on a side street near the waterfront. The town was just waking up. A few local men wandered down to their small boats but, for the most part, the town waited and watched for the war to arrive. Daylight signaled the start of another battle day. A gentle morning breeze carried with it the sound of a few artillery pieces firing from positions to the east. The large caliber shells impacted no more than a few miles from where they stood.

For Neville, the scene was simply too good to let go to waste. "Seems awful quiet for a place where your chickens ain't supposed to have any heads." He delivered his words with just the right amount of sarcasm needed to get a reaction.

"Wait. You wait. Soon as the Yanks start shelling their lines–you'll see."

"Wait for them to start shelling? What do you think they're doing right now?"

Clyde swatted a fly off his nose. "That? That ain't shelling. The Yanks are firing single shots to get their guns zeroed in, real proper like."

"That means the farther we are from zero, the better I'm going to feel. Maybe we should get on the other side of that road to the pier."

"There you go again, trying to sound smart, but I have to agree. It'll be too late to move once they get serious, and I'll bet you my first three beers, that's going to happen as soon as the Yanks finish breakfast."

This is serious, thought Neville. *Clyde never bet three beers on less than a sure thing.*

Even though they felt the need to hurry, they checked all around to make sure no one was paying them undue attention.

With straight backs and rifles on their shoulders, they imitated soldiers on patrol and walked down the street, eyeballs constantly on the move.

The imitation, as far as it went, had them looking like enlisted men on patrol. There was, however one thing setting them apart from other men in uniform. All the Japanese were wearing army uniforms, while Clyde and Neville were dressed as Naval Marines. Dark blue and white clothing with white gaiters covering their US Army issue boots stood out in contrast to brown army uniforms. The only other Marines in the area were his own "Japanese" Marines he told to stay put in the dirt floored building on the outskirts of town.

They kept their hats pulled down to hide their faces and walked with a purpose. Several times they made hasty turns in unintended directions to avoid soldiers coming toward them. "Where the bloody hell are we?" Clyde said out of the side of his mouth.

Neville took a quick peek from under his hat to find the sun. "We need to go left at the next street."

At the corner, they started to turn left followed by an about face done in unison. They moved in perfect synchronization with each other. The maneuver would have made a Sergeant Major proud. An officer stood at the end of the street addressing at least fifty soldiers. Holding their collective breath, the two men desperately hoping to soon be "off the wagon" continued to walk through Tampong, several blocks from the waterfront. Clyde smelled the air, put a hand out to Neville and took in an even deeper breath through his nose. "Do you smell that?"

"Of course I do. Which way is the wind blowing?" asked Neville.

"It's coming from the north."

"Away from the ocean? That don't make any sense."

Clyde stuck his nose up and sniffed again to be sure. "Sense or no, that's where my nose is leading me and that's where I'm going."

They turned and marched down a street crossing the main road. They were at least several blocks from their destination when they saw a full company of soldiers march into view, camouflage, plants living and dead, tucked into their netting covered helmets. Neville gave Clyde a shove and they ducked into an empty storefront's doorway. One quick look at the store's grimy windows said it was empty. A stiff shoulder against the door and they were inside, safely hidden from view in the dark interior.

In a matter-of-fact way, Neville said, "I dare say, ol'boy, there seems to be a few more enemy soldiers in this town than you said to expect, and they all seem to have their heads attached."

When Clyde did not respond, he continued. "What? Chicken have your tongue? And it seems your idea to blend in by wearing these lovely uniforms might not have been your best."

"How was I to know the army and navy wear different uniforms?"

"Oh come on now. We've seen enough Jap Army uniforms in the past three years for you to know the difference."

Trying to save face, Clyde answered. "Well, they was clean. Ain't like we took them off some dead uns' like we done on New Guinea."

As Clyde continued to talk, Neville became aware of a problem. He maneuvered his mate backward a few feet moving away from a staircase leading up to the building's second floor–most likely the proprietor's living quarters. While drawing his pistol, Neville motioned with his eyes, telling Clyde to be careful. Both men, alert to any change in their immediate world, once again heard the staircase creak.

Neville suddenly lunged around the staircase banister, grabbed a handful of cloth and yanked. A startled cry was quickly cut off by Clyde's hand clamping down on the offending mouth. The two men shoved the intruder to the floor. Clyde's knees came to rest on the man's stomach.

Neville flicked on his flashlight to have a quick look at the enemy soldier while his right hand unsheathed his knife. Ready to plunge the blade into the man's chest, he could barely stop himself when the light turned the expected soldier into a person wearing civilian clothes, a local resident. The man stopped struggling, his eyes, wide with fright. Neville put away his knife and flicked the light off. He then put a hand on Clyde's shoulder and gently pulled him away. "Lad, you can't get much closer to your maker than you just did. If you speak English, who the bloody hell are you?"

When the man opened his mouth to speak, Clyde held up a warning hand. "Remember, keep your voice down when you answer, if you want to keep on breathing."

The man, older than he at first appeared, nodded and tried to speak, but no sound came out of his mouth. He swallowed hard and slowly sat up. "I am Felipe Xavier. I live upstairs with wife. I send her to parents when invasion begin."

Neville waved his hand motioning to the store. "What kind of business?"

"Dry goods, clothing and material. I close a year ago. Could not get any material." He looked at the two white men and their Japanese uniforms. "Are you spies? Are the Americans coming today?"

Clyde put his finger to his lips. "Not so loud. Can you tell us where the brewery is?"

"Why do you… Oh. Of course. It has three floors. It is good place to see over city." He got up from the floor and walked to the rear door where he waved for them to follow. "I take you. Help get rid of bad people."

Felipe, dressed in a loose fitting white cotton shirt, white pants, and open toed sandals led them through several alleys and three cross streets. "It is in next block," he whispered. Neville craned his neck to get a glimpse of their goal without seeing it. However, he didn't doubt their guide–the smell of the brewery had strengthened. Clyde's nose, his personal divining rod couldn't twitch any harder. He was in sensory overload.

They got to the rear of the building and except for having a third floor, it looked the same as every other commercial building in town that had corrugated metal walls. Felipe took them to a set of exterior stairs. Cautiously, Clyde and Neville followed him to the roof. The building was set back against a steep little hill. Its position made it a good spot to see what was going on, while the smell from inside made them drool with anticipation. They could see over the trees all the way down the coast to Gakat and five miles out into the bay.

Dominating the center of the scene before them were two destroyers coming north in the main channel. A quick look with his binoculars made Neville smile. American destroyers always had that effect on him when he was in the middle of an enemy held city. Clyde's almost insane desire for good beer had dropped them into another situation similar to several others he wished had never happened. It didn't take a genius to figure out that the situation for the Nips was substantially more difficult than the day before. The chickens were about to lose their heads.

Clyde and Neville relaxed, forgetting for the moment that they were still in danger. They stood on the roof slapping each other on the back. Life was good and about to get better. Very soon, they expected to be drowning in suds. If they were lucky, they might also be bathing in it.

The two ships drifted to a stop a mile from shore and slowly pivoted ninety-degrees. Each one had three five-inch guns and all of them could now fire on the city.

Clyde walked to the edge of the roof. He stood there and waved to the destroyers.

"What are you doing?" asked Neville.

Clyde turned his head to answer while continuing to wave. "Best let them know we're here, don't you think? Can't have them firing on this building by mistake."

No sooner did the words exit his mouth than one ship fired a single round from its after-gun mount. A ranging shot likely to be followed by many more.

Chapter 36

Destiny

October 30, 1944
Late Morning

Captain Boyle of the USS Randall Nelson was the ranking officer of the two destroyers in the bay, a mile from the enemy held town of Tampong. When the men dressed as Japanese Marines on the roof of a building in the town waved at him, mocked him, it was more than he could take. The loss of his older brother on the Bataan Death March three years earlier still burned inside him. Newly assigned to the Pacific after serving four years with the Atlantic fleet, this was his first chance to see his personal enemy up close. Today might be his only opportunity to eliminate, if not the individuals responsible for his brother's death, at least some of their relatives.

The orders for his two-ship group directed him to attack targets of opportunity and disrupt the enemy's lines of communication. He was happy to oblige. "Fire Control, one round, smoke, bearing three-five-one, distance one-seven-five-zero. The building with enemy Marines on the roof just in front of the hill."

Thirty seconds later, the bridge talker repeated to the Captain. "One round, smoke, on the way."

* * *

"Blimey!" exclaimed Clyde, involuntarily ducking at the sound of a shell passing close overhead merged with its explosion on the hillside behind them. Smoke marking where the shell landed quickly enveloped them as it rushed downhill to the sea. Clyde and Neville picked themselves up, their eyes tearing, throats quickly becoming raw from coughing.

Between spasms, Neville rubbed his eyes and looked around for their guide. They were obviously in the wrong place. Being within beer smelling distance of his goal was nice, but his goal wasn't to simply smell the beer, he wanted to get his hands and mouth on it. "Where's Felipe?"

Clyde turned in a circle looking for their guide. He was nowhere to be seen. What he did see however, were the two destroyers rotating their other five guns toward him. "He ain't here. He must be smarter than he looks, and faster too. Come to think of it, why are we still here?" Clyde exclaimed as he led his mate down the staircase at a considerably faster pace than when they went up. The sound of large-caliber shells arriving changed his desire for a large one to a desire for a deep hole in the ground.

They ran out of town the same as everyone else while keeping their eyes peeled for an air raid shelter. The headless chickens conjured up in Clyde's imagination materialized alongside them as flesh and blood men streamed out of town in every direction, but primarily, they headed west. Clyde and Neville went east.

In combat, five minutes is a long time. It turned out to be more than enough time, for the two ships to fire almost a hundred shells into the town. They started at the brewery and worked their way out methodically destroying every fourth building in the town.

The shells fired by the Nelson's guns seemed to have eyes, nipping at their heels, each one ripped out a piece of the town's eastern side. The other ship took care of the western part. Without cellars or slit trenches, there wasn't a safe place in the town to hide.

No one, Japanese or local appeared to take any notice of the unusual Marines. Everyone was in personal survival mode. They ran for five minutes and only stopped when, panting for breath, they were on the outskirts of town. A few yards farther, the street petered out and became a trail through a grove of nut trees.

Once he was able to speak, Clyde could not stop himself, words tumbling out one over the other. "I was standing on it. The mother-load of beer. I could see my lips curling around the rim of a large pint, foam covering my face, four more lined up waiting to be enjoyed, and those tea-totaling Yanks blew it up. I know they don't allow a bloke to enjoy himself on a ship, but I ask you, what have they got against me having a few on land? If I ever meet the low-life on that ship that destroyed *my* brewery, I'll give him a thrashing he won't soon forget.

"He destroyed an entire building filled to overflowing with beer. A man's dream fulfilled, and what do they do, I ask you?"

"Don't ask me. It don't make any sense, so be quiet. You know I feel the same as you, but enough of your crying. We need to see to our men. They ain't trained for this type of work. It's the first time they've been close enough to smell their enemy. No telling what they might do without us around. They…" Neville grabbed Clyde's shirt and pulled him behind a tree as a squad of soldiers thundered by, intent on finding a safe hole in the ground. When the trail looked clear, they stepped back out and determined which way was east. Clyde mumbling epitaphs with every step, they trudged toward Gakat. The loss of their beer might get a normal person upset. Neither of the Englishmen had been described as "normal" in a long time–a *very* long time.

In Clyde's case there, not only was a physical gnawing in the pit of his stomach, but his loss, redirected his dislike for the Japanese to include a part of the Yank Navy. It weighed on his mind as they went to find their volunteers and then finish the trek back to Gakat. Behind them, the town of Tampong burned, fire jumping from one building to the next, signaling a new front line in the war's destruction of a gentle way of life.

* * *

After going cross-country through varying types of jungle, they came across a road that looked in poor enough shape to be the one they were trying to find. Enough sunlight filtered down through the trees to provide them good visibility. With the explosive sounds of war creeping closer, their senses were on high alert. The way the road twisted or turned around every third tree, their ability to see trouble coming took a back seat to being able to hear it.

Japanese troops pulling back in the face of a renewed push by the American Army felt little need for stealth. As much trouble as it was for Clyde and Neville to jump off the road every time soldiers blundered down the trail, it would have been more difficult to try and break a new trail through the jungle. The two-retirement age "Japanese Marines" took a couple of hours to cover the two miles to the hidee-hole where they hoped their men were waiting.

After they found the group still hidden in the building, one man remained on guard duty in the trees while Clyde and Neville took turns asking and answering questions between gulps of water and bites of fresh mango. When talking about the beer, or lack thereof, Clyde tried, with little success, to speak in diplomatic terms about the US Navy, their aim, timing, and choice of targets.

"Sshhh," The man outside the door said. Everyone stopped what they were doing and raised their weapons. Sooner or later, someone was bound to find them in the small building. They needed to be gone before that happened.

Expecting footsteps, instead, a distinctive clanking sound reached their ears. Even sailors knew what it meant. A tank was approaching. Neville waved to Clyde to stay put, as he slipped out the door and lay down under a large broad-leafed bush where he could get a view of the road. Distopolis slipped in beside him. "What you going to do, Mr. Arnold?"

"Hard to say, young man."

The tank, small in comparison to an American Sherman, but ideal for use on South Pacific islands came into view. A file of men, over a hundred strong trudged along behind the vehicle.

"I wonder," whispered Neville, "how many men do you suppose are inside that thing?"

"Don't know. It has to have a driver, an assistant and a gunner."

"What about a commander and loader? Although, it is damn small."

Distopolis looked at Clyde and smiled. "You got a destroyer, now you want a tank, don't you? How you going to do it?"

"Don't really know and probably won't get the chance to find out, but you never can tell what fate might bring. It would be bloody marvelous, wouldn't it?"

Clyde appeared behind them. "Whenever you're finished taking a nap, I say its time to hit the road. If we hurry, we should be able to make it to Gakat before dark."

With the tank and its file of soldiers gone, the group hit the road, moving fast, still wearing their Marine uniforms and hoping to find their personal yacht, Kilroy, patiently waiting for them. When the outskirts of town came into view, Clyde signaled the men to stay put as he and Neville went forward to see if Japanese soldiers had reoccupied the place.

They reached the first set of buildings when voices made them jump out of the ruts and hide, one behind a building on either side of the road. An officer leading a squad of soldiers went by. Almost a minute later, two soldiers came into view guarding three civilians, an elderly man and two women with their hands tied. They pushed their captives along in the harsh manner common among Japanese soldiers.

Neville propped his rifle against the building wall and slipped his knife out of its sheath. He held the blade up for Clyde, across the road, to see. He nodded and did the same. The civilians walked by, followed by the soldiers. The Englishmen took three quick steps. Each one yanked a head back and eliminated his target the way they had taught several classes of new Coast Watchers at the beginning of the war. A gush of blood accompanied several gurgling sounds. In seconds, all that remained were several red puddles and scuffmarks left in the dirt where the dead men had been dragged off the road.

They eliminated the guards so quietly the civilians had no idea anything had happened. Clyde ran up behind the prisoners and tapped each one on the shoulder as he held a finger to his lips. They each reacted the same way when they saw two enemy Marines, each one with a bloody knife in his hand and their wrinkled, smiling sun-darkened faces that did not have slanted eyes. Fear – relief – joy, passed across the three faces. An open mouth, a questioning look, a smile and then…a kiss. Even the man kissed Clyde making him feel uncomfortable, but happy to have saved them from the joys of Japanese hospitality.

Clyde, Neville and their new companions joined their men, who had a hard time not whistling at the slim young woman with shoulder length chestnut brown hair, dressed in soiled light-weight clothes. Distopolis, who was feeling more comfortable with the two old-men than the other sailors, said, "Mr. Arnold, I can't even find me a girl in Brisbane, and here we are in the jungle and you find the loveliest girl I've seen in a long time. How do you do it?"

"Young fella, it's simple. Good things happen if you expect them to."

The little group turned out to be husband and wife, and their twenty-year-old daughter. Distinguished looking, the middle-aged man wore a rumpled tropical weight business suit without a tie. He said, "Senor, thank you for saving me and my family. I am Jaun Hernandez, the Mayor of Gakat. Please, tell me, how can I repay you? Whatever is in my power to give, it is yours."

Before Clyde could think of an answer, they heard and felt the loud crump of exploding artillery shells. The real war was getting close. "I don't think that was the Navy," said Neville. He switched from Clyde to the Mayor. "Right now, we need a place to hide. Wearing these uniforms, we're as likely to be shot by the Yanks as the Nips. Then we need to get to a Japanese barge we left on the beach south of the pier."

Hernandez spoke English well, although his choice of words was somewhat formal. "Ah ha. So you are the people who put it there. The Japanese thought someone from our town must have steal it. That why they arrest us. They going to make me tell them who involved. Of course, they not believe that I do not know anything."

"Did they move it," asked Neville, upset that their transportation might not be there.

"No. They did not take it."

Neville sighed his relief. "Lovely, do you want to come with us?"

"No, that will not be possible."

"That's up to you, Mate. If you change your mind…, but soon as its dark, we'll get our boat and be gone."

"You can not do that."

"Who's going to stop us?" One of the sailors said.

"The American Navy. Two ships were in the channel this morning. Before they leave they destroy your barge."

Clyde's well-browned face turned red. "I'm not only going to kill that bastard, I'm going to strangle him," his hands came up and squeezed an imaginary throat, "and put his head on a stake for the hyenas, or whatever lives around here, to chew on. A man can only tolerate so much before he snaps."

Up until now, Distopolis, like the rest of the men, followed his orders. He did whatever either of the fun-to-be-with, crazy Englishman said. He had never been so uptight, nervous, and scared or enjoyed his time in the Navy more. Even in the short time they had been together, he knew he could trust them to do the right thing, even if the right thing sounded insane. Only now, with Kilroy gone, he momentarily lost control of his emotions. "To hell with your beer," he yelled. "You got us into this, so how you going to get us outta' here? We got Japs in both directions. What's your backup plan?"

"Take it easy there, young man," said Neville. He looked at Clyde with a twinkle of amusement in his eye. "Clyde, do we have a backup plan?"

"Backup plan? Brilliant idea." Clyde gazed up at the sky appearing to be deep in thought, before answering with a smile. "I'm sure we do. Give me a mo' and I'll think of it."

Several of the sailors stepped toward him, their simultaneous words blended into something sounding like the roar of a lion getting ready to charge.

Neville moved in front of them, arms upraised. "Gentlemen, relax. We have not survived this war simply by being lucky, now have we Clyde? We plan our operations with meticulous care. We want to go home as much as you. Don't we Clyde?"

Trying to look as innocent as a twelve-year-old virgin, Clyde responded, "Too right. Now, what do you suggest ol'boy? A stroll through the woods, or a swim in the ocean?"

The noise that sounded like a single lion changed. It now sounded like a pride of lions. No longer able to hold it in, Neville laughed and pointed at the Americans. "Can't you lads take a joke?"

He turned and motioned to Clyde. "Bring that radio over here. Let's see what Commander Cullison can do for us."

The radio transmitter, sitting forgotten against a tree was brought out. In record time they had it ready to transmit. Neville composed and encoded a short message.

> **Finished rece of Tampong. Disorganized enemy on three sides. Need immediate extraction by water from Gakat. Party of twelve.**

Chapter 37

Why?

October 30, 1944
Evening

The messenger hesitated after entering the mess tent on Morotai. He stood in the entrance for a moment blocking others from entering as he tried to locate Commander Cullison. The look on the messenger's face when he caught Cullison's eye, said it all. "Why is it," said Cullison to Harry, "every time I think I have enough time to eat a decent meal, he comes in?"

Harry looked up from his food tray to see the Signals Sergeant winding his way through the crowded tent. "It must be hard being so important, Mate. The war can't seem to get on without you."

"Don't I wish." Cullison extended his hand and took the radio message, a single piece of yellow paper folded over with his name on it. "Good news or bad?" he asked the Sergeant before unfolding it.

"Sorry Commander, I need to get back to the signals hut."

The Sergeant didn't waste any time getting out of the tent. His haste to get away wasn't lost on Harry or Cullison.

"Sight unseen, I'm willing to place a wager on the identity of the person who sent that message. Are you?" Harry drained the remainder of his tea while waiting for a response.

Cullison, in disgust, shook his head. "When the Sergeant doesn't even try to snag a cup of coffee on the way out, the answer is, no."

"Go on, then," Harry motioned to the message. "You haven't heard from those blighters in three days. I'm betting this is going to be interesting."

Cullison read the short message, rubbed his eyes and read it again. Shaking his head, he leaned over the table, rested on his elbows, and scratched his thinning blond hair. "I think they have finally lost it. As I remember things, their last orders were to set up on Limisawa. A day later we find they're on Danawan, and now… Well, I don't even know where this place is, who the other ten passengers are or what they have been doing?"

Harry reached over and gave him a sympathetic pat on the back. "Look at it this way, Bill. How bad can it be? You haven't gotten a call from an Admiral or General regarding those two in months."

Cullison tried to rationalize the situation, knowing he wasn't getting even half the story. Whatever the truth, it had to be worse than he could imagine. It always was. "You have a point there. Maybe I should disconnect my phone as soon we get back to the office."

A chill, a premonition of things to come ran through Cullison. He shook it off, stood and picked up his food tray. "Come on, Harry. Let's find out where Gakat is located."

"Look at the bright side," said Harry hurrying to catch up. "In three days, how far could they have gone? I'm willing to bet they're still in the Philippines."

Cullison opened his mouth, ready to tell his friend to keep his smart remarks to himself. Then, changed his mind. Gakat didn't sound like a name from the Philippine's. *Maybe I should take the bet,* went through his mind, before he realized, betting on what his mad Englishmen were doing was a sure way to lose money.

* * *

Clyde checked the status of his batteries before he signed off. They were getting low. There was only enough juice for two, maybe three more transmissions. He said to Neville, "Morotai said there might be a response. I was hardly able to pick up their signal today. If they do call us, it will be at twenty-two-hundred. By that time I'm going to need to be somewhere in the open where I can get better reception."

Neville looked to the Mayor, who shook his head. "Open space, that is something we do not have, except for the pier. That is where you need to be. It will be safe. No one goes there at night."

The local population of Gakat was still in hiding when the fake Marines walked through town on their way to the large pier. A sliver of moon provided barely enough light for them to see where they stepped.

"Someone must have had grand plans for this place," said Neville as they stood at the base of the long, wide pier. It was five times or more the size of the one at Tampong, a town ten times larger. "I wonder what it was?"

"Can't say, Mate, and it don't matter. Whatever it was, it didn't happen. In fact, I don't think anyone ever forgot about Gakat–to forget this place means that, sometime in the past, it had to have been on a person's mind. How likely is that?"

The sailor carrying the radio interrupted Clyde's verbal thoughts. "Where you want I should put this, Mr. Saunders?"

Neville looked at Clyde. "Where do you want to set up the radio?" He glanced at his watch. "We have an hour before Cullison sends us the pickup information."

Clyde looked around before walking to the side of the pier, bent over and looked under it. The raised pier ran across fifty feet of beach before extending out over the water. He pointed to the sand. "Let's set up down there. I can run an antenna wire along the edge of the bulkhead and we'll be out of the way and what's more important, out of sight. Might still be some Nips in the area."

"Too right." Neville walked over to the family they saved on the trail. "Mr. Mayor, it looks like it might be safe for you to go home now, but before you do–is there someplace where we can get some food? There is no telling how long it will be before our pick-up arrives."

"Why of course. The Japanese are almost all gone, and I pray to God they will not return, but their supplies are still here."

"Here?" Neville turned in a circle. "Where?"

"In our warehouse. I am the manager. Gakat is a small place but we have deep water close to shore. That is why we have our wonderful pier. Almost everything in this part of Leyte that travels by ship uses our little port. You have seen how poor are our roads. That means everything must travel by water. Small boats carry items from here to the other towns. Even supplies for Tampong, come and go by boat from here. Between ships, all of the items must be stored in a protected area."

At the mention of the warehouse, the Mayor's quiet, unassuming wife, dressed in a one-piece sleeveless dress pulled on her husbands arm. He leaned over and she whispered in his ear.

He patted her arm as he quietly said in Tagalong, "Do not worry. We owe them, do we not? Possibly for our lives. I will take them to our building, but they will see only that which I want them to see."

At the mention of the warehouse, Clyde got visibly excited, hardly able to wait for the manager to stop talking. "Where is this warehouse? I need to take a look at the Japanese rations."

Neville reinforced Clyde's request. "Indeed. Our men have had little to eat. Mr. Mayor, please lead the way."

Neville and Clyde stepped aside to allow the Mayor and his wife to show them the way to the unexpected warehouse, where everything−the operative word being "everything"−was stored between ship arrivals. The couple's daughter took advantage of the distraction to slip away and be free of all the men staring at her.

Clyde motioned for several of his men to come along as the group walked from the pier to the building in less than five minutes. Surrounded by trees, except for the dirt road leading to a roll up loading door, the low-slung single-story structure with corrugated sides and roof could not have been less impressive. It's multiple layers of paint were peeling off in large pieces. The predominant color remaining was a brownish-green. They walked around to the far side. Clyde and Neville expected a small building, possibly thirty-feet square. They quickly realized their error in thinking it to be a small operation. The entire town probably worked in or around it. Neville counted his footsteps while walking to the office door. Roughly speaking, the building measured a hundred foot per side, for a total of ten-thousand square feet. Totally hidden, the building was invisible to the rest of the world unless a plane happened to fly directly over it.

While waiting for Hernandez to find the right key from the dozen he had on a cord around his neck, Clyde whispered to Neville, "Something's going on here. This place is big enough to hold everything this island needs from now until the end of the century."

"For once, you're right. Keep your eyes open. No telling what they have in here that we can use."

The inside of the building, except for the three offices along the front wall, echoed like an empty cave but that could be deceiving. The sound of every footstep reverberated back at them. Without windows, the place was as dark and inviting as deep space. The Mayor struck a match and lit a lantern. He walked into the black void, his small cone of light moving unerringly toward its goal. "Come this way." He looked back at them. "I apologize for the lack of lighting. The Japanese have not allowed us any fuel for our generator since June." He pointed to an area against the outside wall. "They kept all of their supplies in Bay number three. It is an area much larger than they needed. Unfortunately, they did not trust me with a key."

Clyde used his handy hammer, the butt of his rifle to remove the lock. Inside the walled-off bay, they found food cartons in several neat stacks. They also found a few cases of ammunition and hand grenades. Clyde turned to his right hand man. "Distopolis, get two men and carry three of each type of food carton back to our campsite. Don't open anything until you have all of it out of sight under the pier. Whatever they ate, we can too. Whether we like it or not, we won't go hungry."

Mayor Hernandez stayed in the building, giving helpful advice when he could. By maintaining possession of the lantern and standing in what appeared to be the building's central corridor, he prevented them from exploring the rest of the building.

Fed and relaxed, the men lay around on the sand under the pier. For the third or fourth time, Clyde looked at his watch. He leaned toward Neville, "What kind of ship do you think the Commander will send? I was hoping for a battleship, but one of those might not fit in here. Probably a cruiser." Clyde nodded to himself. "Yes, I believe a cruiser would be most fitting, don't you?"

"Never can tell what Bill will do. Every time I think I have him figured out, he surprises me. The man has a very erratic personality."

"Doesn't do things in a predictable manner," agreed Clyde.

Neville often argued with Cullison but, as a friend, always stood up for him. "However, when the chips are down, he always comes through for us."

"You're right, of course. I'm sure he'll send something suitable. In any case, we should find out in a few minutes."

Neville whistled softly to himself as he decoded Cullison's message.

> **All transportation in use. Will send more info tomorrow. Army estimated in Gakat in two days. Suggest consider exit through their lines to invasion beach. Admiral Kirkpatrick requires names of your personnel and reason why you are not on Limasawa as ordered.**

Clyde flicked off his flashlight, surprised and annoyed at the tone of the message. "What do you think we should tell the Admiral?"

"Sounds like he might be upset. Don't understand why, though. I can remember meeting him at the bar on Los Negros. That man knows how to drink."

"Then he'll understand us coming here for a few beers. The only person I can think of who wouldn't is Cullison, but even he will after I explain things to Dusty. She'll explain how things are for us."

"That's brilliant. Glad to see you still know how to set the world straight, ol'boy." Clyde looked up at the sky from their position under the pier. "Looks like we might have some weather tonight. We better make sure the lads on guard duty stay awake. Wouldn't want to wake up being hugged by some Nip who stopped by to get out of the rain."

Neville twisted his body into the sand one last time. Sleeping on his form fitting bed, except for the presence of some unusual insects, was better than dirt. The breeze finding its way under the pier was just strong enough to give the flying insects a problem locating their sleeping blood banks. A few feet away, the soft sound of waves lapping at the beach helped his mind relax. All was right with the world, until Clyde said, "We're missing something here. That warehouse? Something ain't right. I don't know what it is, but mark my words, we need to find out. That Mayor had too many keys. No need to lock things up like that. At least, not here."

"Curious are you? Then, go on–I'll reserve your piece of sand if you like, so nobody takes it while you inspect the place." Neville made a "go-away" gesture with his hands. "Go on. Be my guest. Take my flashlight. Sneak over there and take a look. Let me know what astounding thing you find, *after* I wake up in the morning."

"Might just do that after I edit the message you have to write telling the Admiral all of the heroic things we've done."

Chapter 38

Reunion

October 31, 1944
Time – 0630

The unofficial contingent of Japanese Marines woke up to a sound never before heard by man or beast. Eyes popped open with an audible click. They scrambled to their feet and stood erect, eyes wide with fright, unable to see anything from under the pier. One sailor, ran out to the open beach, faced the water raised an arm and pointed as their ears tried to shut out the sound that assaulted them for a second time. The sound, a long drawn out screeching moan came from the damaged foghorn of Clyde and Neville's re-floated Japanese destroyer.

Smiles, cheers and laughter quickly gave way to action. The beer retrieval expedition climbed onto the pier and ran to the very end, arms waving at their shipmates as the ship drifted to a stop nearby. Sailors on the bow heaved a throwing line across. It was followed by a heavy hawser dragged through the water and was soon followed by several more. The ropes, made as taut as possible caused the ship's bow to drift slowly toward the pier. Every few feet of movement required the ropes to be re-tightened until the bow touched causing the stern to rotate. The three-hundred-foot long ship finally came to rest with its rear resting against the end of the seventy-foot wide pier as neatly as if its Captain was a thirty-year veteran.

The Mayor arrived at the same time, huffing and puffing. Ten men followed him, each one carrying a wood packing case on his shoulder. He apologized for not being more hospitable as the first man lowered his case to the ground causing the glass bottles inside to tinkle invitingly. Neville whooped with glee as he grabbed the first bottle. Uncharacteristically, Clyde simply smiled and stood out of the way, as the men took bottles for themselves and those on the ship.

All was right with the world. The Mayor seemed to be sacrificing his personal stock of beer in gratitude for the town's liberation. At least, that's what it looked like.

They emptied the first bottles in record time. The empties placed back in their slots, a second round went almost as fast as the first. A few men started on their third as Clyde finally reached for his first with Neville watching, a quizzical look on his face.

Neville pulled another bottle out of its slot and handed it to Ensign Miller as soon as he stepped off the ship. "Not many Ensigns can put being commanding officer of a warship in their file. How are you feeling?"

As he spoke, a new thought occurred to Neville and his forehead wrinkles deepened. "Ensign, how did you know we were here? We told you we were going to Tampong."

"We met two of our destroyers coming down the channel a little before sunset. They fired a warning shot at us. We were going so slow, stopping was easy. When I talked with Commander Boyle, he said that he destroyed a landing barge in this port, so I came here. Have you been to Tampax yet?"

Clyde threw out his chest. "Of course we have. That was our goal, only that Boyle took it in his head to destroy the town, and *our brewery* along with it."

Miller tried to break in to answer Clyde's previous question, but Clyde had other things on his mind, and asked, "How is our ship?" while running his eyes over the vessel. "Any problems? How much fuel do you have?"

Between gulps of beer and with foam running down his cheeks, Miller answered, "Why...are you in a hurry? Our bow is a little soft and even if it was okay, we can't go very fast, we lost a boiler." He diplomatically didn't clutter up the conversation with unnecessary and embarrassing details. "Where we going? And by the way, Commander Boyle gave us a transmitter, so wherever we go, we can stay in touch."

"A radio? That's marvelous, but I still want to strangle the blighter. All that beer."

Neville broke in. "I thought the ship looked different." He pointed toward the area where the after gun mount had been and said, tongue-in-cheek, "Seems you have a bit more open deck space near the rear end than when we left."

"Sorry about that. We sort of lost it when the boiler blew." Miller quickly changed the subject and again asked where the destroyer was going to go, and when?

"Oh, nowhere," answered Clyde. "Simply want to make sure the ship is ready, in case the Nips come back. Lost it, did you? That gun might have come in handy, but we still have the one up front, right?"

Miller nodded, knowing he wasn't getting the whole story. In fact, he doubted he was getting more than ten percent of the real story. Normally Miller was a trusting person, believing what someone told him, no matter how outlandish, until proven otherwise. However, with Neville and especially Clyde, his intuition had been spot on. They, or at least Clyde, was up to something, and whatever it might be, Miller was ready. These fellows were fun and they were exciting. What more could he ask of a war?

Miller finished off the bottle, put it down and wiped his mouth. "That is *really* good beer. How much did those men bring?"

A quick, two-word answer from Clyde, "Not enough," said it all.

"Too bad." Miller pointed to a half-full case, asking if he could have another.

"Of course, you earned it. Not everyone can raise a sunken destroyer."

In between gulps, Miller said, "I almost forgot. An officer on Commander Boyle's ship is a Japanese linguist. He said the name of our…your ship, is 'Akido'. It means 'to meet or love.'"

Clyde briefly thought about the name. "Sounds as good as anything I was going to give it. How about you, Neville? Akido sound okay?"

"It's good enough for me. Now, we better get things sorted and send a message to Bill canceling our need for transportation. After that, we can get ready to head south." He turned to the Ensign. In a formal tone of voice, he said, "Mr. Miller, I'd be pleased if you would have our ship ready to leave in two hours."

Miller came to attention, smiled and saluted. "Yes, sir. Your ship will be ready."

Neville watched Miller walk away. "I like that lad. Two days ago, I wouldn't give you a farthing for that boy's chances in the Navy. It is amazing, isn't it, how fast a person can change. In war, it's either sink or swim. When we met him, he was playing at being an officer, and now, I think he believes he really is one."

Clyde grunted his agreement as he reached out to grab his partner's arm, but Neville twisted away intent on getting things sorted out. He raised his voice. "Also, Mr. Miller, if you please. See that our crew is properly turned out in the uniform of the day. Some of them seem to be improperly dressed. Look like the enemy. Bad form, Ensign." He shook his head in mock anger. "What would the Admiral say?"

With his second try, Clyde managed to get a tight grip on Neville's arm. "I need to talk with you and then we have to make a decision. After that, we can send Bill that message you wrote."

Clyde led his partner to the far side of the pier where no one could hear them. They sat on the edge with their feet hanging over the water. "Last night when we were going to sleep you said that I should take a look at the warehouse, if I thought something strange was going on."

"That, I did. And…"

"I was right."

"About what?"

They have a generator near the rear of the building."

Neville began to get upset with his mate's roundabout way of telling him something that didn't seem very important. "Well of course they do. The Mayor already said that."

"That he did, ol'boy, that he did. What he didn't say though was that they do have fuel for it. The tank, and mind you, it's a large tank, is over half full. So why do you think they said it was empty?"

"You're the detective, or at least you're trying to act like one. You tell me."

"For someone who thinks he's smart, at times you certainly can be a dull sod. He told us that to keep us from seeing what else is in that building."

"Does it really matter? It ain't ours, whatever it is."

"It ain't ours. Not yet it ain't, but it's what we came for. I think that place is full to the rafters with five star beer. The very same beer we came here to get."

"Did you see it?"

"No, not exactly."

"Well then, I rest my case."

"Sod it all, Neville." Clyde raised his voice as he continued to make his point. "What else can be in there? That Mayor fellow already said everything between Tampong and here goes by water. We know what that road is like. This is the only place a real ship can get close to shore and it's the only way the stuff is going to get out of here. Besides, how many homes do you know of, that keep a dozen cases of fresh beer on the back porch."

Neville hesitated. Clyde was making sense. "All right, for the moment I'll agree with you. Let's say you've got things figured out. What then?"

"That's the problem. I don't know. It ain't like we can waltz in and take the stuff. They're watching us pretty close."

"In other words, we're stuck without that paddle I'm always hearing about. We can't sneak in and steal the stuff and we don't have any money to buy it."

The two men fell silent, chins in hands looking at the water, trying to think of a way to get their hands on the best brew this side of...Manchester. The more they thought about it, the higher up it rose on their list of quality beers, and the farther away was the location of anything of similar quality.

Chapter 39

Decisive Action

October 31, 1944
Late Morning

They sat on the edge of the pier, feet dangling, waiting for an inspirational thought. They needed to find a way to get their favorite liquid refreshment without stealing it from people they considered their friends. Paying for it was out of the quest-ion–they didn't have any money.

After getting all of the men back into their old uniforms, Ensign Miller approached the two coast watchers, who acted as if they had the weight of the world on their shoulders.

"Mr. Arnold, Mr. Saunders, all of the men are properly dressed. You're the only ones here still employed by a hostile power. Your clothes are in the crew's mess."

Clyde looked up and waved a half-hearted acknowledge-ment. He sighed and swung his feet around to follow Miller's diplomatic suggestion. He paused while getting up, someone in the town was shouting. A teenager came into view, running like the devil was about to grab him.

The young man stopped near the Mayor. He bent over, hands on knees trying to catch his breathe. Without any water close by, the Mayor gave the young man a bottle of beer, half of which poured down the boy's parched throat while the rest ran down his chest.

Clyde and Neville joined a group of local men in a circle around the runner as he related his information to the Mayor. English was the only language Clyde and Neville thought necessary, and that was not the language being spoken. Even so, they started to get a sense of what might be happening as everyone's agitation increased, the longer the conversation continued.

The Mayor patted the young man's shoulder in appreciation and turned to Clyde and Neville.

"Bad news, I take it," said Neville.

Hernandez nodded, his eyes downcast. "We thought we had been spared, but that is not the case. Major Oshiri, the commander of this region took his men east to fight the invasion. We hoped never to see him again. This young man," the Mayor placed his hand back on the runner's shoulder, "was sent by one of our local resistance leaders. He tells me that the Major is retreating from the American Army with what remains of his unit. The man who escaped your attack when you landed two nights ago told the Major how you killed the others. The Japanese occupiers are merciless when one of their own is killed. A resistance fighter overheard Oshiri swearing to level our town for what you did."

"And he's on his way?"

"He is approaching as we speak. He has a tank and a number of trucks carrying his men."

"How many?"

"This man says between fifty and a hundred soldiers ...possibly more. I must tell my people to escape into the hills before Major Oshiri arrives. The resistance is sending help." Hernandez looked toward the trees hoping to see help materialize out of the jungle. "But I do not believe they will be in time... if they come at all."

"Aren't you going to fight?"

The Mayor looked around. Some men were already running to their homes to gather up their families. "We have nothing to fight with and the only thing of value is our warehouse. Major Oshiri will take what he wants and destroy what remains, along with the building. My town will starve."

Neville looked at the ground. "And all your beer? He'll either take it or destroy it."

"Yes, he will take it all, if he can," agreed the Mayor.

Neville looked at Clyde, who answered with a smile. Hernandez had confirmed Clyde's deduction. "Told you the place was full of beer, now didn't I?"

"What do you think, ol' boy," said Neville. "Think it would be worth it?"

The Mayor looked at the two Englishmen. "What are you talking about? Would be worth what?"

Ensign Miller hovering behind Clyde, listening to everything tapped Neville on the shoulder. "In ten minutes I can have enough steam up to get the ship away from the pier."

"Not good enough. We need to be out of range of their tank in ten minutes. He puts a couple of shells into the hull and our ship becomes a permanent reef."

"Sorry, Sir. There simply isn't any way to get the ship out of range, unless you can slow down the Japs. I need time."

Clyde turned to Miller. The corners of the coast watcher's mouth began to curve upward as a fresh thought formed. "Ensign, does that cannon on the front of our ship work?"

Miller shrugged. "I gucss so. I didn't see any damage."

Clyde pulled Neville, Miller, and the Mayor into a tight circle to quickly explain his idea.

Halfway through, Miller blurted out, "My God, you really do want one, don't you?"

Clyde ignored the comment, as he asked, "Can you do it?"

"I think so," replied Miller, before breaking out of the group to run the length of the pier and jump aboard the Akido.

Neville turned his attention to the Mayor. "What Miller is doing will buy us enough time to protect the ship, but that still leaves all of Oshiri's troops free to raise the town and kill anyone who tries to stop them. Together, we can stop them, but…"

"You can stop them? What can we do to help? What is it that you need?" He stopped, thinking about Neville's last words. "What is this…but?"

"Clyde and I like beer–good beer. Beer happens to be one of the few things we always agree on. As far as we're concerned, there isn't a brew as good as yours this side of England. It needs to be protected."

What the two old coast watchers were talking about didn't make sense to Hernandez. "You want to protect the beer? Is that what you are saying? What about the people who live here? Are they not important? What kind of soldiers are you?"

"The kind who get thirsty when saving a town from destruction. And, by the by, if we save the beer, we save the town. It would be bloody hard to save one without the other. But, don't forget how last night you didn't trust us. You tried to hide it from us, afraid we were going to steal it."

"That is not true, I…"

Clyde took hold of the Mayor's arm. "Now look, you're a nice fellow and your people like you, why…we even like you. We understand that you're protecting what's yours. Can't say we didn't think about taking some of that beer without your okay. But we didn't, and we're going to try and protect this place. All we're asking is for you to show your appreciation, like the good man you are. Now, that ain't asking too much, is it?"

The Mayor pulled his arm free. "The sale of that beer is all my people will have to pay for food until the brewery can be rebuilt. If we give you half of it, the town will not survive."

Neville broke in. “The man has a point, Clyde. They probably don’t have more than two or three hundred cases?” He kept an eye on the Mayor while he spoke. The crinkles at the corners of his eyes hinted at a smile when the possible number of cases was mentioned and ignored by Hernandez. *Now I know more than you think I do,* thought Neville. *Once we get done with these Nips we’ll see how generous you can be.*

“Damn it, Neville.” Clyde wanted to argue his case, but deep down he was disgusted with himself for sounding like a heartless bastard. He held up a hand calling a halt to the conversation. In a more subdued voice, he said, “Right, you are then. Today will go down in history. The day of the Great Sagat Beer Battle.”

The Mayor couldn’t tell if they were serious or simply a pair of crazy Englishmen who had been too long in the islands.

“Truly? You will do this for us?”

“Not for you,” said Neville, sadly. “The war is about done for us. The Yanks have the Nips against the ropes. A few more months and this war will be over. Come hell or high water, this is our last chance to do something to talk about in our old age.” He looked at his partner. “Right?”

Clyde answered, but with less enthusiasm. “In for a penny…”

Seconds after Hernandez shook their hands, Clyde went to the ship. Men soon appeared on deck, arms filled with weapons used by Japanese land forces. Imperial Navy regulations required the ship to be ready at all times to support land operations. Long belts of ammunition hung from their arms and around their necks.

Neville waved a “come here” gesture toward the ship. Everyone on board, except the crew of the number one gun mount, hurried to the base of the pier overloaded with weapons, ammunitions and explosives. While Neville instructed the men on what they needed to do, the forward gun on the ship rotated to its left.

The barrel lowered taking aim at Neville and his group. Lying on his belly above the gun on its armored shell, Miller yelled directions to the crew below as he hurriedly put together a crude gun sight. The fire director position above the ship's bridge used to aim the guns had been destroyed several days before. The only way for the gun to hit its intended target would be to aim it by hand and eyeball. Fortunate for them, their target would be less than seven-hundred feet away.

Clyde's last action before leaving the ship was to take down the American flag and put the Japanese flag back up. A confused enemy, even if only for a few seconds, might give them an advantage. They were going to need it. For the most part, Clyde and Neville were self-taught soldiers. Their combat in the trenches of France twenty-five years ago provided few lessons that could be applied to the current situation.

On the plus side, however, the two men had good instincts when it came to self-preservation. Seat-of-the-pants fighting suited them just fine. The odds of beating a hundred battle-tested soldiers with sailors, who hadn't shot at anything more dangerous than a bull's eye target, were not good. A lot depended on what happened at first contact. They could only hope that Major Oshiri was a man who until recently had only faced poorly trained guerillas. Overconfidence could be his Achilles Heel.

Clyde and Neville walked to the intersection where the main road through town and the short, wide road from the pier came together. It was the only point from which a person on the main road could see the ship.

Clyde turned to Neville. "What would you have done if the Mayor had not agreed?"

"Bloody hell, you know exactly what I would do. The same as we're doing right now. This place needs help, and we're all there is. You didn't expect me to say good luck, and bugger out, did you?"

Clyde shook his head. "Good man. Now, ol'boy, time for you to get in the trees and take charge of your men." He shook his partner's hand while he put the other on Neville's shoulder. "Be careful, at my age it would be bloody difficult training someone to take your place."

"Be careful? You're the one that needs to be careful." The two men still dressed as Japanese Marines came together and quickly hugged. Neville then disappeared into the thick undergrowth that lined the uphill side of the road.

Alone at the intersection, Clyde looked at his ship. It appeared deserted. They were as prepared as the short time they had would allow. With nothing else to do, he sat down near the intersection, his back to a tree–and waited.

It was a short wait. First came the sound of its engine, similar in tone to an elephant with a stomach problem. Then he heard the clanking of steel treads running through worn sprockets. Clyde stood, and walked to a point where he could see down the road without being seen. The tank came into view as it rounded the last bend in the road. Feigning a man running for his life, Clyde stumbled into the middle of the intersection and waved to the tank crew. He was a lone Japanese Marine hoping to be saved by his comrades. He continued to wave urging them to hurry. A shot rang out and a spurt of dirt kicked up near his feet. He jumped in surprise at the shot, even though he was expecting it.

Once more, he waved urging Oshiri's men to hurry, and specifically, the tank. He pointed toward the ship his saviors could not yet see, before running in that direction. As soon as he was out of sight, he jumped into the underbrush hoping the sight of a Japanese Marine, in distress would prompt them to hurry the pace of their retreat and thereby overlook the ambush about to be sprung. Clyde had done everything he could to lead the tank to an early retirement. Now it was up to Miller.

Thinking himself safe, Clyde peered out from behind a tree. Suddenly, his body stiffened. He remained frozen in position, surprised and ashamed, when he felt a gun barrel poking him in the side. He kept his body still while raising his arms and slowly rotating his head. He could not understand how an enemy soldier could sneak up on him. The battle was over before it even began.

When he was able to see the person behind him, he smiled. The soldier returned his smile and lowered the sawed-off shotgun. The next thing Clyde knew, Captain Nieves Fernandez, the guerilla leader he met while trying to rescue a group of Rangers only the week before, was hugging him and then gave him a quick kiss.

"What in the world are you doing here?"

"We received a message. A Japanese column was retreating in this direction. We offered to help and were told to try to delay them until the American Army is able to catch up. The Japanese can move surprisingly fast when they retreat."

Clyde hugged her again. "Woman, you have an uncanny way of popping up at the right time." He pointed at the tank, now less than a thousand feet away. "My people are set up along the far side of the road. How many did you bring?"

"A few. We will set up here and catch them in a crossfire. What is your plan for attacking the tank? We don't have any anti-tank mines. Do you have some?"

"No, but everything will be fine," Clyde crossed his fingers, "just tell your people not to shoot until mine do."

Clyde stood up ready to run out in the road. Nieves grabbed at him. "What are you doing? They will shoot you."

"Not if you beat them to it. When I get in the middle of the road, shoot a few rounds near my feet, but not too close."

Clyde didn't give the school teacher turned resistance fighter time to slow him down with questions. He stole a quick kiss before crashing through the bushes alongside the road. A few steps later, he appeared in full view of the Japanese tank commander.

Nieves did as she was told and fired four rounds at his feet. Again, spurts of dirt jumped into the air. The tank kept coming. It was only a few hundred feet from the intersection. Clyde ran around in a circle for a few seconds trying to look frightened and brave at the same time before he ran toward the ship. He was an outstanding example of a brave Japanese marine sacrificing himself for the Emperor.

Clyde ran along the side of the road, making sure he got out of the tank commander's view for a few seconds. When he was sure he could not be seen by the Japanese, he sprawled out on the side of the pier road pretending to have been shot.

*   *   *

Miller watched Clyde's act. When the Englishman dropped to the ground, the Ensign knew the tank was only seconds away. For the opening shot, he had the ship's forward gun aimed at the center of the intersection. He kept his eye glued to the makeshift gun sight as the front of the tank came into view. Only a fool would expect to kill the tank with his opening salvo. He needed to see where his first shot landed in relation to where his homemade sight said it would. He could then yell a correction to the crew inside the gun mount. One hit with an armor piercing shell and the tank would be history. Even a near miss might be enough.

The parameters of the meeting, ship versus tank were set with only one fact not settled. Would the Japanese take the bait? With only twenty-minutes, the ship's newly assigned gun crew figured out how to make everything work. Three times, they simulated firing the gun and then tried to calm down to wait. A good crew practiced the same motions for years.

Miller's men were so keyed up, they couldn't stop themselves from talking. Their nerves were as taut as a tight-rope walker's cable. They kept the rear hatch to the turret open allowing men to lean outside and throw up when their nerves got the better of them.

The speed of the tank dropped from slow to creeping. *Come on, come on*, Miller said to himself, willing the tank toward the center of the intersection. A few feet short of Miller's bulls eye, a shot rang out and a bullet ricocheted off the tank turret. In an instant, the tank commander dropped out of sight, his hatch cover slamming shut. The tank's turret began rotating to the right, away from the ship looking for the would-be hero who would shoot a rifle at a tank.

The setup was perfect. Miller yelled, "Fire." His gun crew reacted so fast he didn't even have time to grab hold of a bracket before the gun fired and he bounced backward, his legs ending up hanging out in space. He squirmed forward to get his eye back against the gun sight and waited. It took seconds that felt like minutes for the smoke to clear. The shot landed at the foot of a tree thirty yards in front of the tank. "So much for the element of surprise," said Miller, followed by directions to the crew to change their aim.

The normal action by a tank under fire would be to move. Movement, even more than its armor was a tank's best protection against artillery fire. *He must have a death wish*, thought Miller, smiling to himself when the top hatch popped open and the tank commander waved a Japanese flag at him.

"Loaded," yelled the gun captain.

"Fire," Miller responded, after he grabbed onto a stanchion.

The shell blew a hole three-feet deep twenty-yards from the tank's left side. Clods of dirt fell on the tank before the commander could drop out of sight. He shook himself clean and issued orders to his crew.

The tank rotated to its left to face the ship head on and started forward. At the same time, its turret rotated to bring its short-barreled canon to bear on the new target. Japanese flag or not, the commander, outraged at being fired upon by his own countrymen had to silence the gun. He'd been shot at enough. This, added to the humiliation of a forced retreat by the invading

Americans while constantly being harassed from the air, was more than he could take.

The tank managed to fire an instant before the ship, which was a stationary target while the tank was a small moving target. The armored vehicle had the advantage, but the uneven road balanced the odds. The tank's one-hundred millimeter shell plowed into the remains of the navigation office below the ship's bridge fifty-feet from Miller. A razor sharp piece of shrapnel sliced across his lower back. His back suddenly felt wet, but he could still move his hands and feet.

The five-inch shell from the ship created another hole in the road, this time only a few feet in front of the tank. Three shots and three misses. Time was running out–for both sides.

The tank came to a halt. A stable position would guarantee an accurate shot, if only they could see their target. The ship's last shot, landing in front of the tank blew hundreds of pounds of dirt onto it, obscuring the viewing ports and weighing down the upper hatch. The loader pulled open the belly hatch, dropped down and crawled to the front of the tank. No sooner was he able to reach up to clear a viewing port than a Japanese bullet removed part of his skull. It was the first time Clyde had used his borrowed rifle.

Another crewman exited the tank. Before he could do anything, the ship fired its fourth shot. Miller had been wide left, long, and short. By that rationale, the shot was destined to go wide right, up until the instant it drilled into the body of the tank. The heavy vehicle jumped off the ground, the explosion momentarily contained within it. Then the turret flew off, like a self-propelled rocket with flames shooting out through the decapitated body. The turret landed in the jungle. Other parts of the tank fell in a circle around the destroyed vehicle. Pieces of the crew were spread across the treetops like sprinkles on a cake.

*   *   *

The ship's first shot signaled to the men hidden in the jungle to open fire on the trucks. Surprise was complete. The

Japanese troops being fired upon were in a unique situation. For the first time in their military careers, they were retreating. Never before had they experienced defeat and it showed in their attitude.

The sound of the ship firing came so unexpectedly, many of the men in the trucks were paralyzed with indecision. They quickly succumbed to the withering machine gun and rifle fire mingled with blasts from improvised shotguns, all aimed at them. Despite the sailors and resistance fighters being hidden from sight behind the large leaves and thick trunks of tropical plants, they had a good view of their targets. The future of the Japanese soldiers who reacted quickly and took cover under the trucks looked a lot brighter than for those who remained in the trucks. Both sides took advantage of good cover as a brisk and deadly firefight developed between the opposing sides. An advance by either force on the other's position might still win the day, but there was a problem. The sailors and resistance fighters had never been in a situation where they were on the offensive and the Japanese had never been on the defensive. The role reversal had both sides acting with undue caution.

Clyde, newly revived from the dead, scrambled through the undergrowth to find Nieves. She surprised Clyde with a hug that lasted longer than necessary, before the two of them went in search of Neville. They found him peering out from behind a squat fan palm tree with Hernandez alongside. The shooting, which had started out as a constant barrage, slowed down to individual shots taken at specific targets that were occasionally interrupted by an exploding hand grenade.

"How are we doing, Mate?" asked Clyde.

"Better than I expected, but not good enough. We have the Nips surrounded and killed thirty or forty of them, but our people ain't got the training to pry them out without us losing a lot of men."

"That sounds like a stalemate and that ain't good. No telling when another group of the blighters might come down the road."

"If you're saying we need to get this done right away, I couldn't agree more. We could use a torch to cut loose one of those twenty-millimeter guns on the ship. It might take an hour or two, but it would get the job done."

"That it would," agreed Clyde. "But I have a faster way of doing this." He stripped off his Japanese uniform tunic, leaned over to Nieves and asked her for the shirt one of her men was wearing. He tied the mostly white shirt to his rifle and started waving it above the undergrowth.

Neville and Nieves moved from man to man telling them not to shoot. When the jungle's birds could again be heard, Clyde stood and walked into the center of the road, bare-chested. He stopped when he reached the front of the first truck–standing in the open, he waited and hoped.

He leaned back against the front of the truck and lit a cigarette, looking a lot more relaxed than he felt. On the plus side, he hadn't been shot–at least, not yet.

Major Oshiri looked on, admiring the nerve of the man while seething at his wearing half a Japanese uniform. He took his time thinking about the situation before telling a soldier to create a white flag and walked with him to stand in front of Clyde. It didn't take a mind reader to know how mad and humiliated Oshiri felt being ambushed by some rag-tag group of guerillas. Hearing Clyde's English accent only made it worse, since he had helped defeat the incompetent English at Singapore.

Clyde offered the Major a cigarette, which was refused. *Not a very good beginning*, he thought. "You speak some English, is that right?"

"Hai," said Oshiri.

"All right then. Here is the way I see things. I want to get home and work on my plantation. I presume you also want to get home and do whatever you do. If we keep shooting at each other, and you get lucky, I may die, but however this ends I can guarantee, you will not see another rising sun and no one is going to give a damn. I've been at this fighting thing for three years and I can tell you, things don't look too good for your lot."

"That I not believe true."

"Be that as it may, this is going to be your last battle, unless..." Clyde left his statement hanging, waiting for Oshiri to show some interest in an alternative.

After a longer than appropriate pause, Oshiri said, "Unless?"

"Unless we come to an agreement."

Oshiri stated his position with simplicity. "Japanese soldiers not surrender. We pledge lives to Emperor."

"That's fine with me," said Clyde. "I'd be glad to help you do that. But I'd rather see you lay down your rifles and let some other bloke have the honor. The way I see things, you ain't surrendering. We're simply making a trade. We keep the trucks, you keep your pistols and walk out of here. Do that in the next fifteen minutes, and no one will bother you between here and Tampong."

"That simple? No. It not happen. The others," he motioned toward the jungle, "will not agree. They want blood."

"Probably with good reason, but that's not for me to decide. I'll give you five of my men as escorts to make sure you get to Tampong safely, and you allow them to return unharmed. How's that? Saves face for everyone."

"Hai. But what your rank? Do you have authority?"

"Rank? I ain't got any except Private, and that was when I was in France." Clyde pointed at the destroyer. "As to authority, see that slightly damaged destroyer at the end of the pier?"

"Hai."

"I own it–well now, that ain't quite true. My partner and me, we own it. Is that enough authority?"

"You are civilian. Cannot own warship."

For dramatic effect, Clyde turned in a circle looking for some non-existent person to challenge him. "I don't see anybody trying to take it away from us, do you? So now, do you want to get on down the road, maybe see your family again and someday die in your own bed, or do we start shooting again and you die in the mud under one of those trucks?"

Oshiri took his time making his decision. He needed another option, but there wasn't one. He looked hard at the jungle without being able to find more than three of Clyde's people hidden in the greenery. Tactically speaking, he was on the wrong side of a bad situation and knew it. To die while fighting for the Emperor would be a glorious end, but what would he achieve? The answer was self-evident. The alternative the Englishman spoke of, technically, would not be a surrender. He was being offered a choice. A chance to retreat with some weapons–an honorable exit from the battlefield, or an almost certain death. A death that would be of little benefit to Japan.

"We go," He stated, and looked at his watch. "Fifteen minutes."

"Fifteen minutes it is. I'll meet you right here. Have your men ready to leave. Side-arms only."

As he walked back to Neville, Clyde wondered who he could convince to act as the escorts and how much it was going to cost.

Chapter 40

Report Location

October 31, 1944
Noon

Neville walked around the fresh shell hole in the road and past the smoldering remains of the tank to talk to Nieves when she appeared out of the jungle. “Would you go around to all of our people, as well as your own. Tell everyone to stay out of sight until the Nips are gone. Don’t want the Major to find out how few we are and get ideas about not leaving.”

Clyde saw Nieves and struggled to keep his mind on work as he walked over to where some of his men were hidden. He detailed the first five sailors he found to escort the Japanese to Tampong. He made sure they were equipped with carbines and knew to be jolly quick returning to the ship as soon as they reached the town.

Clyde, Neville, and Nieves then gathered at the intersection. Behind them, they heard snapping and popping as the shell of the Japanese tank cooled. They were the only people Oshiri saw as he led his men, many of them wounded, out of Gakat. How many fighters had forced him out of town remained a mystery he vowed to unravel when he returned after dark.

The Mayor approached the small group who had saved his town as the last enemy troops walked past. "It is hard to believe…they are really gone for good." He stopped to wipe away the tears running down his cheeks. "For the past three years, this is the day we have prayed for. Major Oshiri does not know how fortunate he is that you were here. If it had been up to my people, they would happily have torn his arms out and given him chopsticks to eat uncooked rice. The man knew no mercy."

"Sorry to have ruined your day, except if we hadn't been here…" Clyde didn't see the need to remind the short man that without them, the day would not have ended so well. He looked around and saw one of Nieves people come limping out from behind a tree. "Let's see how our people are doing and who needs help."

"Of course and I must personally thank each of your men. It is only because of your courage that we will sleep in our beds tonight." He hardly stopped for a breath before continuing. "When will you be leaving?"

Barely able to hide the sarcasm in his voice, Clyde said, "In a hurry, are we?"

Hernandez stuttered trying to cover his desire to see the Englishmen on their way. "You are welcome to stay as long as needed, but there are many places that need you, more important than little Gakat."

"Can't argue with that, Sir." Clyde winked at him, got up, and walked toward the road. He saw Distopolis, wearing a bandage wrapped around his left bicep. He called to his personal helper to come over so he could examine the bandage. Not seeing any blood seeping through, he said. "Go down the line of trucks. See if they start. If they do, park them on the pier road. Have the men shove the rest into the jungle."

Nieves posted four men on the road to warn against a surprise return by Oshiri. She sent two others to the town's eastern end, just in case. Flesh wounds from ricochets and tree splinters accounted for eighty percent of the injuries. The other twenty percent, all-serious, but not life threatening, occupied them for another hour. Three had died during the battle–one local man and two sailors. The butcher's bill had been light considering the makeup of the opposing force.

Sailors, resistance fighters, and local residents gathered in groups on the pier wolfing down food brought ashore from the destroyer and relaxed. Today was not their day to die. Adrenaline drained away. For some, sleep easily replaced the excitement of fighting for their lives while others needed to talk their fears away.

Between puffs on a cigarette, Clyde, with Nieves sitting close by his side asked Neville. "How long do you think until our men on escort duty return?"

Neville looked at his watch. "I don't know. Maybe an hour or two?"

"I dare say, that leaves us time for a beer or two before we leave."

"Brilliant idea. There should be enough in those cases brought down earlier to take care of that."

Nieves snuggled close to Clyde and drank a bottle, although her mind was on something else. The beer was distracting Clyde. It was a new problem for her. She had never had an inanimate object as competition.

Neville pointed at the trucks when the Mayor walked by. "You have a nice fleet of lorries there. Fix that road and you'll be able to transport the beer to the warehouse instead of using boats."

Hernandez was stunned. He expected the trucks to be taken away as soon as the American Army arrived. "You are giving them to us? Why?"

"Bloody hell. If you don't want them…" said Clyde.

The Mayor put out his hands to hold Clyde away. "No, no. We are grateful and will use them. They will relieve us of much work. I was surprised, that is all. You are so generous, and I was…"

Clyde said, "Yes, you were."

"Now Clyde," chided Neville. "The man has to look out for the town. We can understand that, can't we? I'm sure he's been thinking about how much money he's going to make off the Yanks when they get here."

Neville's comment got the Mayor's full attention. "But I am told the Americans bring everything with them. Even their beer. Why should they pay us for our beer?"

"After you taste theirs, you'll know why."

"You are certain? How much will they pay? Twice our normal price?"

"Twice?" Clyde blurted out. "Three or four times is more like it."

Hernandez took a moment to think about this, before asking in his stilted English, "You are not making a joke? They have this much money?"

"On my scout's honor," said Clyde with a serious face while holding up his left hand.

The Mayor opened his mouth to say the words Clyde and Neville had been hoping to hear. Before he could, they all turned and faced the main road. The roar of engines and the clank of steel treads reached their ears. A fast moving, mud-spattered American half-track with a twenty-millimeter gun mounted above the driver came to a quick stop.

Neville ran up to talk with an officer in the cab. While talking, five similar vehicles lined up behind. The conversation went on for several minutes. By the increasing volume of Neville, and who ever he was talking to, there seemed to be a difference of opinion.

At the instant Clyde decided he should join the conversation, Neville stepped down off the running board. The six drivers shifted into first gear and sped off toward Tampong.

He turned to Clyde, Nieves, and Hernandez. "They're American Rangers. They broke through what remains of the enemy lines with little trouble, although there are still some Jap units fighting a rear guard action. The Rangers are on their way to Tampong. It seems they don't care about the town, it ain't important, but the road junction on its west side and the bridge over the river is."

"What did you say that got the blighters upset?"

"I simply told the Lieutenant in charge to watch out for Major Oshiri. The young man seemed to take my not personally killing all of the Major's men as a dereliction of duty."

Clyde shook his head. "Ain't good to be so blood thirsty. A fellow makes a mistake and he could end up loosing some of his own men."

With the half-tracks gone, the area returned to its normal quiet. Neville looked around for a moment enjoying the results of what they had achieved, before saying, "I sent Miller back to the ship a few minutes ago. We should be able to get out of here as soon as he has the ship ready. He said he'll have steam up in a half-hour. All we need is for the men on escort duty to get back."

"Too right. We need to be on the high seas before any real officers show up. Don't want to have to shoot some Yanks to keep our ship out of their hands."

"A half-hour?" said the Mayor and Nieves at the same time. One of them appearing happy to see them go, the other, less so.

Trying to sound innocent, the Mayor asked, "How much beer would you like to take with you? If you are right about what the American soldiers will pay, we can spare some to show our gratitude."

Under his breath, Clyde said to Neville. "About bloody time. We gave him enough hints."

"We can handle three or four...," said Neville, intentionally letting the rest of his words trail off in an indistinct mumble. Then, seeming to realize that he was mumbling, he raised his voice back to normal. "Don't want to cause you any hardship, but since you haven't been able to ship any out for several weeks, some of your stock might be getting punky, what with the heat and all. It won't bother us none if you give us some of that. We'll be glad for whatever you can spare us for saving your town. Besides, wouldn't do your reputation any good if you sold some bad product to the Yanks. They might declare the town off limits."

Neville looked at Clyde. "Can you get the transfer organized?"

Clyde faced Neville, acting like a Sergeant Major on parade. "In a half-hour, Sir? Will do, Sir."

Clyde motioned to Distopolis. "Hop to it. Get some men over here and take four trucks to the warehouse. Load up and transfer the beer to the Akito. We leave port in thirty-minutes."

"But, but…" the Mayor stuttered, shocked at losing four truckloads instead of four cases.

Neville tried to sound concerned. "Did you forget something, Sir?"

Hernandez held his tongue. He knew when to acknowledge defeat, and they *had* earned it.

The beer cases moved from the warehouse to the trucks and into the destroyer with lightning speed. Exactly thirty-minutes later, the Akito's foghorn blew, scaring every bird within a two-mile radius. Like children called home after a day playing in the woods, the five men on escort duty came trotting down the road. All of his men, including the bodies of the two casualties, were back in the nest.

Neville walked up to the Mayor and shook his hand. Hernandez smiled. "It was cheap at half the price. Is that not the way you say it?"

Neville nodded. "Brilliant. Glad we agree. See you again, Mayor."

Clyde approached Nieves. Before he could say anything, she hugged him and delivered a long, hot kiss. She pulled away the moment she sensed him responding. "Next time, plan to stay the night," she said, before walking away wiggling her hips. Even wearing loose fitting U.S. Army fatigues, she was able to raise his blood pressure, along with everything else. She only glanced back once, to simply confirm that her hook was well-set in a new species of wriggling fish known as a Clyde.

Neville shook his head in amazement as he cautioned his partner. "You better be careful with that one. I don't think she's the kind that likes to share, and remember, she knows how to end a conversation–permanently."

"What the devil are you talking about?"

"It's simple, my simple friend. What do you think she would do if your two wives decided to come home?"

The popping of far-off small arms fire cut into their conversation. Things were happening and it was time to get a move on. The thick hawsers holding their ship to the pier fell into the water before being pulled dripping wet onto the deck.

The Japanese rear guard was putting up a valiant, but futile effort to hold back the advancing American Army. The remnants of their once invincible army would soon be straggled through Gakat. If the Japanese saw one of their ships in enemy hands, their famous temper and desire for revenge, might overcome their instinct for self-preservation. The town would undoubtedly receive some unwanted attention. Hernandez stood on the pier trying to will the ship on its way.

Ensign Miller stood stiffly against the port side railing careful not to disturb the bandages on his back. He used hand signals to a man on the rear deck who relayed his commands below. Without a harbor tug to help, he needed the ship to drift away from the pier on its own, before sending an order to start the engines. He stood looking down at the very small gap between the ship and pier expecting it to widen, only it didn't. The destroyer had two propellers and their combined span was the same as the width of the narrow ship. With its aft end resting against the end of the pier, he didn't dare start the engines for fear of damaging something.

Clyde and Neville stood near the bow watching.

"He ain't doing anything, is he? Must have taken lessons from you," said Neville looking around. "Seems our ship has taken a fancy to the place. Any suggestions for our young Captain?"

"We could wait for the tide to go the other way."

Neville looked out at the road, as the sound of gunfire grew louder. "Any other suggestions? I don't want to be here when the Nips arrive and I think it best that we are gone before the Yanks show up as well. They're nice fellows, only sometimes they get hung up with all of their regulations. They might not honor our claim of salvage, and then where would we be?"

Clyde motioned toward Miller. "I don't think he wants to use the props with the ship so close to the pier. Can't say I blame him. Let's go back there and give him a hand."

"You…give him a hand? Don't tell me you have an idea. One that will work? I've got to see this."

"Ensign," said Clyde to Miller. "I know the ship has to go forward to get out of here, but is it safe for the ship to move backwards to get away from the pier?"

"Uh…sure, Mr. Arnold, but I don't dare use the engines. We do that and more than likely we'll damage one or both props. Then we won't be going anywhere."

"I understand that, but tell me, how far back do we need to go before you can use the engines?"

Miller looked to the rear of the ship and then forward, trying to calculate the distance he needed to get it safely turned around. "You get this ship to move back seventy-five feet and I'll get us out of here."

Clyde nodded and walked away.

Miller looked at Neville. "What's he going to do, Mr. Saunders?"

"Young man, I have absolutely no idea, but it has a fifty-percent chance of working."

"You think it might work, but you don't know what it is? That's a hell of a way to run a railroad."

Clyde didn't lose any time. He directed men on the forward deck to drag out two hawsers. One end they connected to a large cleat on the pier opposite the non-existent bridge and the other end to the disabled steam winch near the bow. Without any warning, smoke erupted from the forward gun. The entire ship vibrated. Both men jumped and looked to see what it was firing at. Twenty-seconds later, it fired again and continued for two minutes without hitting a discernable target.

Firing the gun caused the ship to lurch backward creating a slack in the hawsers that the men on deck quickly retightened. When the gun stopped firing, the force of the shots resulted in the ship backing up close to the seventy-five feet Miller needed.

The Ensign didn't waste a moment. He sent orders to release the bow ropes and signaled the engine crew for "Slow ahead, starboard engine only." The men in the steering compartment were told to shift the rudder to "Starboard twenty." The center of the ship, still against the pier became a fulcrum point. The stern swung toward the pier as the bow rotated toward open water. When it had swung out to a thirty-degree angle from the pier, the rudder was shifted to its amidships position, and the Akito crept out into the channel.

Smiles, backslaps and a general feeling of well-being overcame everyone. The sailors had their beer and an adventure to tell anyone who would listen, and many who would not. They had defeated an enemy force four times their number and saved a town from destruction. Now they controlled an enemy warship without officers telling them what to do–they didn't consider Miller a *real* officer–and their next assignment would be thirty days leave in the States.

Neville waited until after the ship turned into the main channel from Tampong heading for the Strait before talking to their young Captain. "Have you been checking on the bow? How bad is it leaking?"

"No problem. We run the bilge pumps for ten minutes every hour." A light ten-knot breeze blew through Miller's blond hair as he looked out at the blue water and the cumulus clouds building over distant mountains. "You know, Mr. Saunders, I think I like being in the Navy. The last few days I learned a lot thanks to you and Mr. Arnold."

"Young man, an Admiral couldn't have done any better."

"Thank you, Sir. That means a lot coming from you. Now, where are we going? The main fleet around the other side of the peninsula?"

Neville didn't say a word. He leaned on the railing and looked down at the water sliding by while deep in thought.

"How long will it take us to get back to the Strait?"

"About five-hours."

Without giving any hint regarding his plans, Neville said. "Let me know when we get there," and walked away to find Clyde… and plan.

Later, in the makeshift radio room, Clyde and Neville wrote out their much-delayed report to Cullison. Neville read it aloud one last time prior to Clyde sending it off.

"Seems to cover almost everything. Although, I think we could have used stronger words about them giving us a medal, not that we need one, mind you, but it's nice to have your good judgment and initiative acknowledged." Clyde flipped a switch and started his contact procedure.

* * *

After receiving a legibly written copy of the message, the Signals Sergeant looked around the radio room trying to find someone to deliver it. Strange, all of a sudden, every man in the hut knew when to bury his nose in work too important to be interrupted.

Resigned to having to do the deed himself, he walked over to the mess tent. Clyde and Neville had an uncanny knack of sending Cullison messages at dinnertime. The Sergeant knew without being able to prove it, that they meticulously planned their transmission times to get under the Commander's skin.

This time it was Harry's turn to look up and see the Sergeant. He slowly put down his knife and fork and said, "Bill," before motioning at the Sergeant with his eyes.

"From them?" Cullison asked as he put his hand out.

"Yes Sir, from them."

"How bad is it, Sergeant? Should I get a drink first?"

The Sergeant answered with his facial expression as well as words. "Definitely, Sir, a good stiff one. This here message might be picked for display in a museum after the war."

TO: Commander Cullison, Naval Affairs Coordinator, Morotai
FROM: Commanders, Saunders/Arnold, HMS Akito, Surigao Strait
Completed rescue mission of Army Ranger unit. Imperial Japanese Destroyer, Akito, re-floated and under power. Using operational discretion, moved lookout post from Limasawa to Danawan. Eliminated Japanese naval spotter's position on island. From Danawan assisted Seventh Fleet in location / destruction of Japanese fleet. Rescued thirty sailors from U.S. Destroyer 349 sunk in Surigao Strait. Destroyed Japanese Army units, 100 plus combatants and armor, in and around Gakat, Leyte. Town no

longer under threat. Currently on course to Morotai.

Recommend all personnel involved be awarded appropriate medals for heroism.

Request weather update. Speed, maximum, ten knots.

Request notify all units of new ownership, Japanese destroyer, Akito. Outline recognizable by destroyed bridge and missing after-gun turret. Will require refueling in Morotai for next leg of voyage south and payment of outstanding wages.

Request promotion for Acting Captain/ Navigation Officer, Ensign Miller.

Request sailors currently on board (list to follow) be reassigned for temporary duty at government expense on the civilian-owned Akito not to exceed ninety days followed by standard survivors leave time in States.

Request you notify supply officer, Morotai, of recreational spirits available for purchase, three-hundred cases maximum, market rate, U.S. currency, cash only.

Harry laughed while Cullison silently screamed. Nothing made any sense. Considering that Clyde and Neville sent the message, it was to be expected. He repeated aloud. "Operational discretion? Commanders of HMS Akito? Who do they think they are, and how the hell did they get their hands on it? HMS Akito?"

"I believe they are giving the Japanese destroyer to His Majesty's navy."

He read the message for a third time and wondered where he could find a good bottle of whiskey for the Admiral. Even if he was lucky enough to find his commanding officer in a good mood, it was going to be difficult to explain Clyde and Neville. Cullison knew it was going to take more than a five-minute appointment to tell the Admiral how two over-the-hill civilians could wreak havoc on a well-planned war. And, it only took them two weeks. God only knows what they might be able to achieve if they had help.

Clyde and Neville, the two misfits guaranteed to ignore every regulation and order sent their way had not only survived, they had prospered. And, with the war still raging, there was one thing Cullison knew to be true. They were going to do it again...somewhere.

- THE END -

Authors Notes and Other Things

There are a number of people to thank for helping with this novel, although, no matter who I name, I know I will have left out a few. I apologize here for my error of omission. Thank you to; My love-my wife - Sue, and to Gregory Kompes, Donald Riggio, Linda Weber, Darrah Whitaker, Audrey Balzart, Joe Van Ryne, Debra Dorchak, Amanda Skenadore, Ava Overstreet, Paul Antriedes, Toni Cowen and to all the members of the Henderson Writer's Group – **Thank You.** I cannot overstate my appreciation for the help you have given with your ideas, comments, editing, and support.

A writer draws his ideas from many sources in the process of creating a story. Here are a few that I used:

D-Day in the Pacific, c.2005, Donald L. Miller, Simon and Schuster

History of United States Naval Operations in World War II, Volume XII, Leyte, June 1944 – January 1945, c.1958 Samuel Eliot Morison, Little Brown and Company

Captain Nieves Fernandez – WWII Guerilla Leader in Leyte, Philippines, Michael Sellers.com

Recommended reading:

Ghost Soldiers by Hampton Sides, POW Rescue Mission

Wherever possible, I have tried to stay true to the historical record, however, in the end, history must serve the novel rather than the other way round. I hope readers who are history buffs will forgive me.

Listed below are some facts in the story, which you might have thought I made up.

The invasion of Morotai was conducted without prior on site reconnaissance. MacArthur did not want to alert the enemy. This resulted in the landings occurring on an unsuitable beach. The invasion was moved to a new location when they found a better beach.

Captain Nieves Fernandez was a real person. She was the only female Captain in the Leyte Resistance movement. Prior to the war, she was a schoolteacher.

The Surigao battle between battleships was only the second such battle of the war, and to this day, there has not been another.

I have depicted the movement of the various fleets as accurately as I could within the framework of a novel. The failure of Admiral Halsey to clearly communicate his intentions almost resulted in a Japanese victory.

Clyde Arnold and Neville Saunders have left their mark on Leyte. Their next stop is… Any suggestions?

KRKSoundChoice@aol.com

I hope you enjoyed this, the third installment in the adventures of Clyde and Neville. If you did, may I ask you for a favor? Please post a review on Amazon. Every little bit helps.

Previous Clyde and Neville adventure novels are: **The Coast Watchers** and **New Guinea Rescue**.